THE HOUSE
OF
LASSENBERRY

THE HOUSE OF LASSENBERRY

DANIEL WEBB

Archway Publishing books may be ordered through booksellers or by contacting:

Archway Publishing
1663 Liberty Drive
Bloomington, IN 47403
www.archwaypublishing.com
844-669-3957

Because of the dynamic nature of the Internet, any web addresses or links contained in this book may have changed since publication and may no longer be valid. The views expressed in this work are solely those of the author and do not necessarily reflect the views of the publisher, and the publisher hereby disclaims any responsibility for them.

Any people depicted in stock imagery provided by Getty Images are models, and such images are being used for illustrative purposes only.
Certain stock imagery © Getty Images.

Interior Image Credit: Clark Stoeckley

ISBN: 978-1-6657-0053-5 (sc)
ISBN: 978-1-6657-0054-2 (e)

Library of Congress Control Number: 2020925208

Print information available on the last page.

Archway Publishing rev. date: 12/29/2020

BIRTH

LOVE

LOVE

HATE

DESTROY

REBUILD

DEATH

REBIRTH

— CHAPTER .31 HERE THEY COME —

It was the year, 2020. On the island nation of Lassenberia, inside the GLC room of castle Lassenberia, a young lady of African American descent sat on her throne wearing a long black silk ballroom gown. The gown was lined at the seams with tiny green and red gems. Around her petite waist was a green satin sash. Her shoulder sash was also made of satin, but red.

Her face had a smooth dark complexion. Her hair was jet black with a thick texture, which was twisted into one long braid coming down the middle of her back. Her beauty since birth was considered flawless.

On her head rested a diamond studded tiara. Dead center of the tiara, resting on her forehead was a 3-ounce crystal vial filled with GLC. The vial was sealed with a custom-made diamond cap.

She sat there nervously, staring at the giant double doors that sealed off the GLC room from the rest of the castle. Her left hand was fidgety as she tapped on the arm rest. On this arm rest was an advanced high-tech weaponry and communications control panel. She could hear the muffled sounds of bombs dropping in the distance which sounded like a thunderstorm approaching. She kept glancing down at the arm rest to make sure that her words were still being recorded.

At her feet lay the body of a man whose intestines were exposed due to an earlier battle outside the castle walls. His name was Abdirrahim. He had sworn to protect this young woman of nobility to the very end. She could hear the thundering noise of chaos drawing near as she leaned over to caress the forehead of Abdirrahim's lifeless body. She sat up straight as she heard pending doom outside the double doors. "Here they come." She said into the recorder in a sweat, but dreadful voice.

Her name was Niyale. Queen Niyale, Ruler of the nation of Lassenberia. It was 3 days after her sixteenth birthday, which fell on June 12th. There was no celebration of her birth on that day. Instead, there was blood and dead bodies flooding the streets. "Please! Spirits of my forefathers hear me! Give me strength! Forgive me, for what I've done, for what I'm about to do!" she uttered. She stood tall and proud from her throne. She could hear someone outside tinkering with the double doors as she grabbed a device which happened to be a remote detonator from the arm rest. She had flipped open the lever to this device to unveil a red push button. She had placed her thumb on the red button, waiting for what was about to come through the double doors.

This detonator was the only chance to keep her family's most precious gift out of the hands of her enemies. Her family's most precious gift was the fountain of GLC based in the center of the GLC room.

The fountain was shaped like a giant birdbath made of marble and gold displayed in a swirled design. A device was installed deep within the fountain to cause the GLC to shoot up 4 feet into the air like a small guizer. Within the center of this guizer appeared a 10-foot gold plated perch. On top of the perch rested a 4-foot gold statue of a goldfinch. This was the center of worship for those who believed in the new age faith. Some of the citizens of Lassenberia would kneel before the fountain and recite scripture from the pages of this new belief before applying the GLC to their wounds and illnesses.

Queen Niyale took cover behind her throne once she heard the words, "FIRE IN THE HOLE!" on the other side of the double doors. The queen plugged her ears with her fingers. This still did not prevent the vibration of the explosion from rattling her body.

Before the smoke could clear, 2 flash grenades were tossed into the enormous room. Queen Niyale fell on her back when the force of 240 decibels came in her direction. When her vision cleared, she could see a team of soldiers in full body armor wielding high tech machine guns enter the room in a strategic formation. Her sense of hearing was impaired, but she was capable to stand to her feet and compose herself. The soldiers wore hardened combat masks that covered their entire face but were equipped with mini microphones inserted inside the masks that amplified their voices. "This young lady is a tough one, sir!" one soldier said to the officer in charge. Queen Niyale stood proud, adjusting her tiara as blood trickled from her right ear. She still had the detonator in hand. The strike force, which consisted of six soldiers, had spread out to secure the GLC room. "Clear, sir!" each soldier said to the officer in charge. The officer in charge lowered his weapon, then removed his helmet and armored mask, revealing his dirty blonde mustache. He then donned his helmet. "Queen Niyale! Can you read my lips?" the officer in charge shouted in a precise tone. Queen Niyale reluctantly nodded. "I am captain Trudeau, United States Army! I implore you, your majesty! Drop the device! There's no way out of this situation!" Trudeau said. Queen Niyale just smiled. "This is your final warning, your majesty!" Trudeau shouted as he folded his arms. Queen Niyale's facial expression changed from a smile, to the look of rage. "Bisb da shin bis captain?" she shouted. "What is she saying, sir? What the hell did she say?" one of the soldiers nervously shouted. "Easy corporal! She's speaking Lasserian!" Trudeau said. "What is Lasserian, sir?" the corporal asked. "It's the native language of Lassenberia!" Trudeau said. "Why didn't the top brass give us a heads up about this, sir?" another soldier asked. "That's why I'm here sergeant! I spent 5 years learning to speak fluently in this exclusive language!" Trudeau said. "Icu sheel shin kiltm captain! Bisb da shin bis?" Queen Niyale asked. "Shin ow esim bi re brimik, shis majesty!" Trudeau answered with pride. Queen Niyale looked impressed. "Since you've taken the initiative to learn my language, I will speak yours, for the time being!" Queen

Niyale shouted. "With all due respect your majesty, time is not on your side!" Trudeau said. "Captain Trudeau! It only takes a half of pound of pressure to push down on this red button! You shoot me, and I will still have enough strength in my thumb to activate the thermal nuclear weapon implanted inside the GLC fountain! I don't have to explain to you the effects of such a weapon!" Queen Niyale said. Captain Trudeau had the look of frustration. He took a glance at each of his men. "lower your weapons!" he shouted. "Sir?" one soldier said. "You heard me soldier! Stand down!" Trudeau shouted. "I can take her, sir!" one soldier shouted as he had the young queen in his crosshairs. "God damnit, Marcelle! I said stand down!" Trudeau shouted. simultaneously, Trudeau's men lowered their weapons. "Now! I want everyone to slowly back of the room! The queen and I have a lot to talk about!" Trudeau shouted. "Sir! You sure this is a promising idea?" Marcelle asked. "Sergeant Marcelle! Question my orders again, and I will make sure you don't leave the island alive! Now go! That's an order!" Trudeau shouted. "Yes sir." Sergeant Marcelle said with a defeated tone in his voice. Sergeant Marcelle and the remaining strike force team slowly back out of the GLC room.

Sergeant Marcelle pressed the microprocessor on the side of his helmet. "Core group 1, to Alpha team! Core group 1, to Alpha team! We are aborting the goal! I repeat! We are aborting the goal! Do not fire! I repeat! Do not fire!" he said. As sergeant Marcelle and the remaining team were backing out of the GLC room, captain Trudeau turned in their direction. Give me time to convince her of the inevitable" He said. "You sure about this, sir?" Marcelle asked. "Marcelle!" Trudeau shouted. "Let's go!" Marcelle shouted to the rest of the team. Moments later after Trudeau's men had left the GLC room, he turned his attention back towards queen Niyale. "Captain! Da shin lemakit ot yodamos ksit laym fafyl bigizm?" the queen asked. Trudeau smiled. "Your majesty! Do you realize what you have in your possession? Why in the world would I allow this place to be reduced to rubble?" he said. To convince queen Niyale that he was even less of a threat after placing his weapons on the floor, captain Trudeau gently removed the body armor from his torso. Captain Trudeau put his hands up. With a big smile on his, he waived his fingers. "See! No tricks up my sleeves!" he said. The queen did not look impressed. Trudeau turned to see if anyone was coming through demolished doorway. He turned back towards the queen. "Your majesty I-!" Trudeau uttered. "One moment captain!" queen Niyale. The queen removed the vial of GLC from her tiara. With little effort, she unscrewed the diamond cap from the vial with one hand. while holding the detonator with the other. The diamond cap slipped through her fingers, falling to the floor. She gulped down the entire vial without spilling a drop. As the queen stared dead into the captain's eyes, she flicked the vial on the floor. Moments later, a smile came upon the young queen's face. "Your majesty! Are you ok?" the captain shouted. "No need to shout captain. I can hear you fine now." She said. Queen Niyale turned to brush off the debris from the seat of her throne before taking a seat. The queen looked surprised to see captain Trudeau kneel before her. "You attack my homeland, then you kneel before me! What is the meaning of this, captain?" she asked. "Your majesty! Because of what you have, my little girl lived to see her 8th birthday!" the captain said as his eyes teared up. "Like I said, captain. There is no need to shout. Sound carries in here. How is this possible? I've never given the order to lift the embargo on the United States." She said. "Must I remind you your majesty, just like plans to build a nuclear warhead have leaked over decades to turn nations into superpowers, a small supply of your GLC has slipped under the radar as well." The captain explained. "Are you telling me I have spies, captain?" the queen asked. "What superpower doesn't, your majesty?" the captain said. "Skullduggery!" The queen said to herself. "As I was saying, your majesty, due to your nation's lack of national security, my daughter is healthy and home safe-n-sound with her mother." The captain said. The young queen took a deep breath. "Captain. No amount of your awkward gratitude can justify the horror you've inflicted on my homeland, and to my people." She said. "That is why I have volunteered for this mission, your majesty. I am here to give you the edge on how to end this massacre. It's the least I can do." The captain said. The queen leaned back into her throne, still with the detonator in her hand. "First, tell me about your little girl, captain." She said. "Your majesty?" Trudeau said with a puzzled look on his face. "Your daughter. Tell me about her. How does she look, her favorite toy, her favorite flavor of ice-cream? Since my time maybe limited, why not tell me about her, if I am responsible for her well-being, as you say." The queen said. Trudeau shook his head as he smiled. There was a dead silence in the GLC room for a moment. "Well! She is 8 as I just mentioned. She has the most beautiful blue eyes, like her mother!" he chuckled. "Continue, captain." The queen said. Trudeau had a loss for words for a moment. "She's blonde. She has the cutest dimples." Trudeau said.

It was May 29th, 2002 around 12am in the morning, Central Africa Time. A man lying unconscious in bed slowly opened his eyes. The first thing his eyes gazed upon were the bright lights from the fixtures in the ceiling, which brought pain to his eyes, causing him to squint. His eyes then shift downward. He sees the image of a woman coming into focus. "Hello, handsome!" the woman said. "Kimberly?" the man said as he coughed. "I'm here, my love!" she said. "I have a funny taste in my mouth!" the man said. "It's just the after taste of the GLC!" Kimberly said. Slowly the man sat up from the bed, removing the covers to expose his bare upper body. "Wow!" Kimberly said. "What? What's wrong?" he asked. "Nothing! It's just that you regained your body mass!" Kimberly said with a lustful look in her eyes. "Welcome back, my lord!" a man with a thick accent said in the background. The man leaned to the side to see someone standing behind Kimberly. "Ali?" the man said. "I'm here, my lord!" Ali said with a big grin on his face. Kimberly stood at attention. Ali stood next to her with his weapon in hand. "Long Live the House of Lassenberry! Long Live, Sir Marcus!" Kimberly shouted as she looked down at her husband. "Long Live Sir Marcus!" Ali shouted as he looked straight ahead. "Where the hell am I?" Sir Marcus asked. Kimberly and Ali looked at each other, smiling. "You're in a medical facility. A rehabilitation center, I should say. The Sir Marcus Rehabilitation Center." Kimberly said. Sir Marcus started to blush. "You guys named this place after me? When?" He asked. "Just now!" Kimberly chuckled. Kimberly sat on the bed, close to her husband. She planted a long kiss on his lips. She frowned as she licked her lips. "Yuck! It does taste funny!" she said. "Last thing I remember is getting inside a drum, then everything went black!" Sir Marcus said as he massaged his forehead. "Just give the word, my love, and I'll teach those guys in that tugboat a lesson!" Kimberly said. Sir Marcus shook his head, patting his wife on the shoulder to calm her down. "I have to pee!" Sir Marcus said. Sir Marcus peeked under the covers. He realized he was naked from the waist down. "Get me something to put on, my love!" he said. Kimberly turned to Ali. "Ali!

Run to the warehouse and find something for your lord to wear!" she shouted. "Right away, Ms. Kimberly!" Ali said before leaving the facility. Sir Marcus flipped the covers off himself. He stood from the bed. "Where's the damn bathroom?" he said. "On the other side of that brown door." Kimberly said. Sir Marcus stretched before trekking to the bathroom. "I've never felt so alive." He said. Kimberly watched as her husband walked off to relieve himself. "The GLC must've improved your ass cheeks as well!" she chuckled. Kimberly could hear the trickling of urine as her husband was taking a leak when she reached under the bed to retrieve the cap to the beaker with the remaining GLC inside. Once she put the cap back on the beaker, Sir Marcus comes out of the bathroom. "Are you pregnant?" he asked. Kimberly looked bewildered. "Ah, no!" she said. "I don't know why I asked that! Just had a feeling!" Sir Marcus said. "Are you cheating on me?" Kimberly chuckled. "The question is, are you cheating on, me?" Sir Marcus chuckled. suddenly, there was a knock on the door. Sir Marcus quickly ran back into the bathroom. Kimberly went to answer the door. It was Ali standing there with a stack of neatly folded clothes in his arms. "Sorry, Ms. Kimberly, but I didn't know what size to get!" Ali said. "No, Ali! It is my fault. I should have told you his size before you left. Thank you." she said. The pile of clothes in Ali's arms were about 3 feet high, topped off with 2 pairs of work boots. "You can lay them on the bed, and stand guard outside, please." Kimberly said. "Yes, Ms. Kimberly!" Ali said. "And thank you again, Ali!" Kimberly said as she closed the door behind Ali. Once he heard the door shut, Sir Marcus comes out of the bathroom. "Let's see what we've got here!" Sir Marcus sighed. Kimberly aided her husband in sorting through the pile of clothes. "How about this?" Kimberly asked as she held up a pair of green jogging pants. "I'll pass!" Sir Marcus said. "What about these?" Kimberly asked as she held up a pair of khakis. "Cool!" Sir Marcus said. "Only towards the end of the year! Get it?" Kimberly chuckled. at that moment, Sir Marcus had a flashback in his mind going back to the time when Terrance Haggerty used the words, get it, when he saw all the horrific acts at the National Agreement gathering. Sir Marcus quickly snapped out of his daze. "Are you ok?" Kimberly asked. "Yes! Yes, my love." He said. Kimberly massaged her husband's arm to give him a sense of security. "You've said a while back, that there's a lot of work to do out here. If I am going to lead, I'll need to get down and dirty myself." Sir Marcus said. Kimberly turned to her husband. She put her arms around his waist. "What do mean, if? This is your land! This is our land!" Kimberly said with passionately. Sir Marcus gently stroked the side of his wife's face. "That sounds nice my love, but I have a cousin who's still incharge of the family fortune. Remember?" Sir Marcus said. Kimberly quickly turned away from her husband. She took a deep breath, then turned back towards him. "Let him have his drugs! We have the GLC! We've already built an infrastructure for one third of the island just on credit alone!" Kimberly said with rage in her voice. "It's not that simple! These people! This so-called National Agreement have bound the men in my family for 3 generations at their beckon call! I screwed up and turned everything over to my cousin! So, as far as these people, or if you want to call them people are concerned, everything that my family owns belongs to him! Because at the end of the day, he belongs to them!" Sir Marcus said as he was getting dressed. Kimberly sighed. "Just finish getting dressed, my love. It's time for the people of Lassenberia to meet their King." She said. "King? Look at you all melodramatic!" Sir Marcus said as he was donning his sox. "Me? She said. Kimberly smirked as she hit her husband in the face with a pillow. Sir Marcus grabbed her by the waist. Kimberly screamed with joy as the couple wrestled around on the bed.

Back in the United States, hakim had just pulled up in Butch's car lot which he named Butch's Boeman Dealership. Hakim stopped the car right in front of the parts and services entrance, barely missing a couple of the employees in his path. "Hey! What the hell is wrong with you?" one of the employees shouted. Hakim had a big smile on his face. He turned off the engine before jumping out of the vehicle. The burly white guy in coveralls looked shocked as Hakim trotted pass him with the B.O.I in hand. "Hey! Are you fucking insane, or something?" the man shouted. Hakim stopped, turned around to face the man, who was obviously an employer of Butch's dealership. Hakim looked the man up-n-down, from head to toe with a devious smirk on his face. "Today is your lucky day, man!" Hakim said before turning around and walking away. "Yeah! Thats right! Keep walking!" the man said.

Moments later, Hakim entered Butch's office. He saw one of Butch's goons sitting in a chair reading the newspaper. "Where is he?" hakim asked. The burly dark-skinned bodyguard placed the newspaper to the side and stood up. "Alright! You know the routine!' nigga! Spread'em!" the bodyguard said. Hakim shook his head in disbelief before popping the bodyguard across the face with the B.O.I with a considerable amount of force. The bodyguard cupped his nose, moaning in agonizing pain. "It's general Bates to you, nigga! Know your place!" hakim said. Suddenly, Hakim heard a slow applause from behind. Hakim quickly turned around "If that wasn't so funny, and I wasn't curious about the info you got for me, I would've popped Yo ass on the spot!" Butch said. Hakim was not aware that Butch's bodyguard was rushing towards him until Butch gave him the order to stand down. "The kids' right! He is a general. Show some respect." Butch said. The bodyguard did not say a word. He just gave a nod as he cupped his nose. "Now, go get cleaned up." Butch said. "Who's gonna guard you while I'm in the bathroom?" the bodyguard asked. Hakim and Butch looked at each other and burst out laughing. "Well, it certainly ain't you!" Butch chuckled. butch looked outside. "You came alone?" Butch asked Hakim. Hakim gave a nod. "Step into my office." Butch said. Butch allowed Hakim to step into his office first. As soon as Butch closed the door, Hakim was pushed from behind, causing him to fall to the floor. "What the fuck, man?" Hakim shouted. "What? You thought you was gonna walk up in here, and not get checked?" Butch said after pulling out his pistol and pointing it at Hakim. "Man! I am here to show you some important shit! We're gonna need each other!" hakim shouted, "Get up, and strip down." Butch said in a calm voice. "Come on, man. I tossed it before I got here." Hakim said. "Hey. It's been done to me!" Butch confessed. "Oh shit! Somebody did that to you?" Hakim asked. "Yeah. Now strip." Butch said. "Where's the other generals?" Hakim asked. "They ain't get here yet. Stop stalling! Strip!" Butch shouted. "Damn!" Hakim shouted as he placed the B.O.I on Butch's desk. Hakim did not want to waste any time, so he quickly stripped down to his underwear. Hakim slowly turned around, showing Butch that he was not packing. "Happy now?" hakim shouted as he spread his arms. "You can get dressed now." Butch said. "You mind telling me who made the great Butch Watson strip down to his underwear?" Hakim asked as he zipped up his pants. Butch scoffed at hakim's question.

"You know him very well." Butch said. "Who?" Hakim asked. "You killed the motherfucker to get to where you are!" Butch said. Hakim stood there for a moment pondering who could it be. "Oh shit! Tony?" hakim asked with eyes wide open. Butch nodded with a big smile on his face. Butch looked out the window of his office. "That's fucked up what happened to the Lassenberry people!" Hakim said. "Yeah, kid. But right now, I gotta worry about keeping my own family safe. When me and your fa-, I mean Eddie started out, we took out whole neighborhoods. Men, women, sometimes kids." Butch said. "Goddamn!" Hakim shouted. "Yeah! This was before you were born. Old man Benny ordered us to stop. He said what we were doing was insane. But in 1980, that's when Eddie decided to go after specific targets." Butch explained. There was silence in the office for a moment until Butch saw 2 vehicles pull up to the lot. "Here they come." He said. Hakim and Butch watched as Dubbs stepped out of his Boeman SUV, along with 2 members of his crew. In the other vehicle, which was a Boeman Sedan, Mark (Mookie)Vasquez Jr. was being carried out of his vehicle by his bodyguard and placed in his wheelchair which his driver was holding steady. "Let me look at that book you got." Butch said to Hakim. "Here you go!" Hakim said. Butch flipped open the binder to the first page. At that moment Dubbs and Mookie entered the office. "Where my cousin at, man?" Dubbs asked Butch's bodyguard. "He's in his office!" the guard said as he covered his nose with a wet paper towel. "What the fuck happened to you, amigo?" Mookie asked. "Nothing, man!" the bodyguard said. Mookie just shook his head before following Dubbs and his crew to Butch's office. Dubbs didn't bother took knock. He just burst in. he stopped in his tracks when he saw Hakim standing over to the side. "What's this shit about?" Dubbs asked. "I come in peace, man!" Hakim said. "You check this nigga?" Dubbs asked Butch. "He's clean." Butch chuckled. "This meeting is for generals only! The rest of y'all gonna have to step!" Hakim said to Dubbs and Mookie's people. Butch gave the men in both crews the signal to leave the office with a nod. Dubbs closed the door behind them. "Now! What's this shit about, cuz?" Dubbs asked. Butch sighed. Well, our associate here, got the history of the Lassenberry organization for the past few decades it seems." He said. Butch had a scowl on his face. "What's wrong, man?" Hakim asked. Butch quickly flipped through more of the pages. "What the fuck? Some of these pages are missing!" Butch said. Hakim walked over towards Butch. He looked for himself. Hakim flipped though more of the pages. "This shit skipped from page 50, to page 54! Look at this shit here! It skipped from page 256, to 267!" Butch said. Dubbs walked over towards them to see for himself. He started flipping through the pages. "All I see is shit that everybody already knows about!" Butch said. "Look here! We already know about you killing that girl when you were in high school!" Dubbs said. "Yo, nigga! Watch your mouth!" Hakim said. "¿Qué hay en mí?" Mookie asked. "What the hell is he talking about?" Butch asked. "Don't worry, nigga! We all know about you killing Yo pops-n-shit!" Dubbs said to Mookie. Mookie put his head down for a moment, feeling shame. "Since when you learn to speak Spanish?" Butch asked. "Being around this nigga all the time, you can't help yourself!" Dubbs said. "Never mind all that shit! Turn to the back!" Hakim said. Butch flipped the pages all the way towards the back. He scrolled down on the last page with his finger.

"*It's time for me to face the truth. My generals are not as trustworthy as I thought. On this* day, *May 31ˢᵗ, 2002 I, Edward the 2ⁿᵈ of Lassenberry will make the announcement to remove my 4 Generals from their positions by diplomacy, or by force. I will have no choice to but to replace them with my agents, whose obedience is 100% unquestionable.*" Butch read aloud from the last entry of the B.O.I. "See! What have I told you? That motherfucker wanna kill our black asses!" Hakim said. Hakim looked over at Mookie. "Latino asses, too! Sorry Mookie, man!" Hakim said. "Damn! Thats interesting! Edward the 2ⁿᵈ went 2 days into the future to write this?" Butch asked. "What?" Hakim asked. Butch pointed at the entry date. "He put May the 30ᵗʰ!" Butch said. "So?" Hakim said. Butch looked at Dubbs and Mookie. "It's the 29ᵗʰ, amigo." Mookie said. "Maybe…maybe, he wasn't thinking clearly! Who the fuck knows?" Hakim shouted. "Maybe he didn't write this at all!" Butch said. Butch stared hakim in his eyes, not blinking one bit. Sweat started pouring from Hakim's forehead. "What you nervous about?" butch asked. "Nothing, old man! Are we gonna hit this nigga before he hit us, or what?" Hakim shouted. "You come to me with a book that's missing pages, with incorrect dates, and you want the rest of us to go to war with you against a potential enemy that has 90 times more muscle than we do, huh?" Butch shouted. "I don't know about you cousin, But I gotta go talk to my troops and think about this shit!" Dubbs said. "I know what I'm gonna do. I am gonna hold on to this binder here. I'm gonna arrange a sit down with Edward the 2ⁿᵈ and find out what the hell is really going on." Butch said with a smirk on his face. Hakim became agitated. "Fuck that! I'll handle that nigga myself then!" he said. Butch closed the binder. "You do that, kid. We will go back to making money. You fellas agree?" Butch said. Dubbs and Mookie nod their heads. "When I get rid of that mother fucker, y'all gonna come crawling to me for help!" Hakim said. "Hey kid. You kill him, we'll definitely come crawling." Butch said. "Same here, nigga!" Dubbs said. "Aquí mismo, amigo mío." Mookie said. "Man, fuck y'all!" hakim shouted as he stormed out of the office.

"You still gonna have that sit down with Lassenberry?" Dubbs asked. "Nah! Y'all just keep y'all people on high alert. Nobody hit the streets by themselves. Have your guys stay in groups of at least 3, and packing. Tell everybody if they see anybody approach them in a black suit and dark shades, shoot first and ask questions later. Got it?" butch said. "Got it." Dubbs said. "Tengo la sensación de que sólo va a ser 3 generales pronto!" Mookie said. "I think you're right!" Dubbs said. Before Mookie wheeled himself out of the office, he turned towards Butch. "Hey, what's with this Lassenberia?" he asked. "What?" butch asked. "Never mind." Mookie said before leaving.

Outside, Butch and Dubbs watched as Mookie and his crew drive off. Dubbs waived goodbye as the Boeman Sedan drove off. "What the fuck is wrong with you? you in love, or something?" Butch said. Feeling embarrassed, Dubbs quickly put his hand down. "My gut feeling tells me we're gonna have to worry more about Hakim then Edward the 2ⁿᵈ." Butch said. "You think so?" Dubbs asked. "Get ready. Cause when they find that kid's body in a ditch somewhere, we're gonna have the opportunity to split New Jersey up between the both of us." Butch said. "What about Mookie?" Dubbs asked. "What about him? He can keep his 2 counties. Everything else, is ours for the taking." Butch said.

Suddenly, Butch's employee, the one who had the run in with Hakim comes over. "Say! That kid is a real asshole! Looked like he had blood and brains splattered on his car door!" he said. "Sam. If you mention that to anybody else, I'm gonna personally knock you the fuck out in front of Yo wife-n-kids. Now get the fuck back to work." Butch said in a calm voice. Sam looked terrified as he trotted away back to parts and services.

The next day on the island of Lassenberia, Kimberly and Sir Marcus exit the medical facility hand-n-hand after hours of passionate relations. "The people have been waiting for you to surface from your recovery, my lord." Ali said. "How did they know I was out of my Coma?" Sir Marcus asked. "Forgive me, my lord. But I told one of my nephews of your condition. Obviously, he could not contain this information." Ali confessed. Sir Marcus gently patted Ali on the shoulder. "It's all right, Ali! Its just good to be alive! That's all that matters now!" Sir Marcus said.

Sir Marcus and Kimberly took a stroll down the road, hands still locked together as Ali followed closely behind wielding a high-tech machine gun. Sir Marcus was in awe on how fast so much infrastructure was constructed in so little time. The more they their trekked through this part of Lassenberia, more of its citizens came out of their town houses. Sir Marcus and Kimberly stopped when they realized the crowd had grew around them. "Who are these people?" Sir Marcus whispered to his wife. She smiled at her husband. "These are your people!" she said. Sir Marcus looked upon the sea of different faces. There was no more than 100 people. This small crowd was a diversity of blacks and whites, standing side by side. Men, woman, and children. Suddenly, the crowd parted like the Red Sea. "Here they come!" Kimberly said as a large tribe of African Albinos, about a couple hundred, made their way towards Sir Marcus and Kimberly. "Ms. Kimberly! what is the meaning of this?" Ali whispered behind Kimberly's back. Kimberly turned to Ali. "This is not the time to question me! Just trust me, for now!" she whispered to Ali. "My apologies, Ms. Kimberly!" Ali whispered. Sir Marcus turned to his wife with a bewildered look on his face. "We have a lot to talk about, my love!" he whispered. Kimberly nudged her husband in his ribs with her elbow. She walked toward the Albinos tribe with her arms spread and a welcoming smile. "Kulandira, abale ndi alongo! Ndikhululukireni ngati Chichewa wanga Sali wangwiro!" Kimberly shouted to the crowd. One of the young male members of the Albino tribe approached Kimberly, standing a few feet away from her. "Your Chichewa is perfect. But my people prefer the English language." The young tribesman said. Kimberly exhaled with a sigh of relief. Sir Marcus approached the young tribesman with his hand out in a friendly gesture. "Welcome to the island of Lassenberia I am Marcus." he said. The Albino tribesman looked bewildered as he stared at Sir Marcus's hand. "Mr. Marcus! My name is Ukerewe Torner! On behave of my people, I would like to say, you deserve more than a mere handshake!" the young tribesman said. Sir Marcus stood there in awe as the Albino tribe followed the young chieftain Ukerewe's lead as he kneeled before Sir Marcus. "No need for that, my brother!" Sir Marcus Shouted as he helped Ukerewe from off his knees. Ukerewe was instead embraced by Sir Marcus with a firm hug. The Albino men, women, and children stood by as Sir Marcus released him. Ukerewe had a smile from ear-to-ear, exposing his decayed teeth. "Listen! Wherever you came from, you can be assured that the tyranny you suffered will not be tolerated on the island of Lassenberia!" Sir Marcus shouted. Tim Braxton led the diverse crowd in applause. Kimberly noticed a small percentage of the crowd, who were members of Ali's family, including Ali himself did not applaud. "You've Just cursed this Island, Ms. Kimberly!" Ali whispered in her ear. Kimberly turned to Ali. She did not look pleased. "We will talk about this later! Now, take a few of your nephews to the boat that brought these good people and help them unload their belongings! Now!" Kimberly whispered. "She, Ms. Kimberly!" Ali whispered as he looked down at the ground in shame.

A few days earlier, Kimberly had a discussion with the Prime minister of Tanzania, Tunduru Othman. Their conversation was about the persecution of people with Albinism. The Albino people of Tanzania were, for a long time were either being murdered for their body parts because witch doctors believed they have magical powers, or African natives believed their existence was considered a curse across the motherland. Kimberly's idea for an exodus of the Albino people was told before Prime Minister Othman could finish his sentence.

Kimberly placed her arm around her husband's waist. "What's the next move, my king?" she asked with a smile on her face. Before Sir Marcus could utter a word, Tim Braxton and his brother Simon approached him. "Hello, sir! I'm Tim Braxton, first Baron of the Borough of Braxton!" Tim chuckled as he grabbed Sir Marcus's hand, giving him a firm handshake. Sir Marcus looked puzzled. "The borough of what?" Sir Marcus asked. Kimberly chimed in. "Yes! Tim and his descendants will oversee a region of Lassenberia!" Kimberly said with a smile. Sir Marcus turned to his wife showing a pleasant façade. "Great! We really need to have that talk, my love" he said.

About an hour later, Kimberly was sitting at the desk of her newly furnished office as her husband stood before her reading a pile of documents with concernment. "I have to say, I'm impressed you've gotten so much done in so little time, my love!" Sir Marcus said. Kimberly smiled as she folded her arms, leaning back in her comfortable office chair. Sir Marcus dropped the pile of documents on her desk. Kimberly's smile vanished. "What's wrong?" she asked. "Borough of Braxton? A tribe of Albinos?" Sir Marcus asked. "Yes! A tribe of Albinos! Just a moment ago you welcomed them with open arms!" Kimberly shouted as she leaned forward in her chair. "Of course, I did after you shoved them in my face!" Sir Marcus shouted. "Do you realize what these people have been through? Ukerewe is only 29 years old! The only reason he's leading these people is because his great uncle, who happened to be Albino, was murdered for protesting the atrocities of people with Albinism!" Kimberly shouted. 2 of Ali's nephews could hear Kimberly yelling as they stood guard outside her office door. Sir Marcus sighed. "Ok! You've made your point! Now. What's the deal with the Borough of Braxton?" Sir Marcus asked. Kimberly rolled her eyes sighing. "That, my love, was your cousin's idea to bring them here!" Kimberly said. Sir Marcus scratched his forehead. "Was it his idea to give them a piece of land? Was it his idea to give Tim a title of nobility?" Sir Marcus asked. Kimberly stood from her chair. She walked over to her husband. She put her hands on her husband's shoulders. "What we possess will change the world! When our enemies find out, and they will! They will think long and hard before they attack an island nation with a clan of Caucasians living on it! I had to give Tim and his family an incentive to stay!" Kimberly explained. Sir Marcus closed his eyes for a moment as he exhaled. He put his arms around his wife's waist. "Your father was a genius for bringing you into my life." He said. Kimberly gently poked Sir Marcus in the forehead. "No. my father was a genius for bringing you, into my life!" she chuckled after giving her husband a kiss on the lips. Sir Marcus gave his wife a firm hug.

Moments later, there was a knock on the door. "Come in!" Kimberly shouted as she pulled away from Sir Marcus. Ali entered the office with a grin on his face. "The council is ready for your arrival, Ms. Kimberly. "Thank you, Ali." Kimberly said. Sir Marcus looked confused. Ali stood in the doorway. "Yes, Ali! Is there anything else?" Kimberly asked. Ali dropped his head in shame. He then looked at Kimberly, giving her a sorrowful stare. "I just want to apologize for my words earlier, Ms. Kimberly!" Ali said. "Ali. We'll discuss this some other time. Right now, we need to stay focused on building this island into the most powerful nation on earth!" Kimberly said. "Of course, Ms. Kimberly!" Ali said with a smile on his face. "Would you excuse us for a moment, Ali?" Sir Marcus asked. "Yes, my lord!" Ali said before leaving the office. Sir Marcus turned to Kimberly. "Council? You have a council, now?" Sir Marcus asked. "No, my love! You have a council! Now, let's go so I can officially introduce you to them!" Kimberly said with pride in her voice. "Well, let's do this!" Sir Marcus chuckled. Sir Marcus opened the door for his wife. They exit the office.

Standing outside the office, Ali and 4 of his nephews, whose ages ranged from 14 to 22, were all armed with AK-47 machine guns. "Your vehicle is ready, my lord." Ali said. "Vehicle?" Sir Marcus asked with a surprised look. "Yes, my lord! We have transportation for you and Ms. Kimberly!" Ali said. "How far do we have to go for this council meeting?" Sir Marcus asked Ali. "A little over 3 kilometers, my lord!" Ali said. Sir Marcus looked at Kimberly. she leaned over, putting her lips close to his ear. "2 miles." She whispered. "Jesus! We all look like we're in great shape! Let's walk over there! What do you think, my love?" Sir Marcus asked Kimberly. "Let's do this!" She said. With Ali leading the way, Kimberly and Sir Marcus started their trek down the main road hand -n-hand as 2 of Ali's nephews walked on either side, with the other 2 nephews taking up the rear. This time, Sir Marcus put his lips to his wife's ear. "If the people of Lassenberia are with us 100 percent, why do we need to be surrounded by armed guards?" Sir Marcus whispered. "Perception of force makes enemies and potential enemies think twice. My father's words, not mine." Kimberly whispered. "Jabbo, said that?" Sir Marcus whispered with a surprised look on his face. Kimberly smiled as she nodded.

In a facility resembling a grade school classroom, the potential council members of Lassenberia wait for the heads of state to arrive. Jenna, Kimberly's sister, sat at the oblong wooden table reading copies of documents signed by the prime ministers of Mozambique, Tanzania, and Madagascar. She nodded as she flipped through the pages. "Excellent job, sis!" she said to herself. Tim Braxton paced the room as he read his copy of the documents. "Mmmm! That's interesting!" he said to himself. Ukerewe sat on the opposite side of the table from Simon, who was sharpening his hunting knife with a sharping stone. "That's an impressive weapon you have." Ukerewe said. Simon stopped sharping his knife. "I don't call her a weapon, kid. She's a tool. Weapons are what evil people have. Remember that." Simon said. "May I see it?" Ukerewe asked. "Sure!" Simon said. Simon flipped his hunting in the air, catching it by the tip of the blade. Ukerewe grabbed it by the handle. "Careful kid. She has quite a bite." Simon said. Kent Mooney was leaning up against the wall with his arms folded, staring out the window. He watched as construction crews continued building the roof of the University of Lassenberia across the way. "That is amazing! Fuck America!" he said to himself. Brandon looked agitated as he paced the room with his arms folded. "This is wrong! This is wrong!" Brandon said to himself. "Hey! What's your problem?" Kent asked him. Brandon stopped in his tracks. "Don't pay me any mind! I just have a lot on my plate!" Brandon said. Kent continued to look out the window. Moments later, Deputy Secretary of the United Nations Jawara Soumah entered the room. "My goodness! Did anyone get a chance to use those waterless urinals? Amazing!" he said with a smile on his face. Jenna looked up from reading the documents. "No, but now that you've mentioned it, I can't wait to pee!" she said with sarcasm. Simon chuckled as Ukerewe handed him his hunting knife back. Secretary looked at his watch as he sighed. "How long do we have to wait? I'm a very busy man!" Soumah said. "Listen! I don't know what my sister has in mind, but I'm sure it's worth waiting for! By-the-way! Aren't you the deputy secretary? I'm sure the secretary of the U.N. has everything under control!" Jenna said. Soumah gave Jenna a dirty look before taking a seat at the end of the table. "Do I have to remind everyone that we're about to be a major part in changing the world?" Kent said. "Thank you, Kent!" Jenna said as she rolled her eyes at Soumah. "Smart move to keep the media out of this! This information might be too much for the world to take in all at once." Tim said. "This land is really a blessing from the lord. We need to do all we can to protect it." Simon said. "I smell a war coming, brother. Not a month from now, not even a year from now, but it's coming." Simon said. "Guys! Please! Let's just concentrate on the present and wait for my sister and brother-in-law to arrive!" Jenna said. "Jenna! I know you don't want to hear it, but what Simon said is true!" Kent said. "Kent! I understand what the man is saying, but like I said, let's wait for my sister to come here and lay down the law!" Jenna said. "People! People! The infrastructure isn't nearly done, and you're already bickering!" Soumah chuckled hysterically. There was a dead silence in the room after Soumah finished laughing. Kent shook his head, continuing to stare out the window. "Oh! Here they come!" Kent said.

Moments later, Ali entered the room first, followed by Sir Marcus, and Kimberly. 2 of Ali's nephews stood guard inside by the door, while the other 2 were told to stand guard outside the door. "Good afternoon!" Sir Marcus shouted. "Good afternoon!" the council shouted simultaneously. "Please, everyone! Have a seat!" Sir Marcus said. Everyone but Kimberly and Ali took a seat. Kent sat on Jenna's left, as Tim sat on her right. Brandon sat next to secretary Soumah. Ukerewe turned his chair around to face Sir Marcus.

"For those who don't know, I am Marcus! Sir Marcus! I am the proprietor of this island called Lassenberia! This beautiful woman standing next to me is my wife, Kimberly Lassenberry! The man standing here with the machine gun is Ali! He's the head of my security! I want to make this meeting quick as possible, but we have a ton of things to cover, which might take up the entire day. So, if you would go around the table and introduce yourselves, we can commence afterwards!" Sir Marcus said. "Say, Ali! Unless you're going to fire, take you finger off the trigger! Accidents happen, my friend!" Simon said. Ali looked embarrassed but followed with Simon's request. Sir Marcus slapped his hands together. "Good! Now that we've gotten that out of the way, I would also want to ask, did everyone get a chance to eat, or use the bathroom?'' he asked. Everyone seated looked at each other. "We're good!" Tim said. "Mr. secretary here enjoyed his bathroom experience so much, he had to share it with the rest of us!" Jenna said. Kent smirked as he shook his head. The deputy secretary showed that he didn't find her words amusing by giving Jenna a dead stare. "I guess I'll start. I'm Tim Braxton. The first Baron of Braxton." He said. Sir Marcus turned to his sister-in-law. "Hello everyone! I'm Jenna Marie Jenkins, daughter of the great James Jenkins, also known to everyone back in America as Jabbo!" she said. Kimberly displayed a big smile on her face after hearing that. Sir Marcus then pointed to Kent. "Well, I'm Kent Mooney everyone. I'm a long-time member of the Lassenberry family's legal team, and I manage half the dive bars and bed-n-breakfast establishments for the Lassenberry organization." He said. Sir Marcus then pointed to Ukerewe. "I'm am Ukerewe Torner! Before coming here to take refuge, I lived in Tanzania fighting against the persecution of people with Albinism. Sir Marcus pointed to Simon. "I'm Simon Braxton, everyone! Brother of the Baron of Braxton! Oh, yes! I'm also a small arms expert!" Simon said as he winked at Ali. Ali's nostrils flared as he scowled, but he kept his composure. Kimberly glanced over at Ali, noticing his facial expression. Sir Marcus pointed to the Deputy Secretary. "Your turn, sir!" he said. The Deputy secretary straightened his necktie as he cleared his throat. "I guess it is! Well, my name is Jawara Soumah. I've been the Deputy Secretary of the United Nations for the past 3 years. I'm also a member of the Mandinka Heritage group!" Soumah said with pride in his voice. "Your turn." Sir Marcus said as he pointed to Brandon. Brandon stood from his seat. "With all due respect, Sir Marcus, I would like to refrain from my introduction!" he said. "Why? What's the problem?" Simon asked. Kimberly stepped forward to address Simon's question. "For our protection, our friend's purpose here, needs to be considered classified!" she said. Sir Marcus looked puzzled but did not respond to his wife's statement.

Sir Marcus slowly paced back-n-forth, rubbing his hands together before speaking. Suddenly he stopped in his tracks to face the council. "Okay! Let's get started!" he shouted. Kimberly grabbed a folding chair and sat behind her husband as he stood. "First, I would like to say if any of you, excluding the Deputy Secretary have any reservations on being a citizen of this new land, need to walk out that door now! I promise you, there will be no ill feelings towards any of you!" Sir Marcus said. The members of the council looked at each other. No one said a word. "Good!" Sir Marcus said. Brandon raised his hand. "What?" Sir Marcus asked. "I Have to speak with Kimberly for a moment, outside!" Brandon said. Sir Marcus sighed as he looked at the clock on the wall. "You have 5 minutes!" He said. Kimberly looked infuriated as Brandon walked past her, heading towards the exit. She followed him as one of Ali's nephews held the door open. Ali followed her. "You stay here with lord Lassenberry!" she whispered to him. "Yes, Ms. Kimberly!" he whispered. Sir Marcus slapped his hands together, displaying a grin on his face. "If you all waited this long, I guess 5 minutes won't kill us!" he said. Members of the council looked restless.

Outside the facility, Kimberly and Brandon stood about 20 yards away. "This better be good!" Kimberly said. The sound of construction work going on drowned out their conversation. "This is bullshit! I don't work for your husband! The real head of this organization is back in the states! I've done my job bringing the Braxton people here! Now, I'm taking Terry, and we're going back home!" Brandon shouted. Kimberly glanced over Brandon's shoulder, staring at the Ali's nephews standing guard. "You've seen how weak Edward the 2nd was at the castle! Who can respect that?" Kimberly shouted. "You forget! There wouldn't be an Edward the 2nd if your husband didn't run from his responsibilities! I've heard the story!" Brandon shouted. "The rest of the Lassenberry family are on their way! This place! This is a new beginning for everyone! If Edward the 2nd wants to run a drug empire for those people back there, so be it!" Kimberly shouted as she pointed her finger in Brandon's face. Brandon gently moved Kimberly's finger from in front of his face. "Don't touch me! Don't ever, touch me!" Kimberly shouted. Brandon turned his head for a second, looking at Ali's nephews. He turned back to Kimberly with a smile on his face. "This is a nice set up you're building here! But, how are you going to keep it without that drug empire? That drug money!" Brandon asked. Kimberly folded her arms, shaking her head. "I can tell Edward the 2nd doesn't have much faith in you to tell you the whole story on how all of this is being financed!" she said. "What the hell are you talking about? I have as much security clearance as you do! Maybe more!" Brandon shouted. Kimberly scoffed at his words. "Oh, really?" she said. "That's right!" he shouted. Kimberly was about to come back with a rebuttal, until both she and Brandon heard the screams of a woman over the noise of the construction equipment in the distance. Kimberly turned around. Running down the newly constructed road was Kimberly's sister-in-law Terry. She looked as if she had seen the devil himself. "They're dead! They're dead! They're all dead!" she screamed at the top of her lungs. Brandon bumped into Kimberly as he ran past her to get to his fiancé. Terry was stumbling quite a bit as she ran towards Brandon. "They killed my mommy! They killed my daddy!" she cried. Construction workers looked bewildered as Terry ran by them. Brandon held out his arms as Terry ran towards him. He caught her in his arms, causing them both to fall to the ground. "What happened, baby? What happened?" Brandon shouted. terry was so distraught; she couldn't get the words out of her mouth. "Breathe, baby! Just breathe!" Brandon shouted. Kimberly ran towards the couple. She kneeled next to Brandon, stroking Terry's shoulder. "What happened, sis?" Kimberly said in a calm voice. Tears and snot ran down Terry's lips. "They're…all…dead!" she panted. "Who's dead?" Kimberly asked. Terry looked Kimberly in her eyes, not blinking for one second. "My…family! They're…dead!" she said before passing out. "Take her to the medical facility! Now!" Kimberly ordered Brandon. As Brandon was lifting his fiancé off the ground, Kimberly watched as one of Ali's nieces came running in her direction. The young girl, who looked in her early teens, stopped right in front of Kimberly, breathing heavily. "Maxaa dhacay?" Kimberly asked. "Ms. Kimberly! Ms. Kimberly! it was on the radio broadcast! The Lassenberry family's plane exploded over the Atlantic! The news said there were no survivors!" the girl cried. Kimberly's started to breathe heavily as her nostrils flared and the rage in her eyes surfaced. "follow me!" Kimberly told the girl.

Back at the council meeting facility, Sir Marcus was sitting in his wife's chair, impatiently tapping his foot on the floor. Deputy secretary Soumah looked at his wristwatch as he grew impatient. "Mr. Marcus…" he uttered. "It's, Sir Marcus!" Jenna said. "Ok! Sir Marcus! My people are waiting for me at the dock to fly me back to the motherland!" Soumah said. Sir

Marcus stopped tapping his foot. "Well, since there, your people, they can wait!" Sir Marcus shouted.

Moments later, Kimberly bursts in, looking fired up. Sir Marcus stood from his chair. "What's wrong, my love?" He asked. Kimberly couldn't hold her composure. She covered her face as she sobbed like a child. Sir Marcus ran to her, putting his arms around her. Jenna jumped from her chair. She ran over to console her sister. "What's wrong sis?" Jenna asked as she rubbed Kimberly's back. Kimberly uncovered her face. She stared her husband in his eyes. Sir Marcus wiped away her tears. "Your…family! They're all dead!" She whispered passionately. 'What?" Sir Marcus shouted as his arms dropped to his side. "Terry! She just told us!" Kimberly said. "Where is she?" Sir Marcus shouted. "It was too much for her! She fainted! She's with Brandon, back at the medical facility. Secretary Soumah slowly stood from his chair. "What is going on?" He asked the couple. Sir Marcus turned to face the remaining council members. "Kent! As head of Lassenberia, I'm giving you a decree to draw up a constitution! You have a month to complete it and bring it before me! Jenna! I'm appointing you as the first Prime Minister of Lassenberia!" Sir Marcus said. "This is an outrage! The U.N. won't recognize her as a prime minister! What are her credentials?" Soumah asked. "Secretary Soumah! My sister-in-law is fluent in several languages! We own something that you want! If you want to continue to do business with us, you'll set up a secret meeting for her to meet with the Premier of China, the Prime Minister of Russia, and the President of the National Assembly of Venezuela! You have a month to get it done!" Sir Marcus said. "Why these nations, Sir Marcus?" Soumah asked. "We Have powerful enemies back in the United States! I doubt their arms reach this far!" Sir Marcus explained. Soumah looked around the room for moment. "Very well!" he sighed as he buttoned his suit jacket. "Thank you!" Sir Marcus said in a not so friendly tone. "Can I leave now?" Soumah asked. "Ali! Have your nephews escort the Deputy Secretary to his plane!" Sir Marcus said. "Yes, my Lord!" Ali said. Ali held the door open for Soumah. "Good day, and good luck everyone!" Soumah said before leaving the room. "That guy is a real asshole!" Jenna said. "He's a necessary asshole!" Sir Marcus said. Tim Braxton approached Sir Marcus and Kimberly. "How can we… I mean me, and my family pull our weight?" he asked. "We're going to need a well-trained army! Simon! I want you to gather every abled male citizen of Lassenberia and work your magic!" Sir Marcus said. Simon stood from his chair. "I'm on it!" He said before leaving the room. "Where's Brandon?" Sir Marcus asked. "I said he was with Terry." Kimberly said. "Oh, right! Kent! Do me a favor and get Brandon for me!" Sir Marcus said. "Christ! I went from a founding father, to an errand boy all-of-sudden?" Kent shouted. "Kent! Please! Just do what I tell you!" Sir Marcus ordered. Kent stormed out of the room, agitated. "Do you think it was deliberate?" Kimberly asked her husband. "If it wasn't, it's one hell of a coincidence!" Sir Marcus said. "I need to get back to Jenkins island!" Kimberly said. "Why?" Sir Marcus asked. "Although my family is here, I fear for the hired help, and the livestock!" Kimberly said. "You need to be by my side, my love!" Sir Marcus insisted. "No! I need to take Ali and a couple of his nephews with me!" Kimberly said. Tim grabbed Sir Marcus by the arm. "I'll go with her. I'll bring my brothers, Gabe, and Mathew. All I ask is that you keep our wives and children safe." Tim said. Sir Marcus sighed. He looked at Tim, then looked at his wife. "Be safe, my love!" he said before giving Kimberly a firm hug. "I'll go with you!" Jenna said. "No! if Secretary Soumah fulfills his part of the bargain by letting us meet with these foreign dignitaries, I'm going to need an interpreter!" Sir Marcus said. Jenna gives her sister a hug. "Be safe, little sis!" Jenna said. "I love you, big sis!" Kimberly cried. "Let's not waste any time." Tim Said. "Ok! Let's go! If we go well prepared, we should be at my family's island in 12 hours!" Kimberly said to Tim before they leave the room. Sir Marcus, Jenna, and Ukerewe stayed behind in the facility. Having flash backs in his mind from what took place at the National Agreement gathering, Sir Marcus massaged his temples as he shut his eyes. "What's wrong?" Jenna asked. "I need you two to give me a moment alone, please." Sir Marcus said. "Ok. Let's give him some space." Jenna said to Ukerewe. "Thanks, sis!" Sir Marcus said. "I'm sorry for your loss! We'll get to the bottom us this!" Jenna said as she rubbed her brother-in law's arm. She and Ukerewe leave the room. Moments after, Sir Marcus paced the floor in a small circular pattern, pounding his head with his fists while thinking of the images of his family members. "I'm going to kill you, Terrance! If this was, you're doing, I swear to god, you're a dead man!" he said to himself as he fell to his knees.

Elsewhere, in a room at a rundown motel, just outside Baltimore Maryland, Hakim, along with Clip and Aaron Poole, go over their plans on how to deal with Edward the 2nd. "That's fucked up, man! Chewie was the best of the best!" Aaron said. Clip was peeking through the blinds. "We need an army! I'm talking a couple hundred mother fuckers!" Hakim said. "Man! Most of our street captains and runners ain't gangster like me and Aaron!" Clip said. "Man, I'm talking hundreds just for appearances! We just need a handful of niggas that can actually get shit done!" Hakim said. Clip stood there in his thoughts for a moment. "Yo, Aaron! What's the name of that guy who just got out from doing a bid? The nigga from the Ivy Hill Crew!" Clip asked. Aaron thought for a moment. "Oh! Oh! You're talking about Biff! That's my nigga, Yo!" Aaron shouted. Hakim turned to Clip. "Who the fuck is Biff?" Hakim asked. "That nigga is more fucked up than this kid!" Clip said as he pointed to Aaron. "Will he bleed for me?" Hakim asked. "Yo! All he used to talk about was going out guns blazing for the organization!" Aaron shouted. "I wasn't talking to you!" Hakim said. Hakim looked over towards Clip. "This nigga will fight for you to the death! Me believe me!" Clip said. Hakim sat in his chair rubbing his head. "Damn! I gotta make the call for a refill, soon!" Hakim said to himself. "You sure it's safe for you to go out and give all the crews, even the South Jersey crews their refill if Lassenberry got you in his scope?" clip asked. "Nigga! I still run Essex county, and them cats down in South Jersey regardless! I came too far to give up that shit!" Hakim said. There was a moment of silence in the room. "Find me a piece paper, and something to write with!" Hakim said to Aaron. Aaron scurried around the room looking for a piece of paper and pen. "What you plan on doing?" Clip asked. "Hurry up, Aaron!" Hakim shouted. "I'm looking! I'm looking!" Aaron shouted. Aaron couldn't find a pen nor paper to write on in none of the drawers. "Hold on! I'll be back!" He said. Aaron took his pistol out of its holster and placed it on the bed before leaving the room. "You think we can call a truce with Lassenberry? I've got kids to feed!" Clip said. "Yeah, I'll call a truce, after I put a bullet in that nigga's head! Hold on a minute!" Hakim said before reaching for the phone. "What you about to do, boss man?" Clip asked. Hakim dialed the number to access his drug connection. He turned his back to Clip as he whispered his code 1970h into the mouthpiece of the phone. A few seconds passed, when Hakim violently threw the phone across the room. "What happened?" Clip shouted. "That bulgy eyed motherfucker had my access code denied! I can't get the product to our people!" he shouted. Suddenly, Aaron comes running back in the room. "Had to go to the front desk!" he said breathing heavily. He handed Hakim a sheet of notebook paper and a pen. Hakim turned to the small table and started jotting down a list on the paper. "I've got a real important mission for you, Aaron." Hakim said as he was writing.

Moments before Aaron was about the leave the room, there was a knock on the door. Hakim's eyes grew wide as saucers. Clip pulled out his gun. There was a dead silence in the room as the three men just stood paralyzed, staring at each other in fear. "Who the fuck knows we're here?" clip whispered. Hakim shrugged his shoulders. With gun in hand, Aaron tiptoed to the door. The knocking continued. Before Aaron could utter a word, Hakim, out of desperation, threw the pen in his hand at Aaron, hitting him in the back of the head. Aaron didn't say a word. He turned towards Hakim, rubbing the back of his head. Hakim put his finger to his lips, giving Aaron the signal to keep quiet. "General bates! General Bates! We know you're in there! The manly voice shouted on the other side of the door. "Oh shit!" Aaron whispered. "Lord Lassenberry demands your presence back at Castle Lassenberry, at once!" the voice shouted. "Fuck! How the fuck they find us?" Aaron whispered in a panic state. "There's no way out of this, General Bates! Just open the door and come along peacefully!" the voice shouted. "How do I know you won't shoot my ass if I come out?" Hakim shouted. "We were given strict orders to bring you back alive, General!" the voice shouted. "I didn't know you was a general!" Aaron said. "Shut the fuck up, nigga!" Hakim shouted. "General! If you have any weapons in your possession, it will be in your best interest to place them on the bed!" the voice shouted. "What we gonna do?" Aaron asked. Clip didn't say a word. He just tossed his gun on the bed. Hakim shook his head in disbelief. He looked at Aaron. "Toss it, nigga!" hakim ordered. Aaron walked over to the bed, tossing his gun on the bed. "Your turn, General!" the voice shouted. Hakim looked bewildered. Clip shrugged his shoulders. Hakim slowly pulled out his weapon, tossing it on the bed as well. "Now, I want you and your people to come out slowly with your hands in the air!" the voice shouted. "Go ahead! Open the door!" Hakim ordered Aaron. Aaron slowly opened the door. Hakim and his crew came out as instructed with their hands in the air. Hakim looked around and saw at least 10 NA agents pointing their handguns at them. "As a precaution, General Bates. I need to cuff you." the Caucasian agent said. "Why? We tossed al out shit on the bed!" Hakim shouted. "I know, General, but Lord Lassenberry would feel safe if you were in restraints." The agent said. "This, nigga!" Hakim whispered to himself as an agent placed him in hand cuffs. "Lord Lassenberry also ordered that you come alone." The agent said. 2 agents approached Clip and Aaron from behind before pulling out syringes from inside their suit jackets. They quickly inject both Aaron and Clip, causing them to fall to the floor unconscious. "What the fuck? Why y'all kill my boys?" Hakim shouted. "Don't worry, General Bates. They'll be fine." The head agents said. Another agent entered the room Hakim and his crew was in, coming out with all 3 weapons. "How the hell you know I was still packing? The door was closed!" Hakim asked. "This thermal imaging device made it possible, General." The agent said as he showed it to Hakim. "This way, General." The agent said. As the group of agents and Hakim walked towards the lobby, Hakim noticed more bodies spread out on the floor. "You motherfuckers don't leave nothing to chance, do you?" He said. None of the agents said a word as they escorted Hakim out of the motel. Outside the motel were 4 more agents standing around a black van. After Hakim was aided into the van, the van drives off followed by a black Boeman SUV.

A few hours had passed, when the black van and the SUV had made a turn on to the main road leading to Castle Lassenberry where there was a small garrison of 3 agents standing at a booth on this road. "Here they come." One agent said to another. "Make the call to the main gate." One agent said. As the small caravan passed the garrison, the main gates to Castle Lassenberry.

Hakim was so nervous as the van came closer and closer to the main gate, the agents in the van with him could hear him breathing heavily through his nostrils. Hakim turned to the agent sitting next to him. "So, he wants to kill me himself?" Hakim asked. "General?" the agent replied. "Lord Lassenberry." Hakim said. "That's not for me to say, General Bates." The agents said.

Still handcuffed with his hands in front of him, Hakim was driven on a golf cart, escorted by 3 agents down the halls of Castle Lassenberry, heading towards the west wing. The west wing was where the man incharge of the Lassenberry empire held his exclusive meetings. When the golf cart reached the office doors of Edward the 2$^{nd's}$ office, the agents hopped out, helping Edward the 2nd out of his seat. One of the agents knocked on the double doors. "Enter!" a voice shouted from inside the office. The agent opened the double doors. The other 2 agents grabbed Hakim by his arms. When Hakim entered the office, what he saw shocked him. Inside the office sat the 3 remaining generals. Edward the 2nd stood from his chair with a big smile on his face. "Hakim! What's up, my brother!" he shouted as he approached Hakim with open arms. The agents stood close to hakim to make sure their boss, Edward the 2nd remained unharmed. Hakim looked pissed, but remained silent, for the moment. "I know! I know! You've been through a lot of shit!" Edward the 2nd said as he placed his hands-on Hakim's shoulders. "You're really fucked up, man!" Hakim snarled. "Easy, my nigga. You should be grateful you're still breathing." Edward the 2nd boasted. Edward the 2nd turned to walk back to his seat. "Sit!" he said. Hakim just stood there in rage. "Agents! Put General Bates in a chair!" Edward the 2nd ordered. 2 of the agents forcibly slammed Hakim in a chair next to General Mark (Mookie)Vasquez.

Edward the 2nd sighed as he checked his fingernails for any flaws. He then looked up, probing the office before planting his eyes on one of his generals. "I don't' get it! You give a nigga an assignment, and what does he do, he double-crosses you!" Edward the 2nd said. "You set me up! 2 of my men are dead because of you!" Hakim shouted from his seat. "No nigga! 2 of your men are dead because of, you." Edward the 2nd chuckled. "Listen, man! If it wasn't for me, you wouldn't be sitting in that seat!" Hakim shouted. Edward the 2nd became enraged. He jumped from his seat and stormed over to where Hakim was sitting. His face was inches away from Hakim's face. "Motherfucker! I'm a Lassenberry! I was destined to be in that seat! It is my divine right!" he shouted at the top of his lungs. Edward the 2nd stood upright. He composed himself as he smoothed out the red sash on his uniform with his hands. "Now. The question is- what am I supposed to do with you?" He asked. Edward the 2nd looked over at Butch. "General Watson! You've been in the game the longest. What do you think I should do to General Bates?" he asked. Butch glanced over at Hakim. He sighed. "It's your call, kid." He said to Edward the 2nd. Edward the 2nd folded his arms as he slowly walked in Butch's direction. "What would my uncle do, in a situation like this?" he said as he stood over butch. Butch looked him straight in the eye. "Your uncles' dead, Lord Lassenberry. like I said, it's your call." He said to Edward the 2nd. Ok. Ok." Edward the 2nd said as he turned away from Butch. "What is this shit really about? Kimberly?" Hakim asked with a smirk on his face. Edward the 2nd turned to Hakim with a big smile on his face. "Oh! You wanna play head games? Let's play, this game." He said to Hakim. Edward the 2nd walked over to Hakim. He went to undue his uniform trousers. ¿Que demonios?" General Vasquez said to himself. Edward the 2nd let his uniform trousers drop to his ankles. He then squatted. Within moments, a long light brown turd descended from his anus like a ton brick. Edward the 2nd stood. He didn't bother to clean off his back side. He pulled up his uniform trousers. "General Bates! You have 10 seconds to get on your knees, and without using your hands, I want you to eat that shit like the fucking backstabbing dog you are!" Edward the 2nd shouted. as he turned away. All the generals looked shocked. "Man, you done lost your fucking mind!" Hakim shouted. "Agent! Point your pistol at General Bate's kneecap!" Edward the 2nd ordered. Without hesitation, the NA agent standing the closest to Hakim pulled out his firearm and pointed it at Hakim's kneecap. "If you don't wanna lose that leg, I suggest you get on your knees and start eating, motherfucker!" Edward the 2nd shouted as he pointed to the pile of shit. Hakim shook his head. "You just gonna have to kill me, nigga!" he said. "Don't worry. I just became a vegan last week. It should be a healthy meal." Edward the 2nd chuckled. "This is fucking ridiculous, even for him!" Butch shouted. "Shut the fuck up, old man! I asked you for your advice, and you said it was up to me!" Edward the 2nd shouted as he pointed his finger at Butch. "Like I said, nigga! Kill me!" Hakim shouted. "!0…9…8!" Edward the 2nd shouted. "Hold on! Hold on, for a minute!" Butch shouted. "7…6…5!" Edward the 2nd shouted. "Just take away the South Jersey territory you gave him!" Butch shouted. Edward the 2nd stopped counting. He pondered what Butch had said for a moment. "Agent! Put it away!" Edward the 2nd ordered. The NA agent placed his weapon back in his holster. "Ok! From this day on, the South Jersey territory that used to belong to General Bate's is no longer his! it will stay vacant until I decide who gets it!" he said. Hakim showed a sigh of relief. "Besides, it ain't no fun torturing a nigga that ain't afraid to die." Edward the 2nd chuckled. "You'll lose millions if there's a drought in that area." Butch said. Edward the 2nd turned to Butch. "I ain't broke, old man." He said in a calm voice. "Ok!" Butch sighed. "I want to remind y'all a week from today, memorial services will be held outside the castle walls for my departed family members at 12 noon! I expect y'all to be here in full uniform, an hour before! I also want you to bring the top people from each of your crews! Now, this meeting is over! Agents! Escort the Generals back to the main gate! Uncuff General Bates when he's at the gate! Oh! If I find out any of your people dealing in that territory before I find a new general, best believe, I will hold the General in command of that person responsible! Now! Show your loyalty!" Edward the 2nd said in a stern voice.

Butch and Dubbs stood at attention. One of the agents forced Hakim to stand "Long live the House of Lassenberry! Long live Edward the 2nd!" they shouted before making their way out of the office. "General Vasquez! Let me holler at you for a minute!" Edward the 2nd shouted. general Vasquez sighed as he swiveled his wheelchair towards his boss. Edward the 2nd waited for the others to leave the office before speaking. "What is it, Lord Lassenberry?" he asked. "Whatever you know, or think you know about Lassenberia, doesn't exist! ¿Entender?" He said. "Si mi señor. Entiendo." General Vasquez said. "What?" Edward the 2nd shouted. "I understand, my Lord!" Vasquez said. "Good! Now get the fuck out!" He said. General Vasquez swiveled his wheelchair around once more, dodging the pile of shit on the floor before leaving. Soon as he was alone, Edward the 2nd walked over to the pile of bodily waste. He looked down at it, having a look of sadness on his face. He went over to his desk. He picked up the black phone. "Get someone in here to clean this carpet, now!" he said before hanging up.

Outside the castle walls, one of the NA agents reached in his jacket pocket, pulling out the keys to uncuff Hakim. Hakim watched as the rest of the generals entered their separate limos. "Damn! Hurry up!" he said to the agent. The agent released him from his restraints. Hakim trotted over towards Butch's limo. Hakim leaned over to speak with him. "I just want to say, thanks for what you did back there." He said. "Do me a favor, kid. Unless we're called to a meeting, stay the fuck away from me, and my family." Butch said before ordering his chauffeur to drive off. He watched as the other 2 limos drove off the castle grounds. Hakim turned to the group of agents. "Can somebody give a ride home?" he said

── CHAPTER .32 CHEMTRAILS ──

F lying 5 miles above and 100 miles away from the Florida Keys in an amphibious plane, Kimberly and crew go over their plans once more to set foot on Jenkins' Island. "Somethings wrong. I just have a feeling." Tim said to himself. "What's that, you say?" Kimberly asked. "I think it would be best, young lady, if you would stay behind in the plane until Mathew and I do some reconnaissance!" Tim said. "I'll go along with you! my nephews will keep Ms. Kimberly safe! Besides, you'll need a guide!" Ali said. Tim turned to Kimberly. "He's right. Ali is familiar with the Island." She said. Tim sighed. "Ok!" he said. "One thing I can say, brother, you made the right choice picking this type of transportation." Gabriel said.

Everyone on board went silent when the pilot announced their time of arrival over the PA system. Within moments, the plane skidded off coast of the island's remote side under Kimberly's orders. "Ok! Let us join hands, pray!" Tim said. The prayer lasted about 20 seconds. "You guys locked-n-loaded? Let us go!" Tim shouted.

The co-pilot had exited the plane to tie it to one of the 3 piers on the island. Ali was the first of the recon team to exit the plane. He wielded a sub-machine equipped with a silencer. Tim wielded an AR-15 rifle. Mathew wielded a Steyr AUG assault rifle. "The suns' going down, boys! Switch to night vision!" Tim said. All 3 men donned their night vision goggles. "Let's travel 0.0457 Kilometers apart, gentlemen!" Ali said. "What?" Mathew asked. "50 yards, little brother!" Tim said. "Why?" Mathew asked. "I thought you were a survivalist! If our enemies come for us, they can't take us down all at once!" Ali said. "Who are you, man?" Mathew asked. "I'll tell you in a more peaceful time!" Ali said. The 3 men slowly started their trek into the Island.

5 hours later, in the dark of night, 2 members of the recon team were making their way back to the amphibious plane, this time at a faster pace. Kimberly was awaking from her slumber. Gabriel was the first person she laid her eyes upon. "You look so beautiful when you wake up!" he said. Kimberly had a smirk on her face after the comment. "Where is everyone?" she asked. "No word yet!" Gabriel said. "How long I've been out?" she asked. Gabriel looked at his sports watch. "About 4 hours." He said. There was a moment of silence between the 2. "Why are you staring at me like that?" Kimberly asked. Gabriel began breathing heavily. "I

know it goes against my beliefs, but I just wanted to say, I found you to be the most beautiful woman in the world since I've first laid eyes on you!" he said. Kimberly blushed to the point that she covered her face for a moment. "I'm married!" she shouted with a smile on her face. "I know! I know! I just can't hide it anymore!" he confessed. Kimberly had a serious look on her face. "Do you believe in the future of Lassenberia? Do you believe in my husband leading us to a greater life for, all people across the globe?" she asked. Gabriel dropped his head. He then looked up at Kimberly. "I don't know what I believe at this moment! I've devoted my life to Jesus Christ, but I feel confused! But I'm not confused on how I feel about you!" he said. "Stop it, Gabriel! Stay focused on the mission!" Kimberly said. The pilot and co-pilot were sitting on the pier while Kimberly and Gabriel were alone in the plane. Gabriel looked out the window to see if the coast was clear. He lunged over to Kimberly, with his face being inches apart from hers. "Kiss me!" he whispered. "What?" She asked in a bewildered tone. "Just kiss me! I've spent my life devoted to Jesus, not knowing the feel and affection of a woman!" he confessed. Kimberly gently pushed him away. "One day I'll be a queen! This moment could never be a part of Lassenberia history! If you're going to be a loyal subject of Lassenberia, you must know your place, Gabriel! One day you might be Barron of Braxton! Don't screw that up!" she said. Gabriel disregarded her words. He quickly grabbed Kimberly by her private parts. At first, she physically tried to resist, but soon fell under the spell of lust. Clothes were being pulled off at a rapid pace. Suddenly, Gabriel inserted his penis into the future queen of Lassenberia. They went at it until Gabriel's semen was released. They quickly put on their clothes when they heard the voice of the co-pilot. "Here they come!" he shouted. Kimberly just buttoned the top button of her blouse when Ali opened the hatch. Ali was in shock but focused on his mission. "Ms. Kimberly! I couldn't believe my eyes! Something terrible has happened! As my future queen, you must come with us, now!" he said in desperation. Kimberly glanced at Gabriel before exiting the plane. "Stay close to me, Ms. Kimberly!" Ali said. Tim approached the plane. Tim was out of breath due to his obese physique. "Young lady! This just turned into something real!" Tim said. Kimberly took a deep breath. "Let's go!" she said.

Kimberly and company were making their way through the darkness. "Be careful not to touch anything when we arrive to the village, young lady!" Tim said. "What's wrong?" Kimberly asked. "I can't say for sure, but I believe most of this land was saturated with some type of toxin!" he said. Gabriel checked his weapon, which was a semi-automatic shotgun. Tim turned towards Gabriel. "Check your fly, little brother." Tim said. "My fly?" Gabriel asked. Tim looked down at his brother's work pants. Gabriel caught on, then quickly zipped up his fly. Ali looked over towards Kimberly. she looked away from embarrassment.

The sun was coming up over the horizon as Kimberly's team entered the village. She was so distraught at what she saw. The homes of the hired help, even her home her father had built for her was still intact. The horror of it all, were the bodies and livestock laying lifeless around the homes. Kimberly ran to one of the lifeless bodies. It was the body of old man Salt. She was about to kneel to embrace his body. Tim grabbed her by the shoulder. "No, young lady! We don't know what caused his death, but whatever it was, we don't want it to infect us!" he said. Kimberly couldn't look at her old friend's body anymore. She turned away into the arms of Ali. "if this was an act of our enemies, we will strike back, Ms. Kimberly!" he whispered in her ear. Kimberly pulled away from Ali. She wiped her tears away. "Let's move on! I need to see more!" she said.

As Kimberly and crew searched her families island for signs of life, time looked up at the dreary sky. He stopped in his tracks. "What's wrong, Tim?" Kimberly asked. The formation of the clouds! It just looks odd!" he said. Ali looked up as well. "He's right! The formation of the cloud looks unnatural!" he said. "This is no work of the almighty!" Ali said. "Do you think these clouds have something to do on what happened here?" Gabriel asked. "I don't know!" Tim said. Suddenly, the group turned in one direction, listening to the sounds of a plane coming their way. "It' sounds like more than one!" Kimberly said. The group stared up at the sky in different directions. They noticed 3 turboprop planes crisscrossing each other, leaving a trail of orange smoke behind. "What, in God's names?" Gabriel shouted." "Tim! do you have a container on you?" Kimberly asked. "Yes! Why?" he asked. "I need you to scoop up a sample of the soil! Ali! I need you to carefully pick up one the dead birds and place it in your backpack!" she shouted. "Right-away, Ms. Kimberly!" he said. "I think we need to leave before that orange mist descends! Like now, gentlemen!" she shouted, as she ran back towards the pier.

As Kimberly and the group made haste towards the pier, an orange mist fell upon them. "Jesus! This stuff burns!" Tim shouted. "Hurry! Hurry" Kimberly shouted. Ali noticed the vegetation around him began to slowly melt like wax. "Run! Run!" he shouted. Kimberly and the others scowled as the orange mist concealed to their skin. Tim was lagging. "Come on, brother!" Gabriel shouted. Mathew and Gabriel turned back to rescue their big brother. They grabbed him by the arms, trying their best to lift him as the mist seared through their skin. Kimberly and Ali were yards ahead, screaming in agony while running to seek shelter. Kimberly noticed her arms start to blister. "Ali! Ali!" she screamed. "Come on Ms. Kimberly! the pier is just ahead!" shouted in agonizing pain.

Moments later, the pier came in sight. Kimberly noticed the pilot and the co-pilot were inside the plane, looking up at the sky. Kimberly tried desperately to pull the hatch open. It was locked. She banged on it, screaming at the pilots to open it. Ali raised his weapon towards the cockpit. "Open it, or I'll kill you both!" he shouted. the pilot then gave the co-pilot the signal to open the hatch. Kimberly pushed the co-pilot out of the way, making her way towards the back of the plane. The co-pilot had a look of disgust on his face as Ali entered the plane. Ali's skin was covered in blisters. "Get us out of here! Quickly!" he shouted. Ali fell to his knees trying his best to endure the pain. In the back of the plane, Kimberly went into her backpack. She grabbed a beaker filled with GLC. she drank from the beaker as if she was dying of thirst. Moments later, she could feel the pain on her body lessening, and see the blisters dissipating. She made her way towards Ali. She forced fed him the GLC before he went into shock. Within moments, Ali regained his strength. "Where's Tim, and the others?" he asked Kimberly. "I don't know!" she said. "We have to go back for them!" Ali shouted. "It's too dangerous!" Kimberly said in a calm voice. The co-pilot looked out the window. "Look! There's one of them!" he shouted. "Start the plane! Get us out of here!" Kimberly screamed. Using every ounce of strength left in his body, Gabriel, who was horribly disfigured, made his way to the plane. He pressed the container of soil up against the window of the plane as he was gasping for air. "Open the Hatch!" Kimberly shouted. Ali obeyed her orders, pulling what was left of the Gabriel they knew, inside. His clothes were tattered with burns. The propellers of the sea plane started to spin. "Get me the GLC, Ali!" Kimberly shouted. Gabriel's body went into convulsions as Kimberly held him in her arms. Suddenly, his body just froze. His body began to slowly melt like butter in her arms. Ali quickly sprinkled some of the GLC on Kimberly to keep her from being contaminated. At that moment, the plane began to take flight. Ali poured the remaining GLC on Gabriel. Obviously, it was too late. Ali fell to his knees as Kimberly began sobbing. Gabriel's body had turned into a puddle of goop. Ali shook his head as he scooped up a sample of what was left of Gabriel, placing it inside the beaker.

Miles above the Atlantic Ocean, the sea plane carrying Ali and Kimberly was on it's a way due east towards the continent of Africa. Kimberly stared out of the window in a daze. Ali sat over in the next isle, wiping off his weapon. "I hope you realize Ms. Kimberly; the attack wasn't directly meant for us. It was meant to get rid of the crime scene." He said. Kimberly turned towards Ali. She just nodded, turning back towards the window. Ali looked up from cleaning his weapon when the co-pilot entered the cabin. "Hey! You guys ok?" he asked. Kimberly turned to the co-pilot. She didn't say a word. She just turned back to look out of window. "What's with the green drink?" the nerdy looking Caucasian man asked. Those words grabbed Kimberly's attention. She looked at Ali. Ali looked at her. Kimberly than looked at Ali's weapon. "I have my pilot's license, Ali." She said with a calm demeanor. Without hesitation, Ali pointed his sub-machine gun, with silencer at the co-pilot. The co-pilot's eyes were wide as saucers as he gasped for air. He received a single shot between the eyes. His body fell back like a wooden board. Ali left his seat, heading towards the cockpit, with Kimberly following close behind.

2 days later, around 5pm eastern standard time, Hakim was sitting in a recliner at his Manhattan penthouse. His crew was lounging around smoking marijuana. Aaron had the remote to the TV. He was channel surfing until he came upon a rap video. "Oh shit! This nigga gotta new video out?" he shouted to everyone in the room. There was another young man in the room named toothpick.

William(toothpick)Blane was a tall lanky black guy in his early 20's, who was a lookout for the Dodd street dealers at the East Orange and Bloomfield, New Jersey border. Aaron got wind of his cunning ways of protecting the dealers in that territory. Toothpick was recently brought to Hakim's attention, like Bess. Clip told Hakim he was bringing toothpick over as a potential member of the inner circle.

"Oh shit! MC Gutter! That nigga spit some serious shit, now!" toothpick said as he took a hit of his marijuana joint. "Fuck that nigga, man!" Bess said. Clip turned his attention to Hakim. He noticed that hakim looked pissed about something. "You ok, boss man?" Clip asked. Hakim looked dazed. "What?" he asked. "Don't tell me you still fuming about that shit the other day! We made it out alive!" Clip said. "Fuck that! You realize how much money I lost, because of that motherfucker?" Hakim shouted. "We're still breathing, boss man." Clip said. Hakim stared at the rap video on TV. "♪ *Flossing with diamonds, you see me shining! Watch so bright, it's blinding! Why y'all sleeping, I'm grinding! Pushing weed-n-rocks like Hakim! When he falls from grace, I'll reign supreme!*" ♪ were the lyrics from the young rapper. Hakim hearing those lyrics, became enraged. "Damn! Was that nigga talking about you, boss?" Aaron asked. "You know what? I'm tired of these fake asses, gangster wannabe motherfuckers thinking they can get away with saying whatever they want, without repercussion!" Hakim said with fury in his voice. "What you wanna do, boss man?" Clip asked. "I wanna put a contract on that nigga's head! Put the word out!" Hakim said as he pointed to the TV. "Copy, that." Clip said. "I want It done, like yesterday!" Hakim said. "We should make this a one-man job. Too many niggas involved, shit might get sloppy." Clip said. "Who you got in mind?" Hakim asked. Clip pointed to Toothpick. "You sure?" Hakim asked. "He gotta get his feet wet, if he wanna stay in the core group." Clip said. "Put his ass to work, then!" Hakim sighed.

Back on the island of Lassenberia, the newly formed council, excluding Kimberly, sat around the table discussing the catastrophe that had taken place back on the Jenkin's family Island. One chair at the table remained empty out of respect for the former Barron of Braxton, Tim Braxton. The weapons of the fallen Braxton brothers were placed in the middle of the table, on Sir Marcus's orders.

Sir Marcus stood at the head of the table. "Now, that we members of the council had time to grieve. It's time to get back to work, avenging our fallen heroes, avenging my family back in America, and building this Island into the most powerful place on this planet." He said. Simon Braxton, who was sitting 2 seats down, stood from his chair. "I would like to say, that with all-due-respect, Sir Marcus, I would like to take my entire family back to the United States." He said. Sir Marcus shook his head. "No way I could allow you to leave, at this time!" Sir Marcus said. "It's not your call!" Simon shouted. Sir Marcus walked over to Simon, putting his hand on his shoulder. "You and your family are citizens of Lassenberia now. If you're here, you're safe. If you go back to the states, I can't help you, your children, your wife, your brother's wives nor your nieces and nephews! Please! Help me build an army! I need you! I need you, here!" Sir Marcus pleaded. Simon looked around the table at the other council members. "Lord Lassenberry, pray for me. All of you, pray for me. Keep my family safe, because I'm going to gear up, and head back to the states! If you can be so kind and provide me with the proper documentation to sneak back into the good-ole-U.S. of A." Simon said. Sir Marcus also looked around the table. He shook his head. "No." he said in a calm voice. Frustrated, Simon stormed out of the meeting. "Give him time to think things over. He'll see things your way." Jenna said. Moments later, Kimberly and Ali enter the meeting. Sir Marcus embraced her with a hug and a kiss. "Just ran into Simon. He looked pissed." Kimberly said. "He wanted me to give him the paperwork to go back to the states." Sir Marcus said. "That's suicide!" she said. "Trust me. I wanted to do the same thing after what happened to you back there on your family's island. But I must stay focused on the bigger picture! What did the guys in the lab say about the samples you've brought back?" Sir Marcus asked. "Chemtrails!" Kimberly said. "What?" Sir Marcus asked. "It wasn't the orange mist that killed all the life on the island. It was used to get rid of the crime scene!" Kimberly said as her eyes teared up. "Chemtrails?" Kent asked. Kimberly turned to Kent. "Yes! The white streaks in the sky! It was the cause of the massacre! The same white streaks we've seen for years back home in the states!" she said. "I don't get it! We've been seeing jets fly over us spreading that stuff since we were kids! We're still alive!" Sir Marcus said. "This is nothing new under the African sun, Lord Lassenberry!" Ukerewe said. "Explain yourself." Sir Marcus said. "For decades the motherland has suffered under these chemical attacks. Ethiopia, Sierra Leone, and the Congo have suffered! Poor soil kept crops from growing, turning what was once a rich land, into a waste land! Ever since the Europeans' arrival, there has been nothing but destruction on our homeland!" Ukerewe said. "Hold on now!" Kent shouted as he walked towards Ukerewe. Kimberly gave Ali the signal to intervene. Ali with weapon in hand, stood between Kent and Ukerewe. Ukerewe stood from his seat in defense of his personal space. "It's true! I accuse your kind of Killing off the African to rob the land of its resources!" Ukerewe shouted. "I'm from America, buddy! I didn't kill any Africans! I didn't rob any people of their resources! I certainly didn't try to exterminate any people with Albinism!" Kent shouted before going back to his seat. "Alright, guys! Stop it! Remember! We're all on the same side!" Sir Marcus shouted. Ukerewe slowly sat back in his chair. "Kent! What's the progress on the-?" Sir Marcus asked. Before Sir Marcus could utter another word, in comes a blast from his past. "Hellooo!" the person shouted as he made his grand entrance into the room. "Stephan. It's good to see you." Sir Marcus said. Closely following behind Stephan was Brandon Hart.

Stephan walked into the room wearing a plaid shirt, tight blue jeans, and silver combat boots, with his hair done up in a purple mohawk. He dropped his duffle bag on the floor. "You guys love the latest look?" he shouted as he slowly spun around. Jenna covered her mouth to keep from laughing. Ukerewe sat there in awe. Sir Marcus walked over and shook Stephan's hand. Ladies and gentlemen! I would like to introduce the guy who will make us look presentable, and official to the world!" Sir Marcus shouted. "What is this? A joke of some kind?" Ukerewe asked. Sir Marcus placed his hand on Stephan's shoulder. "No, it's not! This is the guy who will design the finest uniforms for our nobility, and military!" Sir Marcus said. "After what Brandon told me what you offered, I had to get my ass over here, with a quickness, honey!" Stephan shouted as he snapped his fingers. Kimberly and Jenna laughed as they applauded. "Good! Not too far from here, a facility has been set up for you to get started on making all of us look dignified!" Sir Marcus chuckled. "Great, honey! Once I get all your measurements, I can get started! Now! Where's my team of seamstresses and tailors?" Stephan asked. "Jenna! Can you assign a team for our friend here?" Sir Marcus asked. "I'll get right on it." She said. Stephan gently grabbed Sir Marcus's hand. "My condolences deeply go out for your loss, back in the states!" Stephan said as his eyes teared up. "Thank you." Sir Marcus said as he gently pulled his hand away.

The next day, Kimberly sat in her office staring at a beaker filled with GLC. She shook her head, just giggling. Her joyful moment morphed into sorrow. She tried to control her sobbing, but her emotional control fell to the waste side. She placed the beaker on the desk, covering her face as she cried. Suddenly, there was a knock on the door. She quickly composed herself, wiping away her tears. "Come in!" she shouted as she made haste hiding the beaker in one of the desk's drawers.one of Ali's nephews, with machine gun in hand, opened the door, allowing Brandon to enter the office. "You wanted to see me?" he asked. "Yes. Take a seat!" she said. Brandon had a frown on his face, as to say, who is this woman ordering him around. "Where's Marcus?" he asked before taking a seat. "Sir Marcus? Head of the Lassenberry Organization?

Future king of this great land we're on? Oh, he's very busy building his kingdom at this moment! You answer to me, for the time being! Now Mr. Hart, take a seat." she said with a big beautiful smile. Brandon reluctantly sat in the chair across from Kimberly. Brandon looked around the office. So! What's up?" he asked. Kimberly leaned back in her chair. "I've received a coded message from the states. Your presence is requested there. Edward the 2nd says he needs you by his side." She said. "Cool! I'll let Terry know, and we'll catch the next plane out of here!" Brandon said with enthusiasm. Kimberly leaned forward in her chair, with her hands folded on the desk. "Sorry, but it's too dangerous for you to go back. In fact, it's too dangerous for any of us to go back!" she said. Brandon looked bewildered. "I went back to fetch Stephan and made it back in one piece!" he said. "You were lucky!" Kimberly said. "You don't understand! The organization could lose millions if I'm not back there making the transactions!" Brandon shouted. Kimberly stood from her chair. "No! You don't understand! We're moving away from the drugs! At least that kind." She said before shrugging her shoulders. "So, Simon can leave and seek revenge, but I have to stay?" Brandon pointed out. "Simon is a warrior. If he wants to die a warrior's death, so be it." Kimberly explained.

Elsewhere, on a remote side of Lassenberia, away from all the construction going on, Sir Marcus had gathered many of the citizens of the new nation to a meeting. Sir Marcus stood atop of a sand dune, looking down at his subjects. He stood proudly, dressed in full uniform. Jenna, Kent, Ali and Ukerewe stood at the bottom of the dune facing the crowd. Ukerewe held a megaphone, which he used to translate Sir Marcus's word to his people. Standing on the outskirts of the crowd were about a dozen of Ali's nephews wielding machineguns.

"Today is a sad day, my fellow Lassenberians! I've just received news from our allies in Mozambique this morning that one of our most valuable citizens, Simon, Barron of Braxton's plane crashed into the mountain of Monte Binga, killing everyone on board!" Sir Marcus shouted his voice cracked. The screams and cries of the Braxton clan were deafening. Simon's wife fainted even though she was informed and consoled by Sir Marcus earlier. "Even though an investigation is underway, sources say there are spies and saboteurs from the U.S. based near the South African boarder who are aware of our presence here! You are all aware that my wife and Ali barely escaped her family's island a couple of days ago after the demise of the remaining Braxton brothers! To keep these So-called chemtrails from appearing above our skies, I will put into effect, with the cooperation of our friends at the United Nations, a no-fly zone within a hundred-mile radius of Lassenberia!" He shouted. the applause amongst the crowd was faint. Kent looked up towards Sir Marcus, waiting to see what he would say next. Jenna grabbed the megaphone from Ukerewe's hand. "Listen everyone! When this order is put into effect, I guarantee- Sir Marcus guarantees the safety and survival of our families!" She shouted. Ellen, Tim's widow, stormed through the crowd making her way towards Jenna. The 2 women stood face-to-face, inches apart. Ellen's face looked steamed as she grits her teeth. "Your Sister is safe! Your husband and children are safe! Your…mother is safe! My husband is dead! All my brothers-in-law are dead! So, don't you dare speak as if everything's ok! Because it's not!!" she shouted. Ali looked up in Sir Marcus's direction, waiting for orders to intervene. Sir Marcus held is hand up, shaking his head, as to tell Ali not to engage in the situation. Jenna dropped the megaphone to her side. Her eyes started to tear up. She gently placed her hand on Ellen's forearm. "Sweaty! I'm very, very sorry about the loss of your family members! But, consider yourself and the rest of your family, part of our family, from now on!" Jenna cried as she gave Ellen a firm hug. Soon after, both women cried like children in each other's arms.

Back at the more developed side of Lassenberia, Terry was at her luxury townhouse laying down in bed, staring at the ceiling. Moment s later, her fiancé entered the room. He stood over her with a sorrowful look in his eyes. "Honey! Are you, all right?" he asked. Terry snapped out of her daze, slowly turning her head towards Brandon. She smiled. "No." she said in a euphoric voice. Brandon kneeled by her bed side. "Honey! What's going on? Why are you talking like that?" he asked. "I'm…fine. I love…my family." She said. Brandon paused for a moment. "Did you take anything? Did anyone give you something?" he asked. Terry just responded with a smile. Brandon frustrated, punched the headboard of Terry's bed before storming out of the room. About a half hour later, Sir Marcus arrived back at his residence. He unbuttoned the top button of his uniform as he entered his bedroom. In his bedroom, he watched as his wife was playing with his son. In Kimberly's hand was a model airplane. A cargo plane to be exact. She was making sound effects with her mouth as she twirled and hovered the plane above her son's head. Sir Marcus smiled while his son was trying his best to reach for the toy and grab it from his mother's hand. Suddenly, Sir Marcus eyes lit up. He clapped his hands together so hard it startled his wife and son. "I got it! I got it! "Sir Marcus shouted. "My love, please! See what you've done? You made him cry!" she said. Sir Marcus ran over to his wife, kneeling before her as she sat on the bed. "What's wrong, my love?" she asked. I've just came up with the best idea in my entire life!" he said with excitement in in his voice. "What? what?" Kimberly shouted as she held their son in her arms. "This might sound crazy, my love, but bear with me!" he said. "Go ahead! I'm listening!" Kimberly said in a high-pitched tone. "What if we treated the entire island with GLC? He whispered with excitement. "What? Kimberly said with a frown on her. "If and when our enemies find out what we're building here, they might try the same thing with the chem trails like they did on your family's island!" he said. There was a silence in the room as Kimberly smiled, staring into her husband's eyes. "You're right! It does sound crazy!" she said. "Think about it! We get a fleet of crop dusters, dilute the GLC and spray it over the entire island! Not only that! We have all the citizens scrubs themselves down with it as well!" he said in a passionate voice. Kimberly sighed as she stared out the window. She turned her head towards her husband. "You really think it will work?" she asked. Sir Marcus smiled. "Let's give it a shot, my love, and find out!" he said. Kimberly looked at her son. "What do you think?" she asked her son. The heir to Lassenberia only made incoherent noises. "I guess that's a yes!" Kimberly chuckled. Sir Marcus stood. "First we have to go to the holy sight and see how we're gonna get the GLC out of the ground, into vast containers, and into the planes." He sighed. "Holy sight! I like that!" Kimberly chuckled. "Well, it's true!" Sir Marcus responded. "Well, my love. Let's go to the holy sight." She said.

A day later, back in the United States, Edward the 2nd was sitting in an empty restaurant found in Cape May, New Jersey. The restaurant dimly lit. Edward the 2nd sat in the back in booth. There were 3 NA agents there as well. 2 stood on either side of Edward the 2nd, facing the entrance as the third agent stood by the entrance door. It was around one in the morning. Edward the 2nd had downed 4 shots of scotch by this time.

Moments later, Doug Reed entered the restaurant, alone. He was dressed like the average guy walking the streets, then a man that ran northeastern part of the underworld for the National Agreement. He wore a suit jacket with a V-neck t-shirt underneath. The rest of his attire was a pair of baggy jeans and tennis shoes.

"Say kid! How's it going?" he said as he approached Edward the 2nd. "What? No security?" Edward the 2nd asked. Doug just chuckled. "Remember, kid. Your security is my security." He said. "Fuck!" Edward the 2nd said under his breath. "Go over and keep the other agent company!" Doug said to the 2 agents. "Yes, Mr. Reed." One of the agents said. "May I sit, Lord Lassenberry?" Doug said jokingly. Edward the 2nd didn't say a word. He gave Doug the go ahead to sit with a hand gesture. "Now! What's your problem?" Doug asked. "Wanna drink?" Edward the 2nd asked. "Nah, I have to fly up to Rhode Island tonight. Mr. Haggerty needs my help up there. The infighting with those guys never ends I tell ya, being a warlock ain't easy." Doug chuckled. "Anyway! I don't have a transaction man at this time." Edward the 2nd confessed. "Why not? I thought the chubby lawyer's grandson was your guy!" he said. "fuck! He left the country and went somewhere! Now I don't have someone to deliver the product! And I can't be seen on the streets doing that shit!" Edward the 2nd said as his speech slurred. "Listen, kid! I can't continue to babysit your incompetence when it comes to keeping your people in line! Find someone that can do the job, and get the job done! Christ! I took care of that thing for you on Jenkin's island, so you don't have to worry about Jabbo's family! Now they've been taken out, you reign supreme!" Doug said. "What exactly did you do?" Edward the 2nd asked with a dreadful look on his face. "Oh, let's just say we've sprinkled a little fairy dust on the situation!" Doug sighed. There was silence between the 2 men. Edward the 2nd frantically shook his head to snap out of his daze. "Ok! Ok! Anyway! In a few days I'm holding a memorial service for my departed family members. I appreciate it if you would be there in a nice suit, perhaps! I need a hundred-man detail to guard me and the castle while the ceremony is taking place, if you would be so kind!" he requested. Doug shrugged his shoulders. "I have no problem with that!" Doug responded. "Thank you." Edward the 2nd said reluctantly. Doug slammed his hands on the table. "Ok! This meeting is adjourned! Remember! Get another number 2 and get the ball rolling!" he said before leaving. Once Doug left the restaurant, Edward the 2nd summoned his agents over to his table. "I want someone to get in contact with Sleeves Hart, like now! And tell him his presence is in demand at the memorial service! Understand?" Edward ordered. "Yes, my lord!" the agents shouted simultaneously. Edward the 2nd filled his shot glass once more before leaving the restaurant.

― CHAPTER .33 SAMMY PEREZ, ― FROM BLOOMFIELD

The day had come, when Edward the 2nd had to come to grips that 90% of his family were gone forever. The only kinfolk that remained were a few in-laws and distant relatives, who were not invited the memorial service.

This memorial service was big, according to journalists standing outside castle gates. The only catch to this news coverage was that it was pre-recorded, not live. The word was given out to mainstream media to edit programming moments after the live coverage, to protect Doug Reed, Edward the 2nd from the public eye watching around the country. Other drug lords from around the country who showed up at the memorial service, appreciated the media protection, in hindsight.

It was around noon on a bright breezy day. Edward the 2nd had given the order to his generals to bring a handful of their top guys to the ceremony. But his words were ignored. Dozens of street captains and soldiers under each general showed up. This act of disobedience was due to the uneasy relationship between Butch and Hakim. The more men from each camp that came, the safer each general felt.

The memorial service was held on the eastern side of the castle grounds. A hundred-foot obelisk was erected in honor of the fallen Lassenberry family members. The names of each family member were inscribed into the obelisk, starting with Edward the 2nd's aunt, Maggie Lassenberry-Richards.

Standing in an extensive line on either side of the obelisk were hundreds of shady looking characters from the underworld. There was a path cleared, about 5 yards across so Edward the 2nd could make his trek towards the obelisk

There was a militaristic drumline with one bugler in the background, standing near the castle walls. This 50-piece drumline was by far no representation of the united states military, in fact, it was no representation of any nation around the world. Doug Reed had thrown Edward the 2nd an added bone by using poor young souls who were under enslavement of the

MK Ultra program. There were dressed in black uniforms, resembling those of the brain washed Nazi youth back during the 2nd world war. They were trained all their lives to play militaristic songs just for the National Agreement elite when they arrived at a formal gathering. Doug had expressed his braggadocios mentality towards Edward the 2nd by giving him a glimpse of how the National Agreement treat their top people.

The drumline consisting of young men from all different ethnicities, represented professionalism to a Tee. The drum major, dressed in an all-black militaristic uniform stood at attention waiting for his que, wore a black cape which flapped in the breeze.

There were dozens of helicopters and limos parked on the Lassenberry castle grounds belonging to the drug lords who had flown or driven in to see the spectacle. "Holy shit!" Hakim said to himself as he looked at his surroundings in awe.

The 4 generals of the Lassenberry Organization, except for Mark (Mookie)Vasquez, who was wheelchair bound, stood off at the opposite end of the trail that lead to the obelisk. They were also dressed in their traditional uniforms. "This some crazy shit!" Butch said to himself as he stood in line. "What?" Dubbs asked, standing next to him. "Nothing!" Butch sighed.

About a half hour had passed as the crowd stood mingling amongst themselves until the bugler blew into his instrument. Suddenly a silence came upon the crowd. The only sounds heard were the wind and the clicking sounds of hand-held cameras from the paparazzi standing outside the castle gates. These photos would soon after, be found in supermarket tabloids instead of mainstream publications to confuse the public, and purposely feed the appetite of conspiracy theorists.

After the bugler finished, the drum major gave the signal for the drumline to begin their part of the ceremony. The sounds of the snare drums had a totalitarian vibe. As the drumline played on, the giant double doors, that lead to the main entrance of the castle had opened by remote control. Slowly coming through those doors was a Victorian style open carriage, driven by a team of black horse guided by a postillion. There were 3 NA agents posted on the back of the carriage for security. Sitting in the carriage was the head of the Lassenberry organization, Edward the 2nd. Not only did he wear his uniform but wore a hooded black cloak to cover the top part of his face, giving off a sense of mystery. Butch dropped his head in embarrassment. Following the carriage was a customized golf cart driven by a NA agent. Sitting in the back of the cart, all dressed in fine black Italian-made suits were Doug Reed, Sleeves Hart, and Colonel Braxton, known as number3. "This is nice! Not as grandiose as the shit I'm accustomed to, but nice!" Doug said to sleeves. Sleeves didn't respond. He just faced forward.

The horse and carriage came to a complete stop in front of the 4 generals. One of the NA agents jumped off the back of the carriage, walked over and opened the door for Edward the 2nd. He stepped out of the carriage. All eyes on the castle grounds were presumably on him. Soon after, Doug Reed and number 3 stepped out of the golf cart. Sleeves handed his walking cane to one of the NA agents. He was helped off the golf cart due to his decrepit frame. The 3 men followed Lord Lassenberry as he walked down the trail towards the obelisk. At the other end of the trail were 2 NA agents standing on either side of a 5-foot wreath attached to a framed stand.

The wreath 's colors were the same as the Lassenberry coat-of-arms. The Lassenberry flag was flying high on a hundred-foot flagpole, waving in the breeze.

On one side of the trail stood most of the drug lords throughout the country and corporate titans. On the other side of the trail stood the people from the Lassenberry organization. Edward the 2nd paced himself to the sounds of the snare drums as he slowly made his way towards the obelisk. As he was walking, he glanced over to his left where his people were standing. he noticed all eyes were on him except for this one guy, who was rambling on his cell phone.

The guy stood a little over 5 feet tall, with short curly hair. There was a blue mark beneath his right eye. This infuriated Edward the 2nd. This pissed him off so much that he lost his footing and stumbled. He could hear the smirks coming from his left side. He took a deep breath and continued his trek. When he stood before the wreath, as rehearsed, the 2 NA agents grabbed the wreath from the stand and walked backwards towards the obelisk. Edward the 2nd followed them. On the obelisk was a gold-plated hook embedded in it, which was about 10 feet from the ground. Edward the 2nd, along with the NA agents, placed the wreath on the hook. As an added attraction, he kissed his hand and placed it on the obelisk. The sound of the drums came to a halt. The bugler then played taps. Edward the 2nd stood at attention along with the 2 NA agents. After the bugler finished, Edward the 2nd and the agents made an about face. Number 3 trained him to do it properly as done in the military days before.

After the memorial service, Edward the 2nd walked through the crowd getting acquainted and thanking those who showed up. The gathering didn't last long as everyone was heading back to their vehicles and aircrafts. While the crowd thinned out, Edward the 2nd noticed the same guy that was on the cell phone off in the distance. Edward the 2nd looked heated. Butch noticed his facial expression and walked over to where his boss was. "You ok?" Butch asked. "Who's that dude over there?" Edward the 2nd asked. "Where?" Butch asked. "That Spanish looking motherfucker, over there!" he shouted as he pointed to the guy. Butch squinted as he looked pass the small crowd. "Who, man?" Butch shouted. "The mother fucker in the blue jogging suit!" he shouted. "Oh! That's Sammy Perez, from Bloomfield!" Butch said.

Sammy Perez was this fast-talking Puerto Rican guy who ran all the narcotics in Bloomfield, New Jersey. He just finished a 10-year bid in the federal penitentiary about a month ago. It was Jabbo who put in the word for him to move up in the ranks. Sammy made a large profit from selling opioids to the residents in the upper-class Brookdale section of Bloomfield.

"I want you to bring him to the Lodi spot tomorrow, at noon!" Edward the 2nd said. "Hold on, kid! That's Hakim's people! That ain't got nothing to do with me!" Butch responded. "I don't feel like talking to him, right now!" Edward the 2nd said. "I don't fuck with him, either!" Butch said in a high-pitched voice. "Listen, old man! I'm Lord Lassenberry, and you're my general! Just tell him what I told you!" Edward the 2nd ordered. "Alright!" Butch sighed. Before Butch walked away, he leaned in close to Edward the 2nd. "With all due respect kid, the cloak gotta go! You look silly!" he whispered before walking away. Edward the 2nd didn't a say word.

The next day, around 11:15 AM, Edward the 2nd had arrived at the Lodi meeting facility. He sat at one end of a long oak table. He wore a dark-blue silk suit, a pair of dark-blue gator shoes, and on his wrist was a canary-yellow diamond watch. He sat there quietly twirling his signature Lassenberry ring on his finger, 10 NA agents stood on both sides of the table. Placed on the table before him was an unopened bottle of champagne and 2 champagne flutes.

It was 11:50 when a black Boeman SUV pulled up in front of the Lodi facility. There were 4 men inside. The man on the front passenger side, who happened to be Clip, hopped out of the vehicle. He opened the back-passenger door. The first to step out the back of the vehicle was Sammy Perez, Followed by Hakim.

Clip and Sammy dressed casually in jeans, sneakers, and button-up shirts. Hakim on the other hand, was ordered to wear his uniform with the red and green sashes.

Sammy looked nervous as he saw 2 NA agents standing at the front entrance. He turned towards Hakim. "Come on, boss! Please tell me what the fuck did I do wrong?" he shouted. "Calm down, nigga! For the last time, I don't know what this man wanna talk to you about! I was just told to bring yo ass here! Now, let's go do this! Remember one thing. This guy is sensitive, and you got a hell of a mouthpiece. Don't try to out talk him. Please!" Hakim said. As Hakim, Clip and Sammy were making their way to the front entrance, the agents stopped them. "Sorry general Bates, but our orders were to only allow you and Mr. Perez to enter. "one agent said. Sammy looked paranoid at this moment. "I swear to god, I ain't packing!" he shouted. "Stop it! Calm down!" Hakim said. The 2 agents stepped to the side and allowed Hakim and Sammy to pass. Clip went back to the vehicle. "Keep the engine running!" he whispered to the driver.

Inside the facility, hakim and Sammy make their way down the corridor where 2 more agents were standing outside the meeting room door. When they approached the door, one agent tapped on the door 3 times. As the door opened, hakim could see Edward the 2nd. He was sitting at the end of the conference table. "Come on in!" he said. Hakim looked as nervous as Sammy when gazing upon the NA agents. The doors closed behind them. "General Bates! You gonna introduce us to each other?" Edward the 2nd said with smirk on his face. He saw the hate in Hakim's eyes. Hakim inhaled. "Lord Lassenberry, this is Sammy Perez. He runs all our business in Bloomfield." He said. "It's a pleasure to meet you, sir!" Sammy said. "What's that under your right eye?" Edward the 2nd asked. "Man, I had to get tatted because this cat was coming at me when I was in the joint! Next thing I know, dude got shanked! I was rewarded with this!" Sammy explained. Edward the 2nd nodded with a smirk as if he was impressed. "You wanna know why y'all wasn't frisked for any weapons, or recording devices, Sammy?" Edward the 2nd asked. "I guess!" Sammy said. "Hakim!" Edward the 2nd shouted. Hakim was startled. "Tell him what would happen if y'all would've came in here packing or wearing a wire." He said. Hakim turned to Sammy. "He… would… Torture…us, then… kill…us!" hakim said while trying to hold his composure. "Goddamn right!!!" Edward the 2nd shouted. "Now! The reason I called you guys here was to tell Sammy that I didn't appreciate him being on his cell phone at my family's memorial service." Edward the 2nd said. "I…I…I… didn't mean to be disrespectful, sir!!" Sammy said. "Shut the fuck up." Edward the 2nd said in a calm manner. "If that's what all of this is about, I'll handle it." Hakim said. "Hakim. Stop." He said. Hakim didn't say a word. He just surrendered with a nod. "On the other hand, I thought it took a lot of heart to do something that crazy! Anyway! I think that deserves a promotion." Edward the 2nd said. Hakim looked bewildered. "But first, you need to do something before you get that promotion." He said. "I'll do whatever it takes, ah Mr. Lord Lassenberry!" Sammy nervously said. Hakim gave Sammy a hard elbow to the shoulder. "Robot! Bring'em in." Edward the 2nd said to the agent standing closest to him. The agent went into the room off to the side. Moments later, he came wheeling out an elderly man, who was duct taped to an office chair. The elderly man happened to be Stanley (Sleeves)Hart. Hs mouth was also duct taped.

Sleeves had worked as the Lassenberry family attorney for decades. He was one of the original members of Benny Lassenberry's crew. He was behind all the bed-n-breakfast establishments ran by the Lassenberry family. He was the one who saved a lot of low leveled dealers in the Lassenberry origination from doing jail time and get off on probation. It was rumored that no other lawyer in New Jersey could take on a narcotics case. All drug cases were rumored to be represented by is law firm, only.

"This old man sitting here all taped up, didn't do you justice. According to my records, you did a lot of time, because he didn't do his job." Edward the 2nd said. At this moment, Edward the 2nd gave the agent who dragged Sleeves out of the room the signal to pull out a syringe and a camera. The agent placed the syringe on the table near Sammy.

"Listen, man. I'm giving you the opportunity to take this useless mother fucker out by injecting that syringe into his neck." Edward the 2nd said. Sammy didn't hesitate one bit. He took the syringe, walked over to Sleeves, and rammed the syringe into his neck like a hammer. He then took his thumb and pressed the plunger. Sleeves started squirming until his body laid still. Sleeves died with his eyes open. As the syringe was being pulled out of the old man's neck, the Agent with the camera started taking pictures. "I got that idea from my uncle!" Edward the 2nd chuckled as he stood from his chair. Sammy looked faint, leaning up against the table, but quickly composed himself. Edward the 2nd reached in his pants pocket and pulled out a ring. Unknown to Hakim, it was the same ring that belonged to his brother Bex. "Yo! From now on, you're general Perez!" he said as he handed Sammy the ring. Sammy tried the ring on, but found it was too big. "Don't worry. Just get it fixed later. But the next time we meet, it better be on your finger!" he said to Sammy. Another agent had popped open the bottle of champagne, filling the 2 flutes. Edward the 2nd grabbed the flutes, giving one to Sammy. "Hakim! Tell Sammy what he's supposed to say When leaving my presence." He said. "Long live the house of Lassenberry. long live Edward the 2nd." Hakim said. Edward the 2nd put his hand on Sammy's shoulder. "You're gonna run a whole region, instead of a city. Hakim will take you to the counties you'll be running. Burlington, Ocean, Camden, Gloucester, Salem, Atlantic, Cumberland and Cape May is yours now." Edward the 2nd had made clear. "What?" Hakim shouted. Edward the 2nd turned to Hakim. "I'll say it again! Hakim will take you around and introduce you to all the dealers out there!" he shouted. Edward the 2nd turned back to Sammy. "I want you to buy a house out in Cumberland county. If any of your top guys from Bloomfield wanna go with you, let'em!" he said. The 2 men clinked flutes, then gulped down their drinks. "¡Larga vida a la casa de Lassenberry! Larga vida a Edward el Segundo!" Sammy shouted. Edward the 2nd burst out laughing. "Come on, man! Say it in English!" he chuckled. Hakim rolled his eyes as he sighed. Edward the 2nd snapped his fingers as he, summoning

Hakim over. "You go with Hakim, as of right now! But first! I gotta ask! Who the fuck was you talking to on your cell phone at the memorial service?" he asked. "Oh shit, man! I just bought a 2-family house in my hood, on Chapman street. I was calling this fucking guy to finish doing my floors! He talking some bullshit about he can't make it until next week!" Sammy shouted. "Ok. Ok. Y'all just get out there and make that money!" Edward the 2nd before walking the 2 men to the door. As Sammy continued to walk outside, Hakim turned to Edward the 2nd. "I hope you know we're all due for our refill! It's starting to dry up out here!" He Whispered. Edward the 2ND glanced at the NA agents around him, feeling embarrassed. "Come down! I'll get a number 2 guy to make sure y'all get the refill!" He whispered. "Thank you!!" Hakim shouted with an abrasive gesture. Hakim looked over at Sleeves for the last time, shaking his head. "Long live the house of Lassenberry. long live Edward the 2nd." He said before leaving. Edward the 2nd slowly walked over to Sleeves' lifeless body. He just stood there in a daze. "My lord. What do you want us to do with the body?" his favorite agent asked. Edward the 2nd didn't respond. He just stood there staring at the body. "My lord. Are you ok?" the agent asked. He quickly turned to the agent. "Take the body out and incinerate it. But before you do, chop off his arm below the elbow., and leave it here." He said.

Edward the 2nd went into the room where sleeves was being held. He took off his suit jacket, sat in his recliner and grabbed the remote to the flat screen TV. He turned on the TV. Coincidently the TV was tuned to the news. *"Breaking news…New Jersey based hip hop star Anthony Khalif Gaines, known to his fans and to the world as MC Gutter, was gun downed 2am this morning in front of the infamous night club Big shots, located in Newark."* The journalist said. Edward the 2nd had turned off the TV before he could hear the full story. He sat there scratching his head, pondering on what he just watched.

Outside the Lodi facility Hakim and Sammy stood by the SUV. Clip had the back door open for Hakim to get in. "Check this out, man. You made a lot of money for me, and now you're on your own. When you came up short, from time to time, I didn't bitch! But now, you dealing with the devil direct! That nigger in there, gotta big chip on his shoulder! My brother, rest in peace, ain't have the stomach for it! And we both did time in the joint! But all that pressure got the best of him! Oh! One more thing! Don't think you gonna get so big, that you gonna run this guy out of town! There's a force running this country that's allowing him and his descendance to run this state, forever! The crazy shit is, his kid ain't even born yet! He or she gonna run all this shit one day! Now, get your stuff in order, and I'll come up pick you up in a few days." Hakim said before getting inside the car. Sammy known for having the gift of gab, didn't utter a word as he turned to look at the NA agents standing by the entrance. He then entered the vehicle.

A few days later, Sammy and his girlfriend Elizabeth Guzman were driving around the city of Vineland house hunting. Sammy changed lanes while driving on East Landis Avenue. He noticed a grocery store with the words Chavez grocery in big letters. He pulled over, coming to a complete stop. "Why are we stopping here?" Elizabeth asked. "You see that grocery store? That's gonna be my new headquarters!" he said. Sammy put the car in park. "¡Quédate aquí!" he said. Sammy walked inside the grocery store looking confident. He saw 4 young ladies of Latina descent standing at different cash registers. He approached the one who was close by. "Hola cariño. ¿Dónde está el gerente?" he asked. "Él Simplemente se fue por el pasillo 7." She said. "¡Gracias cariño!" Sammy said as he pulled out a wad of cash, giving the young lady a c-note. The young lady had a smile from ear-to-ear. Sammy made his way towards aisle 7, which was the last aisle to the far right. He saw the manager with a clipboard in his hand, who happened to be a tall Latino man, with more European features. "¡Yo! ¿Tu hablas español?" Sammy shouted as he came closer to the man. "Very little!" the man said. Sammy frowned with a disappointing look on his face. "Man! You run a Spanish grocery store, and you don't speak Spanish?" Sammy shouted as he waved his arms around in a cool manner. The man looked stunned. Sammy smiled. "I'm just fucking with you, my dude!" Sammy chuckled. "My uncle owns this place. He's straight off the Mariel boatlift!" the man chuckled nervously. "Yo! You funny, my dude!" Sammy said as he lightly punched the man in the arm. "Check this out, my dude! Is your uncle around? I need to talk business with him!" Sammy said. "No, he's not. He And my cousin, who's the co-owner, should be back in an hour." The man explained. "And, what's your name, my dude?" Sammy asked. "It's Mario!" he said as the they shook hands. "I'm Sammy! Ok, Mario! I'll be back in an hour! ¡Estás a salvo, amigo!" Sammy said before walking away.

An hour and 15 minutes had passed. Sammy was sitting in his car, constantly looking at his diamond incrusted watch. Elizabeth was sitting next to him, looking restless. "I have to use the bathroom!" she said. "Yo! Go inside the grocery store and ask Mario to let you use the bathroom!" Sammy said. Elizabeth sighed as she stepped out of the car, slamming the door.

A couple of minutes later, Elizabeth came back to the car, fuming. "What's wrong?" Sammy asked. "¡Este punk dijo que el baño es solo para empleados!" She shouted. Sammy looked agitated as he pulled out his wad of cash. "Give this to him! Tell him it's from me!" he said as he handed her a c-note. Elizabeth snatched the money from him. "¡Estás loco!" she chuckled. Sammy blew her a kiss.

A couple of minutes passed. Sammy looked in his rear-view mirror as a black Sedan pulled up behind him. He watched as an elderly, chubby fat man stepped out of the passenger side, and a younger version of the man stepped out of the driver's side of the vehicle. Sammy quickly stepped out of his vehicle. "Yo! Pops! Déjame hablar contigo por un Segundo!" He shouted to the old man. The old man turned to Sammy. Sammy ran up on the 2 men. "Excuse me! Are you Chavez? Is this your grocery store?" he asked. "Sí." The old man said. "My name is Sammy. I wanna go inside with you guys and talk business." Sammy said. Chavez and his son looked at each other with confusion on their faces. "Yo! I ain't come here to rob you! look!" Sammy said as he pulled out his wad of cash, which was about 3 inches thick. "¿De qué quieres hablar, Sammy?" the old man asked. The old man glanced at his son. "Ok, Sammy! ¡Sígueme!" he said.

As Elizabeth was coming out of the bathroom, she saw Sammy follow the old man into his office. She went to the office and asked Sammy for the keys to get in the car. "Esto solo tomará un memento cariño!" Sammy said as he tossed her the keys. When Elizbeth left the office, Sammy turned to the old man with a hard look on his face. Listen, my dude! What's your name again?" Sammy asked in a high-pitched voice. "Esteban!" he said with pride. "Well listen, Esteban! Since we're in America, I'm gonna speak English! So, keep up." Sammy said.

"Qué?" Esteban replied. "I wanna pay you a grand a month to turn the storage area here into a meeting for me and my people." He said. "¡Creo que deberías irte, Sammy!" Esteban said. "OK! I'll leave! But I'll be back tomorrow with my people! I guarantee you I'll be sitting in your chair!" Sammy said. He reached into his pants pockets, once again, pulling out his wad of cash. He slammed 2 thousand dollars on Esteban's desk. "That's rent and security right there, my dude! ¡Te veo mañana!" Sammy said before leaving the office. Esteban starting fuming. He picked up the phone and made a call. "Yeah!" the voice said on the other end. "It's me! We have an outsider trying to push his way in!" Esteban said. "Did you get a name?" the voice on the phone asked. "Some Spanish guy named Sammy! He's got some tattoo under his right eye! I Caught a glimpse of his license plates too!" Esteban said. "Spill it!" the voice said.

Hours later, around 4pm, Sammy met up with Hakim in Bridgeton along with the 3 top dealers in that region. The meeting was held in the garage belonging to a friend of a friend of one of the dealers. "What's up, gentlemen?" Hakim shouted.

The 3 dealers at the meeting, Darnell, Kyle, and Jason were the guys still around after the north vs south war. These guys had to lay low after Bex's demise. There was no product coming into that region of New Jersey. Addicts and recreational users had to travel miles into William (Dubbs) Watson territory. Dubbs dare not send his dealers on the streets that used to belong to Bex.

The 3 dealers shook hands with Hakim. "Listen up! This guy right here is Sammy, from Bloomfield!" He said. None of the dealers shook hands with Sammy due to suspicion. "Y'all better get friendly with this guy! He's gonna be your new boss!" Hakim said. Kyle rolled his eyes as he sighed. "This is coming from the top, not me! So, deal with it!" Hakim said. "Ok, new Boss! When we gonna get our shipment? It's dry as a desert out here! And, I gotta pay off the mortgage on one of my houses before they foreclose on my ass!" Kyle asked Sammy. The other 2 dealers chuckled. Sammy looked at Hakim. "I'll talk to the big guy and see what he's gotta say about it! But, in the meantime, y'all get your finances together and get ready to put this stuff back on the streets again!" Hakim said. "I Need y'all to show me to all the safe houses, give me a list of all the police precincts! The runners don't need to see me! Like Hakim said, gather up your loot, and just sit tight!" Sammy said. "That's it! Meetings' over!" Hakim said.

The 5 men leave the garage and the 3 dealers load up into the van. They sit there, waiting for Sammy and Elisabeth to follow them. Sammy and Hakim stand by Hakim's car. "You better get going! You gotta lot of work ahead of you, man!" Hakim said. "I'm making a call. I wanna to bring down Chulio, Crazy Arms and Blasé Mike to come help run shit. I thought I'd run it by you first, my dude." Sammy said. "That's a no…my dude! They don't work under you no more! They work in Bloomfield! Bloomfield is mine! Your people are mine! You got your team over there!" Hakim said as he pointed towards the van. "My dude! I don't know how these niggas work! I grew up with my crew! I know them! I know how they think!" Sammy shouted. "You're gonna make 10 times more money than you were working for me! Stop bitchin, ungrateful ass Rican!" hakim said with a smirk on his face. "Man! That's fucked up!" Sammy said. "You're known for talking the leaves off a tree! Start a camaraderie, or something!" hakim said before getting in his vehicle.

It was around 3pm the following day, Sammy and Elizabeth were standing in front of a modest size mansion on Ascher Rd. in Vineland. On the front lawn was a for sale sign. "This is it! This is it baby!" Sammy shouted. "Shouldn't we call the realtor first?" Elizabeth asked. "Fuck that shit, baby! This is us, right here!" He shouted. "¡Pero es tan grande!" she said. "Yeah, it's big, but this is what we need to start a family!" he shouted. "What are you talking about?" she asked. Sammy pulled out a black velvet ring box. Elizabeth became hysterical. Sammy dropped down to one knee. "¡Cásate conmigo bebe!" he said he displayed a huge sparkling diamond ring. She jumped up-n-down, crying. "It's about time!" she shouted as she smacked him upside his head. He stood up, placed the ring on her finger, and gave her a firm hug. "¡Te amo mucho bebe!" he said. "¡Yo también te amo!" she said. Moments later a beige Boeman Sedan pulled up to the curb. "Who's that?" Elizabeth asked. "That's my new driver. He's from around here. I need you to take the car, head back to Bloomfield and start packing. I got some shit I gotta do out here." Sammy said. "I want to stay with you!" she said. "Come on baby! I can't be in 2 places at one time!" Sammy said. "Ok! Just be careful!" Elizabeth sighed. Sammy gave her a kiss on the forehead. "¡Soy intocable ahora!" he said before walking away.

It was 4:30 when Sammy's driver pulled up in front of Chavez grocery store. The driver shut off the engine. "My dude! Don't just sit there! Get out and open my door!" Sammy shouted. "Alright, Mr. Perez." The driver said.

The driver was Damon, aka Bluto. He was Darnell's younger cousin. He used to sell weed on West Chestnut Avenue, about 2 miles from where they were. Bluto was dark skinned and obese, with a timid demeanor.

Damon walked around the passenger side to open the door for his new boss. As soon as Sammy stepped one foot out the car, a person wearing a ski mask stepped out of the car parked in front of them. "Hey Sammy!" the mask person shouted. "What the fuck?!!" Sammy said as he noticed the masked person coming towards him. Before Sammy could react, Damon received a bullet in the back of the head. The sound of the weapon was muffled with a silencer. Damon's body slumped over on Sammy. "This is from Augustine!" the masked person said before aiming the weapon at Sammy. "Oh shit!" Sammy Said before diving back into the front seat. 2 more shots were fired as Sammy jumped into the driver's seat. People walking in the vicinity couldn't hear the violent act until the windshield was shattered. Sammy hit the gas pedal before taking a bullet in the shoulder and the cheek. Damon's body rolled off the curb as Sammy drove off. The person wearing the ski mask calmly walked back to the car, jumping back into the passenger side. The driver, who was also wearing a ski mask made a quick U-turn and sped off down the street. A crowd started to gather around Damon's body.

Meanwhile, Sammy was swerving down the street holding his face as blood started pouring through his fingers. His anxiety got the best of him when he ended up crashing into a dumpster. The loss of blood from him shoulder wound caused him to pass out.

Sammy had regained consciousness. He found himself in a hospital room hooked up to a heart monitor. He put his hand to his face, feeling the huge bandage on his cheek, as he laid in bed. He looked to his right staring at the get-well balloons and flowers on the end table. He tried to sit up but felt the excruciating pain in his shoulder. He pressed the buzzer by his bedside for help. Moments later a nurse entered the room. "How are we doing today, Mr.

Perez?" She asked. "Where the fuck am I?" he shouted. "Easy with the language, sir!" she said. "Where am I?" he shouted. "You're at the Inspira Trauma Center. You've been in a coma for the past 5 days." She said. "Where's my fiancé?" he asked. "She and a group of people left this morning. She was by your bedside since you arrived. Your friends convinced her to go home and get some rest as soon as your vital signs strengthened." She said. "I gotta use the bathroom!" he said. The nurse retrieved a bed pan. "You can relieve yourself in here." She said.

About an hour later, Sammy had gained enough strength to sit up. His feet dangled off the side of the bed as he pondered his next move.

Moments later, 2 Caucasian men in suits entered the room. Both men introduced themselves to Sammy as they showed their badges. "Mr. Perez. We're glad to see you're still with us." One of the men said. "What you Want?" he asked. "We have a few questions for you, due to the fact you were victim of a crime." The man said. "What happened to my driver?" Sammy asked. The 2 men glanced at each other. "He didn't make it, Sir." The man said. "Can you start from the beginning by telling us how you ended up here, sir?" the other man asked. "I ain't got nothing to say, my dude!" Sammy said. "We're here to help you solve this case, sir. Your life could be in jeopardy. Without any information, we can't help you." the man said. "Listen officer! I ain't got shit to say to none of you guys! I just wanna get the fuck outta her and be with my fiancé!" Sammy shouted. "Are you sure, Sir?' the man asked. "Yeah! Now get the fuck outta here and leave me alone!" he shouted as he massaged his shoulder. The 2 men looked at each other. One of the men went to the door and closed it. The man walked over and stood at attention, side-by-side to the other man. "Long live the house of Lassenberry! Long live Edward the 2nd!" they shouted. "What the fuck?!!" was Sammy's response. "General Perez. By the orders of Lord Lassenberry, we are here to take you before him. So, would please get dressed please." One of the agents said.

A couple of hours later, Sammy arrived in a chauffeured driven SUV at a warehouse found off exit 13a of the Garden State Parkway. The SUV entered the warehouse. Sammy saw Edward the 2nd standing by a stanchion next to Hakim. Both men were dressed in their uniforms. One of the agents opened the car door for Sammy. Sammy was in agonizing pain as he stepped out of the vehicle. He was still in the same bloody clothes, wearing a sling on his arm when he approached Hakim and Edward the 2nd. "Lord Lassenberry! Hakim!" Sammy said as he shook their hands. Sammy looked around and saw about 10 agents spread out around the warehouse. "Damn, man! You look like shit!" Edward the 2nd said. "MY dude! I feel a lot worse!" Sammy said. "You know why you're here?" Edward the 2nd asked. "Yeah! I got shot up!" Sammy said. "No! general Bates! Tell general Perez why he's here." Edward the 2nd said. Hakim took a step forward towards Sammy, standing about 5 inches away from him. "You are here because you fucked up! That grocery store owner you tried to muscle in on, is under the protection of the Philly mob! Listen to me very carefully! You are a drug lord type of gangster, not a gangster who extorts businessmen! Long ago, we made a deal with those people to sell our product without any static! The deal was that we stay out of their business, and they stay out of our business, for a small fee! You almost fucked up that deal!" Hakim shouted. "My dude! How was I supposed to know? All I wanted to do was set up camp there!" Sammy said.

"If you ain't do that shit up north, why you think you could do that down south?" Hakim asked. Sammy had shame on his face. He had no words. "I'll tell you why! You thought that no one knew you, so you thought you could mark your territory without thinking how shit worked! Listen! Sell drugs! That's your position! Sell drugs!" Hakim shouted. "Now that we got that cleared up, go meet up with your fiancé and get that big house you want." Edward the 2nd said. "How you know about that?" Sammy asked. "This meeting is over! By the way, I want you to give that fat kid's family, a hundred grand!" Edward the 2nd said. Sammy and Hakim Stood at attention. "Long live the house of Lassenberry! long live Edward the 2nd." They shouted as Edward the 2nd walked away, followed by 8 agents. Sammy couldn't help but notice the smell of alcohol on Lord Lassenberry and the way he staggered as he walked by him. They piled into 2 limos and drove out of the warehouse. "Now, we gotta have a sit down with the Philly mob and straighten this shit out!" Hakim said before walking towards his vehicle.

CHAPTER .34 AUGUSTINE

It was June 21st, 2002. A week had passed since the incident with Sammy and the Philly mob. Sammy had hired a physical therapist to come to his new home in Vineland the day after closing. His dream home cost him close to a million dollars, which he paid in cash.

Elsewhere on the island of Lassenberia, Sir Marcus and Kimberly stood together watching from a distance as the foundation was being laid for the new castle. The day before a 3-ton dome, made of raw iron, about 6 feet in diameter was placed over the pit holding the GLC. Several of Ali's people stood guard around the clock to make sure any construction crews didn't use the cranes, or any other heavy equipment to lift the dome until the job was completed. Sir Marcus had a huge smile on his face. "It's happening, my love! It's really happening!" he said to Kimberly. Kimberly grabbed her husband's hand and kissed it. "You deserve every bit of it, my love!" she said. "I wish my grandfather could see this! We came from bootlegging, to starting our own nation!" He said. "My father started out shining shoes until he met your grandfather! Life is crazy!" she said. They both started laughing until they heard a voice off in the distance. They turned around and saw Kent Mooney coming towards them. He didn't look happy. In his hand was a long black wine case. Kent handed Sir Marcus the case. "What's this?" he asked. "It arrived about an hour ago by tugboat! Just when you think things couldn't get creepier! Look inside!" Kent said. Sir Marcus slowly removed the cover. The object inside made him and Kimberly flinch. "Is that an arm?" she asked. "Not just any arm! It's Sleeves!" Kent said. Sir Marcus shook his head in disgust. "Know ones safe!" he whispered. The body part was inside a vacuumed sealed bag. "What's that underneath it?" Kimberly asked. Kimberly wasn't repulsed by the arm. She reached in and grabbed what was a note sealed in a plastic baggie. She ripped the seal open and pulled out the note. She unfolded the notebook size sheet of paper. *"I want my number 2 back! Now!"* it read in big bold letters. Written underneath the message was E2. "E2? What's E2?" Kent asked. "Edward the 2nd !!" Sir Marcus shouted. "Krayton?" Kimberly said with a surprise look. "Did you show this to Brandon?" Sir Marcus asked. "No way!" Kent said. "I guess I have to break the news to him and Terry!" Sir Marcus sighed. "Do you want me to come with you?" Kimberly asked. "No, my love. I'm learning that delivering sad news doesn't stop." He said before walking away.

A few miles away, Brandon and Terry were at their town house, snuggled on the couch together. Terry was still feeling the loss of her family members. Prescription drugs was the source of her dealing with her trauma. The GLC only cured the physical side, not the emotional side of being human. "I can't believe it! One day our children will attend the University of Lassenberia, and we're here seeing it being built from the ground up!" Brandon said. Terry laid there, resting on his chest in a daze.

Moments later, there was a knock on the door. "Come in!" Brandon shouted. Sir Marcus entered with a sad look on his face. Brandon took notice. "What's wrong?" He asked. "Can I talk to you in the other room?" Sir Marcus asked. "Baby. Baby! Could you sit up for a moment? I have to talk to your brother." Brandon said. "How you doing sis?" Sir Marcus asked. Terry looked at her brother. She shrugged her shoulders and turned the other way. Sir Marcus walked over and gave her a kiss on the forehead. Both men went into the guest room. Sir Marcus closed the door. "So, what's going on?" Brandon asked. "Can you take a seat?" Sir Marcus asked. "With all due respect, I'd rather stand." He said. Sir Marcus placed his hand on Brandon's shoulder. "Your grandfather. He's-" Sir Marcus said before being interrupted. "Don't tell me he passed away!" Brandon sighed. 'It's worse. He was murdered." Sir Marcus said. "What's?!!!" Brandon shouted with rage in his voice. "He was murdered. They sent his arm to us with a message. I'm sorry, man!" He said. Brandon had to sit down. There was silence in the room for a couple of minutes as Brandon covered his face to hide his sorrow. He wiped away his tears. "What did the message say?" he asked. "The message was from my cousin. It was for you to come back to the states." He said to Brandon. "I was going to go back!!! Kimberly told me to stay here!!!" he shouted. Sir Marcus looked puzzled. "She said that to you?" Sir Marcus asked. Brandon was furious. He stood toe-to-toe with Sir Marcus. "Fuck!!! Yeah, she fucking did!!" he screamed. Sir Marcus was speechless. While he was in his thoughts, Brandon stormed out of the room, and out of the house. Sir Marcus followed him. Terry just sat there in a daze as her brother was shouting at Brandon to come back. Brandon jumped into his jeep and burned rubber on the newly paved road. "Brandon!!!" Sir Marcus shouted.

Kimberly, Kent, and a couple of bodyguards were walking due north, back into town. Coincidently, Brandon spotted them as he was driving in the opposite direction. The jeep fishtailed before coming to a complete stop. He jumped out of the jeep. He rushed toward Kimberly like a bull. "You self-serving bitch!!" He shouted. Kent was shaken. Kimberly stopped in her tracks. Her bodyguards drew their weapons. "IT's ok guys!" she told them. Brandon came so close to Kimberly, she had to take a step back. "It's your fault!!! Your reason my grandfather is dead!!!' he screamed. "Calm down Brandon. I don't know what you're talking about." She said in a calm manner. "You fucking told me I couldn't leave the island and go back to the states because it wasn't safe!!" Brandon shouted as his saliva spewed onto Kimberly's face. "I didn't know Krayton was off his rocker enough to do something that horrible!!" Kimberly shouted. "Well, he did!! Now my only blood relative is dead, and it's on you!!" Brandon shouted. Kent, still nervous, slowly handed the case that held his grandfather's arm. Brandon snatched it away. "That's it! I'm taking terry, and we're leaving first thing in the morning! At least in the states I was somebody! I'd rather be the number 2 man, than be a slave for you and your Husband!" he shouted before heading back to the jeep. As Brandon was leaving, Sir Marcus passed him coming in the opposite direction while being chauffeured in another jeep. Sir Marcus ordered his driver to stop the jeep. He shouted for Brandon to come back but was ignored. He then turned to see his wife, Kent, and to the 2-armed guards running towards him. "What happened?" Sir Marcus asked Kimberly. "It's my fault!" she cried. "What?" Sir Marcus asked. "I told him to stay here and ignore your cousin's orders!" she explained. "My love! Please tell me you didn't!" Sir Marcus said in a wining voice. "I did it for terry!" she said. Sir Marcus dropped his head, rubbing his temples. He took a deep breath. "Ok… As your husband, I love you no matter what. As your king, make it right for him. Ok?" he said before walking back towards the jeep. "Oh, Kent! How far along are you on that decree?" Sir Marcus shouted. "Ah, it's coming along!" Kent chuckled nervously. "Chop! Chop. Man!" Sir Marcus said before hopping in the jeep.

2 days later back in the United States, Edward the 2nd was sitting in his office with a bottle of scotch in his hand. The shot glass in front of him was dry as a bone. He drank straight from the bottle. "How the fuck I'm gonna do these transactions? I don't know shit about fucking, do fucking, selling god damn drugs!" he whispered to himself. Edward the 2nd started sobbing. "I need help!" he cried. Suddenly, there was a knock on the door. Edward the 2nd wiped the tears from his eyes and stashed the bottle of scotch in the drawer of his desk. He pulled out a small bottle of eye drops, squirting a couple of drops in each eye. Finally, he took out bottle of breath freshener. "Come in!" he shouted. "My, Lord. Mr. Hart is at the main gate." The agent said. "Who?" Edward the 2nd said in disbelief. "Brandon Hart, my Lord." The agent said. "frisk him for weapons, other strange devices and bring him here." He ordered.

Minutes later, there was another knock on the office door. "Come in!" Edward the 2nd shouted. the door slowly opened. Brandon stepped.in to the office, with a drained look on his. "What's up?" Edward the 2nd asked. "Why?" Brandon asked. "Why, what?" Edward the replied. "Why did you kill…my grandfather, you motherfucker." He said in a calm voice. Edward the 2nd, being inebriated, had a tough time standing up. He decided to stay in his seat. "I told you when you first came to me that this was a 24/7 job, nigga! If I send you somewhere, I expect you to bring your ass back!" he said. There were 2 agents standing in the doorway. This did not deter Brandon from lunging at Edward the 2nd. Brandon was tackled to the floor. He was struggling like a wild beast to get free. "You ain't leave me no choice." Edward the 2nd said. "Leave you no choice?!!" You killed my grandfather!!" Brandon cried. Edward the 2nd finally had enough strength to stand from his seat. "It was him that brought you to me! That old motherfucker took an oath back when my grandfather was running shit! He knew what this was about! The problem is that you don't know what this shit is about! He thought he was going to sit on the sideline and be a pencil pusher! And I guarantee, you thought the same thing! This gangster shit, nigga! Robot! Lock this nigga in the dungeon! Maybe then he'll understand how shit really is!" Edward the 2nd shouted as his speech was slurring. The one he called robot and the other agent picked Brandon off the floor, dragging him out of the office. As the agents were carrying Brandon out, Edward the 2nd followed close behind. "Watch! You'll see things my way!" shouted as they dragged Brandon down the corridor.

It was June 26th around 1:30 in the morning. A meeting was being held at a gym in south Philly. At this meeting, sitting at a card table, were members of the Philly mob, and members of the Lassenberry crew. The man who ran the Philadelphia and South Jersey underworld was Augustine Cucci. He took over as boss when Mr. Nice passed away from natural causes. Every small business in the Philly, South Jersey area paid Augustine for protection. In addition, a deal was brokered a while back between and Hakim And his brother Bex to make a monthly tribute to Philly, which came to a million dollars.

Augustine was the great nephew of former New York mob boss Alfonse Cucci, who was murdered by his cousin Tony Sangiero years ago. He was tall, muscular, with a head full of jet-black hair. Augustine was one of the youngest mob bosses in the United States. He was around 38 when he took control of his crime family. His former counterpart Ritchie, who was the son of Mr. Nice was passed over for the top position.

Sitting at the card table was Augustine, Ritchie, Bobby, a capo who ran a crew out in Atlantic City, and Salvatore (Dusty) Iaccase, who made millions off the fishing and tourist industry in Ocean county. On the Lassenberry side was Hakim, Sammy and Dubbs.

"Ok! Why are we here? Is it because you people overstepped your boundaries? I would say, yes!" Augustine said after taking a sip of his fruit smoothie. "I just wanna say, it was a lack of communication on our part. I didn't tell my associate here that we don't touch your stuff, and what that stuff was." Hakim explained. "So, where do we go from here?" Augustine asked. "Business as usual, far as I'm concern!" Hakim said. "Fuck that my, dude! I'm sitting here all fucked up! It wasn't like I was robbing the old man!" Sammy, stop it!" Hakim said. "Nah! Fuck them! These niggas shot me up! I demand reparations, my dude!" shoulder!" Sammy shouted as he continuously banged his fist on the table. Augustine's people started chuckling. "I like the balls on this guy! I really do!" Augustine chuckled. "I still got bullet fragments in my shoulder, my dude!" Sammy shouted. Augustine leaned back in his chair. "I know my history, very well! The Gatano family was wiped out! This led to your people not having to pay tribute! The only reparations you're gonna get, is that you get to walk out of here alive!" Augustine explained. "Ok! We're done here! Let's go!" Hakim said as he yanked Sammy out of his chair.

Outside the gym, Sammy confronted the drug lord of Essex County, New Jersey. "Why the fuck you punk out to them pizza making mother fuckers, ?!" Sammy shouted. "You don't get the big picture! If they kill Dubbs just by accident, Butch will call on Lassenberry to get involved! Now, you're talking world war 3, At least in New Jersey! My dream is bigger than that! I won't let you fuck that up for me! By the way! Don't forget to give them their tribute every month, or you'll see more bullets flying!" Hakim explained. "Let's just get the fuck outta here!" Dubbs shouted as he walked towards his vehicle.

Back inside the gym, Augustine sat in his chair pondering his next move. "What on your mind, boss? You wanna clip that Sammy guy?" Bobby asked. "That Hakim. He's a smart one. I have a feeling we're focusing on the wrong guy." Augustine explained.

— CHAPTER .35 SEGREGATION CITY —

2 weeks later, Brandon was slowly withering away in the dungeon beneath castle Lassenberry, as he was stripped of his clothing and having his left ankle shackled to the wall. During his imprisonment he was denied food and water. To make things worse, he was subjected to psychological torture. For the past 2 weeks he was exposed to 60 decibels of continuous humming sounds coming from speakers implanted in the ceiling. After the first week he started mumbling to himself. The second week, he started crying out for Edward the 2nd. Being dehydrated, his cries were becoming fainter over time.

It was July 11th, 2002 when what Brandon thought was an illusion, was Edward the 2nd coming down to see him. "Good morning!!!" he shouted as he banged on the cell bars with an iron pipe. Brandon tried to form words but was groggy. There were 3 agents that accompanied Edward the 2nd' "Open it!" Edward the 2nd said to one of the agents. The agent swiped an electronic card on the control panel, causing the cell door to open. Before Edward the 2nd stepped inside the cell, he had to cover his nose and mouth with a handkerchief from the putrid odor. He kneeled to speak with Brandon, who was sitting on the floor. Technically, Brandon wasn't alone in his cell. Across from him were two decomposed bodies shackled to the wall. "Damn! After all this time down here, those bitches still look good! Tell me something, man! Why the hell did you come back?" Edward the 2nd asked. "To… kill…you!" Brandon said with every ounce of his being. "Come on, man! You know that couldn't happen! Listen. I'm here to offer you a chance to redeem yourself. You can go back to being my liaison, or, stay in this hell hole for the rest of your life. He said. Brandon didn't answer. "Talk to me. Tell me something, man!" Edward the 2nd said. "Ok…ok. Put…me …back…to work." Brandon said. "Good! Agent! Give him the syringe." He ordered. The agent stepped inside the cell. He pulled out a syringe from his jacket pocket. "Doug Reed said this won't hurt you one bit." Edward the 2nd said. "What…are…you…going…to do to me?" Brandon asked with fear in his voice. "Inside that syringe is a RFID chip. It will allow my agents to keep track of your every move. If you take a shit, they'll know exactly what toilet you're sitting on. Ok agent! Stick him." Edward the 2nd ordered. The agent walked over to Brandon. Edward the 2nd had stepped out of the way. The agent carefully injected the syringe into the base of Brandon's neck. Brandon flinched a little. "See! That wasn't so bad!" Edward the 2nd said." What shall we do with him, my lord?" the agent asked. "Remove his shackles and take him to one of bedrooms in the west wing. Tell one of the chefs to make him a decent meal." Edward the 2nd ordered.

Elsewhere on the island of Lassenberia, Kimberly, Ali and other members of the council were standing at the pier welcoming refugees from several underdeveloped countries such as Eritrea, Mozambique, Malawi, Niger, Liberia etc. Kimberly's process of immunization was to have 2 gallons of GLC next to her. There were 2 container ships packed with people searching for a better life. As the refugees exit the ships, they were each given a shot glass of GLC to digest. Within moments the women, and orphaned children felt rejuvenated. Kimberly had to keep one woman from kneeling before her for saving her baby from malnutrition as if she were a deity.

"Kent arrived at the pier moments later. He was in awe as he watched hundreds of people form into separate groups as they set foot on Lassenberia soil. "This is great! I just have one question. Where are the husbands and fathers to these women and children?" Kent asked. Kimberly handed the duty of rationing out the GLC to Ukerewe. She then turned to Kent. "When I was a little girl, I used to stay up late to watch TV. Before the channel would sign off, by playing the Star-Spangled Banner, I'd watch these informercials of kids with flies on their faces, walking through piles of garbage and feces just to find food, and fresh drinking water. I asked myself, where were their fathers? All I saw were white missionaries exploiting them like they were puppies in a shelter. That's why you don't see the men. Understand?" Kimberly said before walking away. Kent went over to help out Ukerewe. He turned around and watched Kimberly get into the jeep and drive off. "I guess I hit a nerve." Kent said to himself.

Later that evening on the north eastern side of Lassenberia, hundreds of tents were temporarily set up for the refugees until the new town houses could properly accommodate them. Miles away, Kimberly and Sir Marcus were cuddled up in bed together in their town house. "How was your day, my love?" Sir Marcus asked. Kimberly yawned. "that bad, huh?" he chuckled. "I feel bad having all those children cramped up in those tents." She said. "Stop it! Because of you, those children are at peak health right now. When the paint dries, and furniture is installed, they'll live like suburbanites." He said. "What about you, my love? How was your day?" She asked. "Let's see. I just appointed your brother-in-law as my personal scribe and biographer. Jenna is on her way to Hong Kong with Prime minister Guebuza and secretary Jawara, along with a sample of GLC of course. We're going to need Military backing more than ever." He said. "I don't think a thousand women and children pose a threat, my love!" Kimberly chuckled. "It's not for them! It's for our friends back in the good ole U S of A!" he said. Kimberly had a worried look on her face when her husband uttered those words. A month later, unbeknownst to her husband, Kimberly hired retired French special forces captain Francois Adour from Pau, France to train every young man with Albinism living on Lassenberia. She also used her sister Jenna as interpreter. These young men were taken to the island of Mayotte in the wee hours of the night by cargo ship. Captain Adour was not paid in cash nor GLC. Blood diamonds were his payoff.

4 months later, these young men returned to Lassenberia well equipped and well trained. Out of 200 hundred young men from ages 12 to 20, only 90 of them returned, alive. Kimberly

named them the Pale Horsemen. A few days later, it was the young men from the country of Eritrea's turn.

An incident had occurred one day when a young man from the Pale Horsemen battalion allowed his emotions to get the best of him. His name was salif. He approached Kimberly, questioning her authority by asking why Ali didn't have to go through the vigorous training his people had to endure. "You really want to know why Ali doesn't have to train? You really want to know?" she shouted. "Yes! I really want to know, my lady!" the young man said. Standing face-to-face with Salif, Kimberly quickly pulled a nine-inch carbon blade from her sheath, plunging it into Salif's jugular vein. Salif panicked, falling to the ground, gripping his neck. Kimberly stood over him. "Do you understand now?!! I asked you a question! Do…you… understand, now?!!" she shouted as Salif was rolling around gasping for air. "That's what General Ali had to go through!! Do you understand?!!" she shouted again. All Salif could do in his panicked state was to give Kimberly a nod. Fortunately, Kimberly had a vial of GLC on her person. She moved Salif's hand out of the way to apply the GLC. Salif was about to pass out until the GLC started to take effect. Afterwards, Kimberly helped him off the ground. "I hope we have an understanding, now!" Kimberly said. "Yes…my lady!" Salif said as he tried to catch his breath. "Now, return to your regiment." She said. Salif trotted away. Kimberly turned to Ali. They both smiled at each other.

While Sir Marcus spent most of his time watching the construction of Castle Lassenberia, Kimberly found time to knight Ukerewe, making him the baron of a piece of land called the Pale lands. Their coat-of-arms was a white flag with the outline of a circle in the middle.

November 1st, 2002 was day the island of Lassenberia was officially recognized as a sovereign nation, with a population of 10,520. Word quickly got out to the media. By this time, 90 percent of its infrastructure was completed. Even though the United nations had approved the request of a no-fly zone over Lassenberia, the age of terrorism gave the United States, the United Kingdom and Israel justification to fly 70,000 feet above the earth using spy planes. Photographs of 6 submarines were captured off the coast of Lassenberia, as well as 2 military bases on the north and south sides of the island.

The next day, Sir Marcus was sitting at his desk looking over blueprints of an underwater transit tunnel connecting Lassenberia to southern Mozambique. Sitting across from him was Jenna's husband Sheldon, who was taking notes. The president of Mozambique wired the plans along with 10 drums of Bentonite, which Sir Marcus found peculiar. "What the hell is Bentonite?" he asked Sheldon. "I have no idea!" he said. Moments later, there was a knock on the door. "Come in!" he said. "Got it right this time!" Kent shouted as he entered the office. Kent handed Sir Marcus the final draft of the decree and Constitution of Lassenberia. "Finally, huh?" Sir Marcus said. "Let's see what you've have for me." Sir Marcus said before clearing his throat.

THE ROYAL EMBODIMENT OF RIGHTS AND REGULATIONS
FOR THE GREAT SOVEREIGN NATION OF LASSENBERIA

THE PROMISE TO THE CITIZENS

By order of the royal family of Lassenberia, all citizens are entitled to their God given right to happiness and prosperity, on the basis that they recognize, respect, and protect the throne of Lassenberia until their last breath, on which he/she who occupy the throne of Lassenberia do the same for his/her citizens. All citizens must take a sworn oath to the crown of Lassenberia once he/she, the citizen reaches 12 years of age.

THE 48 LAWS OF LASSENBERIA

LAW (1) Only those of the royal bloodline can and will ascend to the throne of Lassenberia, despite the sex, the age, and physical condition of he/she who ascend to the throne will not be compromised. If he/she ascending to the throne are believed mentally incapacitated, will allow he/she occupying the high council temporary power until he/she of Lassenberry blood come into fruition. He/she of Lassenberry blood have the right to ascend to the throne of Lassenberia whether he/ she are born on the land mentioned or abroad.

LAW (2) All citizens of Lassenberia must confide in the throne of Lassenberia before traveling abroad, as well as returning to Lassenberia. The high council will decide through a majority ruling on whether a citizen of Lassenberia can leave or return to the nation of Lassenberia if he/ she who sits on the throne is incapacitated to authorize such matters.

LAW (3) Physical harm, towards any citizen of Lassenberia with malice or intent, will not be tolerated. Both victim and alleged offender will be brought before the high council, where there a majority rule, thereafter, will be brought before the throne of Lassenberia for final verdict.

LAW (4) Taxation will not apply to citizens of Lassenberia, nor their spouses coming from abroad, who must present legal documentation of matrimony before the high council.

LAW (5) The export of GLC/ GREEN LIFE CURE is considered illegal, unless authorized by the throne of Lassenberia. Members of the high council and land Barons are not exempt from exporting GLC/ GREEN LIFE CURE. All inhabitants of Lassenberia are subject to physical search, including children, and pets before departing, or reentering Lassenberia.

LAW (6) All narcotic substances are prohibited throughout Lassenberia including marijuana, pain killers of any kind. All citizens of Lassenberia are subject to an annual physical unless called upon due to suspicion of indulging in any illegal substances. Any citizen proven guilty of illegal substance intake or abuse will be subject to exile by order of the throne of Lassenberia.

LAW (7) All citizens of Lassenberia are prohibited private possession of GLC/ GREEN LIFE CURE. Any citizen of Lassenberia, including the high council, and military personnel in need of GLC/ GREEN LIFE CURE must present their case/ request before the high council, unless under dire/ life and death circumstances. Otherwise, final distribution of GLC/ GREEN LIFE CURE to citizens of Lassenberia will be authorized by the throne of Lassenberia.

LAW (8) All items, for example: perishables, livestock, pets, souvenirs etc., will be confiscated from citizens of Lassenberia and foreigners upon entering Lassenberia. If such items are not registered with the high council or the throne of Lassenberia prior to entry of Lassenberia will be prosecuted depending on the severity of the offence.

LAW (9) Unauthorized dumping of toxic chemicals, human waste, electronic, mechanical devices, and non-biodegradable substances off Lassenberia shores will result in disciplinary action, such as imprisonment depending on the volume, weight of such items mentioned in Law (9). Time spent under incarceration of such crimes will be under the discretion of the throne of Lassenberia, if proven guilty in a court of Lassenberian law.

LAW (10) it is prohibited for citizens of Lassenberia over 18 years of age to be involved in an intimate relationship with citizens, or foreigners under 18 years of age without written parental or guardian consent. Such consent will be reviewed by the high council and enforced and interpreted by the he/she who is in possession of throne of Lassenberia.

LAW (11) All citizens of Lassenberia upon turning 18 years of age must serve a minimal of 2 years in the Lassenberian armed forces, whether it be land, sea, or air operations.

LAW (12) Only blood relatives of the crown of Lassenberia, land Barons, and the high council can serve as commissioned officers in the armed forces upon completion of the proper training. All participants of such parties are subject to DNA/Deoxyribonucleic acid testing before entering officer candidate school/ training.

LAW (!3) Citizens or foreigners charged with vandalism, arson, or other forms of destructive acts with intent/malice towards facilities belonging to the crown of Lassenberia, whether it be commercial or residential, will be charged with treason. Such acts are punishable by expulsion by the crown.

LAW (14) all citizens are innocent until proven guilty, having the right to legal representation in the royal Lassenberian court of law.

LAW (15) All citizens of Lassenberia have the right of religious freedom/ faith and ritualistic practices, unless ritualistic practices are performed and or cause to human beings, pets and or livestock.

LAW (16) All land Barons will be held responsible for their region of Lassenberia unless the crown intervenes under justified circumstances.

LAW (17) foreigners buying property throughout Lassenberia for recreational use, example: summer retreats, subletting is subject to search of property due to suspicion of illegal material, substances and or activity by order of the crown.

LAW (18) A maximum of 2 acres of land are the most a foreigner can buy. All purchases must be at least a distance of 6 square miles from the royal palace.

LAW (19) All citizens of Lassenberia must recognize/address the crown or he/ she of the royal bloodline when in the presence of his/her majesty.

LAW (20) All citizens can emancipate themselves from their parent/guardian once he/she has reached 16 years of age once he/she provide form122.4 to the high council, requesting the reason for emancipation. Final decision, after a majority ruling from the high council will be presented to his/her majesty of Lassenberia.

LAW (21) All citizens have the right to protest/rally in an orderly fashion.

LAW (22) Citizens must fill out permit 125.8 5 days in advance to land Barons before conducting grand festivities/ceremonies.

LAW (23) All citizens must fill out from 143.7 to study in an institution of higher learning abroad.

LAW (24) The high council embodiment can be no more or no less than 13 members. The position of high council can be held for life, unless his/her majesty of Lassenberia deem the member of the high council unfit to perform his/her duties.

LAW (25) The birthday of his/her majesty will be recognized as a national holiday until a successor ascends to the throne of Lassenberia, while all labor will cease within a 24-hour period.

LAW (26) The departure/passing of his/her majesty on the throne of Lassenberia will be recognized as a day of mourning, which all labor will cease within a 72-hour period after the day of passing to prepare and arrange for memorial services.

LAW (27) Destruction of Lassenberia's eco system with intent/malice is prohibited. The alleged offender/ offenders will be prosecuted to the highest extent of the law.

LAW (28) Acts of terrorism against the crown and its citizens is punishable by death by public hanging. Final authorization of punishment will be at his/her majesty's discretion.

LAW (29) Any acts of lewd behavior in public is prohibited. Such violations can result in 7 days imprisonment, which can be left at the mercy of the high council.

LAW (30) Any acts of lewd behavior in the presence of his/her majesty is prohibited. Such violations will result in imprisonment at the minimum of 6 months, which will be left at the mercy of his/her majesty.

LAW (31) All foreign dignitaries are not exempt from diplomatic immunity.

LAW (32) Succession to the title of land Baron/Baroness will be kept within the bloodline of said Baron/Baroness.

LAW (33) Footwear shall be removed before entering the interior of Castle Lassenberia.

LAW (34) It is illegal for citizens to carry any type of firearms on their person.

LAW (35) Military personnel, Land Barons, members of the high council can carry small firearms on their person within any region of Lassenberia.

LAW (36) All political parties will not be recognized by his/her majesty, the high council or land Barons. Citizens who decide to form a political party/parties will be considered an act of treason by the crown. Punishment will be at the discretion of his/her majesty. All land Barons/Baroness found guilty of being at the helm of such insurrectional intent, will have their title of nobility, land and property revoked.

LAW (37) any attempt to replicate GLC/GREEN LIFE CURE is considered an act of treason against the crown. Such acts of treason will be under the discretion of his/her majesty.

LAW (38) The consort of his/her majesty can occupy the throne of Lassenberia until the heir to the throne becomes of age.

LAW (39) Form 543.9 must be filled out 3 days in advance by all citizens requesting a personal /one-on-one conversation/meeting with his/her majesty. All requests will be answered in the order the land Barons/Baroness received them.

LAW (40) Unauthorized personal are prohibited to enter/trespass on residence of nobility, military facilities, in port/export facilities.

LAW (41) All citizens are entitled to free mental/psychological healthcare.

LAW (42) It is the responsibility of every citizen to be on alert and report any suspicious behavior throughout the land.

LAW (43) It is the responsibility of all land Barons/Baroness to report any suspicious behavior of his/her citizens in his/her region to the high council, or the crown of Lassenberia.

LAW (44) All inhabitants of Lassenberia will be under 24-hour electronic surveillance outside their place of residence. Any citizen/foreigners captured on any surveillance device is subject to search of their property/land or vehicles, as part of an investigation, which may or may not lead to prosecution.

LAW (45) All children of Lassenberia are intitled to a free education. Home schooling is prohibited. All children will be educated in the facility/facilities provide by the crown of Lassenberia.

LAW (46) Any citizen exposing sensitive material, which could jeopardize the security of Lassenberia to foreigners or the outside world, will face imprisonment for the rest of his/her natural life.

LAW (47) All land Barons/Baroness will be held responsible for the depletion of agriculture produced in their region.

LAW (48) By order of the crown of Lassenberia, the laws written above must be posted in every facility, whether residential or commercial and made visible upon entry.

"This is a major improvement!" Sir Marcus said to Kent. "Glad you approve!" Kent said. "Sheldon. I need you to gather all the council members, so we can all sign off on this, together." Sir Marcus ordered. "Understood." Sheldon said before leaving the office. Kent went over to the window to peek outside. "The population is growing fast!" He said. "Yes. I hear Kimberly is being very selective, too." Sir Marcus said. "With-all-do-respect. Do you trust her judgement on this?" Kent asked. Sir Marcus leaned back in his chair. "I need you to see if the construction crew finished paving Jabbo Road." He said. Kent read between the lines. "Ok! I'm on it!" Kent said before leaving the office. Sir Marcus started rereading the decree.

Later that evening, Kimberly, Ali and 2 soldiers from the Pale horse man were riding in a jeep on their way to the Borough of Braxton. Ali and Kimberly were sitting in the back. Ali glanced over at Kimberly. "Take a deep breath, Ms. Kimberly!" he chuckled. "Why? Do I look that pissed?" she asked.

Moments later, they arrive at the Braxton boarders. Kimberly and company noticed a vehicle blocking the road called Lassenberry, which stretched from one end of the island to the other. Standing outside the vehicle were 3 young Caucasian men armed with shotguns. Kimberly made haste jumping out of the jeep. "Ms. Kimberly! wait!" Ali shouted. Kimberly ignored her bodyguard, quickly walking towards the young men. "Stand down! I said stand down!" she shouted as she came within a few feet from the young men. The 2 pale horsemen and Ali, who were carrying sub-machine guns, drew their weapons at the young men. "You heard her! Drop your weapons!" Ali shouted as he took off the safety of his weapon. The young man in charge of the trio was eldest son of Simon Braxton. "Peter! I'm not going to tell you again! Put down your weapons!" Kimberly shouted. "Alright! Put your guns down, boys!" Peter shouted as he put his shotgun on the ground. The 3 young men put their hands up, showing signs of surrender. The 2 pale horsemen retrieved the shotguns while Ali kept his weapon drawn on them. "Now. Tell me what's going on with you and Filipe? We caught him running down the road all bruised and battered! What happened?" Kimberly asked. "He had the nerve to come out here, play lover boy with my sister and cousin!" Peter explained. Kimberly turned to Ali and sighed. She turned to Peter. "Earlier today, I just signed the constitution called the 48 laws of Lassenberia. You just broke the law number 3, young man!" she explained. "He just can't come out on our land!" Peter explained. "Your land? Your land?!! You live in the Borough of Braxton! Which happens to be a part of Lassenberia!" Kimberly shouted as she poked Peter in the chest continuously. "What do you want to do, Ms. Kimberly?" Ali asked. Kimberly turned to Peter. "Ok. As your queen, I want you boys to return home. I think, it's law 34 that says that I can confiscate your weapons. I'll have a talk with your aunt in the morning. Now go!" Kimberly ordered. Peter and his male cousins didn't give Kimberly any problems. They jumped into their vehicle, heading back to Braxton.

As promised on November 3rd 20002, Kimberly paid a visit to Ellen, Baroness of Braxton. Kimberly wore a long sun dress with flower print, and flip flops.

Since the death of her husband and brothers-in-law, Ellen had become head of the region, which was 30 miles north of Castle Lassenberia. Her home was a 6-bedroom, 7-bathroom mansion. The landscaping was an impressive array of exotic plant and tree life. She was very fond of the Sego Lily which there was a bed of them on either side of the front entrance.

Kimberly was treated like the queen she was soon to be when she entered the Baroness's home. Kimberly came with a 20-man security detail. It was a combination of Ali's nephews and the Pale horsemen. 14 of the men walked the grounds of the mansion, while the remaining men guarded every entrance of the mansion.

2 of the Baroness's nieces served coffee and cookies. Kimberly and the Baroness sat across from each other in Victorian style chairs. Both ladies had their legs crossed showing off faux smiles.

"I guess you know why I'm here!" Kimberly said in a cheerful manner. Ellen took a sip of coffee. "You'll have to forgive me! I'm is still dealing with the departed members of my family! My mind is all over the place!" Ellen said. "Well, I hope you are aware that the constitution is in effect, as of yesterday!?" Kimberly mentioned. "I'm sorry! Why wasn't I there to sign?" Ellen asked with a suspicious look. "Land Barons, shall we say, are not considered law makers! Your job really is to be sort of a caretaker of this region!" Kimberly explained. "Uh! Oh! Caretaker!" Ellen wined.

Outside the mansion there was a stare down between a few of Ali's nephews and Peter and his cousins. What almost caused even more friction between the 2 groups was when one of Ali's Nephews blew a kiss at Peter's 18-year-old sister, Esther.

Back inside the mansion, Kimberly was chewing on a butter cookie. "So, who in God's name sighed this decree?" Ellen asked. "The high council, me and my husband!" Kimberly said with a mouth full of cookie. Kimberly chased down the cookie crumbs in her mouth with a sip of coffee. "Excuse me!" Kimberly chuckled. "Oh, please! I guess If you're the future queen, you can do whatever, whenever!" Ellen chuckled. Kimberly wiped her mouth with a napkin. "What I really came to see you about, was the situation that happened between your nephew Peter and another kid by the name of Filipe. Your nephew claims that he was making a pass at his sister, which I believe is more to it than that, but I'll give him the benefit of the doubt!" Kimberly explained. "So, what do you really believe?" Ellen asked. "Ok! If we must go, there! Let's go there!" Kimberly said. "Lets us go there!" Ellen chuckled. "I just want to remind everyone; we are not in the America anymore! This is a real melting pot! Not segregation city! Do we understand each other?" Kimberly asked. Ellen glanced out her window. She saw African guys with machine guns. She turned to Kimberly. "I guess I have no choice but to understand!" Ellen chuckled. Kimberly looked at the clock on the wall. "Wow! Look at the time! I'm sorry, but I must go." Kimberly said as she placed the coffee cup on the table. "Are you sure? I can make a fresh pot of coffee!" Ellen said. "No. I must go. Don't forget! The coronation is in 4 weeks! I'll have Stephan design you a fabulous gown, fit for a Baroness!" Kimberly said. She gives Ellen a hug. "Remember. This is a real melting pot. "Kimberly said she stared Ellen in the eye. "God bless you!!" Ellen shouted as Kimberly walked out the door.

— CHAPTER .36 DEAR SWEET VIOLA —

Elsewhere in Port Elizabeth New Jersey, Brandon was waiting at the pier with a van filled with hundreds of pounds of illegal narcotics. 6 NA agents surrounded the van. It was around mid-night, when suddenly a small caravan of vehicles was heading in their direction. 4 cars had pulled up to the pier. The first one to step out of their vehicle was Hakim. "It's about God damn time!" he shouted as his entourage stepped out of the vehicle. Butch, Dubbs and Sammy stepped out of their vehicle, along with their crew. Mookie's soldier Bobby represented him because Mookie didn't want to get aid out of the car. Brandon gave the NA agents the order to distribute the product to the drug lords. "You all will receive double the refill. That consists of 2 hundred kilos of coke, apiece, 50 pounds of marijuana, a piece, 10 cases of Oxycodone, apiece from the Gatano crew, as usual. And for the crème de la crème, straight out of Afghanistan, 50 kilos of heroin." Brandon said as he read the manifest. As the vehicles were being loaded, Brandon had 5 large duffle bags filled with cash placed at his feet. "You guys know the drill! There should be a million in each bag! Do you all concur?" Brandon shouted. "Yeah!" Butch said. "Yep!" Dubbs said. "We're good!" Hakim said. "I speak for Mookie. Yeah!" Bobby said. "We're good, my dude!" Sammy said. "Good! I'll see you gentlemen in a week for a refill!" Brandon said before getting in the van. "You see how fucked he looked?" Hakim Asked Butch. "Who, Brandon?" Butch asked. "Yeah! Nigga look like he been tortured or something!" Hakim said. "That ain't my problem, kid. I got my refill, now it's time to get the fuck outta here and chop it up." Butch said. Sammy walked over to Mookie's vehicle. Mookie rolled down hill window. "What's up?" Mookie asked. "Solo quería decir que, dado que somos los únicos 2 tipos españoles que tienen una mierda, ¡debemos unir fuerzas!" Sammy suggested. "Listen, man! Just worry about your own shit for the time being!" Mookie said before giving his driver the signal to take off. "Is that a no?!" Sammy shouted as the car drove off.

The next day around 11pm CST time, a group of men had gathered in a remote area out in Laredo, Texas. This gathering wasn't visible to the point where drifters could intrude because it was being held in a facility 2 miles beneath the surface of the earth. This facility was well lit, and technically advanced.

Screams could be heard through the tunnels leading to the main facility. There were men dressed in lab coats walking about. NA agents were standing guard throughout the facility wearing riot gear with machine guns strapped to their shoulders, while other agents were in black suits.

Walking down the main Corridor was Terrance Howard being followed by 4 NA agents in black suits. Terrance was wearing a pink 3-piece suit, pink poke-a-dot bow tie with white wing tips. As he was walking, a young petite Caucasian woman was running towards him screaming for help. She was covered in blood, wearing nothing but bra and panties. "Helping me! Please help me!" the woman screamed as she grabbed on to Terrance's suit jacket. Terrance was chuckling hysterically. He grabbed the girl by the arms. "What's the matter, sweetie?" he asked. "These, these men! They just killed my boyfriend!" she cried. "They did?" Terrance asked in a taunting voice. "You have to help me! Please." She cried. "Of course, I will, sweetie! Just tell me one thing! How did they kill him?" he asked. I…I… saw them chop his head off!" she cried. "Oh! Wow! Say it again! This time, say it slower, please!" he begged her. "Whaaat?!" she cried with a bewildered look on her face. "Tell me where his body is, you bitch! I want to stick my dick in his neck!" he chuckled as she tried to pull away. Terrance looked over her shoulder, watching as 2 men in lab coats covered in blood were coming in their direction. "Debbie! Why did you run, dear? It's your turn now!" one of the men said in a calm voice. Terrance pushed her in to the arms of the 2 men. "Bye, young lady!" Terrance chuckled as they dragged her down the corridor. "And I thought this was going to be a boring day!" he said as continued his stroll down the corridor.

At the end of the corridor, Terrance and the agents made a right turn to a set of double doors. Standing at the doors were 2 Agents in riot gear. "I'm here to see Dr. Zachmont" He said before the agents opened the double doors. Terrance was shocked at what he saw. "Say Doc! I thought this was going to be a private meeting!" Terrance shouted.

3 days earlier, Terrance was informed that he would have a private meeting with the top Executive in the National Agreement Dr. Alfred Zachmont. It was Zachmont who promoted Terrance, giving Doug Reed his old position.

Inside the room sat not only Dr. Zachmont, but 11 other big shots in the NA. Arnold Luther was mid-west director of the NA, Herbert Cromwell, Hawaii and Alaska's director, Sir Andre Morawiecki, west coast director, Lee O. Patton, assistant west coast director, Michael Bellar, weapons supplier for the NA, Dr. Sherman Tessman, director of the MK Ultra project, Griffen Piter, NA intelligence officer, Dr. Ivan Kashbian, MK Ultra director south west region, Dr. Willem Rutte, MK Ultra director north west region, Dr. Hugo R. Schouten, MK Ultra director south east and Hague Zaanstad, Afghanistan, Columbian and Mexican cartel liaison for the NA.

"Well boys! What it is? What it be like?" Terrance chuckled with his arms spread. Terrance's greeting wasn't reciprocated. There was a dead silence in the earie, unnatural space. "What's the problem?" Terrance chuckled. "Mr. Haggerty! What do you know about Lassenberia?" Dr. Zachmont asked. Terrance's smirk was wiped away. "Oh! That thing! It's just some vacation spot the Lassenberry people built! Nothing serious!" he said. "Nothing serious? It's now a sovereign nation. A fucking sovereign nation!!" Zachmont shouted. Terrance stood there in silence. "I assume this happened on your watch." Dr. Rutte said. "What are you trying to get at, doc?" Terrence asked. "It is because of your bumbling incompetence, we, the regional directors have to do a clean sweep in our own regions, so this doesn't occur again!" Rutte explained. "Give me a fucking break, guys! I already sent a message to Lassenberry, and he's scared shitless! It's business as usual in New Jersey!" Terrance explained. Dr. Zachmont sighed. "We need to find out who's in charge of Lassenberia. Rather, you need to find out who's in charge." Zachmont said. "Why don't we just pay a visit to Lassenberia?" Terrance asked. "We can't if they're under the protection of the United nations, which they are!" Zachmont said. "For fuck sakes! They have thousands of people from different African tribes migrating there! Now why would these people consider this spec of an island the promise land?" Griffen Piter asked. "You're the intelligence guy! You tell me!" Terrance chuckled. "Enough! Mr. Haggerty! You need to find out what you can from Lassenberry, then report back to Mr. Piter!" Zachmont said. "So, that's it? No punishment for a blunder?" Terrance Chuckled. Dr. Zachmont's nostrils started flaring. Terrance could see the evil in his eyes. "On second thought! Agents! Take Mr. Haggerty and feed him to the freaks!" Zachmont ordered. 2 Agents apprehended Terrance. His knees buckled out of fear. "No doc! Please! Just shoot me! Please, just shoot me in the head!" Terrance cried. Becoming so out of touch with his emotions from fear, Terrance lost control of his mental state. He chuckled for the first few seconds, then started balling like a baby as they took him out of the room. His cackling could be heard through the corridors as the agents dragged him away. "Mr. Piter! Go do what you were sworn to do!" Zachmont said.

The one's Zachmont called the freaks were dozens of deformed and violently deranged MK Ultra experiments gone wrong. These so-called human beings were locked away, being fed the warm flesh of illegal immigrants that were captured coming across the U.S. Mexican border.

The next day, there was something grandiose going on at castle Lassenberry in Cherry Hill, New jersey. It was November 5th, 2002 around 3 in the morning when Viola Carr was being prepped and sedated for this special day. Her labor pains were too much to bear as she was hand cuffed to the bed posts. There was a team of pediatricians in the bedroom in scrubs standing over her. The weird thing was there were a group of men standing outside the door.

These men held high positions in the corporate and entertainment world. There was a man who was the CEO of one of the biggest fast-food chains on the east coast massaging his belly, staring at the door like a crazed lunatic. There was another man who happened to be an "A" list actor pacing back-n-forth impatiently. "I have dibs on the placenta!" he shouted as he raised his hand. The other men starting laughing hysterically. Suddenly the door to the bedroom opened. "Gentlemen, please! This is a delicate situation! She's no spring chicken!" the doctor whispered before closing the door. One of the men, who was a Hollywood executive covered his mouth trying to hold back his laughter.

Meanwhile, on the opposite side of the castle, Edward the 2nd sat in his office with a pitiful look on his face as he gulped down his fifth shot of scotch. He was not alone. Sitting across from him was Doug Reed with a big smile on his face as his feet were propped up on the desk.

"Cheer up kid! It could be worse! You could end up with nothing!" he said. Edward the 2nd covered his face as he cried like a child.

Moments later, there was a knock on the door. "Open the door." Doug ordered one of the agents standing guard. The agent opened the door, allowing "A" list movie star Jett Connors to enter. He was wearing a white glove on his left hand. "I have a little sampler for you, Doug!" he said. "That's Mr. Reed to you, you sack of puss!" he said to Jett. "Flattery will get you everywhere!" Jett chuckled. "Come on, what is it?" Doug asked. In the palm of Jett's hand with the glove was a clot of blood mixed with feces. Doug savagely grabbed Jett's hand and began licking the substance out the palm of his hand. Edward the 2nd looked up and began heaving over his desk and floor before making it to the bathroom. Jett laughed hysterically as Doug kept licking his palm.

About an hour had passed. Edward the 2nd had dozed off on the bathroom floor, next to the toilet. His shirt was covered with vomit stains. There was a banging on the bathroom door. The noise had awakened him. The door opened. "Say kid! It's time. you have to come see this." Doug said. Still feeling groggy, Edward the 2nd struggled to stand. "I thought it was a dream!" he said. "No, kid. This is no dream. Come on and let me show you how I, as you colored people say, get busy." Doug said.

Elsewhere in the east wing of the castle, the group of men made their way to the dining hall. They stood off to the side applauding as a golf cart carrying Doug Reed and Edward the 2nd entered the hall. Doug stepped out of the golf cart. Edward the 2nd was too petrified from what he saw that he couldn't step out of the golf cart. "Get over here, kid! I won't tell you again!" Doug shouted as an agent tied a bib around his neck. There was a dead silence as Edward the 2nd staggered out of the golf cart.

Doug sat at the head of the dinner table which was covered with a red and black gothic tablecloth. There were 4 medieval style candles burning at each corner of the table. The group of men formed a semi-circle around the table. "Sit down, kid!" Doug said. "Ok! Ok! Don't rush me!" Edward the 2nd shouted. Edward the 2nd slumped back into his chair which was at the other end of the table while agents dressed as butlers bring in bottles of the finest champagne. The group of elitists stood around as their flutes were filled to the rim. Doug stood. Edward the 2nd just sat there looking miserable. "Gentleman! I would like to propose a toast, to me!" Doug chuckled. laughter was heard amongst the crowd. "Eat! Eat! Eat!" what the men were chanting aloud. A covered dinner platter was laid in front of Doug. Edward the 2nd looked up as he heard the muffling sounds of an animal in caught in a trap. When the cover was lifted, Edward the 2nd tried everything in his power to keep from fainting. It was a sight that horrified him. The life laying on the platter squirmed, still covered in afterbirth. A carving knife and sharpener was placed before Doug. He was the first to plunge his dinner fork into the infant. The cries of the newborn ceased when Doug took his first bite. "Come on, boys! Dig in!" Doug shouted as he waived his fork in the air. The group of men didn't care for forks and knives. In a ravenous fashion, the group of men tore into the infant's body. The men laughed as Edward the 2nd fell out of his seat on to the floor.

When Edward the 2nd opened his eyes, he noticed that he wasn't in the dining hall anymore. He looked over to his left, as he was sitting in a recliner and saw Viola sleeping in the bed. she was hooked up to an intravenous line. Edward the 2nd stood and saw on the other side of the bed 2 bassinettes. He stumbled, hitting knee on the bed post. The noise caused Viola to awaken. "You Ok?" he asked her. "Where am I?" she asked. "You're with me. You're safe." He said. Viola looked to her left. She saw the bassinettes as well. "My Babies!" she screamed, causing one of the newborns to coo. Edward the 2nd stood over the 2 infants. Tears trickled downs his cheeks as picked up one in the blue blanket. "You wanna hold your son?" he asked. "Hand him to me!" she said. Edward the 2nd carefully passed his son to the mother. He looked over his shoulder towards the other bassinette. He carefully picked up the infant in the pink blanket. "Hey beautiful! I'm your daddy!" he whispered as he gazed upon his daughter. Viola started breast feeding her son. She had a concerned look on her face. "Where's my other baby?" she asked. Edward the 2nd couldn't' look her in the eye. "She didn't make it, baby!" he said with dread in his voice. He could see the pain in her face. Viola was strong. She blew off the pain and sorrow with a sigh.

Moments later, Viola was startled when she and Edward the 2nd heard a banging on the door. Doug came into the room like a bat out of hell. "Good morning, my dear sweet Viola!" he yelled at the top of his lungs. "What the fuck, man?!" Edward the 2nd shouted. Doug ignored him, as he flung a bouquet of roses on the foot of the bed. "I Have to run, kids! We have a big party coming up! Well, anyway, congratulations! Ta-ta!" Doug shouted as he waltzed himself out of the bedroom. Edward the 2nd ordered one of the agents to closed the door as soon as Doug left the room. "Who was that?" Viola asked. "Nobody! Just some senile old man!" He said. "Where's Hakeem?" she asked. "Who?" he asked" "My son!" Viola screamed. "Oh! He's on his way, baby girl!" he said. "You still didn't answer my question!" viola asked. "What's that, baby?" he asked with a suspicious look. "Where the hell am I?!" she shouted.

2 days earlier, Viola was home in Hillside experiencing pains. She for one of Edward the 2nd's goons to come in the bedroom. She ordered the burly black man to call an ambulance. Instead, he was ordered earlier to call Edward the 2nd if Viola was going through any difficulties. Edward the 2nd was ordered prior to that to call Doug if anything out of the ordinary occurred.

Moments later, all the goons guarding her home disappeared. A couple of NA agents entered her bedroom dressed as EMT workers. Viola was injected with a syringe, causing her to pass out. She was put on a gurney, taking her out of the bedroom. When they came downstairs, they strolled passed the sofa where her son Hakeem was laid out unconscious.

The ambulance driver didn't head to the nearest hospital, instead he jumped on the Garden State Parkway, heading south. Once the ambulance arrived at castle Lassenberry, the doctors, the group of corporate and entertainment executives, along with Doug Reed were already there.

Edward the 2nd was sitting in his office logging in the birth and names of his children into the B.O.I an hour after leaving Viola in the bedroom. He overruled Viola's decision by naming their son Edward Benjamin Lassenberry. it was Viola who named their daughter Niyale princess Lassenberry.

CHAPTER .37 THE RAPPER

It was November 10th 2002, when Hakim was sitting in the back room of his night club counting stacks of cash from the sales of the last refill. He was sitting with 2 of his top guys, Clip and Bess. "How much you got over there?" Hakim asked Bess. "I got 1.5 mill." He said. Clip had 2 more stacks of cash left to run through the money roller. "How much you got Clip?" Hakim asked. "Give me a second, boss." He said. Suddenly, there was a knock on the door. Clip and Bess pulled out their pistols. "Come in!" Hakim yelled. Aaron entered the room with a shotgun strapped to his shoulder. "Yo, boss! It's this preppy motherfucker outside wanna talk to you." he said. "Did he show a badge?" Hakim asked. "No!" Aaron said. "Tell the boys frisk him, then let him in." Hakim said.

Moments later Hakim met this guy at the bar. "Mr. Bates! I'm Frank Twain, marketing executive for Wormhole Music Group." He said as he and Hakim shook hands. "What can I do for you, man?" Hakim asked. "Can we sit down to talk?" He asked. Hakim looked at the guys in his crew. "Sure, we can! Not in here though. Let's go out to my car." Hakim said. "Ok!" Twain said.

The 2 men went outside in the 40-degree weather to have a meeting in Hakim's Boeman Sedan. They were followed by 2 of Hakim's bodyguards. Hakim sat in the driver's seat while Frank sat in the passenger's seat. "I don't understand why we can't sit in your warm club!" Frank said. "Hey! I got good heat! Besides, my ride might be bugged. So, if I say some incriminating shit, and you vouch for it, we both going down!" Hakim chuckled. "Fair enough!" frank said.

"Well, Mr. Bates, I'm here to talk to you about a hip-hop artist who used to be under our flag. You may have heard of him." Frank said. "Who?" Hakim Asked. "MC Gutter. He was an artist at BIG BAD records." Frank said. "Who?" Hakim asked. "MC Gutter! The rapper! The kid that was shot dead right in front of your club not too long ago!" Frank said. "OK! What about him?" Hakim asked. "It's not about him per se. it's about the booming record sales after his death. You ever heard of ROTTON APPLE RECORDS?" frank asked. "Not really! I'm a hustler, the real fucking deal, not an entertainer!" Hakim said. "I understand that! Anyway, ROTTON APPLE RECORDS is a label under our flag as well. They're based in

California. "Ok." Hakim responded. "There's this gangster rapper at ROTTON APPLE named CHATTER BOX. He and GUTTER were rivaling over who could sell the most records for the longest. Now that GUTTER is dead, CHATTER BOX is like every other rapper. Mediocre!" Frank explained. "What the fuck that shit got to do with me?" Hakim asked. Frank stared out the window for a quick moment. He turned to Hakim. "Come on, man. He mentioned you in his last music video. A man of your stature? That had to piss you off!" Frank said. "Listen, Nigga. I don't know what you're talking about." Hakim said in a calm voice. "I'm just saying, if I was in your shoes, and needed the heat taken away from my business, I would direct it somewhere else. let's say, out west!" Frank said. Hakim sat there looking at Frank in silence. Hakim started to grin. "If you're talking about what I think you're talking about, that's some gangster shit!" Hakim said. "All I can say, once it's dealt with, you'll have the backing of my people, wherever you go." Frank said. "I already got that!" Hakim said. "I have 10 million green friends I can introduce to you." Frank said. Hakim thought about it for a moment. "When can I meet them?" Hakim asked. "You'll meet half of them tomorrow, the other half after the job is done." Frank said. "Mr. Twain. I'm gonna do my personal investigation on you as soon as we part ways. If you are who you say you are, then I'll meet your 5 million friends. Until then, get the fuck outta my ride." Hakim said. "Ok, Mr. Bates." Frank said before leaving the car.

Hakim went back inside the club to the back room. "What happened?" Clip asked. "Yo Bess! Leave us alone for moment." Hakim said. Bess placed the cash in his hand on the table. "I need a drink anyway." He said. Clip and Hakim were alone. First thing. Toothpick gotta go. Then I want you to spy on this nigga, Frank Twain from WORMHOLE Music Group." Hakim said. "No problem." Clip said. "How much on the table so far?" Hakim asked. Ah, about 3 million." Clip said.

It was the following morning when Clip took Toothpick to a diner out in Camden, New Jersey. Clip had a big breakfast consisting of turkey sausage, home fries, scrambled eggs, wheat toast, and orange juice. Toothpick only had a bowl of cereal. "I got 20 grand I gotta pick in Irvington, man." Clip said. "Irvington? Why the fuck we came all the way out here to eat, then?" Toothpick asked. "I gotta drop something off first." Clip said. Toothpick watched Clip scarf down his food. "Yo! You gonna eat all that?" he said to Clip. "Why?" clip asked. "That's why you're so be nigga!" toothpick said. "You judging me? Stay in your lane, kid!" Clip said. "I'm just fucking with you, old man! Chill!" he said as he punched Clip in the arm. Clip just laughed it off.

After Clip finished his breakfast, he donned his ball cap. "Let's go, and get this shit done." Clip said. The 2 men leave the diner. They walk to Clip's car. Toothpick entered on the passenger side. Clip drove off, heading down route 168. "Where the hell are, we going, anyway?" Toothpick asked. Clip looked over at toothpick. "What did I tell you, man? Stay in your lane!" he said.20 minutes into the drive, Clip made a turn off the ramp exit, heading into a wooded area. He pulled over and turned off the ignition. "Why the fuck we stop out here?" Toothpick asked. Clip was a giant compared to the thin frame of Toothpick. He grabbed Toothpick by the back of the neck, pulling him towards him. "What the fuck, man?" Toothpick shouted as he tried to pull away. Clip placed him in a headlock, snapping Toothpick's neck. He then placed Toothpick back in his seat, upright. He then secured Toothpick in his seat belt. Clip turned on the ignition and drove off. As he was driving, Clip frowned as he rolled down the windows. Toothpick had loss control of his bowels in the scuffle.

3 days later, Clip and Bess arrive at LAX around 12 noon. Both arrived carrying only backpacks. They catch a taxi from the airport. Clip tells the driver to take them to an address in Compton. About a half hour later they arrive at their destination. This area was ruled by the most notorious gang in Los Angeles. As soon as they exited the taxi, the driver sped off like lightning. "Damn! Nigga almost ran over my foot!" Bess said. Clip saw a group of black guys on the corner blasting their boombox. Clip knew these were the guys he needed to see because of their gang colors. "You ready to see to these niggas?" Clip asked Bess. "Fuck! I guess." Bess said. "Let's do this!" Clip said. They both go ahead with caution as they walk towards the gangbangers. There were about 14 of them. Some of them had no problem exposing their pistols in their waistbands. As soon as one of the gang members spotted Clip and Bess walking towards them, the blasting music was turned off. "Sup cuz?!" one of the gangbangers said to Clip. "I got a meeting with Crazy K." Clip said. "Who you, nigga?" the banger said as he stood toe-to-toe with Clip. "Tell him N.J. asking for him. He'll know who I am." Clip said. "Alright! Stay yo ass here!" the gang member said. Clip and Bess stayed put as the gang member ran in the house across the street. Clip and Bess stood their ground as the remaining gang members gave them intimidating looks.

About 5 minutes later, the gang member came out of the house, making his way across the street. "Y'all strapped?" the gang member asked Clip. "Nah, man!" Clip Said. "Yo Tre! Pat these fools down!" the gang member said to his associate. Clip and Bess both had their hands in the air as they were being frisked. "They're clean." Tre said. "Come on, old man!" the gang member said to Clip. Clip and Bess follow him across the street into the house. Unknown to them the other gang members who were standing outside walked over and stood on the porch.

Inside the house Clip and Bess were introduced to Crazy K, who ran all the dope in Compton. Crazy K told his soldier to step outside. "Yo! Y'all know y'all niggas got a lot of heart coming out here asking me to do that work!" Crazy K chuckled. "What? You changing your mind now?" Bess asked. "Calm down, man!" clip said to him. "Listen Cuz! Y'all here! Let's do business!" Crazy K said. Clip pulled out a piece of paper from his pants pocket. He showed it to Crazy K. "What's this?" he asked. "We went online and set up an account in your government name and that's the account number. You got a pen and paper? Write it down, cause I'm about to burn it. There's 50 thousand in there. When the job is done, you get another account number for another 50. We'll be staying at the hotel near the airport until the job is done." Clip explained. Crazy K and shook Clip's hand before he left. "Yo cuz! Y'all ain't gotta stay at no hotel! Y'all my guests! I got everything y'all want here! Drinks, bitches, dope! You name it!" he said. Clip and Bess stare at each other. "Nah, man. No disrespect. If some dumb shit goes down, and we don't make it home in 3 days, god help you, nigga!" Clip chuckled. "Man, y'all on some bullshit! That's ok though!" Crazy Z said before Clip and Bess leave.

About an hour later, Clip and Bess were watching TV at a 5-star hotel a couple of miles from the airport. "Man, why I can't get my own room?" Bess asked. "We gotta watch each other's back while we're out here! We ain't packing, and I don't trust them niggas!" Clip said.

"I hear you, man. I can't front though! What he offered sounds tempting!" Bess chuckled. "Let me say something else, man! For that amount of money, we could do the shit ourselves!" Bess said. "We don't need to get our fingerprints on anything out here!" Clip said. "You think we should get reimburse for this, man?" Bess asked. Clip scoffed at his question as he headed to the bathroom.

The next day back in New York, Hakim was at his penthouse with 3 beautiful young ladies. One was a sexy dark-skinned Caribbean, with long wavy jet-black hair, the other young lady looked more middle eastern with a face and body so put together that it would make men melt. The last of the young ladies was a brown skinned African American girl. She had a pretty face but was 50 pounds or so overweight but curvaceous. Hakim was walking around the penthouse in his boxers, while the young ladies, except for the overweight girl walked around in their bra and panties.

As a kid, Hakim learned a lot from Eddie Lassenberry when judging ones' character. Eddie would lay out lures around the house and wait to see which one of his guests would gravitate towards that item. In this case the bait was cocaine. There was about a few grams laid out on his glass coffee table. "If y'all want to take a hit, go ahead." He said. "That's what I'm talking about!" the Caribbean girl said. Hakim went into the bedroom but peaked around the corner to see the reactions of his offer. "Go on! Get some, girlfriend!" the middle eastern girl said to the curvy girl. The middle eastern girl sat in the chair with her legs crossed, filing her nails. The curvy girl was reluctant but did a line anyway. The Caribbean girl was on her second line. The curvy girl didn't like the effects of the drug but was being egged on by the middle eastern girl. A few minutes passed when Hakim had seen enough. He came from around the corner. "Why you let this bitch talk to you like that?" he asked the curvy girl. Hakim could see that she was fighting back her tears. The middle eastern girl was fighting back her snickering by covering her mouth. The Caribbean girl didn't pay any attention because she was busy frosting her gums. "You can't be the mother of my kids! You seem weak as hell! You gotta go!" he said to the curvy girls. The curvy ran into the bedroom, got dressed, then ran out of the penthouse. The middle eastern girl started laughing hysterically. "What are you laughing at, bitch? Get your conniving, manipulating ass the fuck outta here!" he shouted. she stood there looking at Hakim as if how dare he. "You know what? Butch got way more shit going on than you, anyway!" she said as she was putting on her tight outfit. Once her leather boots were on, she poked Hakim on the side of his head. "I guarantee you're gonna miss this pussy!" she said before leaving. Hakim ran out into the hall after her. "You better not snitch, bitch! You might end up missing!" he shouted before going back inside. He walked over to the Caribbean girl. "Listen. If you're gonna be the mother of my kids, you gotta chill with that stuff." He said. The young lady turned to Hakim. She smiled with a nod. "Now, get the fuck out! "he said with a faux smile. Moments later, Aaron came in after standing guard in the hall. "You good, boss?" he asked. "Oh, yeah! I was just figuring out how I was gonna spread my seed." Hakim said as he winked at Aaron. Aaron looked puzzled. "I'm about to get dressed. Call the concierge and have him bring the car around." Hakim ordered. The who?" Aaron asked. "Damn, man! The guys who works the lobby!" Hakim said in a scolding manner.

Later that evening, Hakim walked around greeting patrons at his night club BIG SHOTS.

The base of the club music coming through the gigantic speakers were deafening. He noticed the suit man sitting at a table off to the side with 2 of his goons. He went over to converse with them. "Gentlemen! Enjoying yourselves this fine evening?" Hakim asked. "You're late with payment, Mr. Bates!" the suit man said. "Damn! I thought you Sicilians would be more concerned on how a little Asian boy wacked your boss!" Hakim chuckled as one of the goons jumped out of his seat standing toe-to-toe with him. "You don't wanna start no shit in here! Not now!" Hakim said. The suit man signaled for his soldier to sit. Hakim pulled up a chair and sat next to the suit man. "Here's the deal! fuck the 40 million you were expecting! You'll get half a million a month, same as your people in Philly! That's the only way we're gonna keep the peace! Take it or leave it!" Hakim shouted with a smile on his face. The suit man glanced over at his goons. "Andiamo!" he shouted as he looked Hakim in the eye. All 3 men stood from their chairs and headed towards the exit. "Get home safe, gentlemen!" Hakim chuckled hysterically. Soon as they were out of sight, Hakim looked worried. He reached in his pocket for his cell phone. He hit the speed dial. *"What's up, boss?"* the voice said. "I want you to round up a least a half a dozen of our people and come down here, quick!" he ordered. *"Got it."* The voice said before clicking off. Sitting at the bar, watching his every move was Jimmy Loa. Hakim spotted him as he was shoving his cell phone back into his pocket. Hakim looked infuriated as he walked through the crowd towards Jimmy. "Get the fuck outta my club! Now!" Hakim shouted. "Is that any way to talk to an old friend?" Jimmy asked. "I'm not gonna tell you again!" Hakim shouted. "What you gonna do, pal? Hire some little kid to whack me?" Jimmy said with a serious look on his face. Hakim was speechless. Suddenly, Jimmy burst out laughing. "I'm just fucking with you, man! That's the joke we wise guys tell each other now-a-days!" Jimmy chuckled. "Just get the fuck out and stop spying on me!" Hakim said in a wining voice. "fine! Just grease the palm, and I'm out!" Jimmy shouted. "Follow me to the back!" he said. Jimmy followed Hakim to the door of his office but was told to stand outside. Hakim came out a few minutes later, handing over 5 thousand dollars to Jimmy. "Fuck! "Why so generous?" he asked. "You call that generosity? Times must be hard for you guys!" Hakim shouted. "Between me and you, these zips are draining our fucking pockets like no body's business! Since we can't touch the H or coke, it's just been a fucking struggle!" Jimmy complained. Hakim raised an eyebrow at Jimmy's sob story. "Hey! Rules are rules!" Hakim chuckled. "Fuck you!" Jimmy said before leaving. Hakim pulled out his cell phone again. He hit the speed dial. *"What you want?"* the voice said. "Come on Butch! We're on the same side!" Hakim shouted. *"Just spit it out, kid!"* Butch shouted out of frustration. "We need to get the other generals together, ASAP!" he shouted. *"Why?"* Butch asked. "I smell a civil war brewing between the Gatano people and the Sicilians!" Hakim shouted. *"What the fuck that go to do with us?"* he asked. "Just get everybody together at my safehouse in Irvington tomorrow at noon!" Hakim shouted. *"Don't be wasting my time, kid!"* Butch shouted before clicking off his phone. Hakim was smiling from ear-to-ear before shoving his cell phone back in his pocket.

The next day around noon, Hakim glanced at his diamond encrusted watch as he waited for the other generals to show up. Moments later, Sammy and Mookie were the first to arrive. The 3 generals meet in Hakim's process room where kilos of cocaine were being cooked up by a dozen or so workers. "What's this meeting all, man?" Mookie asked. "I'll tell when Butch and Dubbs show up." He said.

Mookie came in with his assistant Bobby, who was this burly intimidating Spanish guy. Since the incident with Terrance, Mookie had to let go of his former bodyguard. The former bodyguard was found floating in the Passaic river.

15 minutes had passed when Butch and Dubbs walked in the door. "Glad you guys could make it!" Hakim said. "We're here! Let's get to it!" Butch said. "Follow me." Hakim said. The 5 generals left the processing area, heading down to the basement. Mookie needed aid from Bobby and Dubbs to go down the stairs. Hakim flipped on the light switch to unveil an empty but dusty basement. The only items in there were a cardboard box filled with shot guns and AK-47 machine guns.

"We can talk freely down here. I had the place swept for bugs." Hakim said. "Ok kid! We're here! Talk!" Butch said. "I talked to this wise guy at my club last night! He tells me that the Gatano people ain't to happy about the Sicilians coming over here taking over their businesses! I think if we tweaked their ongoing soap opera a little, that'll keep them out of our pockets!" Hakim explained. "I have no problems with Italians!" Mookie said. "You Don't, but Sammy, Dubbs does, and me too!" Hakim explained. "So, what you're saying?" Butch asked. "Let's get Lassenberry to take out the top mob guys from Jersey and Philly!" Hakim said. "You think he's just gonna bend over and do this?" Dubbs asked. "He did it before!" Hakim said. "When was this?" Butch asked. "I can't say! You wouldn't believe me anyway!" Hakim said. "Yo, my dude! Just say the word! Them bitch ass spaghetti eating motherfuckers gotta pay!" Sammy said passionately as he rubbed his arm with the sling. "Hell yeah! That money we give them can go to the cops and judges not on our payroll!" Dubbs said. Hakim's cell phone goes off. He takes it out of his pocket to check who's calling. "Hold on Y'all! I gotta take this call!" he said. Hakim walked over to the other side of the basement while the other generals mingle amongst themselves.

"What's up?" Hakim asked the person on the phone. *"The rapper is dead. Check the news."* the voice said before clicking off the phone. Hakim stuffed his cell phone back into his pocket. He went back over to the huddle with a big grin on his face. "What you smiling about?" Butch asked. "Just got word there's gonna be another East coast west coast rap beef!" Hakim said. "Word?" Sammy said. "Yeah! Somebody took Chatterbox out!" Hakim explained. "So, that's what you're smiling about?" Butch asked. "Ah, no! I was just thinking about this bad ass chick I'm gonna hook up with tonight!" Hakim said. "Yeah, right." Butch said with a suspicious look on his face.

The day before, around 3am PST. The gangster rapper known to the world as Chatterbox was leaving a strip club somewhere in Hollywood with his entourage of 15 guys. Before he could open the door to his 2002 sports car, 2 masked men came running across the street wielding machine guns. Shots were fired. Everyone tried to run for cover. Chatter box, along with 3 others were sprayed with bullets. A black Boeman jeep pulled up. The 2 masked men jumped into the vehicle. The vehicle sped off into the night. His sports car was turned into swiss cheese. Chatterbox's back was riddled with bullets. His body was slumped over his car door.

A couple of weeks had passed, and just like MC GUTTER, no one was convicted of CHATTERBOX'S murder. Just like MC GUTTER, CHATTERBOX'S record sales went triple platinum. Televised tribute concert ratings skyrocketed. Murals of the 2 rappers were all over the United States, Europe, and South Africa.

Hakim received the other half of his cash for a job well done. Unfortunately, Clip and Bess didn't return from their mission. For some reason, Crazy K didn't trust Clip and Bess until the second part of his funds was cleared. After the hit on Chatterbox, Clip returned to Crazy K's hood to give him the account number. The call was then made to Hakim that the job was done, at the same time Crazy k went to the financial institution to retrieve his cash. Whether it was done intentionally or unintentionally, the account number was off by 3 numbers, keeping him from making the withdrawal. Crazy K was so outraged that he didn't think it through to call Clip to straighten things out. He made a phone call to his crew and gave the order to have Clip and Bess clipped.

— CHAPTER .38 ALL OF THESE PEOPLE —

It was November 29th, 2002 when Edward the 2nd's closest confidant, known as number 3 was roaming the halls of the of the east wing of castle Lassenberry. As many times he walked these halls, he was always fascinated will the 50"x50" oil painting of Benny Lassenberry hanging on the wall. This was one out of ten paintings of the former patriarch spread out through the castle.

Coming his way in a golf cart was Viola's son, Hakeem. He was accompanied by a couple of his friends who were joy riding through the castle in a golf cart. The golf cart came down the corridor swerving at high speed. "Move old man!" one of the teenagers shouted as number 3 backed up against the wall. "Poor bastards!" he whispered to himself.

At the west wing area of the castle, Edward the 2nd was in his office logging new entries in the B.O.I with Brandon. "How much did we bring in from the bed-n-breakfast businesses last week?" Edward the 2nd asked. "I have a total 8.5 million." Brandon said as he read from the B.O.I. "That's it?" Edward the 2nd shouted. "That's a 3% jump from the beginning of the month!" Brandon explained. Suddenly, Brandon fell to his knees screaming in pain as he grabbed the back of his neck. "You ok?" Edward the 2nd asked in a calm voice. "My…my neck! My head! The pain!" he shouted. "Oh., really." Edward the 2nd said. Little did Brandon know; his boss had a device that looked like a car remote in his hand. "You sure it was 3%?" Edward the 2nd asked. "I'm positive!!" Brandon shouted in excruciating pain. Edward the 2nd took his thumb off the remote button. Brandon was catching his breath as he stood to his feet. "Wipe the blood from your nose, man." He said to Brandon. Brandon went into the bathroom to get himself together. Moments later, he returned. "Now what's the total on the dive bars?" He asked Brandon.

Suddenly, there was a knock on the door. "Hold on!!" Edward the 2nd shouted. "Put the B.O.I in the safe!" he said to Brandon. After Brandon placed the B.O.I in the wall safe, he placed the portrait over it. "Come in!" Edward the 2nd shouted as he took his seat. The door opened. An agent entered. "My Lord. Ms. Carr is here to see you." the agent said. "Bring her in." Edward the 2nd said. Viola staggered in the office with a zombified look on her face. She wore a long night gown and slippers. "What you doing coming down here dressed like somebody's grandmother?!" Edward the 2nd said. "I just wanna go home! Why can't I go home?" she said with slurred speech. "Bitch! You are home!! Agent! Give her another dose and take her ass back to her room!!" Edward the 2nd screamed at the top of his lungs. The agent grabbed Viola by the arm, dragging her out of the office. Edward the 2nd ran to the door. "You better not even think about hurting my kids, either!!" he shouted before slamming the door. Brandon just stood there in silence with a depressed look on his face. "I don't get this bitch! I give her and that punk ass son of hers everything!! I just don't fucking get it!!" he shouted to the ceiling. Moments later, there was another knock on the door. "Goddamn!... Come in!" he sighed. This time, a different agent entered the office. "My Lord. General Bates is at the main entrance. He says it's important that he has a word with you." the agent said. "Bring'em in but frisk his ass down first!" he said, "Yes, my Lord." The agent said. "You want me to stay for this?" Brandon asked. "Where the fuck else you gonna go?" Edward the 2nd said.

Moments later, there was a knock on the door. "Come in!" Edward the 2nd shouted as he kicked his feet up on the desk. The agent opened the door allowing Hakim to enter. "Hey! I just saw your girl down the hall going off on the help! Is she ok?" Hakim said with a smirk on his face. "Stay out of personal shit. That's an order, and a warning. "Ok!" Hakim said nonchalantly. "What you want?" he asked Hakim. "Can we talk, alone?" Hakim asked, glancing over at Brandon. "He's my right hand for now, so talk!" Edward the 2nd explained. Hakim sighed. "Alright! Alright! This is coming from the other generals as well. We need your help in starting a civil war between Sicilians and the Gatano people, maybe Philly." Hakim said. "Why would I wanna do that?" he asked Hakim. "Why?! I got this Sicilian fucker coming at me for a payoff just about every week! Dubbs gotta pay those Philly gangsters out by the shore! Not to mention what happened to Sammy!" Hakim explained. "The shit I do!" Edward the 2nd whispered to himself. "What?" Hakim asked. "Nothing! Let me think about it! I'll give you an answer when I'm ready!" He said to Hakim. "Think about?! We ain't got time to think about it!" Hakim said. "I said…let…me…think about it!!" he said to Hakim. Hakim was about to leave but checked himself. He stood at attention. "Long live the House of Lassenberry. Long Live Edward the 2nd." He said before leaving. "I want you to get together with number 3 and figure out how it will benefit me if I go along with this fool's plan." Edward the 2nd said to Brandon.

Outside the castle grounds Aaron was sitting in the car, watching as Hakim crossed the mote. Hakim entered the car. Hakim entered the rear passenger side. "What happened" Aaron asked. "Man don't ask me about my business!" "Hakim said. "ok!" Aaron said. "Call clip. See why it's taking his ass so long coming back." He said to Aaron. "I did while you were inside. He ain't pick it. Bess ain't pick up his phone either!" Aaron said. "MY gut feeling tells me, they ain't coming back!" Hakim said to himself. "What's that?" Aaron asked. "Nothing! Drive out to the club!" Hakim said.

The next day around 4:30 pm. Sammy arrived at Mookie's residence in Lincroft, New Jersey. He checked the paper he received from a reliable source to make sure it was the right address. He drove up into the driveway where he was stopped by 2 of Mookie's bodyguards. Both guards were of Latino descent. Bobby came out the house with a disgruntle expression on his face. "¿Qué carajo estás haciendo aquí sin llamar primero?" Bobby said. "Calm down, my dude! You forget I'm a general? I'm going inside to talk to Mookie!" Sammy said. "Acariciarlo!" Bobby said to one of the guards. Because his arm was in a sling, Sammy could only raise one hand in the air. The guard was causing Sammy pain as he searched his sling for weapons. "Take it easy, my dude!" Sammy shouted as he pushed the guard's hands away. "¡Sígueme!" Bobby said. Sammy followed Bobby into the house. Standing in the corridor was Mookie's son. "¿Qué pasa, amigo?" Sammy said to the kid. Sammy was escorted further into the enormous house, into the living room. There he saw Mookie lying face up, wearing nothing but an adult diaper on a massage table with his legs elevated a few inches by a rolled-up towel. Mookie was receiving a massage by his wife.

"General Vasquez, my dude!" Sammy said as he shook Mookie's hand. "General Perez." Mookie said with a look a suspicious look on his face. "This is my wife Rita." Mookie said. "¿Cómo estás, hermana?" Sammy said before kissing Rita on the cheek. "¡Hola! Por favor, a mí!" she said after kissing him on his cheek. "¿Podemos hablar en privado, amigo?" he asked Mookie. "Bebé. ¿Podrías darnos un minute a solas? ¡Poli! ¡Igualmente!" Mookie said to them. Rita gave her husband a kiss on the lips before leaving the room. Bobby stepped outside.

"Bring my wheelchair over." Mookie said. Sammy pushed his chair over next to the massage table. Mookie had the arms of a professional athlete. He was able to pull his body off the table and sit upright in his wheelchair. Sammy sat on the leather sofa next to him. "So, tell me what's so important that you had to come over here unannounced." Mookie said. "Check this out my dude! We're the only 2 Latinos in this organization. my question to you, is why we're working for these dudes, and not for ourselves?" he said. Mookie chuckled for a moment. "Where you really going with this?" Mookie responded. Sammy moved in closer to Mookie to whisper. "I know this dude who's a big timer down in Puebla, Mexico. He's like third in line of this cartel down there! He told me he could throw 400 kilos my way for half the price we're getting from Lassenberry! I say we move Butch, Dubbs and Hakim out of the way, move my product in, and say fuck Lassenberry!" he said. "Your Product? What do I get out of this? Mookie asked. "Simple, my dude! You take north jersey, and I'll take the south!" he said. Mookie shook his head in disbelief as he put his hand on Sammy's shoulder. "Sammy… Sammy…Sammy! ¡Mi hermano! You ever hear the story about my father?" Mookie asked. "I heard bits and pieces." Sammy said. "Well, he had the same dream as you. The outcome was that I had to take over his territory to keep my wife, my kids, and the rest of my family in this luxurious lifestyle. I'll leave it at that. This organization is bigger than Lassenberry, man. You see what happened at the memorial service for his family! I'm here to tell you, that plane accident, was no accident!" Mookie explained. "My dude! We can do this! "¡Somos familia! ¡Ellos no!" Sammy shouted. Mookie shook Sammy's hand. "I'm gonna have to say no, my brother. Do yourself a favor, and forget we had this conversation." Mookie said. Sammy looked infuriated but could do nothing but wave Mookie off and storm out of the house.

It was December 1st, 2002 when the coronation of His Majesty Marcus of Lassenberia and Her Majesty Queen Kimberly was ending. There was nothing this grandiose since the queen of England's coronation on June 2, 1953. Heads of state from 30 African countries, were in attendance, as well several groups belonging to fraternal orders around Asia and Africa. There were characters from not so favorable governments standing in the background. The kings of Lesotho, Morocco and Swaziland were also in attendance.

Queen Kimberly's gown was pearl white, made of silk. She wore the traditional Lassenberry red sash across her shoulder and the green sash around her midriff. Her Tiara was made of gold with diamonds imbedded in it. What made her tiara unique was that she had a 3-ounce crystal vial filled with GLC, closed off with a diamond cap placed in front.

Marcus of Lassenberia wore his traditional uniform with the red and green sash. The display of medals on his left breast increased by 4. Besides receiving medals from Russia, Colombia, and Denmark, he wore the Moroccan Commemorative medal, The Order of the Golden Heart of Kenya, The Zimbabwe Order of Merit, Order of the Seal of Solomon from Ethiopia, etc.

As he sat on his thrown next to his beautiful wife, Marcus of Lassenberia held a 3-foot-long scepter made of gold, which was hollowed out and filled with GLC. There were distinctive markings on the scepter. The tip of the scepter had a diamond shaped Goldfinch, with its wings spread. His crown resembled an Embossed Viking Helmet made of a rare light weight metal, covered with a shiny green and reddish hue, which matched his silk cape that dragged the floor when unattended. Sticking out the top of the crown were 54 tiny horns made of porcelain. There were 3 high ranking representatives from each major religious denomination wanting the honor of placing the crown upon his head. The royal couple sat on thrones that had the traditional appearance of European thrones but known to a small group of citizens they were equipped with ultramodern technology.

The crowd was in awe of the humongous fountain spewing GLC into the air. There were uniformed armed guards surrounding the fountain, keeping the crowd from getting too close. Despite all the security, Marcus of Lassenberia didn't feel safe keeping the precious liquid out of the hands of potential enemies, home and abroad. He and his wife had to make a deal with an unlikely ally to keep their power.

The sun was setting on Lassenberia. The crowd had disbursed, to different festivities throughout the land, or back to their native soil. Marcus of Lassenberia was standing atop one of the towers of his castle gazing across the land standing together with his queen.

"I can't believe it, my love! All of these people are our subjects!" he said. "1,500,673, to be exact." His queen said. "That many, in so little time?" he asked. "You forget, my love? We have a census bureau now!" she chuckled. Marcus kissed the back of her hand. "What would I do without you, my love?" he said. Both the king and queen looked up gazing at the night sky.

They both heard footsteps coming from behind. "Your majesty!" Ali said after bowing his head. "What is it General?" Marcus asked. "He's here." Ali said. "Bring him up." Marcus ordered. "Yes, your majesty." Ali said before leaving. "You sure we're doing the right thing, my love?" Kimberly asked.

Minutes later, Ali returned, but not alone. Accompanying him was a short brown skinned man with a full beard wearing a 2-piece suit. "Your majesty! I present to you the Iranian Minister of Foreign Affairs, the Honorable Akbar Sarmadi Muhammed!" Ali said. "As -Salāmu Alaykum, your majesty." The foreign minister said as he bowed his head.

"Alaykum Salām." Marcus said. Muhammed glanced over at Kimberly. "It's alright Minister Muhammed. My queen is also my partner in foreign affairs." Marcus said.

Minister Muhammed had reluctantly rendezvoused with Kimberly's sister Jenna, because of her being a woman in Morocco a few days earlier. After a couple of days of negotiation, the 2 representatives came to an agreement. The exchange was 2 nuclear warheads for 2 gallons of GLC.

"It is amazing how your infrastructure has developed in such a brief period of time!" the Minister said. "It's amazing what you can get done when the world is in dire need of what you possess!" Marcus said. "Indeed." The Minister replied. "I would like to apologize for our gathering being so discrete. If the western world caught wind of our relationship, we'd be added to that axes of evil list." Marcus said. "The Iranian government wants peace throughout the world. It's a shame that there's hostility towards my people coming from the west. By-the-way, thank you for the sample. I feel like a new man!" The Minister chuckled. "I have no doubt the Supreme Leader will feel the same way." Marcus said. "As we speak, there's a freight liner provided by our friends from china heading this way. There will be 2 containers filled with bottles of rose water, caviar, and other delectable items. You will find our trade within these gifts off the coast of Madagascar. We have a team of nuclear physicists and technicians arriving with the cargo." Muhammed said. "Great! I'll have a security team watching over them around the clock." Kimberly mentioned. "I'm sure they will be safe in your company, your highness." Muhammed said to her. "Well! Since we've cleared everything up, I'd like to bid you a safe journey back home, Minister!" Marcus said. "May your children's children prosper from your endeavors. "the Minister said before being escorted away by Ali. As Kimberly watched as Ali and the Minister walk away, Marcus walked towards the ledge of the tower to stare at the grand statue of his grandfather, Benny Lassenberry.

There was a 100-foot bronze statue of Benny Lassenberry standing outside the castle grounds facing due north. The statue displayed him wearing a long overcoat over a suit and his signature fedora. On the opposite side of the island was Lassenberia's national park near the Borough of Braxton. In the center of the park surrounded by a floral arrangement was a 50-foot bronze statue of Jabbo Jenkins. Jabbo was an unquestionable legend in the United States, especially on the streets of New Jersey.

Back in the United States, Hakim was at this Manhattan penthouse lying on his sofa in a daze, contemplating his next move. It was around 12 in the afternoon. Aaron came inside from standing guard in the corridor. He sat down in the lay-z boy across from Hakim. "You know you're my number one, right?" Hakim said as he stared at the crystal chandelier. Aaron had an ear-to-ear smile on his face, but quickly turned to sorrow. "Man, I know we ain't gonna see Clip and Bess again. You want me to recruit another crew?" Aaron asked. "I got over 400 dealers and runners on my payroll. I learned from Eddie Lassenberry, that every street nigga ain't a killer. Clip was the best at picking killers. Now that he's gone, I'm scared I might pick half ass niggas." He said. Aaron sighed as he looked around the room. "You think we can hold some type of forum with all our people and weed out the sucker ass niggas?" Aaron asked. Hakim turned to Aaron, pondering his suggestion. He quickly sat up. "Goddamn, nigga! You just gave me an idea!" Hakim said. "What's that, boss?" Aaron asked. "This what I want you to do. Get the word out to all our people on the streets to meet at Westside Highschool tomorrow night around midnight." Hakim said. "Westside in Newark?" Aaron asked with a bewildered look on his face. "Yeah nigga!! What Westside you think I'm talking about? Now get the fuck out and make it happen! Oh! Make sure you put the word in everybody's ear that Clip, and Bess was taken out by those gangbangers out west!" Hakim shouted. "For real?" Aaron asked. "Yeah, nigga!" Hakim said. "You sure you're gonna be safe here by yourself?" Aaron asked with concern. "Listen! You know I gotta stockpile in this motherfucker! I'll go out guns blazing if an army come up in here! Now, do what I told you, and get the fuck out!" Hakim ordered.

After Aaron left, Hakim got on hid cell phone. *"Yeah?"* the voice said. "It's me! I need to see you in the morning, ASAP!" Hakim said. *"I told you I'll let you know my decision when I'm ready!"* the voice said. "Forget that! I'm on some other shit now! I need to see you!" Hakim said in desperation. *"Ok! Ok! This better be good!"* the voice said before disconnecting from Hakim.

The next day, around 10 in the morning, Hakim arrived at castle Lassenberry dressed in a black suit and black overcoat. Edward the 2nd watched the surveillance footage in his office and noticed that he'd came alone. There was an agent standing next to Edward the 2nd. "Bring'em to me." He said to the agent.

Moments later, Hakim arrived at the office. As soon as he entered, he didn't give Edward the 2nd time to say a word. "Let's talk outside these walls!" he said. He and Edward the 2nd hopped into a golf cart that was parked outside of the office. Hakim did the driving. Moments later they end up in the courtyard. They took a stroll on the castle grounds. "Now, what you want?" Edward the 2nd asked. "I need your jet and 10 of your agents to come with me!" Hakim said. "Where the fuck you going?" he asked Hakim. "I need to go out to Los Angeles!" Hakim said. "Why?" he asked Hakim. Hakim sighed. "I put a contract on somebody that was a big deal out there! Shit got out of hand! Clip and Bess got taken out because of it!" Hakim confessed. "Who the fuck is Clip and Bess?" Edward the 2nd asked. "You know Clip! My top hitter!" Hakim shouted. "Nigga! All I know is I got 5 generals! The rest of them niggas on y'all roster! Not mine!" he said to Hakim. "Anyway! I gotta bring back the niggas that took him out, dead or alive! If not, my people gonna lose faith in my leadership! I gotta let my troops know I ain't no joke!" Hakim said. Suddenly, Edward the 2nd stopped in his tracks. "Wait-a-minute! This person who was a big deal, ain't a rapper, was he?" He asked. Hakim didn't say a word. "You did it, didn't you?" he asked. "What makes you say that?" Hakim asked. "I think you had something to do with that MC Gutter murder!" Edward the 2nd asked. Hakim looked in every direction but into the eyes of his boss. "Man don't tell me you're the cause of this east coast west coast bullshit I'm hearing about in the news!" he said with disgust. "That bitch ass MC GUTTER was talking shit about me in his videos! I couldn't let that shit slide!" Hakim said. Edward the 2nd grabbed Hakim by the shoulders. "He's a rapper! They ain't real!" Edward the 2nd shouted. "I know that! You know that! But the rest of the world don't know that! These kids think these punk motherfuckers are authentic!" Hakim said. Edward the 2nd released him. "You just can't go out there shooting up the city! Everything is structured! I gotta have a sit down with the top guy running shit out there!" He said to Hakim. "Who is it? I'll go talk to him myself!" Hakim said. "No, you can't! it's way above your pay grade! You will get murdered just for looking at him!" Edward the 2nd made clear.

The man Edward the 2nd was referring to was Jose (Chi-Chi) Mendez. The drug tsar of southern California. He was the one who warned Sir Marcus of the invading gangbangers coming to New Jersey. The National Agreement like Edward the 2nd, chose Chi-Chi to run his territory. According to the information Edward the 2nd received from the B.O.I, his wealth and power was 3 times the size of the Lassenberry organization, but by the rules of the National Agreement, all the drug tsars in the United States were forbidden to conflict with each other. Any beef would result in the death and replacement of the drug tsar.

"I'm gonna have to say, take the loss!" Edward the 2nd said. "Take the loss?!" Hakim shouted. "You heard me!" Edward the 2nd said. "I called on a meeting of all my people tonight! If I don't show up with bodies, it's gonna be anarchy!" Hakim explained. Edward the 2nd though about it for a moment. "What if you drop a body or 2 at the meeting?" He asked Hakim. Hakim's jaw dropped. "I'll give you the agents you need to back you." he said. "Snuff my own people?" Hakim said with doubt in his voice. "I heard stories about my uncle. Once he dropped somebody for getting out of line, everybody else fell in place, with a quickness." Edward the 2nd said. Hakim didn't respond. He stood at attention. "Long live the House of Lassenberry!" he shouted before leaving.

It was around 11:30pm. There were hundreds of drug dealers standing outside of Westside high school in Newark, New Jersey. It was like a block party with systems blasting from tricked out cars. The air was filled with clouds of marijuana smoke. There were crews from Bloomfield, Newark, Irvington, East Orange, West Orange, South Orange, Orange, Nutley, Cedar Grove, Livingston, Caldwell, West Caldwell, North Caldwell, Verona, Essex Fells, Maplewood, Roseland, Millburn, Glen ridge, Fairfield, Belleville, and Montclair. The crowd was a diversity of White, Black, Latino, male and female street soldiers. The age range was between pre-teen to retirement.

The cops that worked South Orange Avenue that night just flew by without a care. This was due to Benny Lassenberry's oldest rule. Always pay off law enforcement. This rule was effective to local and sometimes state law enforcement but didn't hold water with the feds. There were multiple teams of federal agents hiding amongst the headstones in the cemetery next door. Nighttime cameras were used to snap photos of each dealer and runner entering the school. Parabolic listening devices played a part in the surveillance as well.

Moments later, an NA agent came from inside the school with a bullhorn in his hand. "Attention! All of you who work for General Bates are to enter the school in an orderly fashion, and head to the auditorium! For those who do not, must vacate the premises at once!" he shouted.

Inside the auditorium, hakim and Aaron were on the stage sitting at a long folding table with 3 agents standing in the background. The dealers were entering in droves. All weapons were confiscated as people were walking through the metal detectors by the NA agents. "I can't believe this shit!" Aaron said in awe. "Believe what?" Hakim asked. "All of these people! You're incharge of all these people! Damn!" he said. "You got the list?" Hakim asked Aaron. "Ah, oh yeah!" Aaron said as he pulled a piece of paper from his pants pocket. It took about

10 to 15 minutes for everyone to get seated. Edward the 2nd granted Hakim more Agents to guards him.

Hakim was dressed in his uniform with the red and green sashes. He pulled out a cigar to add to his visual dominance. A smirk was on his face as he gazed upon the crowd. "Bring the room to order." Hakim said to Aaron. Aaron stood from his seat. "Everybody! Shut the fuck up!!" Aaron shouted. except for a few whispers, there was quiet.

Hakim stood from him chair walked from behind the table. "It's good to see you all made it!! I called this meeting out of dire urgency!! I have a problem!! We have a problem!! The problem is that we are being prevented from eating!! We have enemies out there who are trying to take me out of the game!! This is the truth!! If I don't supply you all, none of you eat!! You may say to yourself; I can go to another connect or I can get my product from out of state, but that's not how the system works!! I need you all to be more than someone just selling product on the streets!! I need you to be soldiers!! Real soldiers!! I don't want you all to fight and die for me!! I want you to fight and die for your families!! Your territories!! Your very own lives!! I don't care if you're Black, White, Latino!! We are all one family!! Essex county is ours forever!! I have your backs!! And I expect the same in return!!" he shouted to the crowd.

Aaron looked down at the piece of paper in front of him. He stood from his chair. "Long live the streets of Essex county!! Long live General Bates!!" he shouted. "What the fuck?" said one of the dealers in the crowd. "I said, Long live the streets of Essex county!! Long live General Bates, standing before y'all!! Aaron shouted again. "Show them how serious this shit is." Hakim whispered. Aaron walked off to the side of the stage. Moments later he wheeled out someone duct taped to a hand truck. The person was bruised, battered and duct taped from his mouth, to his ankles. That person was Jimmy Loa, who was an associate of the Gatano crime family.

"This motherfucker here, is the reason you all need to be worried!! He and his people want to take the food out of your mouths!! You may say the mafia is untouchable!! I'm showing you proof that they are not!!" hakim shouted as he pulled out a pistol from his holster. Hakim pointed to a teenage white guy in the crowd. "You!! come up here!!" he ordered the young man. The young man sat in the fourth row. He nervously looked around; not sure hakim was talking to him. "I'm not going to tell you again, kid!!" he shouted. "Get up there, white boy!!" one black guy shouted in the background. Some in the crowd were egging the kid on. Finally, the kid approached the stage. It was obvious to Hakim that this kid was nervous. "What's your name? What you do, and in what area you work, kid?" hakim whispered to him. "My… my name is Kenny. I…I sell pot in Essex fells!" the kid answered. Hakim hands the kid his pistol. "If you wanna continue to sell for me and keep feeding your family, take this and put a bullet in that mother fucker's head." Hakim whispered. The kid reluctantly took the pistol. He walked over to where Jimmy was. His hand was shaking as he pointed the pistol at jimmy's face. Kenny could see the fear in Jimmy's eyes. There were a few in the crowd roaring for him to shoot. After a minute of heckling, Kenny pulled the trigger. at that moment, hakim had a flashback in his mind to when Eddie Lassenberry made him do the same thing to a drug dealer when he was a kid. The single shot sounded like bubble wrap being popped but echoed 10 times louder. Kenny dropped the gun by his side. Hakim took the pistol away from him.

"Good, kid! In the morning you'll get a case of oxy. 24 bottles with 75 pills per bottle. You sell them at 20 bucks apiece and take 60 percent, okay?" Hakim whispered. Kenny nodded as he was covered in sweat. There was a dead silence in the auditorium after the pistol went off.

"This young man is a true soldier!! He doesn't have to worry about the mob, the cops, nobody, for the rest of his life!!" hakim shouted as he put his arm around Kenny's shoulder. Suddenly someone from the crowd stood from his chair. "Long live the streets of Essex county! Long live General Bates!" the man shouted. one-by-one, people stood and started chanting the same words until everyone was on their feet chanting simultaneously over and over. Hakim raised his fist in the air as the chanting continued.an agent rolled out Jimmy's lifeless body off the side of the stage.

Hakim and Aaron make their way through the chanting crowd towards the exit. "No one gets their guns back. Take them to the safehouse out in Montclair." He said to the agents standing guard by the exit. "Yes, general." One agent said.

Outside the school grounds, a NA agent held the car door open for Hakim and Aaron. They hop in the back. "You're good, boss! But what's gonna happen when the Italians find out he's missing?" Aaron asked. "Don't worry about it. He wasn't no made guy anyway. Ah, don't forget to bring the white kid Kenny to the penthouse later." Hakim explained. "Got it." Aaron said.

Kenny was 16 years old at the time when he did the killing for Hakim. He was about 5 feet and a couple of inches tall, thin with blonde hair and blue eyes. Kenny didn't look impoverished, or someone who grew up in a trailer park. He looked more preppy like he attended a private school. Soon after Hakim gave him the oxy pills, he named Kenny preppy Ken. Since then, he was one of the most feared white boys in North Jersey. It wasn't until July of 2005 preppy Kev's celebrity was ending. Months after he was given the nickname, he leaned more towards killing people for no reason than sticking to the drug game. When the feds caught up with him, he had murdered at least 18 people. To keep the feds off his scent, Hakim had no choice but to put a contract out on Kenny's head. His body was found in the middle of Wharton State Forest in New Jersey. The rumor was the hit was carried out by a crew in East orange.

After the westside high gathering, Italian social clubs were being vandalized with graffiti and broken windows throughout Essex county, then throughout New Jersey. Sammy's people began following suit, as well as Butch's and Dubb's people. The bosses from the Gatano crime family and the Philly mob caught wind on who the perpetrators were. To prevent a race war and disrupting business on both sides, the suit man and Augustine excepted a payoff of 20 million dollars apiece to leave the Jersey drug dealers alone, for good.

Soon after, Hakim's status became legendary for starting the revolution. It came to a point that he was the most respected out of all the five Generals. This didn't bother Mookie too much because 90 percent of his organization was of Latino descent. It was more of a cultural thing that they stayed loyal to him.

After the agreement with the Italian mob, Hakim, created another inner circle. These guys took an oath to take a bullet for Hakim. James Broker age 22, Alvin (Duck) Pennington age 21, Trevor (Trevy Trev) Williams age 18 were from Newark and Keith (KC) Cotton was age 25, from Irvington. Aaron was incharge of the crew. They had changed their persona and started wearing all black military fatigues and black combat boots, calling themselves the Triple H Crew, which stood for Hakim's heavy Hitters. Every time Hakim would leave the penthouse and head to his night club, they would roll up in 2 black Boeman SUV's.

It was December 22nd, 2002.The sun was shining but the air was bitter cold. The streets of Newark for the most part was quiet. All the dealers were huddled up in the hallways of apartments buildings throughout the city.

Driving around the city in a Boeman SUV were 2 members of the Triple H Crew, James, and Trev. Their job that day was to check up on the dealers in the city. "Where the fuck is everybody?" Trev asked as he made a right turn at the corner of Irvine Turner BLVD. and West Kinney Street. "Pull over!" James said. Trev pulled over, parking in front of a building. "Let's go!" James said to Trev. They both jump out of the vehicle dressed in black fatigues and black overcoats. James pushed in the heavy iron door and saw 4 dealers standing together in the hall shivering. "Why the fuck y'all ain't outside?" James shouted. "Man, it's fucking freezing!!" one dealer said. How the fuck y'all supposed to make a sale if the people don't see you?" James asked. "I hear what you saying, man! We can do about 5 minutes at a time! but that's it!" the dealer said. James didn't say a word. He just walked outside, with Trev following behind. He pulled out his cell phone. He took off his leather glove and pressed speed dial. "Who you calling?" Trev asked. James didn't answer him. "Yo, boss! Niggas complaining about the cold. They don't wanna stand outside." James said. *"Well, do something to make them wanna stand outside, then! Listen kid! I didn't bring you into my circle to have me solve every problem!"* hakim said before hanging up. "What we gonna do?" Trev asked. "We're gonna rent a truck, go to every hardware store around and buy up all the portable heaters." He said. By 10pm, there were over a hundred portable heaters passed throughout the apartment hallways in Newark. "Now we gotta do the Oranges and Irvington!" Trev said. "Bullshit! I'm taking my ass home! I gotta put the lights on the tree!" James said.

Back in Manhattan, Hakim was sitting at edge of his bed, wearing only boxer shorts. Lying next to him sound asleep was his new love interest.

The room was dead silent. The source of light in the bedroom came from a dozen candles. He made his way to the walk-in closet. He clicked on the light switch. In his closet, Hakim had 4 rows of clothing stretching back 6 feet from the wall. There were dozens of shoe boxes neatly stacked about 3 feet high. One row of clothing was nothing but tailor-made suits, while 2 hung rows were button up shirts, sweat suits jeans, overcoats leather blazers and sweaters. The row Hakim was drawn to was the row that had only one outfit hanging. It was his uniform. The uniform granted to him by Edward the 2nd. He plucked a piece of lint off the collar of the uniform. "Damn!" he said to himself. "What are you doing, boo?" the young lady asked as she yawned. "Nothing. Go back to sleep." He said. "That's a cute uniform! Were you in the military or something?" she said. "It's something." Hakim replied. Hakim clicked off the light in the closet. He ran over and jumped in the bed and started smothering the young lady with kisses. She responded with giggles.

— CHAPTER .39 THE GOLD ENVELOPE —

It was December 27th, 2002, when an elderly African American male in overalls was buffing the marble floors of the palace belonging to the National Agreement. The palace, hidden within the deep forests of Maine was a place where the National Agreement held their rituals for decades.

Outside the palace looked like a winter wonderland, but inside would soon be a place of dark, demented intentions. Only those who've received the golden envelope would bear witness or take part in what was about to happen.

Back at castle Lassenberry, Edward the 2nd was sitting at his desk skimming through the pages of the B.O.I. "Holy shit!" He said to himself. What he was reading pertained details of was took place at the last gathering.

As he was reading, there was a knock on the door. He quickly placed the B.O.I in the desk drawer. "Come in!" he shouted. "My lord. Mr. hart is here." the agent said. "Bring him in." Edward the 2nd said. "Yes, my lord." He said. Moments later Branson entered the office. "You wanted to see me?" Brandon asked. "Yeah. I need my uniform cleaned and pressed for this gathering bullshit I have to attend." He said. "Is that it?" Brandon asked. "So far! Just stay in the vicinity, just in case." He said. "Long live the house of Lassenberry. Long live the Edward the 2nd." Brandon said as he stood at attention. After Brandon left the office, Edward the 2nd took out the B.O.I and continued reading. "This is some sick shit!" he said to himself as he was reading.

It was around 1pm when a Boeman SUV pulled up in front of Park Oak Diner in Maplewood New Jersey. Alvin (Duck) Pennington, who was a member of the Triple H crew stepped out of the vehicle, dressed in his black military fatigues. He opened the rear door allowing his boss Hakim and his lady out. Another member, Trev stepped out of the front passenger side. "Yo Trev! Stay in the car." Hakim said as he cautiously looked around his surroundings. Trev nodded. "Is everything ok?" his lady friend asked. "Yeah. Let's go inside." Hakim said. Duck followed the couple inside the diner.

As they entered the diner, a well-groomed middle-aged black man approached them. "Mr. Bates! Good to see you!" he said. "What's up, Chauncey? How you been?" Hakim asked.

"Good sir! Follow me, please!" he said. Hakim's lady friend noticed that there were no other patrons in the diner. Chauncey lead everyone to a booth near the back of the diner. Duck sat 2 booths over. Chauncey placed a menu in front of the young lady. "Would you like your usual, sir?" he asked. "You know what? I'll take a menu this time." Hakim said. Chauncey handed Hakim a menu. "Can I get you 2 anything to drink?" Chauncey asked. "Water for me." The young lady said. "I'll take an orange juice." Hakim said. "Good! I'll be here when you're ready to order, sir." He said before walking away.

Hakim looked into the eyes of the beautiful young lady sitting across from him "Now, beautiful. Tell me your deepest darkest secrets." He said with a smile on his face.

Her name was Taisha Perez. She and Hakim met when she was applying for a bartending job at his night club. She was in her junior year at the most prestigious university in New Jersey. She was of Puerto Rican and African American descent. She was light skinned with thick curly hair. She stood about 5 feet; 5 inches tall with an hourglass figure. What really captured Hakim's heart about her was the color of her eyes, which were hazel.

"Before I tell you my darkest secrets, tell me why we're the only ones in here?" she asked. Hakim leaned back chuckling. "What's so funny?" Taisha asked. "Because it's the way I wanted it." He said. Chauncey returned with their drinks. "Thanks Chauncey. "Are you ready to order, sir?" Chauncey asked. Hakim pointed to Taisha. "I'll have a chef salad!" she said. "I'll have a tuna sub." Hakim said. "Ok. let me take your menus. And I'll be right back with your order." Chauncey said before leaving. Before Taisha could ask Hakim a question, Duck walked over behind the counter and fetched himself a drink from the soda fountain. "I'm charging you for that!" Hakim said jokingly. Duck just shrugged his shoulders. "You own this place?" Taisha asked. Hakim just smiled. "That's cool! What were you doing down at BIG SHOTS at closing hours that day I was applying for a job? You're gonna tell me you own that too?"" she asked. "Ah, yeah." He responded. Taisha almost choked on her water. "Yeah right!" She shouted. "It's true!" he chuckled. "From what I've heard, BIG SHOTS is the place to be on the weekends!" she said. "It ain't easy keeping that machine oiled." He sighed. "One more thing! What kind of Military uniform was that in your closet? I looked online, and I didn't see anything like that in this country!" Taisha said. "It's something that I can't speak on!" Hakim said as he gave her a serious look. "Ah! You don't trust me?" she asked. Hakim smiled as he looked out the window for a few seconds. "The other day when you were at my place, I put some weed, coke and pills on my coffee table. I know you noticed it. I noticed that you didn't question me or dabble in my product! So, to answer your question, yeah, I trust you." he said as he gently held her hands.

Later that evening Hakim and Taisha took a stroll through Weequahic Park. It was cold and windy, but Taisha didn't mind. She felt safe being in the arms of the man that captured her heart. The couple was followed closely by the Boeman SUV.

"Since we didn't get a chance to spend Christmas together, how about coming to my parent's house to bring in the new year?" she asked him. "Let me check my schedule." He said. Hakim looked at his watch. "I'm free!" he said. Taisha punched him in the arm. "You're silly!" she chuckled. "You still didn't tell me about the uniform!" she said. "Come on, girl! Don't worry about that! Focus on us!" he responded.

It was around 10am the following day. Edward the 2nd was sitting in his office reading the newspaper. There was a knock on the door. "Come in!" he shouted. "I already know what you're about say!" Brandon said as he entered the office. "What am I about to say?" Edward the 2nd said with the look of doubt. "You were about to ask me if I had everything prepared for the new year's party." Damn, you're good!" he said. Brandon smiled from the accolades until he noticed something other than the newspaper on the desk. "What's that?" he asked Edward the 2nd. "What? This?" he asked as he picked up a gold envelope. "Yeah, that?" Brandon asked. "Doug gave me this shit a while back! He told me to burn it after I open it! Sick mother fucker!" Edward the 2nd said. "Can I open it?" Brandon asked. "Knock yourself out!" Edward the 2nd said as he tossed the envelope to Brandon. Brandon ripped open the gold envelope. He read the card. "This is odd! This is really odd!" Brandon said. "What the fuck you mean odd?" Edward the 2nd asked. "Look!" Brandon said as he passed it to his boss.

On the card was a code written on it. It also says to dial it from a phone. "What the hell?" Edward the 2nd said. "What you want to do about it?" Brandon asked. "Go get number3 and bring his ass here!" he said. "I'm on it." Brandon said.

About a half hour later, Brandon retuned to the office, along with the old man known as number 3. "What is it? I was taking a nap!" number 3 said. "Take a look at this, old man!" Edward the 2nd said. As soon as number 3 looked at the card, his eyes bulged out as his he'd seen a ghost. He fell back, landing on the sofa. Brandon tried to catch him before his fall. "Yo, old man! You ok?" Edward the 2nd asked. "You were supposed to burn this! You were supposed to burn this!" number 3 whispered.

The sole purpose of giving a gold envelope to an individual was for the person to make the call and confirm the invite. The individual was to burn the envelope afterwards, so there was no trace of the location.

"You fool! Do you realize what you've done?" number 3 whispered. "Watch who you calling a fool, old man!" Edward the 2nd shouted. "What's going on?" Brandon asked. Number 3 rushed over and put his clammy hand over the mouth of Edward the 2nd. "Let's take this conversation outside, young man!" he whispered.

Moments later, Edward the 2nd, Number 3 and Brandon hopped into a golf cart and headed outside the castle walls. The NA agents that were standing guard outside heads turned towards the 3 men walking the courtyard. "Cover your mouths when you speak!" number 3 whispered. Edward the 2nd and Brandon followed number 3. "I have information that these people torture and murder innocent people!" Edward the 2nd whispered. "Where'd you get this information?" number 3 whispered. "That's my business! I just wanna know if it's true?" Edward the 2nd whispered. "Number 3 gave a nod. "What fucked me up the most was that my cousin samara was one of the victims! I can't go to that shit!" Edward the 2nd whispered. "You have to go, young man! These people don't take no for an answer!" number 3 whispered. Edward the 2nd thought for a moment. "What if I send someone in my place to represent me?" he whispered. "Why would you do that?" number 3 whispered. "Because I'm gonna kill every last one of those motherfuckers!" Edward the 2nd whispered. "That's insane! These aren't some thugs from the streets! They have their hands in everything!" number 3 whispered. "I know! I've done my homework, old man!" he whispered. "So how are you going to seek your revenge?" number 3 whispered. "Like I said, I'm gonna need a distraction to take my place and go to this so-called gathering! We're getting the fuck outta of here, and head to Lassenberia!" Edward the 2nd whispered. "What do you need me to do?" Brandon whispered. "You just stay close to me, and make sure this New Year's Eve party runs smoothly!" Edward the 2nd whispered. Number 3 smiled. "What you smiling about, old man?" Edward the 2nd whispered. "I have a plan that just might work!" he whispered.

It was December 29th when Hakim arrived at one of his safehouses in Cedar Grove, New Jersey. This safehouse was ran by an elderly white woman named Sophie Campbell. She had been working for the Lassenberry family for years selling opioids. To her customers she was known as the pain killer queen.

Hakim knocked on the door. He looked up at the surveillance camera above the door smiling. He heard the clicking of multiple locks being unlocked. Sophie opened the door. "Hi handsome!" she chuckled as she gave Hakim a hug. "Hey beautiful!" he said. "Come on in and keep an old lady company! Didn't expect you so soon!" she chuckled. "Yeah, well I thought I'd drive around checking up on everyone to see if business is running smooth." He said. Sophie lead him to the Kitchen. "Made a fresh pot of coffee." she said. "I'll pass." He said as he sat at the kitchen table. "I can't thank you enough for cutting out the middleman! Those jerks were draining my purse, I tell ya!" she chuckled. "That's what I wanna talk to you about." He said. Sophie was pouring herself a cup of coffee. she turned to face hakim. "About what?" she asked. "Your purse. It's not being drained anymore. It's overflowing from what I understand." he said. "What are you talking about?" she asked. "Crack. You're selling crack.'" He said in a calm voice. "You must be joking!" she said. "Everyone has a specific job. Your job is to sell pills. Not crack." He said. Sophie was speechless. Hakim walked over to Sophie. He took the coffee cup from her hand and placed it on the kitchen counter. He gently grabbed her hands. Sophie looked terrified. "Now sweetie. You've been in the game since I was a kid. You know better than anyone on how things run. I'm gonna let you keep the money you've made from selling rocks. But, if I find out you're selling anything other than pills from this day on, I'm gonna have a tough time figuring out how to dispose of your old ass. Understand?" he said. Sophie was shaking like a leaf. "I...I didn't mean any harm!" she stuttered. "Listen to me. If you sell anything other than pills, I'm gonna kill you." he said with a smile. "I'm so sorry, sweetie!" she said as she gasped for air. "Good! Now I'm gonna go and see who else is doing fucked up shit." He said. Hakim kissed the back of her hand before leaving.

Moments later, Hakim was sitting in the back of his SUV, being driven around by Trev until he felt his cell phone vibrate in his pants pocket. He pulled it out. "Yeah, what's up?" he said. *"Lodi. Be there within an hour."* The voice said. Hakim tossed his cell phone on the seat. "Let's stop to get something to eat, then head out to Lodi!" he said.

It was around 2pm when Hakim arrived at the Lodi facility. He pulled out his cell phone and made a call. "I'm here." He said. *"Come around back."* The voice said. "Stay here." He said to Trev. Hakim made his way down the alley. When he arrived in the back of the facility, he saw Edward the 2nd standing there, alone. "Why the fuck we're meeting outside? It's cold as fuck out here!" he said. "It's not safe to talk indoors. I think the place is bugged." Edward the 2nd said. "I thought you were above the law, man!" he said. "I'm above you, nigga!" Edward the 2nd boasted. "What you want?" he asked. Edward the 2nd reached inside his coat pocket.

Hakim jumped back. "Calm down, man!" he said. Edward the 2nd pulled out a sheet of paper. "Read this." He said while holding the paper. Hakim read the instructions on the sheet of paper. "You got it?" he asked hakim. "Yeah!" hakim said. "Well, memorize it! It's your next mission." Edward the 2nd said before setting the sheet of paper ablaze. "Why I gotta go to this place?" hakim asked. "I consider you my second in command." He said. "Oh? So, I'm above Butch?" hakim asked. "Butch is old! Besides, I heard you make a shit load of money, more than anybody. I heard you step on the product so much; your customers won't have a problem passing a piss test." Edward the 2nd said. "Oh, really?" hakim said. "Anyway. I need you to get familiar with the other big shots from around the country!" he said. "I had you all wrong, my nigga!" Hakim said. "Don't forget to wear your uniform. It's a formal thing." Edward the 2nd said before leaving to go back inside the facility.

Hakim had a smile from ear-to-ear while traveling back to Newark. Suddenly, his smile turned to a look of suspicion. He took out his cell phone. "Yo, Aaron! Gather the crew and meet me at the club!" he said.

Back at BIG SHOTS, hakim and his crew sit around the table in the back of the club. "After the new year, we're gonna take a trip out to Maine." He said. "Maine? What's up there?" Aaron asked. "From what I was told, we're gonna rub elbows with the other kingpins from around the country." Hakim said. "Cool!" Jimmy said. "It sounds more suspect than cool." Hakim said. "You think so?" Aaron asked. "I know so! That's why we're going strapped to the tee! I want you to recruit about 30 bodies, just in case!" he said to Aaron. "No problem." Aaron said. "This gathering is on the 4th. We'll leave right after the ball drops in Manhattan to scope out this place." Hakim said. Keith Cotton pulled out his gun and cocked it back. "Let do this!" he said. "Alright. Y'all get the fuck out and make your rounds." Hakim said. Aaron and the crew stood at attention. "Long live the streets of Essex county! Long live general Bates!" they all shouted before leaving. Hakim sat alone, looking worried. "I'll be ready for you motherfuckers!" he whispered to himself.

It was January 31st, 2002. A crowd had gathered at castle Lassenberry that evening to bring in the new year. The crowd consisted of friends and family of Viola Carr. Edward the 2nd made his way through the crowd wearing a silk pajamas and slippers, covered over by a silk bathrobe. He was prancing around to the beat of the music with a bottle of Champagne in his hand. There were those amongst the crowd who looked at Edward the 2nd in a strange way by the way he was carrying on. He was tapped on the shoulder by a tall black man, who happened to be viola's brother-in-law. "Hey, man! Where's Viola?" he asked. "Be cool! She'll be down in a minute! Eat, drink and be merry, nigga!" Edward the 2nd shouted with joy. One of the agents stood between the man and Edward the 2nd. "Please step back and enjoy the festivities, sir." The agent said to the man. "What you say to me?" the man said. "Hakeem grabbed him by the arm. "Come on, Uncle Ron! These guys are serious!" he said. Ron looked around the dance floor and noticed agents scattered about. Edward the 2nd became more belligerent as the night went on. He went over to the DJ booth and grabbed the microphone. "Is everybody feeling good tonight?" he shouted as he was spilling champagne. Only a handful of people raised their glasses. He accidently bumped into the DJ equipment causing the album to skip. "Whoops! My bad!" he chuckled.

There were 2 women standing off to the side. "Where did your sister meet this guy?" the lady asked. "She never told us!" the other lady said. "He's fucking weird!" the first lady said.

It was a half hour left to the new year. Edward the 2nd had already passed out. Viola had finally made her presence to the crowd. She looked glamorous because Edward the 2nd hired a team of stylists to do her hair, make-up and fit her with a dress and heels. She was also given something to sedate her. Her aunt and sister approached her with concern. "Hey baby! You ok?" her aunt asked. Viola was staring off into space for a second until her aunt grabbed her attention. "Yeah. I'm ok." she said in a monotone voice. "You want to leave?" her sister asked. "No! I'm fine!" Viola said. At this time her father came over to console her. "Sweetie! Are you ok?" he asked. "I think there's something wrong! I think they gave her something!" her sister said. "Hi daddy! Why didn't you tell me you suck dick?" Viola cried as she grabbed her father by the collar. She began crying like a baby. "Come on sweetie! let's get out of here!" her father said. Her father grabbed her by the hand, leading her to the exit. One of the agents caught wind of his actions. He went over to intervene. "Sir. Where are you taking Ms. Carr?" the agent asked. "Back off! I'm the secretary of Commerce!" her father said. By this time more agents come over to address the situation. 4 to 5 agents shield Viola and her family members from leaving. The DJ took notice and stopped the music. "Alright people! Take it easy! Let's bring in the new year right, ok?" He shouted the over microphone. Despite what the DJ said, the agents did not allow the family members to take Viola away. Viola's father stood toe-to-toe with the agent. His 2-man secret service detail came over, which led to more NA agents getting involved with the situation. One of the secret service agents pushed a NA Agent out of the way. This was when the NA agents went into defense mode. Guns were drawn on both sides. "Stand down!" one of the secret service agents shouted. "Engage!" one NA agent shouted as he pointed his gun at the head of the secret service agent. Multiple shots were fired, which led to the melee.

It was around 4am when Edward the 2nd woke up feeling groggy. He found himself in the corridor, sitting in a golf cart. Standing near him was a NA agent with blood on his face. "What happened? Where is everybody?" Edward the 2nd asked. "Come with me, my lord." The agent said. "Come where?" Edward the 2nd asked. "Back to the dance hall, my lord." He said. The agent helped his boss out of the golf cart. Edward the 2nd had to lean on the agent as he walked him back to where the party was. "Where the fuck is everybody?" he asked the agent. The agent didn't answer him. "I command you to tell me!" Edward the 2nd shouted. "We had to take you out of harm's way, my lord." The agent said. "Harm's way? What the fuck you mean, harm's way?" he asked the agent. Edward the 2nd's questions were being answered as he saw streaks of blood near the entrance of the dance hall.

Edward the 2nd collapsed in the doorway, bearing witness to the carnage in the dance hall. There were around 10 agents scattered, standing amongst the bodies. "Holy shit!!" he shouted. Edward the 2nd eyes teared up at the site of bodies laid out on the dance floor. "Your orders were to make sure Viola Carr didn't leave the castle grounds. Her family compromised that order. The others were collateral damage, my lord." The agent said. "Where is she? Where's Hakeem?" he asked the agent. "Ms. Carr is safe. She went into shock, so we had to put her under. Her son Hakeem are amongst the casualties, my lord." The agent explained.

Edward the 2nd was devastated. He fell the on his back, crying uncontrollably. "How shall we dispose of the bodies, my lord?" one agent asked.

It was 10 in the morning when Hakim and his crew were holding a meeting inside a rented car parked on Frelinghuysen avenue in Newark. The heat was blasting so that the guys had to take off their coats.

"Let's go over this shit one more time before we head up to Maine. There will be 2 groups. The first group will go with Aaron by plane, and the second group will go with me. You got the plane tickets, right?" Hakim asked Aaron. Aaron gave a nod. "Aaron's group will be on standby, while the rest of us do some surveillance. Did you put enough artillery in here in case we get backed into a corner?" he asked Keith Cotton. "We're straight, boss." He said. "Good!" Hakim said.

It was around 3pm when flight 128 was leaving Newark airport. Aaron purposely set up the seating arrangement so that he and his 30-man crew were spread out through the plane. Their destination was a few miles north of Moosehead Lake, Maine.

Aaron's crew lodged in groups of 5 in separate locations within a hundred-mile radius of their destination. 7 hours later, Hakim and his crew arrive at a cabin near Seboomook Lake. Jimmy paid the owner a substantial amount of cash for privacy. Hakim was in a separate room cleaning his uniform with a lint roller. Jimmy Broker, Trev, Duck and Keith Cotton were doing a final weapons check. They were equipped with AK-47 machine guns, Mack 10 machine guns with silencers, and semi-automatic pistols. "These white motherfuckers up here look crazy as hell!" Duck chuckled. "Yo! If you see a bunch of niggas coming out here in the middle of nowhere, you'll be looking crazy too!" Keith Cotton said. "Yo! This shit crazy! We about do some gangster shit up in this motherfucker!!" Trev shouted. "Calm down, nigga." Keith said. Hakim came out of his bedroom. "We move out in an hour." He said.

It was around 1am EST. Keith Cotton led a small recon team dressed in black through the woods of northern Maine. Given the directions by Hakim, Keith used a GPS device to make his way in the dark. Unbeknownst to Keith and his team, the forest between him and the NATIOINAL AGREEMENT'S palace was contrived with surveillance cameras.

By 3 in the morning, Keith and his team returned to their cabins. Hakim was sitting on the sofa watching TV. Keith walked in. "Yo! You should see that place, man! It's Huge!" he said. "Damn! I can't find anything good to watch!" Hakim said. "Yo, boss! You heard me?" Keith asked. Hakim looked up. "Oh, yeah! What you need to do now, is to tell Aaron What you saw so he can set vantage points if shit goes down. Yeah! Make sure all com links are working properly. I don't wanna lose contact when I'm on the inside." Hakim explained. "No Problem, boss. We about to go smoke some blunts. Call if you need me." Keith said. There was a scowl on Hakim's face. "Hold the fuck up!!" he shouted. "What's wrong?" Keith asked. "I don't want nobody getting high while we're up here! I want y'all to be on point! If I find out anybody smoking, they better not think about coming back to Jersey! Understand?" Hakim shouted. "Got it." Keith said. Keith was about to leave. "You forget something, man?" Hakim asked. Keith looked puzzled for a moment. "My bad, boss!" Keith said. He stood at attention. "Long live the county of Essex! Long live general Bates!" he shouted. "Now, get the fuck out." Hakim said.

It was the day before Hakim was to make his appearance before the NATIONAL AGREEMENT. To relax and take his mind off the event, Hakim decided to rent fishing gear, along with his 3-man crew and head out to Moosehead Lake.

It was a frigid but clear morning. Hakim and his crew were watching the sun come up over the horizon. Their fishing abilities we're quite up to par compared to the locals.

"Damn! This fishing thing is bullshit!" Duck complained. "My father used to take me fishing when I was little. He could catch a thousand trout in an hour! Damn, I miss him!"" Trev said. Hakim looked over at Trev, giving him a look of cynicism. "A thousand in an hour? Stop it!" he said. "I just wanna get the fuck from up here! Just looking at that place creep me the fuck out!" Jimmy said. "Stop sounding like a bitch, man! As soon as I go see what's going on at this palace, we can go home!" Hakim said.

"Hey boys! Are they biting?" shouted a strange voice from out of nowhere. Hakim and the crew were startled. They quickly turned around and saw a police officer standing on the jetty. Hakim laid his pole down. He stood to his feet. "Can we help you officer?" he asked. "From the look of your fishing rods, you look like the one needing help!" the officer chuckled. Hakim starred laughing as well.

The officer looked like he should've retired years ago. He gave off a relaxed demeanor. He had a tough time keeping his pants up over his beer belly. "I'm sheriff Angus!" he said. "Anus!" Trev whispered to Duck. They both began laughing. "What's that you say, son?" sheriff Angus asked. "Don't pay him any mind Sheriff! He's kind of slow!" Hakim said. "Is that so?" the sheriff said. "If you're off duty, would come join us? Maybe you can us something." Hakim said. There was a moment of silence. "You fellas coming from Bath?" the sheriff asked. "From where?" Hakim asked. "I guess not." He said. "What's Bath?' Jimmy asked. "It's a shipyard, about a few hours from here. I'm going be honest with you fellas. The locals out here are sort of nervous about your presence." the sheriff said. "Well, we can't help how others feel, sheriff." Hakim said. "Well, you have a point there!" the sheriff chuckled. "All we wanna do is check out this party going on at the palace, and we're outta here!" Jimmy said. "Zachmont Palace?" the sheriff asked. Hakim turned to Jimmy, giving him the look that he'd screwed up. Jimmy put his head down in shame. "You fellas must be celebrities. That place been creeping me out since I was a rookie." The sheriff said. "See, I told you!" Jimmy shouted. "Shut up!" Hakim said. "Anyway! You boys just make sure you leave the same way to came. Peacefully." The sheriff said. "Will do!" Hakim said. Sheriff Angus turned and walked away towards his squad car. Hakim turned to Jimmy. "Do me a favor for the rest of our time here and shut the fuck!" he shouted.

Back at the Grenville police department, Sheriff Angus gathered his officers together for a meeting. "I paid a visit to our African American guests out in Moosehead." Angus said. "You want us to go over there and bring them up on some kind of charge?" the deputy asked. "Hold on! Take it easy! From what they tell me, they're guests at the Zachmont palace." Angus said. The deputy and 4 other officers looked shocked. "They must be celebrities of some sort." The deputy said. "They didn't say, but I would imagine." Angus said. "You want us to keep an eye on them at least?" one officer said. "Noooo! They look harmless. When their little get together ends, one of you can escort them pass county lines. We don't need the press crawling up our asses!" Angus said.

It was January 4th, 2003, around 9am when Hakim rendezvoused with Aaron by the edge of the lake. Hakim was skipping rocks in the lake as he told Aaron to repeat his part in what was about to take to place that evening.

"I'm glad you know what you gotta do, but there's a slight change of plans." Hakim said. "What's up, boss?" Aaron asked. "I don't trust that Sheriff Angus. I want you to split our little army into 2 groups. I want a 15-man team at the ready, near the palace and the other 15 spread out off the main road. In case the cops come, we can warn the main team at the palace. So, either way, our asses are covered." He explained.

It was around 9pm. Hakim was in his room standing in front of the mirror, fully dressed in his uniform. There was a knock on the door. "Come in!" he shouted. Keith Cotton entered the room. "The car is gassed up." He said. "Cool. Where's that fucking note?" hakim said. "I don't know what you're talking about!" Keith said. "Never mind! I found it." he said. Hakim clipped his com link inside the cuff of his uniform. "You got your earpiece in?" he asked Keith. "Yeah, its in." he said. Hakim walked over to the other end of the room. He held the cuff of his uniform shirt up to his lips. "Testing. Testing. 1,2,3 testing." He whispered. Keith nodded his head to confirm hearing his voice. "Let's go!" Hakim said.

The road leading to the Zachmont palace looked gloomy. Hakim glanced at both sides of the road noticing how high the snow was. The Eastern White Pine trees blocked hakim's view of the night sky. About an hour later Hakim could see the palace off in the distance. Before he could park his car on the palace grounds, he was stopped at a check point. An NA agent approached his vehicle. "Can I help you, sir?" the agent asked. Hakim didn't say a word. He pulled out a note the was signed by Edward the 2nd. The NA agent gave the other agent in the booth the signal to open the electronic gate. "Enjoy your evening, general Bates." The agent said.

Hakim was in awe of the giant fountain as he pulled up to the parking area of the palace. Another agent directed him to pull up to a parking spot. Hakim noticed the fleet of limos and other luxury car parked nearby. He also noticed a couple helicopters off in the distance. As soon as he stepped out of his vehicle, the agent approached him. "Follow me, sir." The agent said. Hakim followed the agent to the main entrance. He looked over his shoulder and noticed another agent guiding a group of men in tuxedos. He recognized one of the men as Frank Twain, the big shot at Wormhole Music Group. He walked away from his guide and approached Frank. "Hey Frank! What's happening, man?" he shouted. "Mr. Bates. Didn't realize you were part of the brotherhood." Frank said as the other men kept walking. "Brother hood? I guess!" Hakim responded. "This place is something, huh? Just wait until we get inside! It will blow your socks off, amongst other things!" he chuckled as he massaged his private parts. Hakim looked puzzled from his comment and where he put his hand. "Let's go inside! It's cold as shit out here! By-the-way, nice uniform!" Frank said as they walked towards the entrance.

Inside the palace Hakim and Frank were stopped at the doorway to be announced. There was a gentleman standing at a podium dressed in a tuxedo. "I present to you Frank Twain of wormhole Music Group!!" the man said over the microphone. Hakim turned over the note to the gentleman given to him by Edward the 2ⁿᵈ. "I present to you general Bates of the House of Lassenberry!!" he shouted. "Come on, Bates! Let's grab ourselves a drink!" Frank said. Hakim noticed hundreds of men from different ethnicities in tuxedos huddled in separate groups mingling.

The music, which was contemporary jazz, was blasting throughout the hall. The servants walked around the crowd passing out drinks and hors d'oeuvres. "Since this is your first time here, I'd advise you not to eat!" Frank chuckled. Hakim with a terrified look on his face, placed the cracker with caviar on it back on the silver platter when a servant walked by. Hakim put his hand up to his face, covering his mouth. "So far, so good." He whispered into the com link. "Come on! Let me introduce you to some of the guys!" Frank said. Hakim followed Frank to a group of guys who were laughing aloud at a joke that was told.

Hakim shook hands with every man in the group. One of the men was Charles Scott, CEO of New World Construction. "Please to meet you, young man!" Scott said. "Same here!" Hakim said. "How's the castle holding up?" Scott asked. "The castle? Oh, yeah! The castle! I don't stay there!" hakim said. Why not? It's a work of art!" Scott said. "My boss lives there! I'm just the number 2 guy!" Hakim chuckled." When I told Eddie Lassenberry, I would build it for him, he was as giddy as a child!" Scott chuckled. "So, that was all your doing, huh?" hakim said with a smirk on his face. "He was a real character! A real man!" Scott said. Hakim had a look of disgust. Moments later, hakim received a tap on the shoulder. He quickly turned around, almost spilling his drink to see a chubby Hispanic man standing there. "What's up, New Jersey?" the man said. "New jersey?" hakim asked. "Yeah! I'm Southern California!" the man said. "Yo, man! I'm from Jersey, but my name is Hakim!" he responded. "I'm Chi-Chi! Man, I'm just going by what the guy before you said! He started the whole coded shit between us!" chi-C hi said. "My bad, man! I just ain't get the memo!" Hakim chuckled as he shook Chi-Chi's hand. "Hey Frank! I'm gonna steal Hakim for a minute and introduce him to the other kingpins!" Chi-Chi said. "Make sure you bring him back before mid-night!" Frank jokingly said as he winked at hakim.

Hakim followed Chi-Chi. He noticed about a few dozen NA agents scattered about, especially at the exits. He looked up at the top of the spiral staircase and noticed a strange looking character wearing a black cloak looking down at everyone. Hakim frowned as he gazed upon his unusually long fingernails.

About a mile away, roaming the through the dense forest were the 15-man strike team lead by Keith Cotton. All were dressed in black, wielding weapons with silencers. They were spread out within yards of each other, slowly trekking their way towards the palace.

2 of the members on the team were just teenagers named Tariq and Alvin. They didn't stick to the plan by keeping a distance of a few yards apart. They were shoulder-to-shoulder, running off at the mouth. "Man, I don't wanna be out this motherfucker!" Alvin said. "Yo, nigga! I'm just waiting to get the word and start blasting somebody, for real!" Tariq said. "You got that blunt on you, man? I need something to calm my nerves!" Alvin said. Tariq pulled out 2 blunts from his pockets, along with a lighter. Alvin took his machine gun under his arm pit and lit up his blunt. "This what I'm talking about, nigga." Alvin said. After a few pulls off

them blunts, Alvin and Tariq leaned their weapons against a tree. "Feel like we're in a fucking horror movie out this motherfucker!" Alvin snickered.

After a while, Tariq and Alvin were far being the rest of the strike team. Alvin was feeling so euphoric from the blunt, he sat down against the tree. "I can't see how you can sit on that cold ass ground, nigga!" Tariq said. "Man, I don't feel shit right about now!" he snickered. Tariq started pacing back-n-forth to keep warm. "You know that bitch Amanda I was fucking with? Man, I found out she had an ass implant!" Alvin said. "Ass implant?" Tariq said. "Yeah, man!" Alvin said. "Why would a black chick want a fake ass?" Tariq asked. "I ain't saying I can predict the future, but I think that shit gonna be normal in the future!" Alvin said. "You saying we're gonna be fucking blow up dolls?" Tariq chuckled. "fake asses, fake titties, weave, all that shit, my nigga!" Alvin said. "Man, I gotta piss!" Tariq said. Don't do that shit next to me! Go over there, nigga!? Alvin said. "Man, I should piss on you!" Tariq jokingly said. "Yeah, and I'll empty this a clip in your ass!" Alvin said. Tariq walked away laughing. Tariq walked about 5 yards away, leaving his weapon behind. After he zipped up his pants, he walked back to where Alvin was. "Yo, man! I think we should catch up with others!" Tariq said. He was startled to see Alvin leaning up against the tree with his eyes wide open and a gunshot wound to the head. "Oh shit! Oh shit!" he shouted as he stepped back. Tariq forgot about picking up his weapon and ran as fast as he could. He made it about 20 yards before being caught by a bullet from behind. His body fell like a log.

Meanwhile, Keith and the rest of the strike team stood fast at the edge of the forest with their eyes on the palace. Many of them were shivering from the cold. One guy from the team came within inches of being caught by a couple of agents passing by. His anxiety from near capture caused his dinner to come out from both ends.

Miles away the lookout team led by Aaron were keeping watch roadside. "Team 2! Check in!" he said over the com link. "Grady, checking in." he said. "Duggie, checking in." "Toby J., checking in." Rasheed here." "Mitch, checking in." "Rich, checking in" "Tahj, checking in." "Nathan, checking in" "black Sean, here freezing my ass off!" "Quill, here!" "Will, checking in." "Big T., checking in." "Junior, here." "Markie, checking in." His was the last voice Aaron heard over the com link. "Yo Biggs! Check in! Biggs?' Aaron shouted. "I'll go find him!" Rich said. Rich left his post to find his cousin.

Rich treaded carefully through the 3 feet of snow crying out for his cousin Biggs. Rich had a bad habit of chain smoking, which caused him to get winded in the extreme cold. He finally gave up, leaning up against a tree to catch his breath. He pulled out a cigarette. After 3 pulls from his menthol cancer stick, rich started wheezing. He bent over and noticed droplets of blood staining the snow. "Shit!" he said before wiping his mouth. As soon as he stood straight, he came face-to-face with a NA agent pointing a suppressed pistol at him. "Those things will kill you." the agent said in a calm voice before squeezing the trigger.

Back at the palace, Hakim was standing next to Frank while bopping his head to the music. He was on his third drink when another member of the brotherhood approached, he and Frank. Hakim was shocked to see this individual, who was a familiar face. "Mr. Bates! Or should I say, general Bates." The old man said. "Sheriff Angus?" hakim said as he was choking on his glass of scotch. "Easy, son!" Angus chuckled.

Sheriff Angus was wearing a black-n-white checkered 3-piece suit, with a matching fedora. Hakim couldn't help noticing the sheriff wearing bright red lip stick and eyeliner. "Yo sheriff! What's with the make-up?" hakim asked. "Son! Before the night is over, my face will be the last thing you'll remember!" Angus chuckled. Frank chuckled along with the sheriff. Hakim looked at both men as if they were insane. "I gotta use the bathroom!" hakim said. "Bathroom? Son! Just go over in the corner and piss or whatever! Somebody will clean up after you! I promise!" angus said. "What?!" hakim responded. Frank slapped Hakim on the back. "Just go over there and do your business!" he said. "Y'all motherfuckers crazy!" hakim said as he went off to take a leak. Hakim walked over to the corner and unzipped his pants. He began relieving himself. No one gave him a second thought as they passed by. Before he finished doing his business, he covered his mouth with the cuff of his uniform. "Standby. I gotta strange feeling about this place." He said on his com link. As hakim was pissing, an elderly white man came over to him. He stood with his back against the wall. The man dropped his trousers to squat. Hakim turned his head in disgust as the man did a number 2 on the floor. Hakim glanced over at the man. "Yo! Didn't I see you on TV?" he asked. "The names' Gates! Carter Gates!" he said. "Now, I remember! I watched you give a speech at the White House!" hakim said. "Defense secretary Gates, son! Welcome to the brotherhood!" he said as he strained to relieve himself. "Oh shit!" hakim shouted. Gates reached out to shake Hakim's hand. "And you are?" he asked. "Get the fuck outta here!" hakim said before walking away. After Hakim walked away, a servant approached Gates with a roll of toilet paper. After Gates wiped his ass, he had no problem flinging his mess on the floor.

It was close to mid-night when guests of the Zachmont Palace were still lingering around with their consumption of alcohol, food, and other things. Suddenly, the music stopped. Most of the crowd looked revved up, expecting what was about to happen next. Coming down the spiral staircase with a microphone in his hand was a slim tall, pasty looking Caucasian man wearing nothing but sandals and a loin cloth. The music was switched from jazz to classical piano. The man came prancing down the stairs to the music. Most of the crowd was howling and whistling at him as if he were a stripper. Hakim cringed at the sight of this guy. He was bewildered that everyone around him was so excited. "Why the fuck everybody going crazy over this weirdo?" he asked Frank. Frank grabbed Hakim buy the shoulders. "It's not about him, kid! Your world is about to change tonight, motherfucker!!!" he shouted in Hakim's ear. "What the fuck you talking about, man?" hakim shouted as frank ditched him to move to the front of the crowd. "Frank! Frank!" he shouted. "Igor! Igor!" Most of the guys were chanting as he reached the bottom of the stairs. "вы готовы к вечеринке?!" he shouted. "What the fuck he said?" Hakim asked. The man they called Igor heard him. "I said, are you ready to party?!!" he shouted. "Damn right!!" one of the drug kingpins shouted. "Before we start the festivities, let's give a round of applause to the man himself, Dr. Zachmont!!!" Igor shouted in a thick Russian accent. Dr. Zachmont came through the crowd escorted by 10 NA agents. The crowd was cheering him on as he grabbed the microphone from Igor. "My people! I would like to say I love seeing all your faces, new and old! The master is pleased with the energy you bring! Now, on with the fun!!!" Zachmont shouted at the top of his lungs. He hands the microphone back to Igor. "Now gentleman! Let's bring out some of the sexiest creatures from all over these great United States!" Igor shouted as he gave one of the agents the signal to open the door to a room of to the side.

One by one about 30 beautiful women in bikinis of diverse ethnicities came out of the room, dancing to the dance hall music that was playing. Everyone was like wolves groping the women. Hakim had a smirk on his face. His smirk was then wiped away when he saw coming out of the room were about 30 physically fit guys in G-strings. "I can't fuck with this shit!" he said to himself. The men in G-strings were being groped and slapped around by those who were into that lifestyle. Hakim noticed the eroticism going to the extreme. Frank came over to Hakim dragging a beautiful blonde woman by the hair. "Come on Hakim! Let's fuck the shit out of this bitch!" he shouted. Hakim saw that the young lady wasn't pleased having her head yanked around, but at the same time she didn't resist. "Nah, man! I'm about to get me another drink!" he said. "You fucking pussy!" Frank chuckled. "Whatever, man!" Hakim said before walking away. As Hakim was making his way through the crowd, he noticed the Defense Secretary fucking one of the men in a G-string in the ass as the man was on his knees eating the pile of shit the Secretary had made.

Hakim was standing off by himself by the buffet table. With his drink in hand, he saw every despicable sex act that a person could imagine. He was sipping on his drink when 3 servants came out carrying platters with ancient daggers on them. Guests in the crowd helped themselves to a dagger. This is when Hakim saw things get brutal. He dropped his drink when a young lady had a dagger pierced through her eye as 3 guests were gangbanging her. He also noticed agents putting chains on the doors. "Engage! Shit is crazy! Engage!" he whispered into his com link. This was the signal for Keith and his strike team to run in guns blazing.

5 minutes had passed as the carnage continued. There was no sign of Keith and his strike team crashing the gathering. "Strike team! Bring y'all ass in here, now!" he shouted into his com link. He kept repeating his cry at least3 more times until he gave up. Hakim noticed Dr. Zachmont and 6 NA agents coming towards him. "Fuck!" he whispered to himself. "General Bates! Don't just stand there like a bump on a log! Come join the festivities!" Zachmont said. "This scene is just too fucking weird for me, man! I'll pass!" hakim said. "Awe come on, General! I insist! Besides, most of your people outside are dead!" Zachmont explained. Hakim's jaw dropped. "Yes, General! We know everything!" Zachmont said. Hakim bent over touching his knees. He began heaving, spitting out the alcohol in his system. Zachmont signaled one of the agents to drag one of the young men in a G-string over. The agent forced the young man to his knees. "Hand over your firearm!" Zachmont said to the agent. The agent handed his pistol to Zachmont. "Now, General Bates! I want you to take this gun and put a bullet into this pathetic soul's head." He said. "Fuck you, man! That man ain't do shit to me!" hakim shouted. "You sure?" Zachmont asked. "Like I said! Fuck you!" Hakim said as he wiped his mouth. Zachmont gave the agent a nod. The agent put his pistol to the man's head and squeezed the trigger. "That's fucked up!" hakim said as the man's body fell to the floor. "Bring them in!" Zachmont said to a couple of agents. About a minute had passed when the agents brought in 3 of Hakim's soldiers. Hakim had the look of disappointment. His soldiers, Aaron, Markie, and Nathan were bound and gagged, bruised, and battered. Hakim was apprehended by 2 agents for Zachmont's safety. "Here's the deal, young man! You're not

leaving here alive unless you finish off your friends!" he said to hakim. "Let them go, man! Put it all on me!" Hakim pleaded. Zachmont signaled over a servant holding a platter with one dagger placed on it. Zachmont took the dagger and handed it over to Hakim. "I want you to plunge that dagger into each of their hearts!" he said. Hakim saw his soldier Markie desperately shaking his head not to be killed. "You have more balls than your boss! Once the night is over, you can go back home and move up in the world and marry that girl you're head over heels for!" Zachmont said with a smirk on his face. Hakim looked at Zachmont. "Yes! I know all things!" Zachmont said. Sweat was trickling down Hakim's face. He slowly walked over towards his soldiers. He looked Markie in the eye. "Sorry, man!" he said before stabbing him in the chest. Hakim stood in front of Nathan. Nathan was struggling to be released. "Just close your eyes, young blood!" Hakim said. Snot and tears were running down Nathan's face on to the duct tape covering his mouth. He did what Hakim told him to do. He shut his eyes tight. Hakim plunged the dagger into him with rapid speed. "Go to sleep! Go to sleep!" Hakim said as tears ran down his cheek. Hakim stood before Aaron. He slowly peeled the duct tape from Aaron's mouth. Aaron began to cry. "My mother told me to stay my ass in school!" Aaron chuckled as he looked towards the ceiling. His chuckling morphed back to sobbing. "See you on the other side!" Hakim said softly as he shoved the dagger into him. Hakim had to turn away as all 3 soldiers twitched on the floor until there was no life left in them. "Can I go now?" Hakim asked. "Oh no, young man! You have to stay for the grand finally!" Zachmont said.

The grand finally of the night is what Eddie Lassenberry and Sir Marcus had to see. It was time for the children to come out and meet their fate.

— CHAPTER .40 PRINCESS TERESA —

It was January 7th, 2003, when Marcus, king of Lassenberia was in his office being interviewed by an Iranian journalist. He was dressed casually in slacks, a button up shirt with the sleeves rolled up. The journalist was a young attractive woman dressed in a blue business suit with a matching Khimar.

"So, your majesty. How does it feel to have half the world at your beckon call?" she said jokingly. Marcus chuckled. "I wouldn't say that! I would say this…Lassenberia in a whole, is at the beckon call of those world leaders who want to give their people a fulfilling fresh start on life!" he said. "What is your relationship the western world, specifically with the United States?" She asked. "At this time…there is no relationship with the United States. There will be no relationship with the United States until it's government stop flooding it's streets with these horrible drugs, whether legal or illegal!" he said passionately. "Legally, you say. I thought America had the best healthcare system in the civilized world!" She responded. "How can one have the best healthcare if you overcharge the people with, excuse my expression, bullshit!" he said. "Can you elaborate, your majesty?" she asked. "For instance. My grandmother suffered from cancer. She was provided with the best care money could buy. Chemotherapy. Prescription drugs. Anything she needed to recover! She was home for a while, then she finally lost her battle!" he said. "I'm so sorry!" the journalist said. Marcus sat up straight, clearing his throat. "The good news is that we, the people don't have to have that fear anymore! What we supply will make chemotherapy and prescription drugs outdated!" he said. "That's wonderful, but do you believe this will create enemies within the pharmaceutical industry?" she asked. Marcus began to chuckle. "We don't worry about that! We have God and the good people of the world on our side!" he said. "Interesting!" she said. Before the journalist could ask another question, there was a knock on the door. "Enter!" Marcus shouted. Ali entered the room with a worried look on his face. "Excuse me, your majesty! There is an urgent situation you must attend to!" he said. "Go see my Queen or Kent! After all, he is my new Prime minister!" Marcus said. "As you wish, your majesty!" Ali said before leaving. "Continue, please!" Marcus said. "Very well! So, is it true you're going on some sort of world tour?" she asked. "Yes, indeed! Not only are we going to tour, we're going to engage in diverse cultures, without being bias!" Marcus said. "May I tag-a-long with my camera man? It sounds like it will be fun!" she said. "I was taking my brother-in-law, but I don't see why you can't tag-a-long!" Marcus said. Marcus's statement put a big smile on her face. "Now, that we've taken a tour of the south side of Lassenberia, how would you like to meet the Baroness of Braxton on the northern side?" he asked. "Of course!" she said.

Marcus and company were heading down the corridor of Castle Lassenberia. Coming towards them was the queen of Lassenberia and 2 armed guards who were Ali's Nephews. Her blouse was stained with a brownish substance. "Excuse me!" Marcus said to the journalist as he ran towards his wife. "What happened, my love?" he asked. "Where were you? I sent Ali for you!" Kimberly shouted. "I was being interviewed! You knew that!" Marcus said defensively. Kimberly looked over her husband's shoulder staring down the young journalist. Her stare was not friendly. The young journalist felt intimidated by quickly looking away. "What's that on your shirt?" Marcus asked. "It's vomit! Your sister tried to commit suicide!" Kimberly said. Marcus looked terrified. He bent over grabbing his knees. "This is no time to fall apart, my love! Your sister needs you!" Kimberly said. "How is she?" he asked. "She tried to poison herself. We gave her a shot of GLC just in time." Kimberly said. "Where is she?" he asked. "She's at the Maggie house. She needs you now." Kimberly said. "Give me a moment, my love!" Marcus said.

The Maggie house was one of the 6 Mansions near castle Lassenberia. They were named after Marcus's father, his aunts, and uncles in their honor. His uncle Eddie was the only one that didn't receive that honor because of his treacherous deeds.

Marcus ran towards the journalist. "I'm sorry Ms. Aziz, but I'll have to cancel that rendezvous with the baroness!" He said. "That's quite alright, your majesty!" she said. "Can we reschedule for another time?" he asked. "Yes! Certainly!" she said. "I'll Have my guards escort you and you're your crew back to the airport." He said.

Even though 90 percent of construction was done, small charter planes were able come and go into Lassenberia Airport under certain circumstances. There was a separate airport fully functional on the other end of the island for official military business, which was called Benjamin Airforce base.

Moments later Marcus and Kimberly arrive at Maggie house. Standing outside were more guards from Ali's clan. Marcus hopped out of the vehicle and made a dash into the mansion. Inside the mansion were more guards from the Pale Horseman division. "Where is she?!!" Marcus asked. "She's upstairs in the bedroom to the left, your majesty." The head of the division said. "Everyone, outside! I want privacy!" Marcus said. Yes, your majesty!" the guard said. Marcus ran up the stairs. He went inside the room and found the head physician of Lassenberia by his sister's bedside. Terry was unconscious. "How is she, Doctor Magumbwe?" Marcus asked. "I gave her a sedative! But I'm afraid she needs a psychiatrist, your majesty!" he said. Marcus stood over his little sister in silence. "No!" Marcus said. "Your majesty?" the doctor responded. "No! she's not getting a psychiatrist!" he said. "Your majesty! Her trauma may run deeper than the loss of her family!" the doctor said. "She needs something to take her mind off her trauma! She needs some sort of responsibility! Trust me doc, I know!" Marcus said.

Later that evening, the royal couple were in bed discussing how to deal with Terry's mental state. Kimberly rested her head on her husband's bare chest. "Do you think we should send her to Madagascar for therapy? I looked online and found information on this therapist that's really popular there." She said as she played with his chest hairs. "No. it's too dangerous. If Terrance finds out there's a Lassenberry still breathing, I just don't want to think about it!" Marcus said. "There's a million things I don't want to think about anymore." Kimberly said before shutting her eyes.

It was March 28th, 2003 when Hakim arrived at the gates of castle Lassenberry, exhausted and dehydrated. He fell to his knees sobbing like a baby. A few yards behind him was a black van. When Hakim fell to his knees, the van took off in the opposite direction. The agents at the gate stood there waiting for Hakim to say something. "I…need…to…see…Lord Lassenberry!!" Hakim panted. "We know, General Bates." One agent said. 2 agents came from outside the gate and picked Hakim off the ground, dragging him inside. As they were dragging him towards the entrance of the castle, Hakim passed out.

Hakim had arrived with his jack boots missing, his uniform soiled and tattered. The feet were blistered and covered in dry blood.

Later, that day around 1pm, Hakim had awakened on the sofa in office of Edward the 2nd. Still groggy, he noticed he was hooked up to an intravenous line and his feet were covered with warm wet towels. He looked over towards the desk a saw Edward the 2nd sitting there reading a magazine. "How was the party?" he asked. "You…motherfucker!" Hakim said. Edward the 2nd left his chair and went over to sit on the sofa by his side. He leaned in close to Hakim's ear. "Listen, man. From what I read about that so called gathering, I didn't think I'd have the stomach for it. You on the other hand, done been through it all." He whispered. With all his remaining strength, Hakim grabbed him by the collar. "They …. made…me…walk…back!!" he said. "I know. But the good thing is, you survived. Don't worry. I had Mookie pick up your product and put it out on the streets for you. I agreed to let him take 20 percent. You lost out on 2 million dollars, but like I said, you survived." Edward the 2nd said. Hakim released his collar and closed his eyes.

As punishment, Dr. Zachmont made Hakim walk from the palace in Maine back to New jersey. To the average person making this trek it would take around a hundred days with rest in between. In Hakim's case, he was followed by 3 agents in a van, not allowed time to stop and rest as he walked interstate 95 south. State troopers from each state pulled over and questioned Hakim's reason for walking the road early in the morning and in the dark of night. Hakim just pointed towards the van behind him. The officer or officers would approach the van, and within a few moments the officer or officers would approach Hakim again and tell him to have a good day before getting back into their squad cars. It was at I 95 running through Massachusetts when Hakim broke down and cried on the side of the road. The agents didn't care for his pain. They were ordered to push him at any cost. He was kicked and shoved until he couldn't bear any more pain. The agents would jump back into the van and continue to follow him.

It was April 1st, 2003 when the royal couple of Lassenberia spent a quiet evening celebrating their third wedding anniversary on a yacht circling the island at 10 knots. They sat at the stern of the ship with a bottle of wine and snacks, both wearing matching white linen pajamas.

They gazed at the clear night sky as they fed each other cheese and crackers. The night was perfect until Kimberly continued to rub her belly. "You ok, my love?" Marcus asked. "I feel nauseous!" she said. "Maybe it's the cheese and crackers. You want me to get someone to bring you a seltzer?" he asked. "I appreciate it, my love!" she said. A few yards away stood a guard from the Pale Horseman Battalion with a machine gun strapped to his shoulder. Marcus signaled the guard to come over. "The queen needs something to settle her stomach! Ask the captain can he provide seltzer water or something!" Marcus ordered. "Yes, your majesty!" the guard said before leaving. At that moment, Kimberly ran towards the handrail to vomit over the side of the ship. Marcus went over to rub her back. "That's it, my love. Let it out. I guess Lighvan cheese is an acquired taste!" he chuckled. Kimberly wiped her mouth with a napkin. "It's not the cheese! I'm pregnant!" she said. There was a big smile on Marcus's face. He turned Kimberly towards him and gave her a hug. She quickly pushed him away to bend over the railing again.

The next day, on the other side of the world in Cherryhill New Jersey, the lord of castle Lassenberry was sitting in the main dining hall along with his aid called number 3. The dish prepared for them was Zillion Dollar Lobster Frittata with edible gold leaf. "Why are we here eating alone? Where's Brandon and Viola?" Number 3 asked. Edward the 2nd pulled out a piece of paper from his pants pocket. He passed it across the table to number 3. Number 3 unfolded and read the note. He didn't respond with words. He just nodded his head. Number 3 passed the note back across the table. The agents standing guard near the dining hall exit didn't react to their secretive on goings. Edward the 2nd quickly balled up the note and shoved it in his mouth. He had gathered up enough saliva to swallow the note. "What is this?" number 3 asked as he looked down at his plate. "Something I saw in a magazine. I ordered the chef to make it. I wanted to challenge my taste buds!" Edward the 2nd said with a smile.

On the opposite side of the castle in the north wing, Hakim was lying in bed still recovering from the long near-death trek from Maine. He was given a pair of crutches to move about the room. His feet were wrapped in a thick layer of bandages. He wasn't allowed to leave the castle until he fully recovered. There were 2 agents posted outside his room to make sure he stayed put. His only knowledge of the outside world was a giant flat screen TV mounted on the wall. He grabbed the remote on the end table and began channel surfing. He stopped clicking the remote when something on the news grabbed his attention.

"Reports from Homeland Security say that the island nation of Lassenberia will be conducting nuclear tests off the coast of east Africa. This is causing great concern with our allies in Europe and North Africa. Tensions between President Lyon and the royal family of Lassenberia have flared since it's king refused an invitation from the president to have a meeting at the Whitehouse. A mystery surrounds the island nation of its day-to-day activities due to its ban on all outside media. So far officials say there is no immediate threat from Lassenberia, just concern. Now, back to jay Thomas with the weather." The reporter said before Hakim turned off the TV.

"What the fuck, man? Shit is about to go down!" Hakim said to himself. Hakim struggled out of bed to grab his crutches. He made his way to the door. When he opened the door, there stood the 2 agents standing at parade rest. One was of African American descent, the other Caucasian. "Can we assist you, General Bates?" one of the agents asked. "Yeah! Get me the fuck outta here!" he shouted. "Our orders are to guarded you until your injuries have healed, sir." The agent said. "Mother fuckers!!" Hakim shouted before slamming the bedroom door.

A couple of days later at the Whitehouse, President Lyon was pacing the oval office, surrounded by a few members of his staff. Moments later the Secretary of Homeland Security entered the room. "Anything, Tom?" the President asked. "Nothing, sir! King Marcus still refuses to hold a meeting with us!" Tom said. "Damnit!! I thought the nuclear testing accusations would scare him into submission!" the president said. "Mr. president. If we don't resolve the situation soon, I'm afraid we might lose the election. The pharmaceutical companies will surly pull campaign funding if rumors of this miracle drug surface to the mainstream media." Tom said. One man stood out from the group. It was Secretary of Defense, Carter Gates. "Mr. president. Would a more tangible scare tactic suffice?" Gates asked. "What kind of scare tactic?" the president asked. "I suggest we move a carrier group off the southern shore of Mozambique, sir." Gates said. President Lyon walked towards the window to think for a moment. He turned towards the men in the room. "We have to do this delicately! I don't want the world to see the United States as bullies! We're still dealing with the alternative media running off at the mouth about 911 being an inside job! We have to keep the perception of the good guy!" the president shouted. "We do have an ace-in-the-hole, sir." Gates said. "What would that be, Mr. secretary?" the president asked. "Members of my staff have information on a Krayton Lassenberry residing in Cherryhill, New jersey, sir." Gates said. "Who?" the president asked. "Krayton Lassenberry, sir. Allegedly, he's one of the most, if not the most powerful drug lord in New jersey, sir." Gates said. "What the hell does some thug in New Jersey have to do with having a meeting with the king of Lassenberia?" the president shouted. Gates cleared his throat. "They happen to be cousins, sir." Gates said.

Later that evening at castle Lassenberry in Cherryhill, Edward the 2nd and his aid number 3 were walking outside the castle grounds discussing the note he had passed to number 3. "These fucking robots are getting on my nerves! I can't even take a minute of alone time now because fucking Doug said they have to protect me 24 hour a day!" Edward the 2nd whispered. "Why did you wait to tell me this days later?" number 3 whispered. "There's was this police chief out in the sticks giving Butch a tough time! I had to call on Doug to set him straight! On top of that, I had to have a sit down with Hakim and Mookie about the 2 million Hakim lost! He tried to run up on Mookie and his people with a walker about money he didn't earn! You believe that shit? How you gonna expect to keep all your money if you weren't there for your refill?" Edward the 2nd chuckled. "Anyway! How do you expect to resolve this problem of being followed?" number 3 whispered. "I gotta get the fuck outta here! My cousin over there living the good life, and I'm here taking abuse from Doug and those other shadow government fuckers!" he whispered. "I have a little secret to tell you, son." Number 3 whispered. "What's that?" he asked. Number 3 looked over his shoulder and noticed 2 agents following a couple of yards behind. "Listen very carefully! If you have a chance to leave the country again, the agents that go with you will be under your total command! Doug and the organization won't be able to command them to return!" he whispered. Edward the 2nd looked surprised. "You fucking with me, old man?" he whispered. "I kid you not, son! Their submission is based on frequency!" number 3 whispered. Edward the 2nd gave number 3 a pat on the back. "Thanks for the heads up, old man!" he whispered.

About an hour later, Edward the 2nd was in the nursery where his children were lying in their cribs sound-a-sleep. He glanced at his daughter as he gently held the tiny fingers of his son Edward. "We're going to rule the world, son." He whispered.

Moments later he made his way to the master bedroom massaging his penis, preparing himself for a night of pleasure. He stood in the doorway, hesitant to enter as he watched Viola drool under sedation. She was sitting on a Victorian style chesterfield with an open bottle of prescription pills in her hand. There were more pills scattered around her feet next to a tipped over drinking glass. Her hair was consumed with large plastic rollers. Her attire for the evening was a pink muumuu. Edward the 2nd looked turned off from her appearance. "Useless bitch!" he said in a soft tone before leaving. He went to another bedroom about 2 doors down where he settled in for the night.

It was April 6, 2003 around 2am when a convoy of black Boeman SUVs arrived at the gates of castle Lassenberry. Open the gate!" Doug reed said to the sentry. "Yes sir." The agent said. The electronic gate slowly opened. Doug and his convoy crossed over the mote. The 3 SUVs parked near the main entrance. Doug stepped out of his vehicle. He looked up at one of the towers of the castle. He took a drag from his cigarette and through it on the ground. "Cocksucker!" he said to himself before entering the castle.

Moments later, Doug was riding in a golf cart down the corridor of the south wing. 2o agents dressed in riot gear were on foot following at double time behind him. He stopped the golf cart and turned to his troops. "Dispatch 6 agents! Have them spread out and find Edward's woman and infants! Bring them to his west wing office!" he ordered the head agent. "Yes sir." The agent said.

When Doug arrived at the entrance to the west wing office. "Is he in there?" he asked the agents standing guard. "Yes sir." One agent said. Doug didn't bother to knock. He pushed open the double doors. He was infuriated as he saw Edward the 2nd sitting on the sofa smoking a blunt with his pants down to his ankles as he was being given fellatio by 2 beautiful blonde women. Edward the 2nd was so relaxed from the marijuana that he didn't bother to get up. "Hey Doug! My man!" he shouted in a jovial manner. Doug took the side arm from his head agent. He cocked it then pointed it at one of the women. Both women received a bullet in the back of the head. Edward the 2nd snapped out of his euphoric state as the 2 women fell at his feet. "Holy shit!! Holy shit!!" Edward the 2nd screamed. Doug handed the agent back his weapon. He rushed over and grabbed Edward the 2nd by the collar. With all his strength, Doug snatched him off the sofa, slamming him on the mound of cocaine on his desk. "He's alive, huh?" Doug shouted. "Who? Who?" Edward the 2nd shouted in terror. "Your fucking cousin! Your fucking cousin, king Marcus!!" Doug shouted as he shook him in a fit of rage. "I don't know what the fuck you talking about, man!!" Edward the 2nd shout. Doug smacked him across the face 3 times. Blood began to trickle from Edward the 2nd's mouth. "Don't lie to me, boy!!" Doug shouted. "I swear to god! I don't know what you talking about!!" Edward the 2nd shouted in fear. Doug gazed into his eyes. He took a deep breath and began to smile. He lifted him off the desk and fixed his collar. "It doesn't matter whether you know, or don't know."

Doug said in a calm voice. "I swear on my kids, man!! I... don't... know...nothing!!" Edward the 2nd cried. "Oh! You swear on your kids? Am I hearing that right?" Doug asked with a wide eye look on his face. "Get on your knees!" Doug said. "I thought you weren't like Terrance, man!" Edward the 2nd shouted. "I'm not! I just have to take a piss!" Doug said. Edward the 2nd looked towards the agents. Their weapons were drawn on him. He slowly dropped to his knees shaking like a leaf. Doug unzipped his trousers. He whipped out his penis and began to relieved himself on Edward the 2nd's face. At the same time, Viola was dragged into the office by an agent. "Don't mind us, sweetheart! I'm just giving your lover here a shower after fucking around with those 2 bitches on the floor!" Doug said. Soon after, 2 agents brought in the babies. "Get up!" Doug said to Edward the 2nd. The head of castle Lassenberry stood to his feet. He was too ashamed to look Viola in the eye. Doug took a whiff of Edward the 2nd, frowning as he smelled the urine on him. "Jesus! I have to change my diet!" Doug said. "What the hell is going on, Eddie?" Viola asked. Doug turned to Viola. "Your boyfriend here swore on his kid's lives he doesn't know anything about his cousin being king of Lassenberia!" Doug shouted. "What is he talking about?" Viola asked. Doug turned to Edward the 2nd. "You almost cost me everything. Even my own life. I must make things right with the gods. I have a little mission for you, kid!" Doug said with a grin.

It was April 8th, 2003. On the Island nation of Lassenberia a ceremony was being held. The coronation of terry, sister of king Marcus was taking place within castle Lassenberia.

45 heads of state from 20 territories in east Africa were in attendance to see and recognize Terry as princess of the borough of Jabbo. The most southern region of the island nation. Out of 1,214 square miles, 10 square miles would be hers.

4 maidservants, who were the nieces of Ali, were assigned to the future princess to make sure she looked her best for the coronation. Her off-the-shoulder, crinoline styled gown was emerald green, made of satin. It was designed by the same man who designed king Marcus's and queen Kimberly's attire for their coronation. Stephan, former owner of Stephan's house of style also designed the uniforms for Edward the 2nd and the 5 generals back in new Jersey.

Her tiara was like that of queen Kimberly's but was not endowed with a vile of GLC centered on top, on the orders of Kimberly herself. Instead, it was replaced by a fine cut 2-inch ruby from the mines of Kenya.

Terry was given a shot of GLC right before the ceremony to clean out her system. Her system was drenched in anti-depressant drugs which caused side effects such as her having constant nose bleeds and ulcers. One thing the council realized that the GLC couldn't cure the mental state of a person.

It was a scene from a fairytale. Terry slowly walked down the isle of the marble floor with a half dozen children following behind her holding the end of her cape.

Her cape was made from the hide of impalas which was dyed the color of ruby red. The edges were the traditional European white with black spots. Its length was about 30 feet long and 4 feet wide.

30 percent of the citizens of Lassenberia were in attendance had lined up on both sides of the isle as terry passed by. Most of its citizens stood outside the castle, watching from a jumbotron.

After Terry kneeled before her brother, he gently placed his hands on her cheeks. "From this day on of April 8th, 2003. I dub you Princess Teresa of the region of Jabbo! May you and your offspring be recognized to the world as such for decades to come! You may rise, Princess Teresa!" he proclaimed. The crowd applauded. The people standing outside watching on the big screen rejoiced with thunderous applause as Teresa stood and curtsied before her brother.

Moments after the jumbotron was turned off and crowd outside started to dissipate, prime minister Kent Mooney approached king Marcus. Kent greeted the king with the gesture of putting his right fist over his heart, simultaneously nodding his head. "Your majesty." he said. "What is it Kent?" Marcus asked. "I've just received a message from the prime minister of Saudi Arabia's staff. They tell me the king would like to hold a private meeting with you, on the condition there will be no media coverage." Kent said. Marcus removed his crown, handing it over to his head of security. He pinched the bridge of his nose, shutting his eyes. He then gave Kent a look of exhaustion. "They're coming out of the woodwork, huh?" Marcus said. "You knew it was going to come to this!" Kent said. Marcus briefly looked around the castle. "Tell the Saudis I'll meet with the king a week from today." He said. "Right away, your majesty." Kent said before leaving. Not long after, the Baroness of Braxton approached king Marcus. "Your majesty!" she said as she curtsied. "Lady Ellen! Did you enjoy the ceremony?" he asked. "Quick, and straight to the point! Just how I like ceremonies!" she chuckled. Marcus shook his head smiling. "So, how's things in the Borough of Braxton these days?" he asked. "Quiet! A mid-western feel, I would say!" she said in a chipper manner. "Good to hear!" he said. As Ellen was engaged in conversation with his majesty, the queen of Lassenberry approached them. Lady Ellen curtsied before the queen but with distain in her eyes. "Your highness." She said to Kimberly. "Would you excuse us? I would like to have a word with the king." Kimberly said. "Yes, your Highness." Lady Ellen said before walking away. "so, my love. I hear your going to pay a visit to the king of Saudi Arabia." She said. King Marcus looked startled. "How in the world did you get this info, when I just heard it seconds ago?" he asked. "Like I've said many times. I'm my father's daughter." She said with a serious look on her face. She flashed a quick smile, then went back to appearing serious. "If the king would like to meet with you, have him come, to you!" she said. Marcus gazed into her eyes for a moment. "You're right, my love." He said. "Of course, I am!" she said in a boastful manner. Marcus looked over towards Ali, who was standing behind Kimberly. "Ali! Make haste and tell Kent there's a change of plans on the Saudi meeting, and that I need to speak with him at once." He ordered. "Yes, your majesty!" Ali said before walking away. "You were meant for me, my love!" Marcus said before gently holding and kissing the back of Kimberly's hand. "Make haste? You sound so medieval!" Kimberly chuckled. "I watched a lot of Tv as a kid with my grandmother!" Marcus said with an embarrassing smile.

It was April the 14th, 2003 when Edward the 2nd was dressed in his ceremonial uniform standing before Doug Reed. Standing next to Edward the 2nd and number 3. Standing behind Doug Reed were 20 NA agents standing in formation. They were all gathered at Teterboro airport. The engines of an Airbus 380 private jet were revved up a few yards away.

"Like I said before kid, you have exquisite taste! This massive piece of machinery isn't even on the open market yet!" Doug shouted. "Hey! If I'm going to be the future king of Lassenberia,

I want to arrive in style!" Edward the 2nd shouted. "This jet is still in its experimental phase! You sure you want to be miles in the air riding this thing?" Doug Shouted. "The risk is worth the reward!" Edward the 2nd shouted with a smile. Doug reached inside his jacket pocket. He pulled out a small vial of red liquid. "Remember! You set up yourself as nobility! When everyone is comfortable with your presence, you slip this into your cousin's drink! Once he's unconscious, he'll slip away forever! No one will be the wiser because it's hard to trace! That's when you establish yourself as king and give us a call!" Doug shouted. "Edward the 2nd took the vial of poison. "What if they search me when I get there?" he asked. "Before you land, swallow it! It'll pass through your digestive system with ease!" Doug shouted. "Are you crazy? What if it breaks in my gut?" Edward the 2nd shouted. "Don't worry, kid! The vial is shatter proof and non-biodegradable! You'll be safe" Doug shouted. "I need just one favor before I go!" Edward the 2nd shouted. Doug shrugged his shoulders." What?" he asked. "I want those agents to come with me!" he shouted. "That's out of the question, kid! You haven't been authorized for that!"" Doug shouted. "Come on! I need to show that I have a strong arm! Besides, you're holding my woman and kids' hostage until I make the call to you guys!" Edward the 2nd shouted. "Hostage is a strong word. Kid! Let's just call it bartering!" Doug shouted. "'I'm risking my life here, man! Don't send me there not feeling safe!" Edward the 2nd pleaded. Doug quickly turned his head toward the agents standing behind him. He then turned to Edward the 2nd. "Go ahead! Take them!" Doug shouted. "Thank you, so much!" Edward the 2nd shouted in a submissive manner. Doug stepped in closer to Edward the 2nd. He put his hands on his shoulders. "If you screw this up, you'll never see your kids again! I promise you!" Doug whispered into his ear. "I believe you." Edward the 2nd said in a timid voice. "Agents! Get on board the jet!" Doug had ordered. The agents formed a single line as they boarded the jet. "Here. Take this transmitter. Say the words Alpha 999 into it. That will let my people know we can step foot on Lassenberia." Doug said. He reluctantly took the transmitter from Doug then slowly walked towards the private jet with a sorrowful look on his face. Number 3 escorted him, whispering his last words to Edward the 2nd. "Don't look so sad, son. Remember. When you leave this land, the agents are yours to command." Number 3 whispered. Before boarding the jet, Edward the 2nd turned to number 3. "I'm ain't sad about what I'm doing, old man! I'm sad about what I have to do once I get to Lassenberia!" Edward the 2nd said before boarding the jet. Number 3 looked puzzled as the hatch closed.

Moments later, the jet rolled down the runway. Doug and number 3 watched as the jet took off into the night sky. At that moment, 20 NA agents come marching out of the hanger bay dressed in riot gear. "Come on. He'll be fine. But I'm not so sure about you…Colonel!" Doug said to number 3 with a smirk on his face. Number 3 looked shocked that Doug knew his identity. The agents surrounded the old man, pointing their weapons at him. "It took me awhile to figure out why they would invite you into the castle from obscurity. Now! I'm taking you to a place where you'll be tortured to the point of begging for death until you tell me everything you told him since you came on the scene!" Doug said. Number 3 looked around at all the guns pointed at him. He then looked at Doug with a smile on his face. Number 3 reached into his pants pocket and pulled out a tiny capsule. "I'll save you the trouble!" he said to Doug. He quickly inserted the capsule into his mouth, cracking it with his teeth. Suddenly, number 3 began twitching as he fell to the ground. His body lay lifeless within seconds. "Shit." Doug said in a calm voice. He gave colonel Braxton a little nudge with his foot. "Yep! He's dead! Chop his body up, save the head for me. It'll go nice on my mantle." He said to the agent in charge. "Yes, sir." The agent said. He ordered 2 agents from the circle to pick up the body and drag it to the hangar bay.

23 hours later, air traffic control at Lassenberia Airport spotted a jet on its radar circling the airspace. The air traffic controller in charge notified both military bases who were aware of the jet's existence as well. *"Alpha command to control tower. We are aware of unidentified planes, heading due south."* The military base commander responded. *"Bravo command to control tower. We are also aware of unidentified planes, heading due south."* The commander of the base responded. "Alert the castle! This is a level 3 threat." The officer of Alpha command ordered.

Inside castle Lassenberia was a military command center east of the throne room. The LCC as it was called, was occupied by 20 staff members around the clock. The technicians who watched the consoles and sophisticated equipment were ex-military from South Africa and Madagascar. It was a requirement that the LCC staff were fluent in the English language.

Kimberly, the queen of Lassenberia entered LCC followed by Ali and 2 other armed guards. The officer in charge was commander Max Ntsay, a retired member of the Gendarmerie at Madagascar. "Ny hatsaran-tarehinao! Tokony ho eo amin'ny sehatry ny seza fiandriana ianao!" he said to Kimberly. "Commander! English please! I'm still learning Malagasy!" she shouted. "Forgive me, your highness! You shouldn't be in here! You and the royal family should be in the safety of the throne room!" he responded. "I'm where I'm supposed to be, commander! Now, what did your computers pick up?" Kimberly asked. "We're waiting for a response from the pilot now!" he said. "Commander! The pilot just said he has Edward the 2nd from the United States on board and wishes to land at once!" the radioman said. "Edward the 2nd?" commander Ntsay asked. Commander Ntsay donned a headset. Before he could respond to the pilot's transmission, Kimberly approached commander Ntsay from behind. "Whatever you do, do not allow that aircraft to land!" she whispered in his ear. "The pilot says he has a short fuel supply and needs to land at once!" the radioman said. Ntsay started sweating as he looked at the radar screen, then turned to his queen. "Your highness! If they run out of fuel, a crash landing is inevitable! If the jet doesn't land in the ocean, casualties will be in vast numbers!" he said. "Once it passes over the water, give the order to Alpha command to take it down!" Kimberly ordered. "Tell the pilot to head towards Ivato!" Ntsay ordered the radioman. Kimberly looked infuriated. At that moment King Marcus, Prime Minister Mooney and 10 soldiers of the pale horsemen entered the LCC. "What's the report, commander?" Marcus asked. Commander Ntsay sighed. "Your Majesty! Please everyone! Let me do my job!" Ntsay shouted. "Watch your tone, commander!" Ali shouted. "Commander! Who's flying above my land?" Marcus asked. Kimberly's infuriated looked was now focused on her husband. "The pilot just announced there's an Edward the 2nd on board, your majesty!" commander Ntsay said. Marcus looked shocked. "commander! Give the pilot permission to land at the airport!" he said. "Commander! Disregard that last order!" Kimberly shouted. Marcus walked over and yanked his wife by the arm, pulling her over to the side to talk in private. "What's your problem?" Marcus whispered. "Take you're your hands off of me!" Kimberly whispered. Ali was about to step towards the royal couple until Kimberly gave him a hand gesture to stand down. "This is serious! Answer me!" Marcus whispered. "I said let go!" she whispered. Marcus released his wife's arm. "He's a threat to us!" she whispered. "A threat? What are you talking about, my love?" Marcus whispered. "He's here to take over! That's what!" she whispered. Marcus rolled his eyes in disbelieve. "He's the reason I'm here! He's the reason we're all here!" Marcus whispered. Kimberly sighed as she closed her eyes for a moment. "You think he did all us this, for us? You're here to keep his seat on the throne warm!" she whispered. "Don't be ridiculous!" Marcus whispered. "You, don't be ridiculous!" She said loud enough for others in the room could hear. Marcus came within inches of Kimberly's face. "Don't embarrass me!" he whispered. "He's going to be our downfall!" she whispered. "Far as I know, he's the only family me and Terry have left!" he whispered. Kimberly grabbed Marcus by the collar. "Your family is already here!" she whispered. Marcus turned his attention to everyone in the room. Everyone quickly turned their heads out of respect. "He's my family! He belongs with us, and that's final!" Marcus whispered to Kimberly. "Ali! Let's go, and let the king do what he thinks is best!" Kimberly shouted before storming out of the room. "Commander! Carry out my last order!" Marcus shouted. "Yes, your majesty!" Ntsay said.

Standing outside the LCC Kimberly pulled Ali to the side. "Before he lands, I want you to assemble a team of your best soldiers and secure the airport! Understand?" Kimberly said. "Yes, your highness!" he said. "Now, go!" she said.

Kimberly went down the corridor and made a left turn which led to a door with an electronic keypad mounted into the wall next to it. She punched in the code causing a 6-inch-thick steel door to automatically open. She punched in another code on a keypad on the opposite side of the door causing it to close. This door was one of many leading to the throne room. Inside this room the council members and the royal family, minus prime minister Mooney and King Marcus lay waiting for the elegit threat to blow over. Jenna approached Kimberly holding prince mark in her arms. She released her nephew, allowing him to run into his mother's arms. Kimberly picked up her son with a big smile on her face. She started tickling him causing him to laugh hysterically. "What's going on out there?" Jenna asked. "We have an unwelcomed visitor flying over our heads, but my dear husband thinks different!" Kimberly said with a faux smile.

CHAPTER .41 BLOODLINE

Under commander Ntsay's orders the jet was able to land at the airport. The airport was approximately 10 miles from the castle. A convoy consisting of 8 military jeeps, headed by Ali was 5 miles away from the airport. "Commander. Send a team from the Pale horseman to the airport. Let them know we're on high alert." Marcus said. "Yes, your majesty!" the Commander answered. Within minutes a 15-man team from the Pale horseman was dispatched, heading towards the airport to meet Edward the 2nd.

On board the jet Edward the 2nd and his NA agents buckled up to prepare for a landing. "Remember! If you're asked to hand over your weapons, do it! I don't want them to think we 're here to light the place up!" he said. "Yes, my lord!" all the agents shouted simultaneously. "Not just yet." Edward the 2nd whispered to himself. Edward the 2nd looked out the window in awe of the landscape of Lassenberia as the jet came closer to landing. "Holy shit! They really did it!" he said to himself.

20 minutes had passed when the jet came to a dead halt at the end of the runway. The pilot told the passengers over the PA system that it was safe to unbuckle their seatbelts. Within minutes, the pilot released the hatch. Edward the 2nd looked out the window and saw the jet enclosed by Lassenberian troops armed and ready for any signs of hostility. "Ok. boy! It's showtime!" he shouted as he headed for the exit. "Do you want to the keep the turbines revved up, sir?" the co-pilot asked. "Motherfucker, I'm home! Once you find a way to refuel, take y'all as back to the states!" Edward the 2nd chuckled. "Yes, sir the co-pilot said.

The first to step foot on Lassenberian land were 2 Agents, followed by 4 more agents. They stood on the tarmac at attention, shoulder to shoulder. Weapons were drawn on them, but they did not flinch nor show any signs of intimidation. 6 more agents stepped off the jet and stood at the bottom of the hatch opening. Edward the 2nd checked himself to see if his uniform was presentable. He then stepped off the jet with a briefcase in hand and a proud look on his face. The remaining agents followed him as he approached Ali and his troops. He held his arms out in a friendly gesture. "My fellow Lassenberians! Is this how you greet nobility?" he shouted with a grin on his face. Neither Ali nor his troops said a word. They remained vigilant with their weapons drawn. "You niggas just gonna stand there, or take me to see the king?" Edward the 2nd shouted. "Wuxuu si qarsoodi ah u eegayaa!" one of Ali's soldiers shouted. The rest of the troops began to chuckle. "What the fuck he just say?" Edward the 2nd shouted. "He said... welcome to Lassenberia, sir!" Ali said. "See! Now that's how you supposed to greet a man like me!" Edward the 2nd said. The troops were trying hard to hold their laughter.

Moments later the Pale horseman troops arrived. They were dressed in bright green combat fatigues. The captain of this team was Kiker Chan. He made his way through Ali's troops. "What is this? Where are you going?" Ali asked. Captain Chan turned to Ali. "We are under orders from the king himself to bring Lord Lassenberry back to the castle! So, step aside and let us do our job!" Chan said. Reluctantly, Ali gave his troops the signal to stand down.

When he approached Edward the 2nd, captain Chan had on a military riot helmet, goggles with black tinted lenses and a black bandana covering the rest of his face as well as the rest of his men. He removed his helmet, bandana, and goggles. Edward the 2nd was startled when he saw his pale pink eyes, chalky white skin, and curly bleached blonde hair. "What the fuck, man? Am I on another planet?" he shouted. "I realize my appearance must be odd to you, sir. We must constantly cover ourselves during the day, being so close to the equator." Chan explained. "Nah, it's cool! The only time I seen niggas like you, was on TV!" Edward the 2nd said. Ali and his troops began to chuckle. Captain Chan turned his head towards Ali's people, trying his best to hold his composure. He then turned back to Edward the 2nd. "Now, if you would follow me sir to meet the king." Chan said. "Hot damn! Let's do this!" Edward the 2nd said as he rubbed his hands together in a jovial manner. "Come on, robots!" Edward the 2nd said to the agents. "They are to stay put and hand over any weapon s they possess!" Ali said. "Cool! You heard the man, agents! Y'all stay put!" Edward the 2nd said. Captain Chan and Edward the 2nd walked past Ali and his men. Edward twirled around twice with his arms spread, breathing in the breezy air. "I love this place already!" he said with a smile. He and captain Chan hopped in the back of one of the vehicles. The Pale horseman convoy drove off. Ali turned to his soldier. "You're right, nephew. He is silly." He said.

As the convoy was making its way south towards the castle, the sight of Lassenberia's infrastructure brought tears to the eyes of Edward the 2nd. It was something out of a sci-fi movie. Every building, public facility, and private home that Edward the 2nd saw looked futuristic. "fucking amazing!" he said. "What's that, sir?" Chan asked. "How can all this happen in such a short amount of time!" he said. Chan chuckled. "Our queen once said if you have something the world wants, your world can change in a matter of seconds! It sure did for my people!" Chan said. Edward the 2nd looked at Chan with disdain. "Your queen, huh?" he said. "Yes! She is an amazing woman!" Chan said with pride. "I see you and the troops back at the airport ain't to fond of each other." Edward the 2nd said. Chan expressed a moment of sadness on his face. "Back in the motherland, my people have suffered a lot from prejudice and hatred! Here, the queen demands that we be treated with respect, despite what you've witnessed back there!" Chan said as he wiped away a tear. Edward the 2nd looked out the passenger window nodding his head repeatedly. "Is that so?" he said to himself.

When the convoy finally pulled up the castle gates, Edward the 2nd shook his head in disbelief. "This shit is huge!" he said to himself. "Follow me, sir." Chan said as they exited the vehicle. At the entrance of the gate a blonde-haired girl pulled up in a custom-made golf cart. She looked to be in her early twenties. She wore a sky-blue uniform with a white sash draped over her shoulder. "Who's that? Edward the 2nd asked. "That sir is corporal Braxton. She's second in command of the castle's interior." Chan said.

Corporal Christina Braxton was the niece of the Baroness of Braxton and the daughter of the late Simon Braxton. She was one of the few from the Braxton clan that volunteered to join the Lassenberia's military. Edward the 2nd couldn't take his eyes off her. To him, she was picturesque until she grabbed captain Chan by the sleeve of his uniform and gave him a peck kiss on the lips. "You know that is forbidden while we're on duty!" Chan chuckled. "Write me up!" she said jokingly. "Sir. The corporal will take you inside the castle." Chan said. "Damn! A blue eyed blonde-haired white girl, and an albino! You 2 have kids, they'll definitely run for the hills before the sun comes out!" Edward the 2nd said. "Sir?' Chan responded. "Nothing! Just joking!" he chuckled before getting into the golf cart. "See you tonight!" the corporal said to the captain before driving off.

The difference from castle Lassenberry on the island nation and castle Lassenberry back in the United States was there was no mote to cross over. The castle on the island appeared more grandiose from the outside. Edward the 2nd was taken on a semi-tour before being taken to his destination to meet his cousin. He was elated by the interior of the castle. "I tell ya corporal, this is beyond fucking amazing!" he said as he stared at the artwork on the 50-foot-high ceiling. "look up there on the wall to your right, sir. If I'm not mistaken, that's a giant mosaic portrait of your grandfather!" she said as she pointed at the 15x15 foot portrait incased in glass and surrounded by a gold hand crafted frame. Edward the 2nd shrugged his shoulders, tilting his to look at it from a different angle. "Nice! What I wanna know where's the portrait of my uncle hanging?" he asked. "Sir? The corporal responded.

The security level was reduced throughout the castle once it was confirmed that Edward the 2nd was in close vicinity of the king and queen. "We're almost there, sir!" Braxton said. "Shit! It's like a city within a city up in this motherfucker!" he said. Corporal Braxton just giggled.

Within moments the golf cart made a stop outside the private study of king Marcus. There were 2 Somalian guards standing at parade rest by the double doors. When Edward the 2nd stepped out of the golf cart, the soldiers stood at attention. "Follow me, sir." Braxton said. The guards opened the doors to allow the corporal and Edward the 2nd pass.

"Cousin!!!" Marcus shouted as he stood in front of his desk with his arms spread. Corporal Braxton looked flabbergasted because usually she would make a formal announcement to her king about who she's bringing before him. "Okay, your majesty! May I introduce Edward the 2nd from the United states!" she chuckled. Edward the 2nd payed it cool. He walked towards his cousin with a certain type of swagger and a smirk on his face. The 2 cousins hugged each other. Marcus's hug was firm and genuine, while on the other hand Edward the 2nd's hug seemed bogus and disingenuous.

"How are you, cuz? You look good!" Marcus said as he held his cousin's shoulders. With a smirk on his face, Edward the 2nd slowly and gently removed his cousin's hands from his shoulders. He looked around the study with an impressed look on his face. "You've done good here." He said. "I owe it all to Kimberly! Without her, none of this would be possible!" Marcus said. Edward the 2nd turned to corporal Braxton. "Could you excuse us?" he said. "Sir?" she asked with a confused look on her face. Marcus sensed the comfortable look on his cousin's face. "It's ok, corporal! Leave us, please!" Marcus said with a nervous smile. "As you wish, your majesty." She said with a look of concern before leaving. Edward the 2nd turned to his cousin. "Kimberly? you sure about that, cousin?" he asked. "Listen! I know you sent her here, but you have to admit she did a hell-of-a-job!" Marcus said as he walked around the other side of his desk to sit down. Marcus leaned back resting his elbows on the arm rest. He interlocked his fingers, having a calm demeanor. "The question I have for you, who's running the store back in the states?" he asked. "When I got off the jet, I said to myself in so many words, fuck the store!" he said. "So, this is trip is one way, is what you're saying?" Marcus asked. "You can say that!" Edward the 2nd chuckled. "Be mindful, cousin! You're leaving behind a lot of money and property our grandfather worked for his entire life!" Marcus said. "Our grandfather? Come on, cuz! I think we had this conversation before! It was Uncle Eddie that made everything possible! Don't worry. I put every family heirloom in storage. I made a shit load of money selling all the family's legitimate businesses. Far as the dope game is concerned, I decided to let the generals sort that out themselves. I got the real important shit in here." He said as he cradled the briefcase in his arms. "What's in there?" Marcus asked. "Man, I'm tired! I need a place to rest my head for a while, man!" Edward the 2nd said. Marcus paused for a moment. "Of course, cuz!" "I know you heard about the shit that happened back in the states. They're all gone, cuz!" Edward the 2nd said. "Don't worry, cuz. We'll get our revenge." Marcus said as his voice cracked. Marcus put his wristwatch up to his mouth, then pressed a button on the side of the watch. "Corporal Braxton. Return to my study, please." Marcus said. "Oh! Could my agents come to the castle too?" Edward the 2nd asked. "Ah! I'll set up quarters for them in a facility in the neighboring town." Marcus said. "Cool! Then I'll stay where they're staying, for security reasons of course!" he said. "Security reasons?" Marcus asked. "Yeah! Your people gotta funny way of pulling out the welcome mat!" Edward the 2nd mentioned. "I'm sure the Pale horseman division didn't show any hostility!" Marcus said. "The albinos? I wasn't talking about them, cuz!" Edward the 2nd said.

Moments later, corporal Braxton returned to the study. "Yes, your majesty?" she said. "Take Mr. Lassenberry to the town of Edward and have him and his agents settled in." Marcus said. "I prefer lord Lassenberry cuz. Oh, thanks for naming a town after me!" Edward the 2nd said. "Corporal. Take...lord lassenberry to his quarters. The town is still in development. Consider yourself its first citizen! You know What? I'll make you the Earl of Edward, or something!" Marcus chuckled. "The Earl of Edward? Really?" Edward the 2nd said with a look of disappointment. "Fuck it! I don't mind! Just do me a favor, cuz! Make sure my agents arrive in Edward in one piece. Now young lady! Take me to Edward, please!" Edward the 2nd said. "Follow me." She said.

Once Edward the 2nd and corporal Braxton left the study, Marcus went to the laptop on his desk. "Mr. Mooney! Find out who's holding those agents at the airport! Give them the order to stand down and escort them to the town of Edward." Marcus ordered. "Mr. Mooney? So formal, dude!" Kent said. "Just get it done!" Marcus said. "No problem, your majesty."

He said. Marcus looked disappointed once he ended communications with prime minister Mooney.

It was May 1st.2003. Clayton Watson, a.k.a Butch was having a one-on-one conversation with Tommy Falcone, a soldier from the New Jersey faction of the Sangiero crime family. Falcone looked tired. Like a man who was beaten down by life. The meeting between the 2 men was taking place at Butch's cabin out in Franklin Lakes, New Jersey. It was around 2 in the morning. Falcone had arrived a half hour after Butch.

"You wanna drink? Gotta fresh bottle of grappa with your name on it!" Butch said in a cheerful voice. The old man didn't look impressed. Falcone slammed his liver spotted hand on the oak wood table. "You think I'm some naive girl easily distracted by booze? Where's my 6 kilos of powder?" Falcone shouted. "Take it easy! My connect is missing in action right now! just give me another day! I guarantee you; I'll have the stuff by then!" Butch said. "I got fucking 90 thousand in cash sitting in the car! I expect 6 kilos on this table! I gotta deadline to meet! Voi neri! Non si può fare nulla di giusto!" Falcone shouted. "I promise I'll throw in half a key, on the house!" Butch said. "You don't understand! If I don't kick up a half a million to the bosses by the end of the week, I'm a dead man!" Falcone shouted. "Shhhh! You hear that?" Butch asked. "Hear what?" Falcone asked. "I heard a thumping noise, coming from outside! You sure you came alone?" Butch asked. "Of course, I did!" he responded. Butch rushed to the window to look outside. It was pitch black. Falcone began to panic. He slowly stood from his seat. "What you trying to pull?" Falcone asked. "Just be quiet!" Butch whispered. Butch pulled out his pistol from the holster attached to his belt. He gave Falcone the signal to stay put. He went to the door and slowly opened it. Once the door was wide open, butch felt something fly pass his face. He quickly turned in Falcone's direction. Falcone was nowhere in sight. "Tommy! Tommy!" Butch whispered after closing the door. He crept over to see what had happened to Falcone. He approached the table and saw Falcone on the floor, laid on his back with a bullet hole in his forehead. "Oh shit! Oh Shit!" he said to himself. The cabin door slowly opened. Butch quickly turned towards the door, firing his pistol at a rapid rate until the clip was empty. Out of the darkness 2 NA agents dressed in riot gear wielding machine guns with silencers entered the cabin. "General Watson. Drop the weapon and come with us, please." The agent said in a calm voice. Butch slowly placed the pistol on the floor, then put his hands in the air. "What the fuck you want with me?" he asked. "Again, general. Come with us, now." the agent said. Butch turned to the body on the floor. "What about him?" he asked. "We'll take care that, sir. Now come with us." The agent said. With his hands still in the air, butch followed the agent's orders and slowly walked towards the door. Moments after butch entered the black van, he noticed a team of agents exit another black van and entered his cabin. "Hey! There's 90 thousand bucks in his car that belongs to me! I need to go get it!" Butch said. "That's not of importance, sir." The agent said. "Not of importance? What the fuck?" Butch shouted as the van drove off.

It was 4pm central standard time when a black helicopter landed near a hanger bay on the outskirts of Corpus Christi, Texas. Exiting the copter were 2 NA agents and a man with his head covered with a black sack cloth. The 2 agents physically escorted the man towards the hanger bay. Inside the hanger stood Doug Reed wearing a fighter pilot's jump suit. The jump suit barely fit him because of his protruding beer belly.

One of the agents removed the slack cloth from the man's head, who happened to be Butch. He didn't look frightened but confused. He glanced around the hanger which was empty. He then placed his focus on Doug. "You like the outfit? Cool, huh?" Doug asked as he struck different poses. "What the fuck is this all about?" Butch asked as he pulled away from the agent's grip.

"Mr. Watson! Or general Watson, I should say! Today is the best day of the rest of your life!" Doug said. "What the fuck you talking about?" he asked. "You, my friend, have been promoted!" Doug said. "Promoted to What?" Butch asked. "As of today, you are the man that will run New Jersey for us!" Doug said. "First of all! Where the fuck am I?" Butch asked. Doug looked bewildered from his response. "Didn't you hear what I just said?" Doug asked. "Yeah, I heard you, but you still didn't answer my question!" Butch said. "OH! I won't speak on that! I'm just here to bring you the good news!" he said. "Where's Lassenberry, and where's our shipment?" Butch asked. "As far as we're concerned, there is no more Lassenberry!" Doug said with fury in his voice. "What the fuck? you kill him?" Butch asked. "When we get our hands on him, it's a 99.9 percent chance that will happen. But, let's talk about the good things in life!" Doug said with smile. "I'm up there in age! I just wanna get my product and feed my family!" Butch said. "Because you're up there in age, makes you the perfect candidate!" Doug said. "What about the other generals?" Butch asked. "What about them? Either they go along with the flow of things, or they just go." Doug explained. "Listen, motherfucker! One of those generals happens to be my cousin! So, watch yo mouth!" Butch said. Doug burst out laughing. "That's why you're the chosen one! your loyalty is legendary!" Doug said. "Leave me and my family out of this hierarchy bullshit! Give the position to Hakim or one of the other guys!" Butch said. "Speaking of Hakim, that's a definite no." Doug said. "Why not? He's young, vibrant!" Butch said. "He's a troublemaker!" Doug shouted so loud, it made butch flinch. "I guess this is the part where you tell me I don't have a choice!" Butch said. "Well, either go with the flow or you and members of your family go to jail for a long time, general. You forget, your criminals?" Doug said. Butch sighed. "Alright, motherfucker! You got me!" he said. "Don't think like that! Your grandchildren will be set for life! Shit! Your great grandchildren won't have to worry about theirs bill, ever!" Doug said. "Ok! is this meeting over?" Butch asked. "Just one more thing. General bates must go. So, deal with it." Doug said. Butch looked as if he had the weight of the world on his shoulders before the agent placed the sack cloth over his head.

The next day around 7am, Hakim was sitting at the kitchen table eating breakfast with his fiancé Taisha. They were being served by middle-aged black woman named Pat whom Hakim hired from an ad online.

"So, what are we doing today?" Taisha asked. "Well, since business is at a standstill for the moment, I say we head out to the beach and rent a boat and go sailing!" Hakim said. "Let's do something simple, like go for a walk-in central park!" she said. "You forget I got bad feet?" Hakim said. "I'm sorry, sweetie!" she said. "Where the hell is my cane, anyway?" he asked. "It's in the dining room. I'll get it for you." Pat said. "Thank you." Hakim said. "Let's get the boat and go then!" Taisha said. Moments later, Pat came back into the kitchen with Hakim's walking cane. "It's been a while since I've seen any of your friends come around! Is everything ok?" Taisha asked. Hakim dropped his fork on his plate. He sighed for a moment. "In my line of work, people come and go." He said. Suddenly his cell phone began to vibrate. Hakim took out his phone from his pajama pants pocket. He recognized the number. "What this nigga want?" he said to himself. "Who is it?" Taisha asked. Hakim ignored her. "What's up?" Hakim asked. *We back in business. Come down to the spot and pick up yo shit.* the voice said. Hakim put the phone back into his pocket. "Who was it?" Taisha asked. "That was an associate of mine. I'm gonna have to postpone our date today." He sighed. Taisha gently grabbed his hand. "Seriously?" she said. "Bills gotta be paid, baby!" Hakim said. "So, what am I supposed to do while you're gone?" she sighed. "I gotta few thousand dollars in a shoe box in the closet. Take it and take your mother on a shopping spree, or something. I promise I'll call you as soon as I'm done." Hakim said before giving her a kiss on the cheek. "Pat! Could call down to the lobby and tell them bring my limo around front within an hour?" Hakim asked. "Yes sir." She said. Hakim grabbed his cane. "I'm about to go jump in the shower. You wanna join me?" he asked. Taisha smiled and started unbuttoning his pajama top.

It was around 9am when Hakim's limo pulled up to the pier at Port Elizabeth. "Stay here." He said to his new limo driver before exiting the vehicle. Hakim noticed dock employees at work off into the distance. He didn't see any of the other generals, nor agents. Being cautious, he pulled out his pistol from inside his jacket as he limped further down the pier. As he came to the end of the pier, he saw Butch sitting on a crate, staring out into the ocean.

"Yo! Where is everybody? Where's the shipment?" Hakim shouted as he approached butch. Butch didn't bother to look at Hakim. He continued to stare at the calm waters. "The shipment already came." He said. "So, where the fuck is my product?" Hakim asked. Butch turned to Hakim. "Put the gun away and sit down next to me, kid." He said. "I'm a general, nigga! You don't talk to me like that?" Hakim shouted. "And I'm the new boss! Now, put the gun away and sit the fuck down!" Butch shouted. "What the fuck you mean you're the new boss?" he asked. Hakim ignored Butch's orders and continued to stand with his gun pointed at him. "It's over, kid. The whole Lassenberry regime is done. I've been given the order from up top to run the state." Butch said. Hakim looked around, and still saw no one in sight. Not butch's people nor any agents. "So, you killed Krayton, now you're gonna take me out even though I gotta gun pointed at you?" Hakim said. "I don't know what the fuck happened to that nigga! Far as me and you are concerned, I've been given the go -ahead on what to do with you!" Butch said. "All I gotta do is pull the trigger and it's over for yo old ass!" Hakim said. "You pull that trigger, not only will you die, that pretty Latina girl of yours and her whole family dies!" Butch said in a calm voice. Reluctantly Hakim put his gun away. "If you're gonna kill me, then get it over with! Just don't touch my woman!" Hakim pleaded. Butch walked over to Hakim, standing face-to-face with him. "Doug wants you dead, for whatever reason. I was there when you took your first step. I was there when you got your first tricycle. Yeah, for a time I wanted you dead, but I reconsidered. You'll get to live. But It'll be behind bars." Butch said. "Man! I can't go back to jail! Fuck that!" Hakim shouted. "You wanna die? Is that what you want?" Butch asked. "I can't be caged in no more, man!" Hakim shouted. "Listen. I'll make sure your commissary is stacked." Butch said. Hakim turned and walked a few steps away from Butch. He then turned to Butch. "You know that mother fucker said the same thing you said! Not one time did he pay me a visit! Not one time!!!" hakim shouted. "You had a chance to live a regular life when you came home! You chose to come back! Now, this is the price you gotta pay!" Butch explained. Hakim stood there teary eyed. "When they coming for me?" Hakim asked. "In 3 days, the feds gonna knock on your door. Get your paperwork and personal shit in order before they come. Now go spend time with that pretty girl of yours." Butch said. "Who's gonna run my territory? Hakim asked. "That's none of your business, kid! Now, go!" Butch said. Hakim limped away with his head down.

Back in Lassenberia Edward the 2nd was roaming the streets with 2 of his agents in a neighborhood with much of the population being Somalian. He and his agents were dressed in civilian clothes.

It was around 5 in the morning UTC, on a Sunday. There were a handful of little kids playing soccer in the middle of the pristine street. They looked happy except for an Albino boy standing off to the side. Edward the 2nd noticed how they ignored him. He over to the little boy to console him. He asked the boy why he was so sad. The boy looked at him with an odd look. "I said, what's wrong with you, kid?" he asked. The boy looked at him, speaking in a different language. Edward the 2nd walked away shaking his head. "I gotta do something about that shit." He said to himself.

As Edward the 2nd and the agents continued their stroll down the street, a military jeep pulled up alongside them. "How are you Mr. Lassenberry?" the soldier said. "I prefer to be called lord Lassenberry." Edward the 2nd said. "Very well then, Lord Lassenberry it is!" the soldier replied. "What's your name?" Edward the 2nd asked. "Private Kayre Abdi, sir!" he said. "I noticed the group of kids playing back there. There was this one albino kid who was treated like an outcast. What's the deal with that?" he asked Abdi. Private Abdi looked around in all directions. "They are disgusting people! But her majesty the queen said we are all equal! We all must be as one if we are to lead the world to true freedom!" he whispered. "The queen told you, a private, that we all are equal. Wow!" Edward the 2nd said sarcastically. "Yes!" the private said in a jovial manner. Edward the 2nd stood silent for a moment. "Private Abdi! How would you like to be my personal driver?" he asked. "Forgive me, lord Lassenberry, but I must speak with my superiors on such matters!" Abdi said. "Listen, man! I'm part of the royal family! So that makes me your superior! Understand?" Edward the 2nd said. "But my lord!" Abdi uttered. "No buts, man! Take me and my men on a tour!" Edward the 2nd said as he signaled the agents to get in the vehicle. "But my lord! I am on patrol!" Abdi said. "I just gave you a fucking order, private!" Edward the 2nd shouted as his agents hopped in the back of the vehicle. Even though he had a pistol strapped to his waist, the young private looked intimidated as Edward the 2nd entered the front passenger seat. "I like you, man! You stick with me; you'll be standing by my side when I'm on the throne!" he chuckled as he slapped Abdi on the back. "On the throne, my lord?" Abdi asked nervously. "Relax, man! Just drive!" Edward the 2nd said as he smiled. Abdi drove off, heading south towards the borough of Jabbo.

Moments later, Abdi crossed the border line, entering the borough of Jabbo. The sun was coming up over the horizon. Edward the 2nd had a better view of his surroundings as

Abdi drove on. He noticed the new town houses lining the whole block on both sides of the streets. At the end of the block he ordered Abdi to slow down. At the end of the block was an immaculate mansion, resembling a small castle. Coming out of this mansion was a black woman walking as if she was in a daze. She was wearing a night gown. "That lady! She looks familiar!" Edward the 2nd said. "That's Princess Teresa, My, lord!" Abdi said. "Pull over! Now!" Edward the 2nd shouted at the top of his lungs. Abdi hit the brakes hard, coming to a screeching halt. Edward the 2nd hopped out of the vehicle. His 2 agents hopped out as well. "Stay here!" he ordered them. The 2 agents stayed put by the vehicle. Edward the 2nd trotted a few yards to catch up with his cousin. He finally reached her, stopping her in her tracks. When he looked into hers eyes, he noticed she was in a drug induced state. "Terry! Terry! Are you ok, cuz?" he asked with concern. For a moment terry didn't say a word. She gazed at her cousin as if she were staring right through him. "Terry! It's me!" he shouted as he shook her by her shoulders. He snapped his fingers in her face. After a moment of shaking and yelling at her to get her attention, terry snapped out of her zombie state. "Krayton?" she asked. "Yes, cuz! It's me!" he said. "Krayton?" she said in a euphoric manner. "You ok, little cuz?" he asked. Suddenly her look changed. Sadness fell upon her face. "They killed my mommy and daddy!" she cried. Edward the 2nd hugged his cousin firmly. "I know! I know!" he said. "They killed my family!" she cried. He released her from his hug. "Listen, cuz! I'm gonna set things right! They're gonna pay for that shit! You hear me? We're gonna get all them mother fuckers!" he said. Terry said nothing. she just burst out in tears, giving her cousin a long firm hug.

Abdi came running toward them. "Is everything alright, your highness?" he asked. "I got this, man! Go finish your patrolling!" Edward the 2nd said as he waved Abdi off. "As you wish, my lord." Abdi said before running back to his vehicle. The 2 agents came to their master's aid. "I'm taking her back into the house! You 2, stand guard outside until I call on you!" Edward the 2nd said. "Yes, my lord." The agents said simultaneously.

It was May 5th, 2003 around 8pm EST. it was a clear night sky in New York City with a mild breeze. Hakim and Taisha were at his penthouse snuggled up sitting on the sofa binge watching a TV show. They were sharing a big bowl of popcorn. "Come on girl! Save me some!" Hakim said. "What you expect from a pregnant woman?" Taisha said. "You're right baby! I'm sorry! Eat your pretty little ass off!" he chuckled. Taisha threw a piece of popcorn in his face.

Hakim went from laughing, to having a serious look on his face. He grabbed the remote and clicked off the TV. "¿Por qué demonios haces eso? They were coming to the good part!" Taisha shouted as she snatched the remote. Hakim gently took the remote from her and placed it on the coffee table. He gazed into her eyes. "What's wrong, baby?" she asked. Hakim took a deep breath. "Sabes que te amo, ¿verdad??" he said. "I love you too! Now, what's wrong?" she asked. Hakim removed his arm from around her shoulder. He got up and went into the bedroom. "What's wrong?" Taisha shouted. a few minutes later he came out of the bedroom with a small stack of papers in his hand. He placed the stack of papers on her lap. "What's this?" she asked. He sat down next to her. Always fearing that his home might be bugged, hakim didn't say a word. He showed her what was written on the stack of paperwork, which happened to be legal documents and a note. "The note read that he had the diner, a gym out in Newark, 2 apartment buildings out in Kearny, a condominium out in Bloomfield and BIG SHOTS, and 4 million in cash stashed away in storage out in east orange, right off freeway drive east. "I went to my lawyer and had everything signed over to you." he said. "Why are you doing this?" she asked. Hakim put his head down for a moment. He turned to Taisha. "The life I've been leading since I was a child, comes with a price. Now, it's time for me to pay the price!" he said. "Where do you plan on going?" she asked. "Wherever the wind takes me, baby!" he sighed. Taisha stood up. "No! No! You're not leaving me to raise this baby by myself!" she screamed. Hakim's eyes started tearing up. "I don't wanna leave you! I swear I don't, but the truth is if I don't leave, you won't be safe! Besides, you're having my baby! I need to keep my bloodline going!" he said. "You need to stop talking crazy!" she said. "Come. Sit next to me, please!" he pleaded. Taisha calmed herself and sat down next to Hakim. "Everything's gonna be alright. You're gonna be alright." He said before kissing her on the lips

Later that evening, Taisha was sleeping in Hakim's king size bed. she was tossing and turning until she was wakened out of her sleep by the combination of the doorbell ringing and hard banging on the door. She looked over and noticed that Hakim wasn't next to her. She called out his name as the ringing and banging continued. She grabbed her robe at the foot of the bed and turned on the newly installed monitor hanging on the wall in the bedroom to check who was at the door. The colored monitor showed a group of 8 men and 1 woman at the door, all wearing dark blue windbreakers. 1 of the men slightly turned for a moment showing the letters FBI on the back of his windbreaker. Taisha put her hand over her mouth, looking shocked. She ran out of the bedroom whispering Hakim's name before heading to the door. Hakim didn't appear. she checked one of the bathrooms in her last attempt to find him. She turned the knob to open the door which was locked from the inside. She tapped on the door many times before the feds burst in with guns drawn.

"FBI! We have warrant for the arrest of Hakim Bates!" the female agent shouted. the federal agents had spread throughout the penthouse when Taisha came down the corridor. The agent practically shoved the documented warrant in Taisha's face before she could utter a word. Taisha was placed in handcuffs and forced to sit on the sofa. "You just can't invade our privacy like this without a warrant!" Taisha shouted as 4 of the federal agents were searching the place. "This is a warrant in my hand, ma'am! Now where is Mr. Bates?" she asked. "He's... in the bathroom down the hall!" Taisha reluctantly said. 3 of the federal agents crept down the corridor with guns at the ready. When they approached the bathroom, 2 of the federal agents positioned themselves on either side of the door. The main federal agent played with the knob realizing the door was locked. "Mr. Bates! FBI! Come out slowly with your hands up!" the main federal agent shouted. the main agent nodded his head, giving the other 2 federal agents the signal that he was going in. he kicked in the door. To his surprise, he and the other 2 federal agents saw Hakim's body on the floor with an empty pill bottle next to him. The main federal agent kneeled over the body checking for a pulse. "Call an ambulance! Quick!" he shouted. 1 of the federal agents made the call from his cell phone. The other federal agent came running down the corridor where everyone else was. "What happened?" the female federal agent asked. "The fucker overdosed! It's faint, but there's a pulse!" the federal agent responded. "Did you call an ambulance?" she asked. "They're on the way!" he said. Taisha began screaming hysterically. "Everything will be fine, young lady!" the female federal agent said as she consoled Taisha by rubbing her back.

The FBI agents were shocked that the paramedics happen to show up sooner than expected. What was different about these EMT workers wore dark shades even though it was 3 in the morning. "Is there an eclipse?" one of the federal agents jokingly asked as the EMT workers walked by to get to the bathroom. There was no response from the EMT workers.

As Hakim's unconscious body was being hauled out on the gurney, the federal agents turned their attention towards Taisha. "We're taking you into custody, young lady." The female federal agent said. "Can I get dressed first?" Taisha asked. "Of course! I'll take you into the bedroom." She said.

Once outside, the federal agent looked puzzled to where was the ambulance. The female federal agent asked the other agents that were posted outside what happened to the ambulance. They were just as puzzled. They were told it was a matter of urgency that Hakim's body be transported to the nearest hospital.

"Get me a helicopter! Now!" the female federal agent shouted into the 2-way radio. It suddenly became clear to the federal agents posted outside that the EMT workers weren't on the up-n-up.

Taisha was standing there in handcuffs, wearing jeans a t-shirt and sneakers. At her behest, a jacket was placed over her head to protect her identity from the cameras and journalists that were waiting outside. She was rushed into one of the unmarked cars. "Did someone follow the ambulance?" the female federal agent shouted. "Yes, ma'am!" one federal agent responded.

The ambulance driving down Amsterdam Avenue, with lights flashing and sirens wailing, was closely followed by a couple of federal agents in an unmarked vehicle until out of nowhere the vehicle was t-boned by a burgundy Boeman pick-up truck coming off 59th street. The federal agent's vehicle flipped over several times crashing into oncoming traffic. The ambulance sped up weaving through traffic finally making a sharp right turn on 110th street. Within the back of the ambulance, Hakim unconscious, was hooked up to an intravenous tube. "Diversion was successful." The EMT worker sitting with Hakim said as he looked out the small back windows. "We'll be within our destination in approximately 45 minutes." the driver said.

It was around 5:30 am when the EMT workers with hakim arrived outside at a shack in the middle of Mashomack Preserve on Shelter Island, off Long Island. Inside the shack, Doug Reed was sitting silently at a small table. There were 6 NA agents standing around him facing the exit. Moments later, Hakim was rolled in on the gurney by the 2 EMT workers.

About a half hour later, Butch arrived outside the shack, along with his driver and his son Kevin. "Ok. it's showtime." Butch said. "Pop! Why I gotta be out here?" Kevin asked. Butch stopped in his tracks. He placed his hand on his son's shoulder. "Son. If you wanna be a part of this world, you gotta see this shit up close and personal!" If you can't handle it, stay yo ass in the car!" Butch said before walking away. Kevin looked around the wooded area before pressing on to follow his father. "Hey, pop! Why you ain't wearing your uniform?" Kevin asked. Butch turned to his son. "Today is a new day, my boy! The streets of New Jersey belongs to us now!" he said proudly.

There was an NA agent standing outside the shack. Butch approached the agent with his hands raised. His son followed suite. "Good morning, general Watson." The agent said. "It's Mr. Watson! Just pat us down, so we can go inside!" Butch said. "Yes, sir." The agent said. After being patted down, Butch and his son entered the shack. Butch looked shocked when he saw Hakim's body lying on the gurney. "What's this shit?" he asked. "General Watson! You don't seem to get the picture on how I work! Let me give you a crash course! I told you to kill this son-of-a- bitch! Why did he try to commit suicide?" Doug asked. "How the fuck I'm supposed to know?" Butch shouted. "I assume the Lassenberry family didn't tell you, we run every inch of this pathetic country! We are everywhere!! We know all!" Doug shouted. Doug gave one of the agents a nod. The agent kicked the back of Kevin's leg, causing him the fall to his knees. He then put his pistol to Kevin's head. "Hold the fuck on, now!" Butch shouted. "I'm going to give you another chance to kill this fucker, because I'm pressed for time!" Doug shouted as another agent slid a hunting knife across the table. "I want you, General Watson, to take this knife and carve out general Bates's heart!" He said. "fine! Fuck it!" Butch said. Butch reached for the knife. He walked over towards Hakim's body.3 of the NA agents closed in, keeping Doug from potential harm. Butch raised the knife above head without hesitation. "Christ! You are a natural!" Doug said. After Butch plunged the knife into Hakim's chest. Hakim's body gave a knee jerk reaction. Without hesitation, Butch sawed through the bone of his chest cavity. "His son puked his brains out, trembling like a leaf. After removing the bone, Butch inserted his hand into the body. He then yanked out the heart. "Good! Now, eat it!" Doug said. "What the fuck?" Butch shouted. "Give me the god damn thing!" Doug said. Butch tossed the bloody organ to Doug. He didn't hesitate to bite a chunk out of the heart. As he chewed on it, he expressed a look of bliss on his face. "Now, it's your turn!" Doug said as he chewed with his mouth open. Butch snatched the heart from Doug. He nibbled at the heart, expressing disgust on his face. As Butch continued to nibble, Doug closed his eyes, softly chanting to himself. Butch had enough. He looked at Hakim's lifeless body. Damn, kid!" he said to himself. Doug opened his eyes. "Get up, son." he said to Kevin. Kevin stood to his feet. "Be proud, kid. You're now the prince of New Jersey!" he said.

CHAPTER .42 Я НАШЛА НОВОГО ДРУГА

It was June 6th, 2003. Marcus, the king of Lassenberia was holding a meeting at the castle with his sister-in-law Jenna. Her husband Sheldon was also there as the scribe.

"I had a back-ground check done on this new Russian prime minister. Before his time in the KGB, this man is a total mystery!" Jenna said. "The lassenberry family did business with former KGB operatives in the past. I just hope we can reconnect, with this guy." Marcus said. "The life expectancy of Russian men was incredibly low during the cold war. it's slowly rising, but maybe we can give them a quick boost!" Jenna said. "When the Saudi king came here, he not only offered 30 percent control of his oil refineries, but one of his daughters to marry my son just for a gallon of GLC!" Marcus chuckled. "Little Marcus? A husband?" Jenna said as she burst out laughing. "Crazy, right?" Marcus chuckled. "Far cry from the American way, huh?" Sheldon chuckled. "Yeah! I told him the refineries would suffice!" Marcus chuckled.

After the laughter, a silence fell upon the trio. "So! How do we get this guy's attention? Any suggestions?" Marcus asked. "Trust me! We have this man's attention. We have the whole world's attention at this point!" Jenna said. "The question is, how we get his attention without letting those in America knowing?" Marcus asked. "Don't worry. I'll just go undercover as a journalist from Havana. I still have friends in Miami that can get me through the door." Jenna said. "No disrespect, Marcus. But I gotta lot of concerns about my wife's safety!" Sheldon said. Marcus turned to Jenna for a response. "Sweetie. I'm Jabbo's daughter. As the kids say now-a-days, I got this!" she chuckled. "I just want to say, that we're the only ones that know about this, and I want to keep it that way. Not even your sister needs to know about this! The Russians are on their way to being a superpower again. Once we got them as our European muscle, those creeps in America won't be able to touch us!" Marcus said. "What if this new prime minister wants to connect with us, more ways than one?" Jenna asked. Marcus scratched his head pondering what to say. "We'll just feed them some GLS, a spoon full at a time." Marcus said with a smile. "What's my window of time? "Jenna asked. "Is your passport still valid?" Marcus asked. "Ah, yeah!" Jenna said. "Well, let's get going! Use your charm and be back within 2 weeks!" Marcus said. At that moment, Sheldon put away his ink pen and closed the royal journal called the J.O.E (Journal of Eternity), which was created by Marcus himself. He told his wife Kimberly that they needed to wipe the slate clean as far as their family's past activities were concerned.

It was June 8th when Jenna arrived off the shores of Havana Cuba by seaplane. There, she rendezvoused with long time Jenkins family friend, Hector Orlando from Miami. He arrived from Canada a day before. They met and hugged in the middle of Old Square Plaza. "Ha pasado mucho tiempo, hermosa!" Hector said as he gave Jenna a firm hug. "Me alegro de verte de nuevo, amor!" She shouted with joy. They released each other, continuing to hold hands. "¡Me gusta el earring! ¿Cuándo lo conseguiste?" she asked as she tugged on his earlobe. "My ex bought it for my birthday. Anyway! How's Sheldon and the kids?" he asked. Everyone's great! The girls are growing so fast!" she said. "Your sister?" he asked. "She's doing great as well! You know she had a boy, right?" she said. "Wow! That's great!" he said. "He's about 3, now!" she said. "I heard about the tragedy that happened on your family's island! I'm so sorry" he said. "We're still going through the motions, but we'll pull through this!" she said. "MY heart goes out to all the families who lost love ones! Did they find out the cause?" he asked. "It's still under investigation! I believe it was a lethal dose of pesticides! But what do I know?" she said. "Well, my dear, what can I do for you?" he asked. "I need you to get me into the Russian embassy so I can get an interview with the prime minister!" she said. "Since when you became involved with the media?" he asked. "I didn't!" she said. Jenna gazed at her surroundings. She stepped in closer to Hector. "I'm on a mission!" she whispered. Jenna wore a gold necklace. Hanging from that necklace was a small vial of GLC, which she clutched as she was asking Hector for help. "I need to get this to the prime minister!" she whispered. "What is that?" he asked. "It's the key to my family's safety!" she whispered. "¿Es algún tipo de veneno?" hector asked jokingly. "Stop it! Can you get me in there, or not?" she asked. Hector sighed. "I have a cousin who's a top liaison to the ambassador. Ya veré. Yo lo que puedo hacer." He said. "Where are you staying?" she asked. "The Grand El Candil Hotel." He said. "I'll get a room there then!" she said. "Nonsense, my dear! I was stuck with double beds! You can stay with me! "he said. "Gracias, cariño.!" she said as she hugged him. "I have to tell you, my dear! This type of contact doesn't come free!" he whispered. Jenna also wore a gold bracelet. Dangling from that bracelet was a clear marble size ball filled with GLC. She held it up to his face. "Don't worry, sweetie! I've got that covered!" she said.

The next day, around 2pm UTC, hector and Jenna were having lunch at the Fontana café. "So, what do you have for me, sweetie?" Jenna asked. Hector looked at his watch. My cousin should be here any minute now!" he said. "Good! This Arroz con pollo is delicious!" she said. "You should try this Mojo Criollo!" he said.

Moments later, an attractive Latina wearing a business suit approached them. Hector stood up to greet her. "Hola, primo!" he said before giving her a kiss on both cheeks. "Hola, primo! te extrañé tanto!" she said. "Isabella, me gustaría conocer a un querido amigo mío, Jenna Jenkins.!" he said. "¡Por favor, para conocerte!" she said to Jenna as they shook hands. "Lo mismo aquí!" Jenna said. Hector pulled out a seat for her. "¿Comiste todavía?" hector asked. "¡Soy bueno! ¡Tuve una ensalada antes!" she said! "Vamos a ir a las señoras de negocios! ¿no?" hector said. "¡Sí! ¿Qué es esta reunión sobre?" Isabella asked. Jenna picked up a steak knife. "Déjame ir directo al grano. Dame tu mano, querida." Jenna said. Isabella looked nervous. "¿Qué planeas hacer con ese cuchillo?" she asked. "Confía en mí! sólo Dame tu mano, por favor!" Jenna said. "Sólo confía en su Isabella! ¡ Confía en mí!" hector said. Reluctantly, Isabella stretched out her hand. Jenna quickly made a gash on her index finger. Isabella flinched. Jenna yanked the marble from her bracelet. She cracked it open on the table. She quickly sprinkled its contents on Isabella's finger. Hector and Isabella were both shocked to see how fast her wound healed. "¿Cómo es posible que en el mundo?" Isabella asked. "Tengo una larga historia. Lo que necesito de ti, es una reunión con el embajador ruso. Si haces esto por mí, te prometo que serás muy recompensado." Jenna said. Hector and Isabella looked at each other, overwhelmed with joy. "¿Necesitas un traductor Ruso?" Isabella asked. "Sólo apunta en la dirección correcta, cariño. Yo me ocuparé del resto." Jenna said. "Tengo que volver al trabajo. Nos vemos en frente de la Embajada a las 8 am." Isabella said. "Estaré allí. Jenna said before she and Isabella shook hands. Hector and Isabella stood and gave each other a hug. "¡No seas un extraño, primo! estar en contacto más a menudo!" Isabella said. "Hasta pronto, Jenna.!" She said before leaving.

Within the next 2 days, under the guise of a journalist, Jenna was on the next commercial flight to Moscow from Havana. Besides having a necklace and bracelet holding the GLC, she also wore earrings shaped like marbles filled with miracle drug. Jenna noticed that she was 1 out of 4 on this flight. There were 4 Caucasian men wearing civilian clothes. They were spread out in each corner of the cabin. 2 sat up front, while the other 2 sat way in the back. She turned to the gentlemen in the back, smiling at them.

Hours later, Jenna had awakened. She looked out the window as the pilot announced they were above the Khamovnski District. There was heavy turbulence as the plane was preparing to land. Jenna buckled her seat and held on tight to the arms rests preparing for the worst.

It wasn't too long before the plane came in for a landing at Vnukovo international airport. One of the men sitting up front left his seat, opening the overhead compartment. He pulled out a fur coat. He walked over to Jenna and tossed it in the seat next to her. "You'll need this, Ms. Jenkins. You're far from sunny Havana." He said.

The plane came to a complete stop. The hatch was opened. "Follow us, Ms. Jenkins." The man said. Jenna felt the cold brisk wind as she stepped on the tarmac. There was a military vehicle waiting for them. Beside the driver, there was an elderly man sitting in the passenger seat. "Good Morning, Ms. Jenkins. I am your interpreter, Boris Yuri. How familiar are you with the Russian language?" He asked. "I know a little!" she said. "Don't worry. I'm here to help." He said. Thank you!" she said.

About a half hour later Jenna and her interpreter arrived outside the Kremlin, followed by the 4 men in an unmarked vehicle. Jenna was in awe of the Kremlin and the bright colors of the surrounding towers. Jenna and her escorts passed by 2 guards of the presidential regiment. They were cleared to enter the facility known as the Russian White House.

Once they arrived outside the office of the prime minister, Jenna was told to stay put until called upon. Sitting on a bench across the hall reading a newspaper was a redheaded woman in a dress wearing shaded glasses. Jenna didn't dwell on it at first until she noticed the woman kept glancing at her and that the newspaper she was reading was up-side-down. Jenna covered her mouth to keep from laughing.

Moments later Boris comes out of the prime minister's office. "Ms. Jenkins. Follow me, please." Boris said. Jenna entered the room first. There were a handful of secretaries at their desks hard at work until Jenna walked in. They all froze for a moment, watching as she was led to the prime minister's office. There were 2 uniformed guards standing at attention on either of the prime minister's office door. When she entered his office, she saw sitting behind a polished wooden desk a stocky middle-aged Caucasian man in a dark-blue suit. "Ms. Jenkins! I present to you prime minister of the Russian Federation, the honorable Volodin Sergey." He said proudly. Prime minister Sergey stood from his seat. He walked around his desk to greet Jenna. "Please to meet you, Ms. Jenkins!" he said as they shook hands. "Это честь, премьер-министр!" she said. Prime minister Sergey looked impressed. "It seems Ms. Jenkins is linguistically capable!" the prime minister said to Boris. "Вам нужны мои услуги, сэр.?" Boris asked. "You may leave us." Sergey ordered. Boris gave a nod to the prime minister and Jenna before leaving the office.

"Садись, дорогая." The prime minister said. Sergey aided her as she sat down. "With-all-do-respect, Mr. prime minister, I'd rather interview you in English. If it's ok with you." she requested. "Why certainly, my dear!" he said.

Jenna brought along a leather handbag. Inside that handbag she pulled out a note pad, ink pen and a tape recorder. She took a deep breath. "Shall we begin?" she asked before clicking on the tape recorder. Sergey gestured her to begin with her questions. Instead of asking her first question, she took off her necklace. The prime minister looked puzzled. Jenna then ripped off a sheet of paper from the note pad. She then folded the paper, creating sharp creases. "Can you give me your hand, sir?" she asked with a seductive smile. "Very well!" he said reluctantly. With one quick swipe she caused a paper cut on 2 of his fingers. Sergey flinched. She quickly cracked the vial of GLC on the desk and poured it on his wound. "Хорошие небеса!" he said as his paper cut healed within seconds. "Good heavens is right, sir!" she chuckled.

The following day, Jenna was given a personal tour of all the architectural wonders in Moscow. From Red Square to the Spasskaya Tower, to the Basil's Cathedral and the Bolshoi Theatre. Jenna was in awe giving praises to the structures, at the same time giving a faux interview. Except for Boris, none of the aids and security accompanying Jenna and the prime minister knew the real reason for her visit.

Her questions to the prime minister were innuendos not to his patriotism to his country, but how his loyalty would be to Lassenberia. "How far would you go to defend the citizens of Russia who fell victim to the collapse of the economy after the cold war?" was one of her questions really directed towards Lassenberia. "I would come out of my own pocket and give every last citizen of my homeland a sense of security!" he said. "What is the relationship between the United States and Russia after the cold war?" she asked. "Well, I have a great deal of respect for the United States and its infrastructure! But the United States must respect and recognize Russia as a force to be reckoned with, when it comes to the global economy!" the prime minister said. "What are your thoughts and policy on terrorism, sir?" she asked.

"To invade ones' country is despicable! The president and I, despite what took place in 1979, are crusaders of fairness and prosperity! The Russian government is willing to lend a helping hand to those in need!" he said after giving Jenna a wink.

Volodin Sergey came on to the political scene after the fall of the iron curtain. He served in the Russian Army until rising to the rank of Полковник, equivalent to a U.S. army colonel. During the cold war, he served as a KGB operative. He is cousin, by marriage, to Russian mobster, Igor Brezhnev From Brighton Beach in Brooklyn.

Day 3 of her visit, Jenna was invited to a formal dinner at the prime minister's residence in Shvedskiy Tupik. Those in attendance were part of Sergey's inner circle. The president and other Russian officials had no idea this cotillion was being held.

Unbeknownst to his wife, prime minister Sergey bought Jenna a luxurious ballroom gown. It fit her curvy physic like a glove. The strapless gown was powder blue, made of silk. Sergey couldn't take his eyes off Jenna even though his wife was standing by his side. When it came time to feast, Sergey insisted that Jenna sit to his right as his wife sat to his left.

The crowd of at least 30 people were impressed that Jenna spoke fluently in their language. It didn't take Jenna long to notice that those sitting close to her, including Sergey's wife weren't familiar with the English language. This gave Jenna the upper hand to lean over and talk business to Sergey as they dined. This also gave Sergey the advantage over his wife to whisper sweet nothings into Jenna's ear as he tried to slide his hand across her lap, which Jenna kept resisting by pushing it away. She kept her composure and stuck to talking business.

"I hope you realize, siding with us will piss off the politicians in the United States." She said before sipping her glass of wine. "Who said they have to know?" Sergey chuckled. "What about your president?" she asked. "What about him?" he asked with a smug look on his face. "Ok!!" Jenna said with surprise. Sergey leaned into Jenna. "Between Lassenberia and the Russia that I will create, we can conquer the world, my dear!" he whispered. Sergey's wife looked disturbed by his gestures towards Jenna. She quickly changed her composure, not to be off her game in front of the other guests.

A couple of days later at the International Security &Surveillance building in Washington DC, the director of intelligence was sitting at his desk sipping on a cup of coffee when around 10am EST one of his staff members burst into his office. "Damnit! Can you knock?" the director shouted. "Sir! This is really urgent!" the assistant said. The assistant dropped a folder on the director's desk. The director looked puzzled. "What's this?" he asked. "Open it, sir!" the assistant said. The director opened the folder. Inside were black and white photos. "Again, I ask! What's this?" he asked. "Sir! One of our field agents snapped these photos of the prime minister escorting this black woman to Vnukovo airport in the dead of night, on a private jet!" he said. "So!" the director said. "She landed hours later at Maputo airport in Mozambique, according to our agents assigned there!" the assistant said. "Like I said! So?" the director said. "Sir! She chartered a sea plane to the island of Lassenberia! We ran her image through the computer and found out that she's Jenna Jenkins! An in-law to Marcus! Their king!" he said. The director had a smile on his face. "So, our little upstart nation is involved with the Russkis!" he said. "Shall we notify the president, sir?" the assistant asked. The director scoffed at his question. "The president?" he said. "Don't worry. I can take it from here." The director said. "Yes, sir." The staff member said before exiting the office. The director, instead of using the landline phone on his desk, pulled out his cell phone. The director entered a code into his cell phone. "*Yes. What is it?*" the voice said. "Sir. The new nation. It's suspected their doing business with the Russians." The director said. "*Are the joint chiefs or the President aware of this?*" the voice asked. "Of course not, sir. You're the first to know." The director said. "*Well done. Keep me posted.*" The voice said before ending the call.

Elsewhere, in Cherryhill New Jersey, Butch and his son Kevin stood outside the gates of castle Lassenberry. "Hey you!" Butch shouted at one of the NA agents standing guard by the gate. The agent approached Butch. "Yes. May I help you, general Watson?" the agent asked. "The Watson crew is taking over this castle now! so, open the gate!" Butch said. The agent gave the signal to have the gate opened. "We'll be your security from now on, general." The agent said. "Oh! That's about to change in a few minutes!" Butch said. "I don't understand, sir." The agent said. Butch ignored the agent. "Well, son. It's all yours now." Butch said. "I drove by here a few times, stood outside the walls during the wedding, but I never thought I'd get to go inside, let alone own it!" Kevin said. Moments later, 4 vehicles pull up. 20 men of diverse ethnicity exit the vehicles. "We're here, boss! What's up?" one of the men asked. "You see these clown ass mother fuckers in the black suits standing guard at this place?" Butch asked. "Yeah." The man said. "My sons' gonna be moving in here soon. I want y'all to make sure these, whatever they are, are gone by the time he unpacks his first suitcase. Understand?" Butch said. "You got it, boss man." The man said. "Give them a warning first. If they don't get the fuck out, force them out." Butch said before he and Kevin walked off towards his vehicle. The man, who was one of Butch's top soldiers stared down the agent, trying to intimidate him. The agent did not back down, nor showed any aggression. The man, named Carry, who was given the task by Butch, was a 6-foot muscle bound black man smiled. "This gonna be easy." He said to himself.

No less than 20 minutes had passed, when Butch and his son were riding on the Garden State Parkway heading north when Butch received a called on his cell phone. Butch and his son Kevin were sitting in the back seat while his bodyguard was sitting in the front passenger seat. "Yeah!" Butch answered. Butch could barely hear the call coming in because of all the melee in the background. "Hey! What the fucks going on?" He shouted. "*Boss! Boss! They got us pinned down! we dropping like flies out this mother fucker!!*" his top soldier shouted. Butch could hear the gunfire and screaming. "Fuck!!" Butch shouted. "What's wrong, pop?" Kevin asked. "What's wrong, boss?" his bodyguard asked. "Damn!! Them mother fuckers at the castle taking out our people!" Butch shouted. "Let's turn this mother fucker around then!" the bodyguard said as he cocked back his pistol. "No! let me think this through!!" butch shouted as he put his cell phone on speaker. Guns shots could be heard going off until they were heard far and few in between. Suddenly, there was a dead silence on the phone. "Hello!! Hello!! Yo!" butch shouted. "What the fuck we waiting for, boss? Let's go back there and help!!" the bodyguard shouted. Butch looked depressed as he clicked off his cell phone. "Forget it. Them niggas dead." He said sorrowfully. Butch dropped his cell phone. "Take us home, man!" Kevin said to the driver.

It was around 2pm when Butch and his crew arrived at one of his homes in Morris County,

New Jersey. Coincidently, there were a team of NA agents standing outside his home. They weren't dressed in black suits like other agents but dressed in civilian clothes. Butch and his crew sat in the vehicle for a moment. "What you wanna do boss? Go out guns blazing, or what?" his bodyguard asked. "Nah. Everybody throw y'all weapons out the window. They got us out gunned." Butch said. After they tossed their weapons, one of the agents approached the vehicle. "General Watson. Mr. reed would like to see you inside." The agent said. "Y'all mother fuckers broke into my house?" Butch shouted. "Follow me, general." The agent said in a calm voice.

It was a quiet upscale neighborhood. The nearest house was about 100 yards away. There were no pedestrians walking on the streets. Expecting a police squad car to randomly pass by was rare. Even cops on Butch's payroll didn't drive by unless he gave them a call for a favor.

Butch and his crew came out of the vehicles with their hands in the air. "You can lower your hands, gentlemen." The agent said. The agent told Kevin, the driver and the bodyguard to stay outside while Butch was being escorted inside of his house.

When Butch entered his home, he saw Doug reed sitting on his plush sofa with a cup of tea in his hand. "Hey Butch, my man!" Doug said with a big grin on his face. Butch looked heated. He was about to go after Doug's throat until 2 agents restrained him. "Why you let that shit happened to my men at the castle?!!" Butch shouted. "You just don't get it! Your people are obsolete! My agents watch over you now!" Doug shouted after he smashed the teacup into the wall. "You sick mother fucker!" Butch shouted. "No. No. No, sir! Terrance was a sick mother fucker! I'm being reasonable! That's why I'm going to let you live! That's why I'm going to let your son and the rest of your children live!"" Doug shouted. "What the fuck do you want from me?" Butch asked. "I want you to run the drug business in New Jersey, that's all!" Doug said. Butch dropped his head. Doug stood to his feet. He approached Butch. "From now on, these 8 agents will be your shadow. They will protect you from the law and enemies far and near." Doug said as he reached in his jacket pocket. He pulled out a gold envelope and a note. He handed both to Butch. Butch reluctantly took the envelope and note. This is a list of all the businesses you'll be buying from per unit, at retail prices. Don't open the letter until I'm gone. After you read it, burn it." Doug said before leaving.

Back in Lassenberia, Jenna was at her home with her husband Sheldon having passionate, wild sex. After 15 minutes or so, he rolled off her onto his back, breathing heavily. "Jesus! You weren't like this since our honeymoon!" Sheldon said. "I don't know! Maybe it was the Russian air!" she chuckled.

Moments later, the doorbell rang. Sheldon went to the door wrapped in his bathrobe. "Yeah?" Sheldon shouted through the door. "Sir! His majesty would like a word with the prime minister at the university!" the voice said. "She'll be there!" he shouted. "Yes, Sir!" the voice said. Sheldon headed back towards the bedroom. "Who was it?" Jenna asked. "Your brother-in-law wants to see you at the university." He said. "Oh, god! He wants the report on the Russian mission!" she sighed. "You said the mission was successful! It doesn't matter if your report came a few days later!" Sheldon said. "I know. I know! But we must realize we're not in America anymore, and he is our king." She explained. She pulled her husband towards her, giving him a kiss on the lips. "Marcus is a pussycat. Trust me. he won't blow his top." She said. "He'd better not! I don't want to give a king a black eye!" he said. Jenna and Sheldon stare at each other for a moment in silence. They both burst out laughing. "You're crazy, baby!" she chuckled. "Go, jump in the shower, and see what the man wants!" Sheldon chuckled as he smacked her on her butt cheek.

As Jenna was being driven through the streets in a limousine, and followed by 2 military vehicles, she noticed as she looked out the window 2 NA agents standing guard outside of princess Teresa's mansion. Within that moment, Edward the 2nd came out of the mansion, smiling. Jenna had the look of suspicion on her face but didn't bother to tell her driver to stop to investigate.

Jenna arrived at castle Lassenberia being escorted by 2 Ethiopian born soldiers dressed in Lassenberry uniforms, who happened to be wearing the Ethiopian emblem as an arm band. This was by order of queen Kimberly to have every soldier of Lassenberia to display their country of origin to put an end of confusion between the different refugees.

Inside his chambers, Marcus stood in front of his mirror gazing upon his image. "I am the king. I am the king." He said repeatedly. This was a ritual he held by himself before having a meeting with someone since his coronation.

Once notified of his sister-in-law's arrival, Marcus took a deep breath, checking himself in the mirror once more before leaving his chambers. They met in the throne room, alone. "Hey, sis!" he said cheerfully. "Hello, your majesty." Jenna said as she bowed her head. "Where the hell were you?" he said in a high-pitched voice. "If you must know, spending time with my husband! You're the one who gave me a 2-week period, remember?" she said with sass in her voice. "Come on, sis! I must know what's going on right-a-way!" he shouted. "With-all-due-respect! Calm down!" she said. "I can't calm down! I'm running a country! Not some corner grocery store!" he shouted. "Where's my sister?" she asked. What?" he asked with a confused look. "My sister! Where is she?" she asked. Jenna instantly changed his train of thought. "She's still away, making trade deals." He said. "She been gone for a while now!" she said. "India's' a big country!" he said. "How's your cousin dealing with his new surroundings?" she asked. "He dealing. Why you ask?" he asked. "Just asking, that's all!" she said. "Can we get back to the Russia thing, now?" he asked. Jenna started laughing. "I'm 100 percent positive, I found a new friend." She said.

CHAPTER .43 BRANDON

It was June 23rd when Butch and his son Kevin returned to castle Lassenberry. "You sure you're up for this, son?" Butch asked. "Yeah...I got this, pop." He said. "Let's go, then!" Butch said as they drove pass the gates. As they exited their vehicle, a NA agent approached them. "General Watson. The garrison is ready for your orders, sir." The agent said. "Stop with this general shit! Just call me Mr. Watson!" he said. "Very well, sir." The agent said. "Take us in inside." Butch said. "Yes, sir." The agent said. The agent signaled another agent to pull up in a golf cart. Butch and Kevin hopped in the golf cart. They were driven over the mote as the giant entrance doors were opening. Kevin was in awe as the cart entered the main corridor. "Damn! No wonder they had porter potties at the wedding! My ass would've got lost in this place!" Kevin said.

As they continued their journey riding down the south wing of the castle, Butch frowned upon the aftermath of the skirmish between his men and the NA agents. He shook his head as he stared at the blood stains smeared on the walls, which were parallel to the trail of bullet holes. "Stop! Stop the cart!" he shouted. the driver stopped the cart midway down the corridor. "Is there a problem, sir?" the agent asked. "We'll walk the rest of the way!" Butch said. He and Kevin step out of the cart. "Would you like me to stay around. Sir?" the agent asked. "No! I been in here enough to know my way around! Bye!" Butch said. The driver made a U-turn, heading back towards the exit. "Come on, son! Let me give you a personal tour." He said. Kevin followed his father, heading towards the west wing. "What's that funky smell?" Kevin asked. "Death. Get used to it." Butch said. "You know I can't get that shit out of my head!" Kevin said. "What?" Butch asked. "Pop! You ate that dude's heart!" he said. Butch stopped walking, grabbing his son by the collar with an enraged looked on his face. "I know what the fuck I did! You ain't gotta throw that shit in my face!" Butch shouted. "I meant no disrespect, pop!" Kevin said with fear in his eyes. Butch released his son's collar. "You here now, kid! Ain't no turning back!" Butch said before continuing his walk. Kevin stood there looking up at the elaborate artwork on the high ceiling. "First thing you need to do, is get these guys to clean up this blood-n-shit!" butch's voice echoed through the corridor.

45 minutes had passed. Butch and Kevin were on their way to the north wing after a little

sightseeing. They were critiquing how the place was unkept. "fuck! I gotta take a leak again! The bathroom should be down this hall!" Butch said. He and Kevin went down the corridor until Kevin spotted the sign, restroom. "There it is pop!" he said. "This what happens when you get old, son! It's like carrying around a leaky faucet!" Butch said. Kevin snickered. "Wait here." Butch said. Butch trotted into the bathroom. The bathroom had 5 urinals, 5 stalls and 3 marble top sinks. Behind the sinks was a huge mirror, framed by bright white lights. After doing his business, he stood in front of the mirror to wash his hands. "Fuck!" he shouted when he realized there was no hand soap in the dispenser. He punched the paper towel dispenser when he found it was also empty. He waved the excess water off his hands. He was about to leave until he heard a faint noise coming from one of the stalls. He kicked open each stall until coming to the one closest to the wall. Butch balled up his fist to prepare himself for an attack. He kicked opened the stall. "Don't shoot!!" the man sitting on the toilet shouted. "Brandon? What the fuck you doing in here?" Butch shouted. "I didn't want to get shot!" Brandon said. "Man! You been in here all this time?" Butch shouted as he covered his mouth and nose from the stench coming from the toilet. "Goddamn! I'm about to puke!" Butch shouted. "I heard a bunch of gun fire! I stayed in here! I didn't want anybody to hear the toilet flush!" he explained. "flush the toilet, and let's get outta here!" Butch said. Brandon stumbled when he got off the toilet due of losing feeling in his legs for sitting down for so long.

As they were making their way down the corridor, the 3 men ran into 2 agents. "Mr. hart. Would you come with us, sir?" one agent said. Brandon looked nervous. "Why? I didn't do anything!" said cried. "Take it easy! He's with us!" butch said. "Sorry, Mr. Watson. Ours orders are from Mr. reed, if Mr. Hart is found, were to take him with us." the agent said. "I'm giving you an order agent! Leave him be!" Butch shouted. "Protocol forbids your orders to override that of Mr. Reed's." The agent said. The 2 agents apprehended Brandon as he struggled to free himself. Kevin lunged forth to help before his father grabbed him. "Stay out of this one, son. Let's finish searching this place." Butch said.

Brandon was taken outside, handcuffed from behind and forced into a black SUV, accompanied by 4 agents. The SUV drove off the castle grounds. About a mile away from castle Lassenberry, a black sack cloth was placed over Brandon's head. The sack cloth was pulsating from Brandon's heavy breathing underneath.

Hours later, Brandon felt the vehicle come to a complete stop. He heard the engine cut off. He was then dragged out of the vehicle. After being led to an undisclosed place, the sack cloth was lifted from his head. He found himself Standing in the middle of some creepy looking laboratory straight out of a 1950's science fiction movie. "Where am I?" he asked. The agents did not answer him. Suddenly 2 figures came into the room. The first to step to the door was a middle-aged Caucasian man wearing a lab coat. The other person entering the room was wearing a suit, but had a demonic ceramic mask concealing the person's identity.

"Mr. Hart?" the man in the lab coat asked. "What do you want from me? Why am I here?" Brandon asked. The man walked over to a stainless-steel table and uncovered a jet injector syringe. He walked over towards Brandon. Without hesitation, he put the injector to Brandon's neck and squeezed the trigger. Brandon did not flinch from the injection. "What the hell you put in me?" Brandon asked. The man uncovered a microscope that was also on the table. "Bring Mr. hart here." The man said to the agents. "Take a look through the lens of the microscope, Mr. Hart." The man said. Brandon was hesitant. "Come on, Mr. Hart. It's just a microscope. It won't bite." The man said. Brandon leaned over to investigate what was through the lens of the microscope. "It looks like some type of microchip!" Brandon said. "Exactly, Mr. Hart!" the man said. "Is that the thing you injected into me?" Brandon asked. The man didn't say a word. He reached into the pocket of his lab coat and pulled out a small round red object. The object had a stem protruding from it. He reaches into his other pocket and pulled out a cigarette lighter. He lit the stem and tossed it across the room. It then exploded, causing everyone in the room except for the 2 agents to flinch. The sound caused temporary deafness to everyone. The man then pulled out a small object resembling a car remote. The man then handed the remote to the person wearing the ceramic mask. "That chip you've just seen has the same amount of concussive force as that cherry bomb, Mr. hart." the man said. The person wearing the ceramic mask approached Brandon. "Listen very closely, Mr. Hart. You now belong to me. If you want to live, you'll do as exactly what I instruct you to do. "Why are you people doing this to me? I was just a go-between!" Brandon cried. "Stop sniveling! I'm sending you on a mission to the island nation of Lassenberia! There, you will assassinate king Marcus! After your mission is complete, you will rendezvous with one of our agents in South Africa, where you may return to the United States. We will then extract the chip from your neck. Then Mr. Hart, you can live your life as a free man." The man wearing the mask said. Brandon dropped his. "When… do you want it done?" he asked in a defeated tone. "There's a plane waiting for you as we speak. Oh! One more thing, Mr. Hart. This remote has an unlimited range. If you're not in South Africa within 5 days, BOOM!!!" the masked man said before the sack cloth was placed over Brandon's head.

June 24th was when the plane carrying Brandon Hart arrived in Kempton Park, Ekurhuleni, Gauteng, south Africa. Before leaving the plane, he was uncuffed and had the sack cloth removed from over his head. Brandon was literally tossed off the plane onto the tarmac, landing on his stomach. Brandon got up and brushed himself off. "5 days, Mr. Hart!!" the agent shouted over the sound of the spinning turbines before closing the hatch. Brandon had to quickly run from the plane as it made a U-turn down the runway.

After hours of trekking on foot from Kempton Park, Brandon finally arrived on the outskirts of Johannesburg. He was stripped of all his cash before leaving the plane. All he had on his person was his driver's license and a pack of chewing gum. Tired and exhausted, Brandon couldn't help but notice giant posters of Marcus and Kimberly dressed in royal garb, holding hands on the side of high-rise buildings, with the sunrise behind them in the background. The sign below the poster was written in English, Zulu, Afrikaans, and Xhosa. It read in bold letters, **A NEW AND BRIGHTER FUTURE HAS COME TO JOHANNESBURG.**

Brandon had stopped one of the locals on the street. "Is there a Lassenberian embassy around here?" he asked. The old black man didn't speak a word of English. "Forget it!" Brandon said before taking off into the thick of the city.

Moments later he came across a (SAP) officer at a traffic intersection, directing traffic. "Officer! Officer! please tell me you speak English!" he desperately asked. "What is the problem?" the officer asked. "I need to know if there's a Lassenberian embassy here, in the city!" Brandon asked. "It's not in operation. The facility itself is still under construction." The officer said. "Is there another one, in the neighboring countries?" Brandon asked. "The nearest Lassenberian embassy is in Maputo, Mozambique, about 500 kilometers from here." The officer said. "Listen! I don't have a dime to my name, officer! I need to get to Mozambique as quickly as possible!" Brandon said. "That is your problem, sir! I'm busy! Now please step back and let me do my job!" the officer said. "fuck!" Brandon screamed before taking off. "Ngikuthuka, wena mulatto bastard!" the officer said before blowing the whistle to direct traffic.

The following day, Brandon made it far as the Witbank Nature Reserve with the help from an Afrikaan man belonging to a nearby yacht club. The old man took mercy on Brandon's plight. Brandon's story was that his wife was leaving him and taking the kids. The old man empathized with Brandon's story. Brandon had a big smile on his face as he listened to the man's war stories until things took a turn for the worse. The old man's vehicle blew a tire, rolling into a ditch off the Albertina Sisulu Road. Brandon made the decision to help the old man change his tire. Not only did he help with the tire, but he also stayed with the old man until roadside help arrived to tow the vehicle out of the ditch. An hour had passed when the tow truck showed up. Brandon noticed the old man and the tow truck driver went off to have a lengthy conversation. Once they were done conversing, the old man walked over to Brandon. He looked towards the sky. "It's getting dark!" he said. He reached into his pocket, pulling out his wallet once again after paying the tow truck driver. He pulled out a wad of cash, handing it over to Brandon. "What's this for?" Brandon asked. "Sorry, young man. This is where we part." He said. "Why? I need you right now!" Brandon shouted. "Ever since the end of apartheid, they aren't too fond of whites where we're are going, especially at night!" he said. "I really need your, help!" Brandon cried. "That's 13 thousand Rands. That should be more than enough for where you're going." He said. "How am I supposed to get there? On foot?" Brandon asked. The old man sighed. "Here. Take my car." He said. He handed Brandon the keys. "You're letting me take your car?" Brandon asked with skepticism. "I'm very well off, young man!" he said with a grin. He pulled out a pen a paper. "This is my number. "Give me a call when you reach your destination. I'll have someone come retrieve the car." He said. Brandon began to get teary eyed. He gave the old man a firm hug. "Thank you, so much! I owe you, big time!" he cried. Brandon ran over and jumped into the vehicle. He sped off into the night.

It was June 26th. The sun was coming up over the vast horizon when Brandon arrived in Maputo, Mozambique. He asked officials where was the Lassenberian embassy. They pointed him in the right direction.

It wasn't too long when he drove up to the embassy gate. He was exhausted from his long trek, but it didn't stop him from getting into the embassy. He begged the officials to get him in contact with someone from Lassenberia.

It took a few hours until he contacted Kent Mooney. "Kent! I need to get to the island!" he said. "What's wrong?" Kent asked. "Since Edward the 2nd left, I've been kicked out of the loop! My life might be in danger!" Brandon cried. "Where are you?" Kent asked. "I'm at the embassy in Maputo! It's in Mozambique!" he said. "I know where it is!" Kent said. "Can you get a plane or boat out here, quick?" Brandon asked. "We're still getting the bugs out of air traffic control. It might take a day or 2. As far as a boat, I'll have to go through the proper channels." Kent said. "The proper channels? Son-of-a-bitch! My life is on the line, here!" Brandon shouted. "Take it easy! I'm just pulling your leg!" Kent chuckled. "You're a real jerk!" Brandon said. "I'll have a boat come get you tonight. Be at Port Maputo by mid night." Kent said.

Brandon was on the pier of Port Maputo waiting for his ride. it was 15 minutes after midnight when he started to panic, pacing in circles, constantly staring at his wristwatch. He grabbed his neck and started scratching at the spot where he was injected. The locals working on the pier stopped to see why this man was acting crazed. Brandon began crying out for help when he realized all eyes were on him. Suddenly, the sounds of a motorboat was heard of inf the distance. "Brandon? Brandon Hart?" the voice coming from the boat shouted. Brandon heard the voice and began laughing hysterically. He began jumping up and down, waving his hands in the air. "Over here! Over here!" he chuckled.

The motorboat pulled up to the pier. There were 3 albino soldiers on board. One of them hopped on the pier to greet Brandon. "Mr. Hart! I am Keita, captain of the Lassenberian search and rescue-." He said before being interrupted. "Yeah, yeah, yeah! Let's just get fuck on the boat and get out of here!" Brandon shouted. "Ok, sir. Let's go!" Keita said. He helped Brandon come aboard. The motorboat took off into the night across the choppy waters.

About a half hour later, they arrived on the southern shores of Lassenberia. Brandon was taken to the search and rescue facility. "We can have an escort to take you to your fiancé, princess Teresa, sir." Keita said "Never mind that! Take me to see the king!" Brandon said. The soldiers looked at each other with puzzled looks on their faces. "Sir. We just can't let you see the king without going through the proper channels." Keita explained. "Fuck the proper channels! I'm practically part of the royal family! Now, take me to see the king!" Brandon shouted. "It's late, sir. I promise you; you'll see the king at first light" Keita said. Brandon bent over, grabbing his knees. "Fuck! he shouted as he stood tall. Keita pressed the button on his commlink. "Search and Rescue to Bravo command, in come." Keita said. *"Bravo command to search and rescue. Report."* The voice over the commlink said. "I need a vehicle to take Mr. Hart to the borough of Jabbo." Keita said. *"A vehicle for Mr. Hart. Copy."* The voice responded. "Your ride should be here any moment, sir." Keita said. "This is un-fucking believable! "Brandon shouted. "Are you ok, sir? What are those marks on your neck?" Keita asked. "Nothing! I had an accident!" Brandon said. "Wait here." Keita said. Keita went into his office. He stood before a computerized safe. He then punched in a 6-digit code. He unveiled many vials of GLC. He grabbed one before securing the safe. He then grabbed a cotton ball from the first aid kit. He went back to where Brandon and his men were. "Here, sir." Keita said. Brandon took the cotton ball and the 1-ounce vial of GLC. He dabbed the green cure-all on to his wound. Within seconds it disappeared. "This is amazing!" he said. Brandon then tilted his head back, allowing the remaining GLC to drip into his mouth. "sir!" Keita shouted. "I have a cold!" Brandon said as he shrugged his shoulders.

It was around 3 in the morning when the vehicle carrying Brandon arrived in front of princess Teresa's mansion. Standing outside the mansion were 2 NA agents. "What the hell is this? Why are these guys here?" Brandon asked the driver. "Forgive me, sir. My English is not so good." The driver said. "Never mind! You can let me out here!" Brandon said. "Sir?" the driver said. Frustrated, Brandon just hopped out of the vehicle. Once Brandon left the vehicle, his driver drove off. Brandon then approached the 2 NA agents. "State your business, sir?" one agent asked. "I'm here to see my fiancé, princess Teresa!" he said. "The princess is preoccupied, sir. Unless ordered by the king and queen of Lassenberia, no one is to see the princess." The agent said. "Are you kidding me?" he asked. The agents said nothing. "Fuck this!" Brandon said as he was about to barge his way through. One agent grabbed him by the wrist. "Hey! Let go!" Brandon shouted. "Sorry, sir. I can't allow you to enter the premises." The agent said. Brandon found it hard to break away from the Agent's grip.

Moments later, the agents and Brandon were blinded by the bright headlights of a military vehicle coming down the street. The young soldiers driving in the jeep were from the Ethiopian clan called Zewde, named after the woman who led the migration from Addis Ababa. The soldiers were just children in their early teens, yet they were trained in hand-to-hand combat and firing small arms.

"What's going on here?" one soldier asked. "Hey, kid! Tell these guys to move out of my way!" Brandon said. "Who are you, sir?" the young soldier asked. "I'm Brandon hart! Fiancé to princess Teresa!" he said. "You heard the man! Let him pass!" the soldier demanded. "We are not to let anyone pass unless it's ordered from the king or queen." The agent said. The 3 young soldiers grabbed their sub-machine guns and hopped out of the jeep. "I'm not going to tell you again!" the soldier said as he pointed his weapon at the agents. "Hold on! Let me move out of the way first!" Brandon shouted out of fear. Before things could get out of control, Edward the 2nd came out, covered in a bathrobe. "What the hell?" Brandon shouted. "Oh, shit! It's Brandon! How the hell are ya?" Edward the 2nd said with a smile. The soldiers lowered their weapons and stood at attention. "forgive us, Lord Lassenberry for disturbing your sleep!" the soldier said. Brandon looked infuriated. "My Lord! Can I talk to you, in private?" he asked. "Of Course!" Edward the 2nd cheerfully said. "Could you tell this agent to let go of me?" Brandon asked. "Let him go." Edward the 2nd said. He led Brandon over to the side of the mansion. "I thought we were going inside to talk!" Brandon said. "Oh! I 'm going back inside! But I don't know about you going in!" Edward the 2nd said. "Where's Teresa?" Brandon asked. "She's safe inside!" Edward the 2nd said. "Can I see her?" Brandon asked. Edward the 2nd glanced up at the night sky before staring Brandon in the face. "She's not feeling good. She's still fucked up from what happened to our family. I decided to stay by her side until she snaps out of it." He said. "It's ok! I'm here! Now, could you take me to see Marcus?" Brandon asked. "Does he know you're here?" Edward the 2nd asked. "No." Brandon said. "Agents!!' Edward the 2nd shouted, alerting his 2 agents. They came running around the side of the mansion. "Yes, my lord." One agent said. "Take Mr. Hart to my residence. Make sure he doesn't come out until I say so." Edward the 2nd ordered. Brandon looked shocked. "What?" he shouted. "Come with us, Mr. Hart." The agent said. Brandon tried to make a dash for the entrance of the mansion but was apprehended before he could grab the doorknob. The young soldiers looked puzzled. "Help me! They're taking me away!" Brandon shouted.

"Y'all ain't gonna do a god damn thing!" Edward the 2nd shouted as he came from around the side of the mansion. "Sorry, Mr. Hart. Lord Lassenberry just gave us an order." The young soldier said. "You're damn right I gave you an order! Now get back in your jeep and start patrolling, or whatever you boys do!" Edward the 2nd ordered. "I have to see the king!! I have to see the king!!" Brandon shouted as he struggled to slip away from the agent's grasp. "When you get back to my place, bring back more agents to double my security! While you're at it, get rid of those soldiers! Quietly. Make it look like the albinos did it." Edward the 2nd whispered to the agents. "Yes, my lord." One agent said before they hauled Brandon away. The young soldiers returned to their jeep and drove off. Edward the 2nd went back inside the mansion.

It was around 4 in the morning when Brandon was pacing the attic of Edward the 2nd's residence where he was confined to. He knocked over shelves and smashed the mirror on the dresser out of desperation. He kept banging on the door. "Let me out!! I must see the king!! It's a matter of life and death!!" he cried. There were 2 NA agents standing on the other side of the door at parade rest. Brandon's begging and pleading went unanswered.

Around 8 in the morning, IST Time, a 300-foot yacht called the Jabbo was leaving the Tuticorin seaport. On board the luxury vessel Kimberly stood at the stern waving back at her hosts, who were President Singh Bihari and his family.

The yacht was being escorted out to sea by 4 Indian frigates. Kimberly's trusted aid and bodyguard, Ali stood by her side cradling his sub-machine gun. "So, what do you think, your highness?" Ali asked. "4 gallons of GLC in exchange for buying up all the land in Assam, Madhya Pradesh, Uttar Pradesh and Karnataka? I'd say we came out on top." Kimberly said. Standing in the background were 52 Lassenberian soldiers, most of Somalian descent were clowning around. Ali took notice of their unprofessional behavior. "Excuse me, your highness!" Ali said as he went off to discipline his troops. Kimberly watched as the shores of Tamil Nadu became more distant. She wore a red sari given to her as a gift from the first lady of India. She began massaging her belly. "It's seems like we're coming closer to ruling the world, kid." She whispered to her unborn child.

As soon after Edward the 2nd landed in Lassenberia, Kimberly gathered Ali and his troops to leave for India, which she planned to visit a month earlier. Only her husband and Ali knew of her mission. She decided to take the royal yacht instead of taking the royal private jet. Her first stop was in the city of Dwarka at the Gulf of Kutch. President Bihari new of her arrival and what Lassenberia had to offer. He told his staff that it was odd that the queen of Lassenberia would come to India by water, and not by air. Still-in-all he decided to fly from New Deli to greet her.

Kimberly, her entourage, and her security team were amazed by the sights and architecture of places like Kochi, Kolkata, Bengaluru, Agra Mumbai, Jaipur, and Deli. It was all impressive to Kimberly, but when flying over Madhya Pradesh Kimberly asked the president why he didn't mention the region below. His explanation was that it was the land, like so many others, the land of undesirables. Kimberly requested to land in Madhya. President Bihari was reluctant to have the plane land in this region. But he gave in because of the rumors he heard about the miraculous effects of the GLC. "Undesirables deserve a chance for a prosperous life." Were her words to the president.

Bhopal, the governor of Madhya made a last-minute effort to accommodate the president and his honored guest.

To make the tour of Madhya more interesting, Kimberly rented a herd of elephants for the group to travel the land on. It was an amusing ride for Kimberly and Ali until they came upon a small village who looked like the poorest of the poor. "This is sad, your highness! It reminds me too much of my homeland before you and the king arrived!" Ali said.

Malnutrition and leprosy were common amongst these people. "What is the world health organization doing about this?" Kimberly asked. "To be honest, your highness, there's little to do! Not just here, but across other regions! Fresh clean water is scares! We bring water trucks to the area once a week, but babies are still dying from poor hygienic conditions! To be more profound, the pharmaceutical companies are drain on our economy!" the president said. "Until now, Mr. president!" Kimberly boldly said. "What do you mean?" the president asked. "Ali! When we return home, I want 10 cargo ships transported here!" Kimberly ordered. "Yes, your highness!" he said. "Mr. president! I'm going to change the landscape here, and in other regions that are in need!" Kimberly said. "I think we're in the company of a savior." The presidents said to the governor. "I don't consider myself a savior, Mr. president." Kimberly said.

Back in Lassenberia Brandon was still in the attic trying to figure out how to escape without alerting the NA agents on the other side of the door. He tried to open the window, but it was sealed tight due to a bad paint job done by a worker from the painting contractors. He looked at his watch. He realized that his time was ending. He had one day to complete his mission. He had one day to assassinate the king of Lassenberia and make it back to Johannesburg.

A few hours later, the royal yacht Jabbo returned to the shores of Lassenberia after a long trade mission. The queen saw the heads and aids of the different regions of Lassenberia standing on the pier to greet her. Lady Ellen, the baroness of Braxton. Stephan, head of Lassenberia's textile industry, Ukerewe, Baron of the Pale lands, prime minister Jenkins, Edward the 2nd, Earl of Edward, members of the high council from the Zewde clan, Kent Mooney, founding father, keeper of the 48 laws of Lassenberia and Yevi Bantu, governess of little Africa.

There were 12 NA agents gathered around Edward the 2nd as his security. He made his way through the crowd with their aid to be the first to greet her. "What's up, your highness!!" Edward the 2nd shouted with his arms spread out. Kimberly looked terrified as she stood at the top of the gangplank. "Stay vigilant!" she whispered to Ali. Ali was locked and loaded as he stood behind his queen. "Come on down!! We missed you!!" Edward the 2nd shouted with a big grin on his face. Kimberly's showed a sigh of relief when she heard the words- "Make way for the king!!" Someone shouted amongst the crowd. Edward the 2nd on the other hand, looked like a defeated man as he turned towards the crowd. The crowd parted like the sea referenced in the bible. King Marcus gallantly walked through the crowd, escorted by 12 soldiers of the Pale Horseman.

Back at the residence of Edward the 2nd, Brandon had his face pressed against the window as he watched off in the distance the luxury yacht and the ant size crowd of people standing at the pier. He had one day left to fulfill his mission and make it back to the United States.

He looked down at the ground. He stepped back away from the window. He walked over and stood on the bed to practice jumping off it to simulate the perfect landing. He kept staring at wooden chair across the room. The agents standing outside the door looked at each other as they heard the thumping noise coming from inside. Neither agent bothered to investigate.

Back at the pier, Edward the 2nd stepped to the side so his cousin could greet the queen. "Must be good, to have it all." Edward the 2nd said to Marcus as he walked by. Marcus ignored his cousin's words and continued his walk towards the top of the gangplank. Marcus bowed to Kimberly then kissed the back of her hand. "Damn, nigga! Why don't you just bend her over and lick her asshole?!" Edward the 2nd whispered to himself.

"How was your mission, my love? Marcus asked Kimberly as he led her by the hand down the gangplank. "Very lucrative!" she chuckled. "Sounds exciting!" Marcus said. "So, what's been going on since my departure, my love?" she asked. "Kent just told me for the first time today that Brandon arrived a few days ago and nobody knows where he is!" Marcus said. "Did you have them check Teresa's estate?" she asked. "Yeah! But still no sign of him!" Marcus said. "We should have all available personnel check every borough and every home." Kimberly said. "Sounds like a plan." Marcus said.

The crowd bowed their heads as the royal couple reached the bottom of the gangplank. Ali had previously ordered him troops to make sure the crowd made room for them to pass by. Edward the 2nd made it his business to walk alongside them. One of the soldiers approached Edward th2nd to separate him from the royal couple. "What the hell is your problem, young man?" he shouted. "Stand back, sir!" the young soldier said in a stern voice. "It's alright, soldier. Stand down." Marcus said. The young soldier then released Edward the 2nd's arm.

There was an armored plated SUV waiting for the royal couple to take them to the castle. Another young soldier from the Zewde clan held the back-passenger door open for them. Queen Kimberly waved to the crowd before entering the vehicle. Marcus entered after her. The royal couple was shocked when Edward the 2nd scooched himself in the vehicle next to Marcus. "What is your problem?" Kimberly asked. "Am I not part of the royal family? Am I not heir to the throne?" Edward the 2nd asked. "Heir to the throne?!!" she shouted. "Yes! I am next in line, cuz!" he responded. "You forget, I have a son?" Kimberly said before the soldier closed the door. The vehicle drove off. "He's a toddler!" Edward the 2nd shouted. "Both of you, stop it!" Marcus shouted. "No disrespect, cuz. But right is right." Edward the 2nd said. "I said stop it!" Marcus said.

"It was said Brandon arrived here. Do you know where he is?" Kimberly asked. "I ain't nobody's fucking babysitter!" he shouted. "And you want to be king?!! Please!!" Kimberly scoffed. "Let's talk about this at the castle, please!!" Marcus shouted as he glanced at the driver and Ali, who was sitting up front. There were also 4 armed guards hanging on to the side of the vehicle as it was heading towards the castle.

When they arrived at the castle, Kimberly spotted her son being accompanied by the nanny. "Mommy!!" the little prince shouted as he yanked away from the nanny and ran off towards his mother. Kimberly kneeled and grabbed her son, lifting him high into the air. "Ain't that sweet! Edward the 2nd said. Kimberly turned to him with her son in her arms. "How are you and Viola coming along? You guys make any babies yet?" she said in a sarcastic tone. Edward the 2nd played the question off with a chuckle. "I was done with that 5150 shit for a while now. I'm out here staring out fresh!" he said. Oh, really? Who do you have your eye on?" Kimberly asked. Edward the 2nd turned to his cousin Marcus. "How's relations with your African subjects?" he asked. "Well, anyway! I've prepared a dinner show for your return, my love!" Marcus said. "Thank you, my love!" Kimberly said before planting a kiss on her husband's cheek. "I invited a bunch of dignitaries from the motherland and the middle east! This is going to be a phenomenal night! Let me tell you, the entertainment I brought over here, is off the chain!"" Marcus boasted. "I am invited, my queen?" Edward the 2nd said to Kimberly jokingly. "Yeah, sure!" Kimberly said nonchalantly. "Say, cuz. Can we meet up in a little bit, so you can debrief me on what's going?" Edward the 2nd asked Marcus. "No problem! Meet me in the throne room in a couple of hours." Marcus said reluctantly. Edward the 2nd summoned over a soldier standing at his post. The soldier came over. "Yo kid. Give me a tour of the surrounding area." He said. The soldier nervously looked over towards Marcus for confirmation. Find your relief first, then take him!" Marcus said. "Yes, your majesty!" the young soldier said. Edward the 2nd followed the young soldier. "I don't think it's safe to involve him in our foreign relations." Kimberly said. "My love! He is a Lassenberry! me, our son, Terry, and our unborn child, is all what's left of our bloodline! It would be a sin to leave him out of the loop!" Marcus explained. "But my love!" she cried. "But nothing! Just meet us in the throne room later!" Marcus said before walking away. Ali approached Kimberly. "Is everything ok, my queen?" he asked. "I don't know! This is what I want you to do. Get a couple of your troops and keep an eye on Edward's residence tonight. Tell them to keep their distance, if possible." She said. "Yes, your highness." Ali said before getting back into the vehicle. Kimberly began playing with her son by tickling his belly.

After Edward the 2nd was given a tour of the castle and the area surrounding it, he was escorted to the throne room by the young soldier. In the throne room Kimberly, King Marcus, Kent, and Sheldon were waiting for him to show up. 2 guards entered the room. "Your majesty! I present the Earl of Edward!" one of the soldiers shouted. Edward the 2nd entered the throne room in a jovial mood. "What's up my people?" he shouted. Marcus glanced at the digital clock on the wall. "Take a seat." he said.

There was a round wooden table set up in the middle of the throne room. Edward the 2nd took a seat in one of empty chairs. "What on the agenda?" he asked as he rubbed his hands together. "You already know Kent. He's now the protector of our laws and what we hold dear." Marcus said. Kent and Edward reached across the table to shake hands. "Long time, no see!" Edward the 2nd said. "Good to see you again, Lord Lassenberry." Kent said. "This our prime minister and the queen's sister, Jenna Jenkins. "Marcus said. Edward the 2nd walked around the table to shake and kiss the back of her hand. Sheldon had a grimace expression on his face. "I think we met before! Anyway, it's a pleasure to meet you cousin!" he said. "And finally, this is her husband, Sheldon Bartholomew. He's the royal scribe, or shall I say, the keeper of secrets!" Marcus chuckled. Edward the 2nd walked over to shake his hand. "You must be a secure nigga, her not taking your last name…I'm just fucking with you, brother!" he chuckled. Kimberly sneered at his comment. "Let's settle down and get to the business at hand!" Marcus said. Marcus turned to his wife. "Well, my visit to India was a positive. We now have 4 provinces there. On top of that, we have a large migration of women and children with serious physical deficiencies scheduled to come to our shores." Kimberly said. "How many people we're talking about?" Edward the 2nd asked. "We have sufficient space." She said. "You approve of this shit, cuz?" Edward the 2nd asked Marcus. There was a moment of silence coming from Marcus. Edward the 2nd could see the uncertainty in his face. "Yes… I have confidence in my queen's judgement." Marcus said. Jenna and Kent glance at each other, also noticing Marcus's hesitance. "For the record! Do we have a number of migrants coming?" Sheldon asked. "!0 cargo ships. I would say a thousand per ship. Give or take a few hundred." Kimberly said. "God damn!" Edward the 2nd shouted. "Like I said! We have the space!" she said.

Suddenly, the meeting was interrupted as one of the guards standing outside entered the throne room. "Your majesty. I present to you commander Ntsay with a very urgent message!" the guard announced. Ntsay stepped in and approached the table, dressed in uniform. He greeted his king with the Lassenberian salute by placing his right fist over his heart, simultaneously bowing his head. "Speak, commander." Marcus said. "Your majesty. The bodies of 3 soldiers from the Zewde clan were just discovered floating off the shores of the Pale lands." He said. Marcus quickly stood from his seat. Everyone except for Edward the 2nd looked shocked. "From what the reports said it appears their necks were snapped, your majesty." Ntsay said. "Damn! I thought those albinos were nice people!" Edward the 2nd said with a smirk on his face. "Where's Ukerewe?" Marcus asked. "He has a team of his Pale horseman investigating the crime scene, your majesty." Ntsay said. "Shut down the island, commander! No one comes in or out, until further notice!" Kimberly shouted. "No, my love! We have important guests arriving tonight! It'll be bad for business if we cancel! Commander! Make sure no one leaves the island until I give further notice!" Marcus said. Edward the 2nd looked impressed. "Yes, your majesty." Ntsay said before leaving the throne room. "So, what'll we do?" Jenna asked. "What you're going to do, is make sure the gathering runs smoothly tonight! I want the highest level of security posted within a 2-mile radius around the castle!" Marcus said.

It was around 8pm UTC time, when Brandon continued to quietly pry open the window that stood between him and freedom from the hands of Edward the 2nd. He had 4 hours to complete his mission and get back to the motherland to be extracted by the NA agent. Some success was made until a crack appeared in one of the windowpanes. Instead of pushing from the sides, he began applying force more towards the sill. Even though he was being held captive against his will, Brandon was not denied a great deal of sustenance. A diet of fresh fruits, vegetables, and a south African stew called Potjiekos kept him from hunger. The downside was that the nearest bathroom was one level down from where he was being held. He was only given a metal bucket and a roll of toilet paper to relieve and clean himself. The smell of his own excrement and a plate of rotting leftovers became too much to bare causing him to cover his nose and mouth with a pillowcase.

Back at castle Lassenberia, Edward the 2nd played as his older cousin's shadow, following King Marcus around as guests started arriving. He and Marcus were both dressed in their traditional lassenberry uniforms originated by their uncle. The difference was that Marcus's uniform was decorated with 5 extra medals from foreign dignitaries that considered the royal family of Lassenberia as allies. Marcus received the Royal Order of the Ndlovukazi from the king of Swaziland himself, with the title of Grand Master. The African king considered Marcus his brother across the water.

Kimberly was in her private quarters on the south side of the castle getting ready to greet the guests. She stood in front of a body sized mirror incased within a gold frame as 4 of her aids tended to her hair, make-up, and wardrobe. She had a worried look on her face as she stared into the mirror. "What is wrong, my Queen? Are you not pleased with your hair style?" one aid asked her. "No of course not, Edna! It looks fabulous! It's just my woman's intuition kicking in!" she said. "You're what, my queen?" Edna asked. "Never mind!" Kimberly said with a sad look on her face.

Elsewhere in the ballroom, a handful of foreign leaders, their spouses and top aides were standing around mingling with each other. There were giant flags mounted around the walls being each nation's heads of state in attendance that night. In the middle of the ballroom were 2 50-foot long solid oak wood tables with white linen table clothes draped over them. Servants were walking around dressed in black tie and tails carrying trays either with flutes of expensive champagne or appetizers on them. There was a 40-piece orchestra performing classical music on the newly constructed stage built on the opposite of the exit.

"Why can't my robots help with security, cuz? You know as well as I do, they're way more capable then these fucking refugees!" Edward the 2nd whispered. "You're right about one thing, cousin. They're, your robots, and you should keep them as far away from my troops!" Marcus whispered. "At least give them their weapons back!" Edward the 2nd pleaded. Marcus turned to him, placing his hands on his shoulders. "Relax! I have a whole army and navy now, cuz! Can't nobody touch us!" Marcus whispered before walking away. "Tell that shit to those 3 kids that got their necks snapped!" Edward the 2nd whispered to himself.

It was around mid-night when Brandon's luck had changed. He was finally able to wedge his fingers between the sill to slowly open the window. He checked the door before lifting the window high enough so that his head could fit through. He crawled out the window headfirst. He focused his attention on the bushes below before taking the plunge. He landed face first into the bushes causing scratches and bruises. His legs landed on the concrete, causing him to dislocate his right knee. The excruciating pain from the fall showed on his face but he stood to his feet limping to his goal. Brandon stayed away from the streetlights, lurking behind houses and other structures. He came across a signpost. On the signpost was the figure of a castle with 30km printed next to it. "30 Kilometers?!! Fuck!!" he whispered to himself. He followed the arrow on the signpost.

Back at the castle, the party for queen Kimberly was in full swing. There were politicians, high ranking military officials and people of nobility from all parts of Africa, Madagascar and the other neighboring island nations mingling with one another as the orchestra played classical jazz music. The crowd applauded as Kimberly made her grand entrance. As Kimberly was making her way through the crowd, one of the guests, who was the prime minister from Ethiopia asked the queen about princess Teresa's wellbeing. "She's doing much better!" was her answer.

Kimberly's gown was emerald green made of silk with a red silk shoulder sash. Her emerald, diamond studded ball room heels were hidden due to her gown reaching the floor until her sister Jenna told her to raise her gown. Her fingernail and toenail polish, which had diamond studs embedded in them matched her gown as well. Her locks were done a in traditional Somalian hairdo which stood high as 2 feet.

Edward the 2nd sat in a corner with a drink in his hand, watching her with a sneer on his face as she made her way through the crowd. His losing battle with alcohol became obvious when he threw a piece of ice from his glass at one of the guests as young lady walked by. The young African woman felt the object being thrown at her and turned towards Edward the 2nd. "What the fuck you looking at?" he said. It was quite clear that the young woman didn't understand English. She just smiled and walked away.

Well into the party, Edward the 2nd's consumption of alcohol was so out of control, he staggered through the crowd bumping into guests, making his way to his cousin. Standing next to king Marcus was Kimberly and the king and queen of Morocco. Both couples just finished making a toast to future endeavors. It was Kimberly who spotted Edward the 2nd coming towards them. "Oh, my god! Not this again!" She whispered as she gave off a faux smile gritting her teeth. "What's wrong, my love?" Marcus asked. "Would you all excuse me?" Kimberly said as she handed her husband her drink. She quickly intercepted Edward the 2nd before he confronted Marcus. "Where do you think you're going?" she asked as she grabbed his arm. "Why the fuck there ain't no statue of my uncle around here, when he started all this shit!" Edward the 2nd shouted. "Get over here!" she shouted as she pulled him to the side. Guests standing nearby noticed the uneasiness between the 2. Edward the 2nd yanked his arm away. "Get your damn hand off me! I'm the true king! Y'all belong to me!" he said slurring his speech. "If you don't calm down, I'll have you arrested!" she shouted as she looked around for aid. "Excuse me!" Marcus said to his quests. He rushed over to where his wife and cousin were standing. Marcus looked furious. "What's the problem?" he asked. "The problem dear cousin, is that you're disrespecting Uncle Eddie's legacy by not having a giant ass statue of him on this fucking island!" Edward the 2nd said. "That's it!" Marcus said before snapping his fingers, summoning 2 armed guards over. The 2 guards made their way through the crowd. "Yes, your majesty?" 1 guard said. "Escort Lord Lassenberry out of here and have someone drive him to his residence and keep him there until further notice!" Marcus said. "Yes, your majesty." The guard said.

About a couple of miles away from the castle, Brandon was literally hopping on one leg as he approached the first line of sentries. "Halt!" 1 guard shouted, pointing his machine gun at Brandon. "You have to let me get to the castle! I have to see the king!" Brandon shouted as his hands were raised in the air. At this time, 4 more guards came over, forcing Brandon to the ground. "Who are you?" the guard shouted as Brandon was being searched. "I'm Brandon Hart! Fiancé to the King's sister, Terry!" he shouted. "Your, who?" the guard asked. "I said I'm Brandon Hart!" he shouted. "This is the man they've been looking for!" the guard said. "Radio into the castle that we're bringing in Brandon Hart!" another guard as the other guards helped him off the ground. At the same time, Edward the 2nd was being escorted in a dignified manner to a vehicle, despite being loud and using explicit language towards the guards. "Y'all niggas better recognize a true king when you see one!" he shouted.

Before the vehicle carrying edward the 2nd could pull off, the jeep carrying Brandon pulled up. Edward the 2nd was focused enough to see Brandon being aided out of the jeep. "Oh, shit!" he said to himself. Brandon was leaning on one of the guards as they were headed to a golf cart to enter the castle.

Inside the castle, Marcus captured everyone's attention by clinking his champagne flute with a fork. "Everyone! Everyone! Could I have your attention please?" he shouted as Kimberly stood by his side. The crowd became silent. "I would like to thank all of you for coming out from such great distances! I would like to end the evening in a final salute to my lovely wife and queen of Lassenberia, Kimberly! so, if you all would follow me outside so you all can enjoy the festivities!" he shouted. "What are you up to?" Kimberly whispered in his ear. "You'll see, my love!" he said. The crowd was excited to see what Marcus had in store for the queen as they followed the royal couple and a few armed guards outside. Ali was walking next to Kimberly. "What surprise does the king have for me?" she whispered in his ear. "Rumor has it, my queen, there will be a fireworks spectacle." He whispered. Kimberly nodded her head, smiling.

It was around 2am UTC time when the crowd arrived outside. Moments later the first skyrockets burst into the air. The crowd was in awe as the night sky lit up. Kimberly had a smile from ear-to-ear. Her smile didn't last long as she saw Brandon and the guards coming towards her. Marcus looked concerned as Brandon was coming closer. Prior to this, Brandon had grabbed the side arm from one of the guard's holster. He used every ounce of his strength to pull away from the guards, hopping on one leg towards the royal couple. The other guards ordered him to halt, but their words were ignored. Shots were fired. Brandon took 2 shots to the back, then fell to the ground. He struggled to stand to continue his trek. The crowd looked shocked and ran for cover. Marcus walked past the guards that were protecting him. They, along with Kimberly tried to stop him from getting caught in the crossfire. Brandon came about 2 feet from the king before the guards could tackle him. He pointed the weapon at Marcus's face. "I'm sorry!" he said before squeezing the trigger. Lucky for Marcus, the safety was still on the gun. Brandon fell to his knees sobbing, realizing that he had failed at his mission. One of the guards snatched the gun away from him. Instead of being pissed, Marcus approached Brandon with a sorrowful look. He kneeled to look him in the eye. Marcus gently raised his head. "Why would you want to do this to me?" he asked Brandon. Before Brandon could answer him, his head began to tremble. Suddenly his entire head combusted like a small explosion causing Marcus to be thrown on his back. The guards standing over Brandon's headless body suffered minor burns to their face and hands. Kimberly screamed at the top of her lungs. Most of the women in the crowd covered their faces from the horrific sight. Kimberly ran to her husband, falling to her knees to cradle him. Marcus's left side of his face was severely burned down to his skull from the explosion. "GLC!! Someone Get me some GLC!!" she screamed. Ali kneeled and gently rested his hand on his King's chest as his eyes teared up. "It too late for that, my queen!" he cried. The crowd began to regroup and huddle around the queen and her guards. The guards ordered the crowd to stand back as the fireworks continued. The soldiers in the vehicle carrying Edward the 2nd had driven off before the melee occurred.

Moments later, the sounds of civil defense sirens were set off through the entire island nation. For his own protection, the soldiers escorting Edward the 2nd ordered him to stay inside of his residence. The NA agents did not react until Edward the 2nd told them to protect him by standing guard inside and outside his residence. Miles away, the men and women of the Braxton clan armed themselves as soon as the sirens were set off. It was Philip, one of the sons of Simon Braxton, that ordered the Borough of Braxton to be shut off from the rest of the population. Their head of state, Ellen Braxton, was one of the guests at the party currently.

Edward the 2nd looked out his window as a swarm of military vehicles drove by heading towards the castle. he ran up the stairs towards the attic where Brandon was being held captive. He pushed the agents standing guard outside the attic to the side to enter. He went to the window. He noticed that it was cracked opened enough for a body to slip through. He called upon the agents to come into the room. "You worthless fucking robots!!" he shouted as he threw a foreign object across the room. Neither agent reacted. "I order you to fight each other to the death! I want the winner to dispose of the loser's body!" he shouted. "Yes, my lord." They said before Edward the 2nd left the room. He locked the door to the attic. He could hear the rumbling sounds of a tussle before walking away.

CHAPTER .44 RALPH (EL INTRÉPIDO) FERNANDEZ

It was June 29th, on a hot sunny day on the streets of Bloomfield, New Jersey. Sammy Perez was home sitting in front of his 65-inch flat screen TV watching the news. He was shocked to see the breaking news.

"Breaking news. Tragedy has stricken the fledgling island nation of Lassenberia when an alleged coup d'é·tat has taken the life of its king, who happened to be the heir to the defuncted Lassenberry drug cartel. Just last year the entire Lassenberry family, excluding king Marcus and his wife and son were victims of a plane explosion coming out of Teterboro airport." the reporter said before Sammy clicked off the TV. "Fuck!!" Sammy shouted as he threw the remote across the room. Elizabeth came running into the room. "What was that noise?" she asked. "¡Nada! ¡El control remoto se escapó de mi mano!" he said. Elizabeth looked across the room and saw the remote on the floor in pieces. "Really?" she asked with doubt in her voice. "Can you tell the maid to fix me a sandwich, baby?" he asked. "Whatever!" she said before leaving the room.

Sammy sat there for a moment in silence. He then pulled out his cell phone. He hit speed and waited for a response. "My dude! Where you at?" he asked. Sammy sat there listening. "Meet me at the boathouse in Warinanco park at 3!" Sammy said before clicking off his phone.

It was around 2:45pm when Sammy was already standing outside the boathouse checking his watch. About a mile away there was an unmarked car with 2 federal Agents inside taking photos with a high-powered lens camera. About a mile away in the opposite direction, sitting in a black van were 2 NA agents with high tech binoculars watching the federal agents. About 10 minutes later, a black Boeman SUV pulled up to the boathouse. 2 burly Spanish guys exit the vehicle, while the driver remained inside. 1 of the guys went to the back of the vehicle and pulled out a folded wheelchair. The other guy opened the back-passenger door, reaching inside pulling Mookie out, cradling him in his arms. The wheelchair was unfolded and placed on the ground. Mookie was carefully placed into the wheelchair. He was then wheeled to where Sammy was standing. "¡Más vale que sea importante! ¡Soy un hombre muy ocupado!" Mookie said. "My dude! Everything I do is of import ants!" Sammy chuckled. "What you call me out here for?" Mookie asked. "Can we talk in private?" Sammy asked. "Espera en el coche hasta que los llamo chicos." Mookie said to his men. The 2 guys gave a nod and went back to the vehicle. "Talk!" Mookie said. "Did you watch the news today?" Sammy asked. "The Lassenberia thing? Yeah!" Mookie said. "My dude! That's all Butch!" Sammy said. "What the fuck you talking about?" Mookie asked. "My dude! You don't get it? Hakim is gone! He takes control of Newark, and now, he and his son take the castle too! Wake the fuck up!" Sammy shouted. "Watch yourself! You're talking to a general!" Mookie said. "I'm a general too! So, fuck you!" Sammy said. Sammy saw that Mookie was trying his best to keep his composure. "Listen, my dude! My beef ain't with you! I'm just saying we gotta look out for each other. Between him and that goofy ass cousin of his, they're sure to come and try to take our shit too!" Sammy said. "Didn't we have this talk before?" Mookie asked. "I don't' remember!" Sammy said. "I think we did." Mookie said. "My dude! Are we gonna join forces, or not?" Sammy asked. "I ain't worried about shit. My people got my back to the end." Mookie said. Sammy gave off a cynical look. "¡ Mi amigo! Si tuvieran tu espalda, no estarías en una silla de ruedas.!" Sammy said before walking away. "This shit bigger than Butch, mi hermano! Mookie shouted. "Al carajo con él, y su gente!" Sammy said to himself as he walked past the SUV.

Shortly thereafter, Sammy returned home. He sat outside on his patio scrolling through the names in his cell phone. "Yes!" he said to himself in a victorious manner. He opened the screen door. "Baby! I'm going to Uncle Ralph's! I'll be back before mid-night!" he shouted. "Acabas de llegar a casa!" she shouted. "I'm out!" he said to himself.

His uncle was Ralph Fernandez, known on the streets as the fearless one in the hood. He was short and lean in stature but was one of the most respected men Essex county. Ralph wasn't involved in the underworld. He was a retired civilian and Vietnam veteran. He owned a condominium in Bloomfield New Jersey with his wife Carmen, who happened to be Mookie's distant cousin on his mother's side.

It was around 7pm when Sammy pulled up to his uncle's driveway. Sammy stood outside his car honking his horn like a mad man. "Yo! ¡Tío Ralph!" he shouted as he continued to honk the horn. A couple of his uncle's neighbors stuck their heads outside their windows. They recognized who Sammy was and went back inside. "That's right! Mind y'all damn business!" he shouted. "¿Qué demonios? Ralph shouted when he stepped out onto his balcony. "Buzz me in!" Sammy shouted. "See if I gotta package in the hallway!" Ralph said before going back inside. Once he was buzzed in, Sammy saw a huge package on the floor underneath the mailboxes. He read that it was for his uncle and grabbed it. When Sammy entered the house, he and Ralph greeted each other with a hug. "¿Qué pasa, sobrino?!" Ralph said. "Same shit, different day." Sammy said. "Congrats, nephew! I heard you moved up in the world!" Ralph said. "How the hell you find out?" Sammy asked. "Who you think you're talking to, nephew?" Ralph chuckled. "My fault!" Sammy chuckled. "Have a seat! You want a drink? Ralph said. "Ah, no. I'm good. Where's auntie?" Sammy asked. "She went down to the hospital to see her mother." He said. "How she doing?" Sammy asked. "She's holding up. "Y'all need anything?" Sammy asked. "We're good, man." Ralph said while channel surfing with the remote. "Ain't seen you in a while, nephew! What's up?" ralph asked. Sammy sighed before answering his question. "You know Butch running things now?" he said. Ralph looked shocked. "Holy shit!" he said. "Yeah! He got Newark now!" Sammy said. "What happened to that kid, Hakim?" Ralph asked. Sammy looked at his uncle, shaking his head. "Damn! That's fucked up!" Ralph said. "That's why I came here, to talk to you." Sammy said. "Why? He's the reason you took them bullets?" Ralph asked. "Nah! That was on some whole different shit." Sammy explained. "I know it's all evil shit out there, but I rather have Butch running the streets then that psycho Eddie Lassenberry!" Ralph said. "That's why I came to you." He said. "What's up?" Ralph asked. "I need you to talk to Butch and see if me and him are on good terms." Sammy said. Ralph burst out laughing. "Don't tell me, he got you shaking in your boots?" he chuckled.

Ralph and Butch go back to their freshman year in high school. Butch spent most of his time in school selling Marijuana for the Lassenberry crew to the other students. One of his customers was Ralph. For those in school who didn't buy from Butch became targets of physical abuse and ridicule. It was until one day Ralph was in the hallway and saw Butch had his future wife hemmed up against the locker. Ralph noticed that Carmen looked uncomfortable. None of the other boys in the hall would step up to defend her. Ralph dropped his books on the floor, took a deep breath and went over to confront the situation. He tapped Butch on the arm. Butch turned his head. "What you want?" Butch asked. "Come on! Leave her alone!" he said.

Ralph was a lanky kid standing about 5 feet tall at the time. butch on the other hand, lifted weights and stood almost 6 feet. Even back then, butch had a reputation of knocking out some of the boys in school with one punch. Rumors spread that he knocked out one of the teachers. That rumored had yet to be proven. Butch turned to Ralph, grabbing him by the collar. "Mind yo fucking business before I cut off your supply, Chico!" Butch said. The kids in the hall stood frozen out of fear and curiosity. This was when Ralph's life changed. He balled up his fist and gave Butch a left cross in the eye. Butch released him, going into temporary shock. He shook it off, but before that, ralph took another swing, landing a hit on his jaw. Butch stumbled back. He shook it off again. He put his fists up. He and Ralph went toe-to-toe landing wild punches on each other. The crowd was roaring and cheering for their favorite. Butch eventually came out the victor when he landed his famous knockout punch. Carmen came to Ralph's aid. Butch stood over them. He gently pushed Carmen out of the way. He gave Ralph a few taps on the cheek until he regained consciousness. One of the teachers came running down the hall. Butch took off in the opposite direction towards the nearest exit. That was the last day butch came to school. Even though he lost the fight, the kids gave praise to Ralph for standing up to Butch. As time passed, it was Butch who spread the word on the streets, giving Ralph the nickname the fearless one, which led to Carmen becoming attracted to him.

After high school Ralph and Carmen were married. Ralph joined the marines during the early days of the Vietnam war. Butch on the other hand, after dropping out of high school, became a foot soldier in Eddie Lassenberry's crew.

"I can't believe my uncle clowning me!" Sammy shouted toward the ceiling. "Take it easy, nephew! I'll go have a talk with Butch. We ain't speak to each other in years but we still have a mutual respect." Ralph said. Sammy slapped his hands together in a joyful gesture. "Muchas gracias, tío Ralph!" he said. "Just make the call to Butch so we can talk." He said. Sammy sprung from his seat, feeling better than when he arrived. "Alright, unk! I'm outta here! I gotta whole bunch of dope fiends to feed!" he chuckled. "You need to stop!" Ralph chuckled. "It's true!" Sammy said. "You sure you don't wanna stay for a drink?" Ralph asked. "I'm good! I'm good, unk!" he said before giving Ralph a hug goodbye.

It was May 1st 2003, around 3amwhen Ralph was sitting at a 24-hour diner on Broad street in Bloomfield. He was a regular patron who was served his usual omelet, home fries and coffee without even mentioning it. He was constantly looking at his watch as he had the waitresses and manager laughing hysterically at his lewd jokes. The diner was practically empty except for 2 old white guys sitting at the counter chatting with each other.

About 15 minutes later 4 black men walked into the diner with serious expressions on their faces. They were in t-shirts and jeans, or either button up shirts or dress pants. "Alright people! The diner is closed!" one of the men shouted. "What's this about?" the manager asked. "Mr. Watson is about to come in here! That's all you need to know!' the man said. That was enough for the manager to get rid of the customers and tell the waitresses, dishwashers, and the cook they were off duty. Ralph stayed seated as he said goodbye to the waitresses. One of the black guys flipped the open sign to the closed side as he guarded the door. The manager went back into the kitchen and stayed there. Moments later, Butch entered the diner followed by 2 more bodyguards. One of the guards locked the door.

Butch was dressed in a dark blue silk suit, and a flower printed necktie. The color of his shoes matched his suit. He wore a diamond encrusted watch along with his Lassenberry ring. "Butch, baby!!" ralph shouted with a mouth full of food. "Long time, no see, ralph." Butch said in a calm voice. Ralph wiped his mouth with a napkin before getting out of the booth. "Hold on, old man." One bodyguard said before frisking him. "He's clean." The man said. "Come over here and give me a hug, man!" Butch said. Ralph and butch embrace each other. "How've you been, man?" Butch asked. "Good, bro!" he said. "Now, your nephew said you wanted to talk to me. So, talk." Butch said. Ralph rubbed his hands together. "Ok, bro. this is the deal." he said. "Come, on, man! Get on with it! I got shit to do!" Butch said as he moved his hand in a circular motion. "Of course, bro!" Ralph said. He gestured Butch to take a seat in the booth. "Alright!" Butch sighed. As they were sitting, 4 of the bodyguards had spread out through the diner. One of them went behind the counter and poured a cup of coffee adding cream and sugar. He went over and placed it in front of Butch. "It's about my nephew. Let me be honest. He's kind of nervous that you're running everything, and just wanna know is everything good with you 2." Ralph explained. Butch took a sip of his coffee. "Listen to me, ralph. I respect you, and everything! But…but your nephew ain't got no fucking business coming to you about anything concerning me! Eddie Lassenberry asked you to hook up with us a long time ago, and you said no to us! With that said, don't ever call me about my business! Understand?' Butch said as he slammed his hand on the table. "We're cool, bro! forget we ever had this conversation!" Ralph said as he reached his hand out. Butch scoffed at his hand gesture but smiled before they shook hands. "You need anything? A new house? A new car?" Butch asked. "I'm straight. Oh! You can pay for my breakfast! "he chuckled. "Come on, man. Give me a hug so I can get the fuck outta here!" Butch said. Both men stood and embraced each other once again. Butch reached in his pocket and pulled out a wad of cash, peeling off a c-note, placing it on the table. "You take care of yourself." Butch said to Ralph before leaving the diner. His bodyguards followed him out. The last bodyguard turned the closed sign back around to the open side of the sign, then gave ralph a half ass salute before leaving. The manager peaked his head out of the double doors. "Are they gone?" he asked. Ralph then grabbed the hundred-dollar bill off the table and stuffed it in his pants pocket. "Everything's cool, bro! I gotta get outta here and check on my wife! By-the-way, butch said breakfast was on him!" he said before leaving the diner. The manager scratched his head with a puzzled look on his face.

— CHAPTER .45 EDWARD THE ADDICT —

It was the darkest day, metaphorically speaking, for the island nation of Lassenberia since queen Kimberly discovered the toxic dump site on its shores. At the same time, it was literally a bright sunny day when Edward the 2nd came out of his residence looking disheveled, rubbing his head after being in isolation for the past couple of days. He looked up at the blue sky. He spotted a flock of goldfinch nestled in a tree across the street.

The goldfinch weren't native to Lassenberia. just like all the other animals on the island, they were exported from various parts of the world on the orders of Kimberly and King Marcus. This species of goldfinch was exported from North America. King Marcus chose these birds because there is an image of one pictured on the Lassenberry family crest. About 300 goldfinches were shipped from a zoo in West orange, New Jersey.

Moments later a military jeep carrying 3 young soldiers of Somali descent pull up in front of his residence. A few NA agents stood between Edward the 2nd and the jeep. "What's up?" he asked the soldiers. "It's urgent that you come with us, Lord Lassenberry!" one soldier said. "What was the air sirens about the other day?" he asked. "I think you should come with us, my lord!" the soldier said. "Alright! Alright! Goddamn! Let me jump in the shower and get dressed! You know what? On second thought! Where we going, anyway?" he asked. "To the castle, my lord!" the soldier said. "fuck it, then! I'll have my men bring me there!" Edward the 2nd said. "You are to come with us, my lord, on the orders of the Prime minister!" the soldier said. "I said I'll have my men bring me there!" he said. This was when more NA agents started to crowd around the jeep. "Trust me! You don't want no problems with these guys!" Edward the 2nd said to the soldiers. The young soldier in charge looked around. He realized that they were outnumbered even though he and his men were armed with machine guns. "Let's go!" he said to the driver. The NA agents cleared a path for the jeep to drive off.

About an hour and 4 cups of coffee later, Edward the 2nd appeared from his residence dressed in his uniform and jack boots. "Let's go!" he said to 9 of his agents. They jump into 2 SUV s. "Let's go to the castle!" he said to the driver.

At castle Lassenberia, the entire perimeter was off limits to the citizens of the island nation. The area just outside the castle walls were so quiet, you could hear a pin drop. The same spot king Marcus met his end was the same spot where his wife sat on the ground cradling his corps for the past couple of days. The dried blood stains from Brandon's body remained on the ground. Kimberly gave Ali the order to forbid anyone to come near her and her deceased husband. The guards surrounding the queen had bandanas cover their mouths and noses from the stench of the king's rotting corpse. She sat there stroking the uninjured side of his face, continuously whispering words of love into his ear.

The prime minister, Jenna Jenkins and her husband Sheldon stood off in the distance looking sad, grieving for their sister. "Honey. Don't you think it's time we take the body and give him a proper sendoff?" Sheldon asked. "Not just yet! Give her one more day, and hopefully she'll snap out of it! I don't even want to think what Princess terry would do if she saw this!" Jenna said. "When should we break the news to her?" Sheldon asked. "Let Kimberly do it! It's only right!" she suggested.

Moments later Jenna, Sheldon and the guards heard vehicles approaching. They turned to see the 2 SUVs pull up. Edward the 2nd was squinting his eyes to make sure it was Kimberly and his cousin that he saw on the ground. "What the fuck?!!" Edward the 2nd shouted before getting out of the vehicle. "I don't know whether to cry or jump for fucking joy!" Edward the 2nd whispered to himself. He approached Jenna and Sheldon. "Where the hell you've been?!! I sent soldiers for you!" Jenna shouted. "Come down! now, tell me what happened!" Edward the 2nd said. "We didn't witness it, but they're saying Brandon tried to kill Marcus, then his head exploded!" Jenna said. "His what?!!" Edward the 2nd shouted. "Did I stutter?" she shouted. "That's enough of that fucking sass talk from you!" Edward the 2nd shouted as he pointed his finger at her. "Watch how you talk to my wife!" Sheldon said. "Fuck y'all! I don't have to stand here for this!" Edward the 2nd said before walking away. He slowly approached the guards surrounding the royal couple as the NA agents stayed by the vehicles. The guards drew their weapons at Edward the 2nd. "Stand the fuck down! I'm a Lassenberry! I'm responsible for all of you being here!" he shouted. "What do you as prime minister, have to say about this?" one guard said to Jenna. This was the moment when Edward the 2nd gave the signal to the NA agents to come to him. Jenna and Sheldon were making their way towards Edward the 2nd but were cut off by the NA agents. "What the hell you're doing?" Jenna shouted. "From this day on, shit changes! The king is dead! The queen is having a moment! I'm a Lassenberry! enough said! Now stand…the fuck…down!" Edward the 2nd said to the guards. They looked at each other, then lowered their weapons. Kimberly was so out of it; not hearing the hostility going on. Edward the 2nd walked past the guards. He squatted in front of the royal couple. Kimberly didn't notice his presence as she continued to stroke her husband's face. Edward the 2nd grabbed his cousin's hand. He cringed and started to heave as he saw maggots crawling in and out of his eye socket. He glanced up towards the sky then looked at Kimberly. "Listen bitch. You had a good run, and now it's over." He whispered to her. Still, Kimberly didn't notice his presence. He released his cousin's hand, letting it fall to the side. Edward the 2nd stood tall. "Listen! I'm in control of our defenses from now on! I don't think Mr. Hart would've committed suicide!! I'm going to find out who was behind this, but I'll need your help! I promise you all, we will avenge our beloved king! Long live the house of Lassenberry! long live the house of Lassenberry!" he shouted as he raised his fist in the air.

The guards looked at each other. They slowly but simultaneously raised their weapons in the air. "Long live the house of Lassenberry! long live the house of lassenberry!" they screamed. Edward the 2nd walked away from the crime scene, walking towards Jenna and Sheldon. "You see! The Lassenberry bloodline is strong, no matter what!" he said to them. "I'm the prime minister! It's my job to oversee things under the royal couple!" Jenna said. "It's my island! My nation, and I can prove it! If you wanna take it to the United Nations, let's do the damn thing! Now, if you don't mind, arm my agents with weapons before the day is out! I gotta prepare for my cousin's funeral, which I'm leaving you incharge of!" he said before leaving. "What do you think?" Sheldon asked. "I think we're witnessing the beginning of the end!" Jenna said.

Hours later, Edward the 2nd went to visit the borough of Braxton. He was escorted by 10 of his agents, who were armed with pistols and machine guns.

Citizens of Braxton watched as the caravan drove through the streets heading for the capital building. The capital building was where Ellen Braxton conducted all business concerning the diverse community. The SUVs parked in front of the capital. There were 2 guards of Mozambique descent standing at the top of the stairs in front of the entrance. Edward the 2nd proudly marched up the stairs with a big grin on his face followed by his agents. "Make way for your new king, you sons-of-bitches!" he shouted jokingly. "What is your business here, Lord Lassenberry?" one of the guards asked. "I come to see the white chick!" he said. "Lady Ellen is not present now. She's visiting the pale lands." The guard said. "Well, show me to her office, and go fetch her for me!" Edward the 2nd he ordered. "But lord Lassenberry! I can't leave my post!" the guard said. "Do you wanna be arrested for disobeying a direct order from a member of the royal family? Your soon to be king?" he shouted as he grabbed the young guard by the collar of his uniform. The guard looked nervous. He was spared further embarrassment when Lady Ellen's chauffeured vehicle pulled up. Her security detail stepped out of the vehicle. One of her security guards, who was her nephew Bartholomew, was the son of Simon Braxton. Lady Ellen stepped out of the vehicle. "Lord Lassenberry? What are you doing here?" she asked. "Lady Ellen! So, go to see you on this fine day!" he said with a grin. "Fine day?!! Your cousin the king, is dead!!" she shouted. "My cousin died days ago. Can we talk in your office? We need to talk about your future." He said.

In another area of the island, princess Teresa was sitting on her couch alone in her mansion when she started rubbing her belly. She became nauseous. She began to vomit on the floor before she could make it to the bathroom. Her commlink was on the coffee table. She crawled towards the coffee table as she continued vomiting. She reached for her commlink and pressed the button. "Get...me...doctor...Magumbwe! Now!" she said before passing out.

When Teresa became conscious, she saw Doctor Magumbwe standing by her bedside. "Welcome back, princess." He said. "Where am I?" she asked. You are in the hospital, princess. You've just been transferred to the maternity ward." He said.

The hospital where princess Teresa was being cared for was called the Benjamin Lassenberry Universal Hospital. Construction of this ultramodern medical facility was completed 2 months earlier. Since its establishment, the hospital has only cared for pregnant women. The other wards, such as cancer ward, cardiology, emergency etc. room have never been occupied due to the miraculous effects of the GLC.

"Maternity ward?" she asked. "Coagulations, princess. You're pregnant." He said. As she laid there, a tear trickled down the side of her face. "Where's my brother? I would like to see him, please!" she said. The doctor sighed with a sad look on his face.

Back at the Braxton Capital building, Edward the 2nd had just finished having a meeting with Ellen. "Now, let's go pay a visit to these albinos." He said to his agents as he stood at the top of the stairs of the capital building.

After leaving the 24-hour diner, Butch and his caravan of bodyguards were heading towards Newark, driving down Bloomfield avenue. "Where you wanna head next, boss? You wanna get out here and check on the troops?" the driver said. "Nah. I'm gonna leave that to my son. He's gotta learn the business eventually. Head down to McCarter Highway. I thought I saw an abandoned factory down there the other day. If it's for sale, I'll turn it into a safe house." Butch said. "Copy that." The driver said.

Just when they were about to cross the border from Bloomfield to Newark, they heard a car horn behind them honking continuously. Butch looked behind him watching as a town car speeding up dodging traffic. The vehicle pulled up beside them. "Yo! What the fuck is this shit?" the bodyguard in the front passenger seat shouted as an old white man driving close to Butch's vehicle waving his hand, shouting at his driver to pull over. "You want me to smoke this mother fucker?" the bodyguard in the passenger seat said to Butch. "Hold on! Is that Jimmy? Jimmy Cupo?" butch shouted.

Jimmy (Rock Star) Cupo was a soldier in the Gatano crime family. His reputation went back to the days of Benny Lassenberry and alleged boss, Alfonse Gatano. After the massacre in 1997, all the crews in the crime family were in disarray for the time being. Jimmy survived the massacre because he was just an associate at the time and wasn't invited to attend the wedding of Gatano's daughter. Jimmy was known for shake downs of small business and breaking and entering. Before taking the oath to the Gatano crime family, Jimmy Cupo spent his leisure as a guitar player for local rock bands He did 3 years in the same prison, at the same time Hakim did for getting caught red handed breaking into a mansion out in Alpine New Jersey. The younger members of the crime family gave him the nick name rock star because he always had his hair long, in a ponytail and his expertise on 80's hair band trivia.

"Pull over! Let me see what this knucklehead wants!" Butch said. "You Sure, boss?" the driver asked. "Just pull the fuck over!" Butch said. The driver pulled over to the curb. Jimmy pulled up in front of them. Jimmy stepped out of his vehicle wearing a blue jogging suit and sneakers. Butch's driver and bodyguard pulled out their weapons. "Take it easy boys. This old man looks like he needs to be hooked up to an EKG machine. Get on your phone and tell the others not to get out of the car." Butch chuckled. "Got it." His bodyguard said as he pulled out his cell phone. Jimmy walked up to butch's vehicle. He knocked on the rear passenger window. Butch rolled down the window. "Jimmy Cupo! How the hell are ya?" Butch said. "I saw you drive off from the diner when I pulled up! Mike told me what happened! Who the fuck told to you; you can shut down one of my collection spots?!!" he shouted before spitting on the ground. Butch was doing his best to keep from laughing at the old man. "It was no more than 5 minutes!" butch said. "I don't give a fuck if it was 5 seconds! That's my bread-n- butter, not yours, you fuck!" Jimmy shouted. "I had a meeting!" butch said. "Have a meeting in your own fucking spot!" Jimmy shouted. "Say jimmy. How would you like to make a couple of bucks doing a job for me?" butch asked. "What?" Jimmy asked. "You heard me." Butch said. "I don't work for you spooks! If I had my way, you'd be working for me!" Jimmy shouted. "Come on, jimmy! It ain't like you can't use the money! I know your crew is barley scraping by since that thing back in 97!" butch said. Jimmy calmed himself. "Butch! I tell ya, things ain't been the same since!" Jimmy said as he was breathing heavily through his nose. "See! I know these things!" Butch said with pride. "These fucking Sicilians! They're coming over here in droves! I feel like I'm the last of a dying breed! I'm so stressed, I gotta take 3 different pills every morning! I heard rumors the Lassenberry people got some miracle drug oversees that can cure anything! Is it true?" he asked. "I don't know! I'm over here with you!" Butch explained. "Now, what you were saying about a job?" Jimmy asked. "Let's take a walk." Butch said. Butch's driver and bodyguard heard butch mention Sammy Perez in their conversation as he and jimmy walked across the street. "I think some shit about to go down!" the driver said as he turned to the bodyguard.

It was May 5th, 2003, about 5 in the morning when the feds came knocking on Sammy's door. There were 4 unmarked cars parked outside his home in vineland New Jersey. There were many FBI agents roaming the around his mansion. Sammy had a bodyguard standing outside of his home until the feds arrested him for illegal possession of a firearm. He was placed in a one of the cars as agents banged on Sammy's door. Sammy came to the door in his bathrobe. "What the hell is this?" Sammy asked. Morning. Mr. Perez. I'm FBI agent Presley and this is my partner agent Delgado." Presley said as he showed his badge. "Delgado? What are you, Puerto Rican?" Sammy asked. "No. Dominican." Delgado said. "¡ Lamento oír eso, amigo mío! ¡Todos no podemos ser perfectos!" Sammy chuckled. "That's a good one." Delgado responded. "We're here to inform you, Mr. Perez, that there's been a contract put on your head. Also, we have a warrant for your arrest for violation of parole. We know you're affiliated with the Lassenberry organization because you were seen on surveillance cameras rubbing elbows with low level members of the organization." Presley said. "Man, I don't know nothing about no lassenberry shit, my dude!" Sammy said. "Ok! read him his rights." Presley said to Delgado. "Goddamn, my dude! Let me get dressed and talk to my wife!" Sammy said. "Sure thing. But we're coming inside with you." Presley said. "Whatever, my dude!" Sammy said as he went back in his mansion.

The next day Butch was at his home he just bought in Nutley New Jersey. The movers were bringing in furniture for the dining room. Butch was in the kitchen chatting with his Daughter and youngest son when one of his Bodyguards came in, "Boss! We gotta problem!" he said. "Follow me." Butch said. He led the bodyguard into another room to speak in private. "Talk to me!" butch said. The word is, that my dude guy, just got taken in by the feds along with the old Italian man! The old man flipped! There's no news on my dude saying anything!" the bodyguard said. Butch didn't say a word. He just gave a nod. "Stay here." Butch said. Butch went back into the kitchen. "Hey! Daddy has to go away on a business trip for a while!" he said to his kids.

It was around 6pm when Butch and his driver were sitting in a vehicle outside a movie theatre in Newark. A few minutes later, a Boeman Sedan with dark tinted windows pull up next to them. "Is that him? The driver asked. The window rolled down halfway. Someone stuck their hand out the rear passenger window, waving at Butch to come over. "I guess that's him! Wait here!" Butch said to his driver. Butch walked over and entered the back seat. "What took you so long? I've been waiting out here for 2 hours!" Butch shouted. "Take it easy! I'm here, ain't I? Jesus! You think you're the only king pin I gotta babysit?" Doug Reed said. "Anyway! I gotta problem!" Butch said. "What is it?" Doug sighed. "The feds got one of my generals! I gotta leave the country until I figure out my next move!" Butch said. Doug began laughing hysterically. "Oh! I didn't realize I just told a fucking joke!" Butch said. "I'm sorry! But I should've told you how things work!" Doug chuckled. "How what works?" Butch asked. "You're untouchable!" Doug said. "What the fuck you mean, untouchable?" Butch asked. "Yeah! You're with us. You can do whatever the fuck you want, as long as you do as I say!" Doug said with a smirk on his face. "You mean to tell me that me and my generals can't be touched by the feds?" Butch asked. "You're untouchable! Your generals, on the other hand, can be replaced like batteries in a TV remote!" Doug said. "So, what am I supposed to do with Sammy?" Butch asked. "What the hell you asking me for? You're the jersey king pin!" Doug said. "I also got a problem with a mobster." he said. "Like I said, you're untouchable! Now, get the fuck outta my car!" Doug said. Butch exited the vehicle with a grin on his face. Butch went back to his car. "What happened, boss? You still wanna get that plane ticket?" the driver asked. "Just take me back to the house in Nutley! I need to find me a new general!" he said as he rubbed his hands together. "Don't look at me! I don't want the headache! I'm fine behind the wheel!" the driver said. Butch began laughing as they drove off.

Later, that evening, Doug reed was preparing a late-night dinner. He and his alleged guest were in a house in upstate New York. There were about a dozen NA agents standing outside this house patrolling the area. Doug grabbed a pair of oven mitts when he heard the timer go off from the oven." Dinner is ready, my dear!" shouted as he opened the oven door. He pulled out a black roasting pan, placing it on the top of the stove. Minutes later, he entered the dining room carrying the main course on a platter. "This smell scrumptious!" he said to the person sitting at the dining room table. "Come on! Don't cry! I guarantee you'll enjoy this." He said to the person. The other edibles on the dining room table were steamed vegetables, mashed potatoes, and warm pumpernickel bread. Doug with a smile on his face, as he stuffed the linen napkin in his collar. There were 2 NA agents standing in the room as he prepared to dine. His guest began to scream when she saw the main course. "I told you, and I told Edward the 2nd this was going to happen. If your kid's father, or should I say your baby daddy would not return to the states, completing his mission, I was going to eat his kids! I think this is baby Niyale if I'm not mistaken!" he said with a confused look. He took a closer look at the roasted corpse. No penis! Yeah! This is the girl!" he said. "You evil son-of-a-bitch!!" Viola screamed as she tried to break free from her handcuffs, which were secured to her chair. "Please don't make this harder than what it is! I gave him more than enough time to return! It's not my fault he doesn't give 2 shits about you and these bastard babies!" he said as he was carving up the dead infant. He placed the arm of the infant between 2 slices of bread. He placed the morbid sandwich. On her plate. "Dig in, my dear! After all, it's your kid!" he said with a serious look on his face. "I'm going kill you!!!" she screamed. "If you are going to be difficult, I'll have to force feed you like a child! Agent! Hold her mouth open!" Doug said. The agent squeezed her jaw, forcing her mouth to remain open. Doug walked over and force fed her the sandwich. Viola began to gag. The more Doug forced the sandwich in her mouth, the more Viola began to regurgitate. "I know what you need. You need something to chase down your meal." Doug said. He went to the kitchen and opened the freezer. Inside the freezer were 3 ice trays and another frozen infant wrapped several times in plastic wrap. He grabbed an ice tray, then filled a drinking glass with 3 ice cubes. He opened the cupboard and grabbed a bottle of warm blood. He then went back into the dining room. "There's nothing like a glass of vital fluids on ice to chase down the taste of baby!" he said. He poured the blood into the glass and put it to Viola's mouth. "Hurry up! Drink it before it congeals!" he said. Most of the blood ended up on her chin and her lap. "You bitch!! He said as he slapped her across the face. Doug became agitated. "Take her, and chain her back up in the basement!!" he shouted. "There's rats down there!! Please don't!!" she screamed. The 2 agents uncuffed her and had to practically drag her to the basement as she was kicking and screaming. Doug went to sit back down. "No sense of wasting all of this tasty food!" he said to himself. He began to eat in a ravenous fashion.

It was May 8th, 2003. Edward the 2nd had made it clear that he was the heir to the throne of Lassenberia to every community. His cousin, the late king Marcus was entombed within a sacred room inside the castle. the day of the funeral was one of the biggest ceremonies in the world since the last president of the United States was assassinated. Every foreign dignitary from the continent of Africa, some part of Asia and Indonesia were in attendance. Queen Kimberly was too distraught to attend. She stayed huddled up in her chambers, still in her ball gown she wore that fatal night, cradling her son, surrounded by a few servants. Princess Teresa was in attendance under the influence of opioids. Edward the 2nd found fault that Jenna authorized the media to attend. After the ceremony he unofficially outlawed the foreign media for the fear of spies especially from the United States.

June 6th was the day Edward the 2nd chose to have his coronation. This was a significant day to him because it was the birthday of his favorite uncle, Sir Edward. Before this day came, there was turmoil within the ranks of the Somalian community. Ali lead a faction that believed all citizens of the island nation were equal under the lectures of queen Kimberly and the 48 laws, contrary to the beliefs of his trusted soldier, commander Abdirrahim. His faction believed in the old superstitious ideology that people with Albinism were an abomination and the Braxton clan could not be trusted because they were Caucasian. He made it clear that he did not want these people around him through public speeches. Kimberly was not there to oppose him. Edward the 2nd saw it as an opportunity to increase his power over the people.

It was June 3rd when Edward the 2nd approached Abdirrahim in private at the commander's residence. Edward the 2nd did not want to make him feel uncomfortable, so he arrived without his agents.

When he entered Abdirrahim's home, Edward the 2nd noticed how proud he was of his Somalian heritage. The artwork, the furniture, and even Abdirrahim's attire all stood for his native land. "it is an honor that you came to visit me. Lord Lassenberry!" he said. Abdirrahim's wife served the 2 men samosa and Shaah tea. Edward the 2nd took a sip of the tea. His eyes lit up. Abdirrahim could not help but to laugh. "Wow! This has kick!" Edward the 2nd said. "My apologies my lord for laughing." He chuckled. "That's ok! it's just something I'll have to get used to!" he chuckled. "May I ask? How is the queen's condition?" he asked. "Hopefully, she'll come around. She's a tough woman." Edward the 2nd said. "When I arrived here, I heard it was her that discovered the GLC!" he said. "They forgot to tell you that it was me who had to approve it for human consumption." He boasted. "Of course, my lord!" Abdirrahim said. "I was meaning to ask you. what made you decide to become a citizen of Lassenberia?" Edward the 2nd asked. "Just like everyone else here, I wanted a fresh start for my wife and children! Ali is a childhood friend of mine. If it were not for him, I'd still be a fisherman just scraping by." He said. "How is the fishing industry over there?" Edward the 2nd asked. "It's great for the huge corporations, but for an independent man such as myself, it was a struggle! They would hire henchmen to keep us out of the area! So, I had to learn deep sea diving when the huge boats came near. I learned how to use a harpoon gun and bring my catch to the surface!" he explained. "Oh! I guess you can hold your breath under water for a long time, huh?" Edward th2nd asked. "I held the record in my village for holding my breath for 4 minutes and 25 seconds!" Abdirrahim said with pride. "That's great!" he said. "I prefer commanding troops, my lord!" Abdirrahim chuckled. "On a serious note, I know that you and Ali are close, but disagree on the politics of Lassenberia." he asked. Abdirrahim looked uncomfortable. "It's ok, man! You can talk to me!" Edward the 2nd said. Abdirrahim leaned forward in his chair. "Those cursed pale people! They're like a plague!" he whispered. "When you say pale people, who are you talking about? The Braxton clan or the albinos?" Edward the 2nd asked. "All of them!!" he whispered passionately. "I hear you." Edward the 2nd said. "You must understand, being of African American origin! Descendant of slaves!" he whispered. "You don't have to tell me twice! My grandfather served 2 masters for a period, until my uncle, the great Eddie Lassenberry cut it down to 1! Then there is me! I serve no man! If I have men like you by my side, I guarantee your children, and your children's children paradise!" he said. What Edward the 2nd said brought tears to his eyes. "It's ok, my friend. It's ok." Edward said as he rubbed Abdirrahim's shoulder. "Together, we can make momentous changes! First, I gotta change these ridiculous laws! Well, some of them. Certain people on the council have to abide by my changes or be removed!" he said. "Tell me what you need me to do, my lord!" Abdirrahim said. Edward the 2nd leaned back in his chair. He just stared at Abdirrahim for a moment. The room was silent. "Your underwater skills may come in handy for what I want done." He said.

The next day Edward the 2nd and his NA agents stopped by the office of Kent Mooney. Kent did not hold any authority over the military like Ali, Jenna, Ukerewe, and Ntsay, yet he was held in high regard for bringing civility to the island nation by creating its laws, even though he could not enforce them. The Mooney hall of records were named in his honor. It was where Sheldon and his staff stored all hand-written events about Lassenberia. Kent and his staff would then enter the information in Lassenberia's computer database. Kimberly and Marcus did not put too much trust in technology. They feared one day the grid would be shut down from outside forces. At the same time, they feared losing all handwritten literature to something disastrous like a fire.

In his hand, Edward the 2ⁿᵈ carried a briefcase he brought with him from the Unites States. Edward the 2ⁿᵈ and his agents did not schedule an appointment to meet with Kent. They just barged in, not in a threatening way but by show of entitlement.

"Hey! What's up Kent?" he said in a cheerful voice. Kent was sitting at his desk with his feet kicked up reading a report sent in by one of Sheldon's staffers. Kent did not stand when Edward the 2ⁿᵈ entered his office. He just smiled. "What's so funny, man?" he asked Kent. "How's everything, lord Lassenberry?" he asked. "You didn't answer my question, man!" Edward the 2ⁿᵈ said. "After all the stuff that is been happening lately, a man must smile, or he'll lose his mind! I didn't see the tragic events concerning your cousin, the king, but it's not pleasurable reading the sick shit in detail just as well" Kent explained. Edward the 2ⁿᵈ opened his briefcase. He pulled out a binder journal and placed it on Kent's desk. "What's this?" Kent asked. It is the most important piece of literature on this island! It's the B.O.I!" he said. "What?" Kent asked. "The book of information! It was started by my grandfather, who passed it to my uncle, then my cousin. Now, I have it." He said. "What do you want me to do with it?" Kent asked. Copy it. Put it in the Lassenberia history books!" Edward the 2ⁿᵈ said. Kent took the binder. He flipped through the pages, then closed the binder. "What's wrong? Edward the 2ⁿᵈ asked. "I'm sorry, Krayton! But I can't enter this into our database!" Kent said. "What the fuck you just call me? Say it again, so I can have my agents beat the shit out of you!" Edward the 2ⁿᵈ said furiously. "Alright! Lord Lassenberry! Jesus!" Kent said. "Why can't you put it in?" Edward the 2ⁿᵈ asked. "Because it is part of United States history, not Lassenberia history. The queen wanted us to start with a clean slate. Every memory of the old days of slinging dope die with us. I'm gonna marry one of those Braxton girls, raise a family and never have to worry about some pusher like yourself throwing cocaine and pills in my kid's face." Kent said. "Like me, huh?" Edward the 2ⁿᵈ said. He took back the binder. "Since I'm gonna be the new king anyway, I guess I can wait!" he said. "How so? For you to be in succession to the throne, the queen must abdicate all authority to you. I highly doubt she will do that since she has a son. More than likely she'll let you sit on the throne for appearances while she runs everything" Kent said. "Yeah, I forgot about my little cousin, the prince!" Edward the 2ⁿᵈ said. "I heard rumors about princess Teresa being pregnant. I wonder how the fuck that happened? I know it's your cousin, but you think she fucked any of those African boys?" Kent asked. Edward the 2ⁿᵈ tried his best to hold back his rage. He flipped gritting his teeth into a faux smile. "Forget about all that for now! I was getting a few of the locals together tonight to celebrate my coronation on the royal yacht. Since it is all about my little cousin's future, we can celebrate that!" Edward the 2ⁿᵈ said. "I don't know! I'm backed up with work since the King's death!" Kent said. "Come on, man! You need to chill for once in your life!" Edward the 2ⁿᵈ said. "I'll pass." Kent said. Edward the 2ⁿᵈ stood there for a moment thinking of a way to convince Kent to loosen up. "Corporal Braxton will be there!" he said. "Christina?" Kent said. "Oh, yeah! She said she's got this brand-new outfit for tonight!" Edward the 2ⁿᵈ said. "Well, since you put it that way." Kent said. "See! I knew you would change your mind!" Edward the 2ⁿᵈ chuckled.

That evening, Edward the 2ⁿᵈ went to visit his cousin princess Teresa. She had soldiers from the Zewde clan stand guard outside her mansion. She had given them orders not to let anyone approach her doors. When Edward the 2nd and his NA agents showed up, it became a standoff. "Listen to me! I do not care what the princess told you motherfuckers! I am the future king! The last thing you wanna do is piss me off!" he shouted. "With all due respect lord Lassenberry, we have our orders!" one soldier stood forth and said. There were over 20 Zewde soldiers facing off against 7 NA agents. "You boys ain't got the numbers or the experience right now to go toe-to-toe with my men!" he said. Edward the 2nd gave signaled his agents to draw their weapons. The Zewde soldiers did the same. Edward the 2nd put on a brave face but slowly backed away, hiding behind his agents. "You have 3 seconds to put away your weapons!" Edward the 2nd shouted. "You don't want to do this, lord Lassenberry!" the Zewde soldier shouted. "Fuck it! 1…2…" Edward the 2nd shouted. "Stop!!" princess Teresa shouted from her 2nd floor window. The Zewde soldiers slowly lowered their weapons. Edward the 2nd ordered his agents to do the same. "Cousin! Come on down so we can talk!" he shouted. "Ok!" she said. Moments later the front entrance opened. "Come in." Teresa said. "Stay here and keep these boys company." Edward the 2nd said to his agents. "Yes, my lord." One agent said. Edward the 2nd went inside.

Teresa snuggled on her plush sofa holding a throw pillow in front of her to cover her midsection. "You don't have to hide yourself from me, cuz. You're not even showing yet." He said. "So, you've heard?" she asked. "Yep!" he said before sitting in the chair across from her. "I can't believe my brother is gone! I don't want to believe it was because of Brandon!" she cried. "Hey! I am here! Little mark is here! Your bloodline ain't going nowhere! The Lassenberry name will never die! We are forever, little cuz! That's what's important right now!" Edward the 2nd said with a smirk on his face. He went over and sat next to Teresa. He gently grabbed her hand. "That baby inside you is special! Whether it is a boy or girl, it's going to rule the world one day! Hopefully, it's a boy!" he chuckled. "The scary thing is…I don't remember being with anyone! I don't know who the father is!" Teresa cried. Edward the 2nd had a guilty look on his face. He got up and kneeled before his cousin. "After our family died in the plane crash, I…I…thought we would die out! Uncle Ed-, I mean Sir Edward did not do what he did to allow that to happen, cuz! I felt it was up to you and me to keep our bloodline going!" he said. "What are you talking about?" she asked. Edward the 2nd closed his eyes. He began to tremble nervously." Tell me! Tell me what's wrong!" Teresa demanded. He opened his eyes. "The father of your baby…is…me!" he whispered. Teresa looked surprised. She began shaking her head in disbelief. "No! No… No!!!" she screamed. Teresa began smacking him in the face. "Get out!! Get out!!" she screamed as she continued smacking him. Edward the 2nd jumped back. He stood at attention as Teresa continued sobbing. "Long live the house of Lassenberry!!" he shouted before walking out the door. Teresa buried her face in the pillow crying and screaming.

Outside her mansion Edward the 2nd gave his agents the order to follow him. The Zewde soldiers just stood there with bewildered looks on their faces.

It was around mid-night when the party Edward the 2nd hosted on the royal yacht was in full swing. Everyone was getting hammered with all kinds of beer and liquor. "I love this shit! We can get shit faced and all we have to do is take a couple of drops of GLC, and no hangover!" Kent shouted to the crowd. The crowd cheered as they raised their glasses. Kent went over to Christina. Edward the 2nd was watching his every move that night. He walked away from the crowd. He pulled out a vial of GLC which he stole from the medical supply and quickly guzzled its contents. Within seconds he sobered up. "I would like to toast to my sister, Queen Kimberly!" Jenna shouted as she raised her glass. The crowd cheered as they raised their glasses. Sheldon was feeling the full effect of many glasses of whiskey when he staggered over to where Edward the 2nd was standing. "I'm so glad you've accepted the fact that Kimberly is our leader and you decided to support her!" Sheldon said. "I know my place, man. It is what it is." Edward the 2nd replied.

The royal yacht was anchored 2 miles off the coast of Lassenberia. Edward the 2nd invited only the heads of state to the party. He told the ship's captain that it would be undignified for the citizens to see them carrying on recklessly.

Edward the 2nd excused himself from Sheldon's presence and his annoying chatter. He went over to the port side of the yacht. He looked over the side and saw a dark figure hanging on to the anchor. Most of the crowd was scattered on the starboard side. He saw Kent trying to put his arm around Christina. He also noticed that she looked annoyed. "Hey Kent!" he shouted as he signaled for him to come over. Kent just stood there wobbling as Christina walked away. He finally staggered over towards Edward the 2nd. "Hey buddy!!" Kent shouted into his ear. Edward the 2nd was also annoyed with his belligerent behavior. "Look down there!" he said to Kent. "Where?" Kent asked. "Down there! I thought I saw a shark!" Edward the 2nd shouted. "A shark?!! There's no sharks around here!" he shouted as he looked over the side. As Kent was looking over the side, Edward the 2nd quickly grabbed him by the ankles, tossing him to flip over the rail. Kent went headfirst into the water. He struggled to stay afloat as Edward the 2nd quietly walked away. Before Kent could yell for help, he was yanked under water. He fought for his life to resurface, but something or someone had a strong grip on his ankles. Kent fought and struggled until he had no more strength. His lifeless body did not have a chance to float to the surface. He was dragged away further out to sea while still submerged.

It was around 5 in the morning when a search party was sent out to look for Kent. There were 5 teams from search and rescue on motorboats scouring the area. They went out as far as 10 miles searching for Kent's body. Sadly, Jenna called off the search when his body was found washed ashore on the Union of the Comoros. His cause of death was presumed accidental.

Edward the 2nd became infuriated when Jenna, by popular demand, held a nation-wide memorial service for Kent on the day his coronation was to take place. It was Jenna who gave the eulogy. She signed the order to have his body entombed outside the hall of records. **"KENT J. MOONEY/ FOUNDING FATHER/ JANUARY 4, 1956- JUNE 4, 2003"** was written at the base of his tomb.

July 3rd, 2003 was when queen Kimberly finally came around to her senses and reestablished her duties as queen. The first thing she did was christen Edward the 2nd as lord protector of Lassenberia in a private ceremony instead of the grandiose ceremony he had envisioned. After the ceremony Edward the 2nd and Kimberly went off to have a one-on-one conversation on the pier where the royal yacht was docked. They did not face each other in conversation. They both watched the clear blue sky, the sun beaming above the horizon, and the calm ocean.

"I realize I was out of it, and not in my right mind. But I'm back now." Kimberly said. "I understand! You lost your husband, and I lost another family member!" Edward the 2nd said. "The reason I wanted to talk to you alone is that I understand you have the legal documents to be in the position you originally wanted to be in." she said. "So, you do realize I can pull the plug on your whole bullshit reign of power?" he said in a calm voice. The queen and the lord protector continued to stare out into the ocean. "The people loved my husband. The people love, me. You should be grateful that I raised your status." she said. Edward the 2nd began to chuckle. "Ok! let us play this game. You can play queen for a day. But as soon as you step out of line, your ass is mine." He said. Kimberly turned towards Edward the 2nd. "Don't forget. I am the only one with access to the GLC. Plus, I have an actual army, navy and soon to be air force to back me." She said. Edward the 2nd turned in her direction. "But the island is legally mine." He said with a smile. At that moment, Kimberly's calm demeanor crumbled right before his eyes. "Don't fuck with me! I swear on the life of my unborn child! If you want a war, you'll get one!" Kimberly said before walking away. "You sure you wanna do that, girlfriend?!!" he shouted as she walked down the pier. Edward the 2nd began laughing hysterically as he faced the sun set.

As time went on, the division in ideology between Ali and his childhood friend Abdirrahim grew to the point that there were protests in the streets. Followers of Abdirrahim demanded that the population with albinism be deported. At the same time thousands of refugees from India's poorest regions were pouring in by the boat load.

The Indian population, mostly women and children, were placed in a region of Lassenberia bordering the pale lands. Just like the other refugees, they were all given a shot glass of GLC. All forms of disease were cured before the crowd had gathered to take an oath to the queen of Lassenberia.

Between September 4th to the end of November 10th, 2003 dozens of Abdirrahim's followers, who were mainly teenage boys of Ethiopian descent were transported to detention centers in Madagascar for brutal nighttime attacks on children with albinism. Edward the 2nd began losing favor with Abdirrahim. He remained behind the scenes, not showing any signs of supporting Abdirrahim's cause.

Edward the 2nd was at his residence watching old gangster movies. One reminded him of Christmas with his family back in the United States, he said to one of his agents standing guard by the door. They don't even celebrate Christmas around this motherfucker!!" he said to the agent. The agent had no opinion on his rants. He just stood there doing his duty. "What the fuck I'm talking to you for? It's like talking to a wall!" he said. Edward the 2nd went to the door. He summoned another agent who was standing guard outside the door. "I need you to deliver a message for me." He said to the agent. Edward the 2nd grabbed a pen and pad from off the coffee table. He began writing. Once he had finished writing, "I want you to take this letter, go to the castle and give it to the queen." Edward the 2nd said as he folded the letter and handed it to the agent. "Leave your gun here! I do not wanna start no unnecessary hostility! Now go!" he said to the agent. "Yes, my lord." The agent said.

About an hour later, the agent arrived at the main entrance of the castle with letter in hand. He told the soldiers his business for being there and was thoroughly searched for weapons. He was then allowed to pass with an escort to see, the now sergeant Christina Braxton. Sergeant

Braxton, along with 5 soldiers, briefly interrogated the agent in a small room after taking the letter. She gave the letter back to the agent where he followed her to meet the queen. Before he had the chance to deliver the letter to the queen, the agent had his hands and ankles shackled as an extra precaution. He was then led to the throne room where the queen was waiting for his arrival. Once the doors opened to the throne room, the agent stood before queen Kimberly, who was sitting on her throne. Her husband's throne remained where it was first placed.

"Queen of Lassenberia, I present to you a message from lord Lassenberry." the agent said. "You can bring the message to me." She said. The agent approached the throne and handed her the message. Kimberly read the letter. The message read that Edward the 2nd would like to trade the queen ownership in 50 percent of the island for a substantial supply of GLC. She began to chuckle. "Tell your lord that I'll think about it" she said before dismissing him.

When the agent returned to Edward the 2nd, he relayed the queen's response. "That, bitch!" he said as he flipped over the card table with a unfinished jigsaw puzzle on it. Later that evening Edward the 2nd had trouble sleeping. He was tossing and turning in bed until he decided to head to the bathroom. He opened the medicine cabinet where there was a bottle of Teresa's medication he had taken from her home. He worried that it would be harmful to her unborn child. He popped a couple of pills, hoping it would relax him. A couple of hours later he still could not sleep. The pills were taking effect on his sense of reality. He started seeing images of Kent Mooney walking around his house. suddenly the image of Kent stopped and came towards him. "How the hell you get in my house?" Edward the 2nd asked. The image did not answer him. Kent's image lunged at him, causing him to jump back and fall against the wall. Edward the 2nd started kicking and screaming for help. The agents standing guard outside kicked the door in looking for the culprit attacking their boss. Edward the 2nd stood up and grabbed one of the agents by the collar. "Go after that motherfucker!!" he shouted. "Go after who, my lord?" the agent asked. "Get out my fucking way!!" he shouted as he grabbed the gun from the agent's holster. He went outside and started yelling down the street waving the gun in the air. "Come here! Bring Yo bitch ass here!" he shouted at the night sky. Guards patrolling the area noticed his erratic behavior. Edward the 2nd took the safety off the gun and squeezed off one shot before being tackled. 5 of his 18 NA agents confronted and overpowered the young soldiers, leaving them unconscious. "Let's get him inside." One agent said. "Get off of me!" Edward the 2nd shouted once they got him back in the house. "My lord. What about the soldiers?" the agent asked. "What soldiers?" he asked. "The soldiers outside, my lord." The agent said. "I don't fucking know! Get rid of them!" he said to the agent. The agent incharge gave a nod to the other agents to carry (out the order. "You are dehydrated, my lord. You need medical attention." The agent said. "Yeah! I need water!" Edward the 2nd said. The agent put him over his shoulder and carried him to the bathroom. He then laid him on the shower floor. He turned on the showerhead, shooting chilly water on to his boss. Edward the 2nd was so out of it, he did not flinch one bit. "Did you find him?" he asked the agent. "Find whom, my lord?" the agent asked. "Fucking Kent!!" he shouted. "He's dead, my lord." The agent said. "Uh, oh! There he is, behind you!!" he shouted. "That's impossible, my lord." The agent said. Edward the 2nd lunged forth in the agents direction to attack the image. The agent was trained to react in a hostile environment within milli seconds. He gave Edward the

2nd a sharp blow to the chest with the palm of his hand causing him to bang his head on the shower wall, knocking him out cold. The agent checked his vital signs. He then turned off the shower head.

It was around 10:30 in the morning when Edward the second had awaken in his bed. he put his hands to his head and felt that his head was bandaged up. "Fuck!!" he said to himself. There was a knock on the door. "Come in!" he shouted as he held his head. "My lord. Can I get you anything?" the agent asked. "Yeah! Coffee, a glass of water and the bottle of pills in the medicine cabinet!" he said. "Yes, my lord. The agent said before leaving.

Moments later Edward the 2nd was standing in front of the mirror of his bedroom with the bottle of pills in his hand. He just stood there looking at the pills. He then stared at his reflection. He went to the bathroom and stood over the toilet. He began to empty the bottle into the toilet. He went back to his bedroom burying his head in the pillow. The sounds of his yelling was muffled by the pillow. "That fucking, bitch!" he said to himself. He leaves the bedroom, running back into the bathroom. Once again, he stood over the toilet contemplating his next move. He dipped his hands in the toilet, scooping the pills out of the toilet before they could dissolve. His hands were stained with the chalky residue from the pills. He placed the pills on a dry head towel. He then began to lick the chalky substance from his fingers. One of the agents stood in the doorway, watching as this was taking place. "What the hell you want?" Edward the 2nd asked. "The bodies have been disposed of my lord." The agent said. "What bodies?" Edward the 2nd asked. "The Lassenberian soldiers from this morning, my lord." He said. "Yeah, sure! Excellent job, robot!" Edward the 2nd said. "If I may say so, my lord. The pills you've taken could be problematic to your judgement." The agent said. Edward the 2nd looked surprised. "Since when you started thinking for yourself? I'm lord lassenberry! Edward the 2nd! Not Edward the addict! Now get the fuck back to your post!" he shouted. "Yes, my lord.!" The agent said before leaving his boss's presence.

— CHAPTER .46 OPERATION BAD GUY —

It was November 27th, 2003, around 5 in the morning. 2 elderly Caucasian men were taking a walk through the desert, about 10 miles away from a top-secret military base in the state of Nevada. One of the men was Dr. Zachmont. "I just can't believe it! We have had total control over these savages, nationwide for years! For reasons I do not wish to speak about, we've allowed these fucking Lassenberry people to slip through our fingers!" he shouted.

The other man he was venting to was United States Secretary of Defense, Carter Gates. "I promise you sir, I am doing everything I can to convince the president to break down Lassenberia's defenses! My people in Washington are now saying they've banned all foreign media!" he said. "Maybe that'll work to our advantage." Zachmont said. "How so, sir?" carter asked. "If we're blind to their every move, that means the American people are blind as well." Zachmont said. "I'll need to form a think tank." Carter said. Zachmont stopped in his tracks. "Screw a think tank! I am your think tank!" he said. "Of course, sir!" carter said. "I think it's time to set the wolves loose." Zachmont said. "The wolves, sir?" carter asked. "I'm talking about allowing certain drug kingpins in the country the freedom to cross borders." He said. "How will that lead us inside the walls of Lassenberia, sir?" carter asked. "Simple. We do a takeaway." Zachmont said. "A takeaway, sir?" carter asked with a puzzled look on his face. "We can put a freeze on suppling the kingpins on the eastern seaboard from getting their narcotics. Allow New Jersey to still stay in business, while the rest of the region will see them as the enemy and wage war on them for survival. Every junkie in the region will travel for miles to New Jersey to feed their addictions. The media will look for the source of all the chaos, which you will explain to the President and the Secretary of Homeland Security that Lassenberia's arm has reached the shores of this great nation, and the Lassenberry drug cartel is stronger than ever." Zachmont boasted. "Brilliant, sir!" carter said. Zachmont grabbed Carter's shoulders. "You pull this off, and master will reward you greater than you can imagine!" he said. "When shall we start, sir?" carter asked. "I'll contact you when the fuse is lit." Zachmont said. "Very well, sir." Carter said.

The 2 men continued to walk until they came upon a black limousine. Dr. Zachmont pulled out a small remote from his pants pocket. He pressed the red button on the remote.

"Ready for pick-up." He said into the remote. Within minutes a red prop plane appeared in the sky. It landed a few yards away from where the men were standing. "Well, this is where we part ways, Mr. secretary." Zachmont said. "Will you still be at the house for thanksgiving dinner, sir?" carter asked. "Of course! Will your youngest daughter be home from college?" Zachmont asked. "I believe so, sir." Carter said. "For your sake she'd better be! Good lord, she has a nice pair of tits! After dessert, I would like to have sex with her. You can have the privilege of watching." Zachmont said. "It would be an honor, sir." Carter said. "Good boy!" he said as he gently smacked carter on the face. Zachmont began to walk towards the plane, at the same time secretary Carter headed toward the limo.

It was late February 2004 when the crime organization, still going under the name Lassenberry began to feel the effects of what the Department of Homeland Security and the Drug enforcement agency would later call **Operation Bad Guy**. As boss of the Lassenberry organization, Clayton (Butch)Watson began to expand his drug empire across the Hudson river since New York City was suffering from a narcotics drought. Only Butch had access to pills, marijuana, heroin, and crack cocaine. After a week, the drought had spread as far as Maryland to the south and Connecticut to the north.

Butch received word from the streets that his entire family was in danger of being kidnapped by other crews outside of New Jersey's boarders for his product. He decided to move his wife, children, cousins, nieces, nephews, aunts and, uncles into castle Lassenberry as a precaution.

Elsewhere, on the corner of Ellsworth and North Washington street in east Baltimore Maryland, 2 black men were having a conversation about how bad business was on the streets. "Damn! I'm down to my last pound of weed!" one of the men said. "You doing better than me! I got an ounce left! I'm so stressed the fuck out; I'm about to smoke this shit myself!" the other guy said. "You better hold on to that shit, my nigga!" the first guy said. "I'm hearing them niggas up in Jersey holding all the weight!" the second guy said. "I can't believe the fucking state of Maryland dry as fuck!" the first guy said. "I'm about to take that ride up to jersey and stick somebody for their shit! You with me?" the first guy asked.

For weeks dealers have been migrating to States unscathed by the drought. Unfortunately, most of them were either chased back to their own territories or ended up dead in the streets.

In the case of New Jersey, Butch had to hire soldiers from the Gatano crime family, and the Philly mob to keep his streets safe from outsiders due to the national Agreement pulling back their agents for support. "I can't believe I hired one devil to protect me from the other devils!" Butch once said to his cousin Dubbs. To make things even more disastrous, Zachmont ordered the drought to be pushed back further west as far as the Appalachian Mountains. Drug kingpins from Ohio and Tennessee started to feel the effects of not receiving any product. There were a few independent meth labs still around in certain rural areas of Nashville and Chattanooga.

Mookie had fortified himself and his family in their home with 30 hired guns on the premises. From time-to- time, he would connect with one of his dealers on his walkie-talkie, he would sometimes hear continuous gunfire on the other end. He told his wife Rita it was becoming a losing battle to continue to do business on the streets because of outside invasion. "Creo que todo esto pasará, nena!" she reassured him.

Butch spent most of his time during this ordeal in the west wing office stressing over the situation. He confessed to his cousin Dubbs that he felt he was trapped in a cage. Dubbs told him that the feeling was mutual. The product was flowing, the money was coming in, but at a great cost.

It was March 17th, 2004, when white House press secretary Kelly O'Bannon was about to give a press briefing on the drug war sweeping the eastern seaboard of the United States. She made her way to the podium wearing a emerald green dress. She adjusted the microphone before speaking.

"Good morning, and happy St. Patrick's Day!" She said in a uplifting voice. The room of journalists reciprocated her greeting. "Today, the president and his cabinet are concerned with the on-going drug war in streets of more than 15 states, including here in Washington DC. Our intelligence and drug enforcement agencies have informed us that allegedly, the source of this horrific turn of events reach far as the rouge island nation of Lassenberia, who have cut off communications from the outside world since the assassination of their head of state, King Marcus. We are working very diligently with our allies in Europe and in Asia to bring an end to this catastrophe. Now, I will take questions." She said before pointing into the sea of journalists. She zeroed in on one journalist raising his hand. "Tom?" she said. "Does anyone know who assassinated the king of Lassenberia?" he asked. "Like I've just stated. Communications have been cut since then. Karen?" Kelly said. What type of illegal drugs do you think are being exported from Lassenberia?" Karen asked. "All of them!" Kelly said. The room filled with laughter. "Susan?" Kelly said. "Are there other nations involved in assisting the Lassenberian drug trafficking?" Susan asked. "That is still under investigation. Bob?" Kelly said. "Who is occupying the castle in new jersey allegedly owned by the lassenberry family?" he asked. "We are not sure at this time. Jill?" Kelly said. "Is military action being considered? Jill asked. Not at this moment. Jared?" Kelly said. "What does the president plan to do about the ongoing violence in the streets of our cities?" he asked. "We're leaving that up to local and state authorities. We are are more concerned with the source of the problem. Brenda?" Kelly said. "There are rumors of a secret order infiltrating the government who are behind the violence in the streets of our urban communities. Care to comment?" she asked. Kelly smiled. "I know we're living in the conspiracy theory age. But I can assure you there is no agency infiltrating our national security. Now, if there are not any more questions, I'd like to thank you all for your time." Kelly said before stepping down from the podium. A roar of questions came from the crowd as she was leaving the press room.

Elsewhere... "What do you mean, they're missing?" Jenna asked sergeant Braxton. "From the report. The soldiers haven't shown up to muster in days." Braxton said. "This is getting ridiculous! We have more of our troop's bodies either washing up on shore, or just vanishing! "Jenna said. "I propose we shut down the island, your excellency; until we get to the bottom of this." Braxton said. "Our allies depend on the GLC. We depend on goods and services from them." Jenna said. "I didn't mean stop trading, your excellency. I meant stop bringing in new immigrants." Braxton suggested.

On the other side of the island, Edward the 2nd was boarding the royal yacht. He had about 7 NA agents going with him. The rest were left behind to guard his residence. He had ordered the captain to take him to the coast of South Africa.

After captain and the crew docked the yacht in Durban Harbor, Edward the 2nd and his agents visited the metropolitan area looking to trade a vial of GLC for a bottle of prescription pills that he had begun to use to self-medicate from stress. Once he found his drug connection, he convinced the dealer that one vial of GLC was worth all the pills he had to offer. By giving the dealer a sample of the GLC, he was convinced that Edward the 2nd had was worth its weight in gold. After a day of touring the city of Durban and enjoying the night life with female companionship, Edward the 2nd and his agents returned to the yacht with 4 cases of the preferred opioid which he had no problem getting through Lassenberia's customs due to his status on the island nation.

Under the influence of the opioids, Edward the 2nd would throw lavish parties on the royal yacht or at his residence. He would only have the most attractive teen-age girls as his guests. Since he was lord protector, no one, not even the queen herself questioned his decadent activities. Kimberly said to her sister that if wild parties would keep him out of her hair, then so be it.

For a while Lassenberia was calm and peaceful when security was tightened, immigration came to a halt and Kimberly was free from any interference from Edward the 2nd. It was until Jenna, the prime minister of Lassenberia, received communications from the United Nation's deputy secretary that the United states would sanction Lassenberia because of the drug wars taking place on the east coast. Kimberly became outraged when receiving the news. She knew it was based on her control of the GLC. The United states began to force its hand on countries economically conspiring with Lassenberia.

Kimberly had called a meeting with the council to discuss the economic war the United States had put into play. She urged the council and the citizens to tighten their bootstraps until she returned from the United Nations in New York to resolve the situation. Before leaving to visit the United States, Kimberly feared a power struggle would occur within the royal family. She had the council sign a decree that her children, 4-year-old Mark and 4-month-old son James Benjamin would be put under the care of the council and to succeed her to the throne if she did not return. This was to protect them from not only Edward the 2nd but another Lassenberry as well. A month after Kimberly had given birth to her son, princess Teresa went missing after giving birth to a baby girl whom Edward the 2nd named Niyale. Edward the 2nd knew that his children from Viola would not survive the hands of Doug Reed after being double crossed. Teresa was so distraught about giving birth under incestual circumstances, she had threatened Edward the 2nd many times that she would kill her child. It was rumored that she had taken a motorboat and headed towards Mahajanga in Madagascar.

Being the prime minister, Jenna insisted that she go visit the United Nations in place of her sister. Kimberly could not sit around and watch her subjects be starved to death from the sanctions.

During this time, Edward the 2nd had increased his dosage of pills. He began seeing images as he walked the streets in a zombie state. The NA agents would protect him by forming a circle around him as he staggered about. Citizens walking by were concerned about his well-being, but the agents would not allow them to come near him. The next day when he woke up, he found himself in his bathtub naked. He turned on the showerhead. The agents standing outside in the living room could hear the high pitch screams as he was sprayed with the freezing water. When he came out of the shower, there was an Agent waiting to hand him a towel to dry himself off. "Give me a report, robot!" Edward the 2nd said. "My fellow agent has reported that the queen is preparing to leave for the United States to negotiate the terms of the sanctions placed upon Lassenberia." the agent said.

NA agents were not only in hand-to-hand combat, fluent in 100 different languages, weapons training but espionage as well. They were programmed to analyze, assess, and conquer their environment no matter how intellectually superior or inferior their master's competence.

"Now would be the perfect time to set your plan in motion to claim this island, my lord." The agent said. Edward the 2nd looked at the agent with suspicion. "That's funny! I do not remember giving the order to spy on the queen! But thanks!" Edward the 2nd said.

Edward the 2nd went to his bedroom to put some clothes on. Afterwards he went down the hall to another bedroom where another NA agent was caring for his infant daughter Niyale. "There's my little princess!" he said as the agent handed her over to him. "She's been relieved of flatulence after feeding, my lord." the agent said. "You mean you burped her?" Edward the 2nd asked. "Yes, my lord. "Why don't the fuck you just say that?!!" he shouted. "Is there anything else you need done, my lord?" the agent asked. "Get her dressed. I am taking her outside for a stroll. She needs to get used to her kingdom!" he chuckled. 'Is there anything you have in mind I should dress her in, my lord?" the agent asked. "Yeah! Clothes, Motherfucker!" he shouted.

Edward the 2nd went downstairs. He was searching frantically through his residence for something. He practically turned the place upside down as he used explicit language out of frustration. One of his agents approached him from behind. Edward the 2nd became startled. "What the fuck you doing sneaking up behind me like that?!!" he shouted. "Forgive me, my lord! Is this what you were looking for?" the agent asked as he held a small object in his hand. Edward the 2nd went from being angered to looking relieved. "You robots are fucking amazing!" he said.

The agent held the vial of poison given to Edward the 2nd by Doug Reed back in the United States. The vial of poison had passed through Edward the 2nd's digestive system once he arrived in Lassenberia to fulfill his goal.

"After the queen leaves for the United States, I want you to go the prime minister and schedule a formal dinner for us to discuss business." Edward the 2nd said. "Yes, my lord." The agent said before handing over the vial of poison. "We'll see who runs shit around here!" Edward the 2nd said to himself.

It was a sunny breezy afternoon. Edward the 2nd had a big smile on his face as he pushed his daughter in her stroller. 6 agents were guarding them as they walked down Jabbo road. The citizens of Lassenberia who were driving by would pull over to greet Edward the 2nd and his daughter. The agents were apprehensive to let anyone near the infant. "Let the people gaze upon the future ruler of Lassenberia!" he said to the agents. The women were in awe of Niyale's smooth brown skin and beauty. She had a full head of curly hair, chubby cheeks, and alluring eyes. "Ni jambo jema yeye haionekani kama baba yake!" one of the women of Tanzanian descent commented. The women around her began to chuckle before getting back into their vehicle. Edward the 2nd did not know the language but felt that there were no kind words coming from the woman. "What the fuck she say, robot?" he asked. "The woman said it's good that the baby doesn't look like her father." The agent translated. Edward the 2nd stood there for a moment with a hurt look on his face. "Find out who she is and make her disappear!" he said to the agent. "Yes, my lord." The agent said before walking away.

Later that evening, Edward the 2nd went to visit Sheldon at the hall of records. Sheldon and his staff were busy preparing a speech for the queen to speak before the United nations. They were working against the clock. They planned to have it in her hands before mid-night. She has scheduled to leave first thing in the morning.

"What's up, my brother?" he said to Sheldon as entered his office. "What brings you out this evening, lord Lassenberry?" he asked. "Oh, I'm just making my rounds. I just came from visiting the borough of Braxton and the pale lands. Those albinos are very closed off people!" he said. "You would be too, if you were persecuted since birth!" Sheldon said. "Maybe. But you need to pay extra attention to these people, and have your people record their every move. I just got bad vibes from them." He said. "Is this coming from the queen?" Sheldon asked. "Listen. I'm lord protector, assigned by the queen. And you were just given an order." Edward the 2nd said with a faux smile. "Ok!" Sheldon sighed.

Edward the 2nd started looking through files. "Anything in particular you're looking for, lord Lassenberry?" Sheldon asked. 'What? You have something to hide?" he said. Sheldon had the look of embarrassment in front of his staff. Edward the 2nd began laughing. "I'm just fucking with you, man!" he chuckled as he continued to look through the paperwork. There was a nervous laughter amongst the staffers. "You'll have to excuse us, lord Lassenberry. We have to get this speech to the Queen." Sheldon said. "You gonna be there when she make the speech?" Edward the 2nd asked. "Ah, yes!" Sheldon said. "Cool! I approve." Edward the 2nd said. "You approve?" Sheldon asked. "Well, I gotta go! You have a safe trip and give the queen my best." Edward the 2nd said before leaving with his entourage of agents. "That was odd!" one of Sheldon's staffers said. "Yes, it was." Sheldon said as he sat there in deep thought. "Get me on the line with general Ali." He said to one of his staff members.

Back at castle Lassenberia Kimberly's staff were running around preparing for her departure. Her trusted aid Ali had a 10-man detail geared up and ready to make the trek to the United states. Given diplomatic immunity, Ali and his men were able to carry small arms such as high-powered rifles, pistols, and light machine guns into U.S. territory.

Commander Ntsay was on duty in command central when he received a call from Sheldon to get in contact with Ali. Once Sheldon gained communication with Ali, he urged Ali to increase his security detail going to the United States. Ali questioned Sheldon's judgement. Sheldon told him his it was based on intuition. Being a man of reason, Ali heeded his words and tripled his security detail.

It was March 21st, 2004, when queen Kimberly's plane was preparing to land in New York City. There were dozens of military vehicles, state, and local authorities on the tarmac waiting for her arrival. There were fighter jets circling the air space on full alert. Coast guard ships and local police patrolled the harbors of New York. The actual airport was shut down, causing cancelations and delays of arrival, and leaving flights.

Once the plane came to a halt, 4 black limousines quickly pulled up next to the plane. Due to the elevated level of security, not even the local and foreign media were aware of the queen's arrival. Once everyone loaded up into the limos, the limos quickly sped off escorted by military vehicles, 20 police officers on motorcycles and emergency rescue vehicles. There were federal agents posted on top of skyscrapers equipped with high powered rifles along the route towards the Hardenbergh hotel where the queen and her people would rest before her speech to the world.

Instead of pulling up in front of the luxury hotel like other foreign dignitaries, queen Kimberly and her entourage entered through the service entrance. Flags from other countries were hoisted above the hotel when heads of state arrived. Due to the situation with what was going on in New Jersey, orders came from the secretary of Homeland Security not to raise the Lassenberian flag.

At Kimberly's request, she and her entourage were given the top 3 floors of the penthouse, which each suite cost twenty thousand dollars at night. Kimberly stayed on the top floor with a garrison of her men guarding her.

Later that evening, Kimberly was looking at the New York skyline from the roof top as the moonlight reflected on the Olympic size swimming pool. She began pacing around the swimming pool, being followed by 2 armed Lassenberian guards while reciting the speech given to her by her scribe/ brother-in-law Sheldon. He stayed up with her, sitting on a Victorian style patio chair, with a copy of the speech in his lap coaxing Kimberly to make the speech genuine.

"It seems like I'm kissing these peoples' ass!" she said out of frustration. "Not at all! It's saying that you're willing to do whatever it takes for the citizens of Lassenberia!" Sheldon said. "I told you before we came here, what this is about! Someone got wind of the GLC!" she said. "Like I told you, it's up to you to take this stigma off the Lassenberry name by having them lift the sanctions and stop the killings here in America!" Sheldon explained. Kimberly stood quietly in thought. She took her copy of the speech and tore it in half. "Screw this! I will not be bullied into surrendering our most precious resource! They threaten us with sanctions, we will expose their motives to the world! If they deny the accusations, we'll just take our ball and go home!" she said before heading towards the exit. Sheldon sighed as he fell back into his chair.

Elsewhere in the city of Camden New Jersey, an incursion was taking place on 2 African American street dealers from the Lassenberry organization as they were fighting for their lives to protect 20 kilos of pure cocaine stashed in the trunk of their Boeman Sedan.

One guy was nick named Colgate because of his straight teeth and perfect smile. His partner was nick named Booda. They were forced to detour into Johnson park and trade bullets with 6 other black men from Baltimore.

"How the fuck they find out we're holding product?!!" Booda shouted. "How the fuck I'm supposed to know? Nigga! I don't think we gonna make it to the safe house and mix this shit!!" Colgate shouted. "You think?!!" Booda said with sarcasm in his voice. Their car was being riddle with bullets. They were pinned down between their car and a huge oak tree. Booda caught a piece of glass in the eye from the shattered windshield. "I got glass in my eye!! I can't see shit!!" he shouted as he aimlessly returned fire. Colgate took down one of the guys with a shot to the head. "I'm down to one clip, man!!" Colgate shouted. "My fucking eye!!" Booda shouted as he crouched down in the back seat. Colgate took cover behind the driver's side door before taking a bullet to the ankle. He jumped back, landing under the steering wheel. "Fuck!! I'm out!!" he shouted. "Here, man!!" Booda shouted as he tossed his last clip in Colgate's aim was off, landing on the dashboard. Colgate took a bullet in the palm of his hand when he reached for the clip. "Goddamn!! We're done, man!!" he shouted as their attackers began to move in on them. "I'm getting the fuck outta here!! They can have that shit!!" Booda shouted as he scooched backwards to exit the car. With one hand, Colgate grabbed the clip, shoved it into his pistol, and began firing. "Come on, motherfuckers!!" he shouted as his attackers moved in for the kill. He squeezed off shots until his clip was empty. Just like the car holding their stash, both he and Booda were riddled with bullets.

The 5-man hit squad moved in, checking the bodies for movement. "These niggas dead." One of the men said. "Check the trunk!" another man said. The trunk was popped opened, and as they were tipped off earlier, there lay the 20 kilos in plastic shrink wrap with a big capital letter L stamped on each kilo. "Let's load this shit and get the fuck out before the cops come!" one of the men said. Off in the distance a black van was parked. There were 2 NA agents of African American descent sitting in the van, watching everything that took place. "They've found the drugs, as directed. Let us go." One agent said to the other.

The next morning, Kimberly had risen from her bed. she covered herself with silk robe. Before she headed toward the mirror, she opened the drapes to let in the sunlight. She stood in front of the mirror and began sobbing. She regained her composure when there was a knock on the door. "Enter!" she shouted. "Is everything alright, your majesty?" Ali asked. "Of course! Tell the girls to prepare my wardrobe and come up to do my hair and make-up." She said. "Yes, your majesty." Ali said. He and Kimberly glanced out toward the terrace, watching the silhouette of 2 guards standing at their post.

A couple of hours later, Kimberly's 'handmaidens were putting the final changes on her hairdo to compliment her diamond tiara. Her outfit was put together in a more conservative fashion. She wore the traditional Lassenberry black top with the red and green sash, having her Husband's medals pinned on her. Her bottom attire was a long black pleated skirt falling below her knees, with sheer pantyhose and black high heel shoes.

It was March 22nd 2004 when queen Kimberly was on her way to make the most important speech of her life before the free world. Even though the United Nations building was less than 5 minutes away from the hotel, Kimberly's entourage insisted that she be driven under tight security to her destination.

The queen's envoy was sent to the United Nations building hours before the queen's arrival for a final security check. Bomb sniffing dogs, debugging devices, and metal detectors were used to make sure the queen's safety was certain. Fortunately, the security team found a duffle bag filled with homemade pipe bombs near one of the exits. It seemed the botched terrorist attack did not have the chance to place the bombs to be set off. When Kimberly received notice about the situation, she still thought it was too important to make her speech then to turn around and run back to Lassenberia.

When Queen Kimberly entered the halls of the United Nations, the 192 members from each nation watched in silence as the queen made her way down the red carpet towards the podium. All non-English speaking members donned their earpieces for translation. She looked impressed once she stepped on stage as she gently rubbed her hand across the Lassenberian flag mounted in the background. She quickly changed to a more serious expression when turning toward the audience.

"Good afternoon fellow delegates. I am going to make this brief. First, I would like to thank the Secretary-General, the UN President and hopefully after the day is over, the President of the United states for this especially important invitation." She said. Members of the assembly began to chuckle. "I am the former Queen consort, Kimberly of Lassenberia, now serving as absolute monarch upon the death of my husband, king Marcus. I come to you today to talk about the horrific accusations towards my country and my family name. I understand that the Lassenberry name has been synonymous with drug trafficking here in the United States during the last 5 decades or so. But I assure you that the crimes committed in the cities of the state of New Jersey due to the illegal narcotics trade are not the fault of the Lassenberry family." She said. The sounds of the assembly chatting amongst each other could be heard, causing Kimberly to pause. "I believe, like so many others around the United States that this scourge falls upon a shadow society within the American government. I also believe that the sovereign nation of Lassenberia is under the threat of being extorted for its most precious resource, which could be beneficial to the world's population. I come here before you all and demand that you denounce and retract the media's slanderous attacks brought on allegedly by this shadow society. Then, and only then, there will be a time to heal the world of pestilence and traumatic injuries." She said. The assembly began chatting amongst themselves once more. "I would like to close with this, ladies and gentlemen. It would not be wise to bite the hand that can supply a cure-all across the world. Thank you." she said before stepping down from the podium. Ali, who was standing off in the wings, rushed to her side to escort her out of the room. UN soldiers swarmed around them as they were heading toward the exit. They led Ali and the queen to the underground tunnels of the UN where the rest of her security team was waiting. Before they could drive off, 2 secret service agents ran towards them. "Your majesty! The president of the United States would like to invite you as his quest at the White House!" the agent panted. "With-all-do-respect to the president, the queen has nothing else to say!" Ali said. "No, Ali! Let us take the president up on what he has to say!" Kimberly said. Ali leaned in towards the queen. "We must leave, your majesty! I have a bad feeling about this!" he whispered in her ear. "We'll wait at the hotel for the president's." Kimberly said. The queen's caravan made a U-turn out of the under-ground garage, making their way back to the hotel.

Back at the hotel suite, Ali was continuing to convince the queen they should leave the country as soon as possible. "We have these people wrapped around our fingers! The longer we stay, the more they feel our uncertainty, your majesty!" he said. "I believe once we have President Lyon in our back pocket, the rest of our adversaries will follow!" she said. "I hope you're right, your majesty! I hope you're right!" he sighed.

That evening at castle Lassenberry in Cherry Hill New Jersey, Butch was walking down the corridor of the east wing, followed by 2 armed bodyguards. Suddenly he was approached by his cousin Dubbs. "Yo! Did you hear?" Dubbs asked. "Hear what, nigga?" Butch asked.

"We got New York and Rhode Island to back off!" he said. "Back off from what?" Butch asked. "Warring with us!" Dubbs said. "Where you get this from? Doug?" Butch asked. "I put spies out on the streets!" Dubbs said. "Y'all stay here!" Butch said to his bodyguards. He grabbed his cousin by the arm, pulling him away so they could talk in private. "I run shit, here! Don't ever make moves behind my back again!" He whispered. "I ain't I a general too?" Dubbs asked. "Fuck that general shit! Before this shit is over with, it's gonna be just us! Mookie and his inner circle gotta go! We'll just say to everybody that he was a casualty of war!" Butch whispered. "Why? Mookie always stayed in his lane!" Dubbs said. "I said what I had to say!" Butch whispered before walking back towards his bodyguards.

The next day Edward the 2nd had risen from his bed, stretching as he yawned. He had a smile on his face as he made his way to his daughter's room which was being guarded by 2 NA agents. He stood over her crib. "How's my future queen?" he said as he stroked her hair. He went to the door. "Did y'all feed her yet?" he asked one of the agents. "Not yet, my lord." The agent said. "Ok, then. Have someone make my breakfast. I'm going outside to get a breath of fresh air." He said before heading downstairs. When Edward the 2nd stepped outside in his robe and pajamas, there were 2 NA agents standing guard at the entrance. "What a wonderful day! Don't you think so, robot?" he asked one of the agents. "If you say so, my lord." The agent responded. Suddenly they saw a young African woman running down the street screaming off in the distance. "Waziri Mkuu amekufa! Waziri Mkuu amekufa!" she shouted. "What the hell she screaming about?" Edward the 2nd asked. "She just said the prime minister is dead, my lord." The agent said. Edward the 2nd smiled. "Like I said! What a wonderful day!" he said as he folded his arms.

When Edward the 2nd offered an invitation to have a one-on-one business dinner with Jenna. She was reluctant at first but eventually caved into his offer. The dinner was held at his residence the day after the queen and her entourage left for the United states. Jenna made sure that her security was close by, meaning that soldiers from the Pale Horseman division were standing in the room as they dined. Edward the 2nd had his agents clear the room to make the prime minister feel secure. The real threat was in the front pocket of Edward the 2nd. In his possession was an empty vial that held the poison meant for king Marcus. Edward the 2nd took it upon himself to prepare the meal as a friendly gesture. With the help of a cookbook, he prepared a hearty meal for the prime minister, which consisted of garlic mash potatoes, steamed mixed vegetables, corn bread, and for the main course grilled chicken. For dessert, he served strawberry cheesecake. The strawberry sauce was the same color of the contents that was in the vial. As Doug Reed said, the poison was non traceable. "I have to be honest with you, because of the disappearance of princess Teresa, my trust in you has fallen drastically!" Jenna said. Edward the 2nd looked stunned. "She was my favorite cousin! I hope your soldiers are doing their job to find her!" he said. "We are! I hope for your sake, with-all-do-respect, she is unharmed!" were her last words before she took her first bite of strawberry cheesecake. Jenna went to bed that evening with a full belly, and never woke up. Her assistant called upon help from one of the soldiers to break into her bedroom when she didn't respond to the knocking on the door.

"Well, I guess I best get dressed and get ready for the bullshit!" Edward the 2nd sighed.

"Very well, my lord." The agent said. The agent remained outside at his post while Edward the 2nd went back into the house.

Usually it takes weeks for the president of the United States to prepare to meet with foreign dignitaries. In the case of President Lyon meeting with Kimberly, it took place the same day queen Kimberly made her historical speech at the UN. Kimberly had changed clothes for the occasion, leaving her tiara being at the hotel, which was being guarded by a garrison of her security detail. At this meeting dozens of journalists miraculously swarmed the oval office. The flickering sounds of cameras were heard as Kimberly and the president sat next to each other and shook hands for a photo op.

"What is the relationship between the U.S. and Lassenberia, Mr. president?" one journalist asked. President Lyon and Kimberly looked at each other. They both cracked a smile. "As you can see, it's a good one!" the president said. "Mr. president. When will there be an official trade agreement with Lassenberia?" another journalist asked. "Soon! Very soon." The president said. "Your Majesty. How does it feel to be in the oval office?" another journalist asked. Kimberly paused for a moment, pondering the question. "Refreshing." She said showing off her beautiful smile. The crowd began chuckling. "Mr. president. When do you plan to visit Lassenberia?" another journalist asked. "Soon!" the president said. "Your majesty. Is it true that your private family resort was attacked by a rival drug cartel?" another journalist asked. "That'll be enough questions! Thank you!" the president said. The camera men and reporters in the room could see the sorrow in the queen's face before being rushed out of the room by secret service and staff members.

Once the oval office was cleared, President Lyon placed his hand on Kimberly's shoulder. "Everything will be fine, young lady." He said. "I hope so." She said. "It will be an honor if you and your brother-in-law would join me and the first lady for dinner tonight." The president said as he handed her his handkerchief. Kimberly nodded her head as she wiped away her tears.

Sheldon and Ali were standing outside the oval office. "I don't like this, sir! We should be on the plane to Lassenberia!" Ali whispered to Sheldon. "Quiet!" Sheldon whispered. Everyone standing in the corridor made way for an important figure heading toward the oval office. The man who the secret service agent opened the door for to the oval office was secretary of defense Gates. The door was closed behind him at once, giving Ali a glimpse at his queen.

"The queen of Lassenberia! it's an honor to finally meet you, your majesty!" Secretary Gates said with open arms. "Your majesty. I would like you to meet secretary of defense, Carter Gates." The president said. "No need to get up, your Majesty! The honor is mine!" Gates said as he shook her hand.

— CHAPTER .47 THE RENEGING NIGGER —

It was March 24th, 2004 when Edward the 2nd had a one-on-one meeting with Abdirrahim on the royal yacht. NA agents were scattered about the vessel keeping a lookout for unwelcomed guests as it was tied to the pier. They sat on beach chairs at the stern of the ship sharing a bottle of wine. Edward the 2nd stared out at the sun coming over the horizon, sipping his glass of wine. "Lord Lassenberry. Lord Lassenberry!" Abdirrahim shouted trying to get his attention. "What?!" Edward the 2nd responded. "What was the reason you summoned me, sir?" he asked. "Yeah! Yeah! Uh! I need you by my side more than ever now!" he said after snapping out of his daze. "How can I serve you, sir!" Abdirrahim said. "When the queen and Sheldon return from, whatever the fuck they're doing, they're gonna be more than pissed when they find out the prime minister is dead!" he said. "What was the cause of death, sir?" Abdirrahim asked. "According to the doctor, it was of natural causes!" he said. "At least she passed in her sleep. I have seen more traumatic forms of death in my lifetime. Abdirrahim said. "Tell me about it!" Edward the 2nd said. "The first time when I was 6 years old." Abdirrahim said. Edward the 2nd looked confused. "It was just a figure of speech! Jesus!" he responded as he shook his head. "Oh. Sorry, sir." Abdirrahim said. "Something is still bothering me about the dinner we had together." Edward the 2nd said. "What is it, sir?" Abdirrahim asked. "The pale horsemen was her security that evening! They looked as if they were up to something devious!" Edward the 2nd said as he quickly cut his eye towards Abdirrahim to see his reaction. Abdirrahim shook his head looking fired up. "It figures, sir. I was always told as a child these creatures were an abomination in human form! They probably put a curse upon the dear prime minister!" he said. "The energy in the room was so…disturbing! I feared for my life! But I kept a cool exterior!" Edward the 2nd said. "If I find out those wretched creatures were responsible for the prime minister's death, lyaga oo dhan, waxay u dhiman doonaan geeri naxdin leh!" Abdirrahim said with hate in his voice. "I don't know what the hell you just said, but it sounds scary as shit!" Edward the 2nd chuckled. "I said-!" Abdirrahim was about translate. "I don't give a fuck! As long as it wasn't about me!" Edward the 2nd chuckled as he gently elbowed Abdirrahim on the arm. "I'm going to draw up a search warrant in a couple of hours. I want you to take a team into the pale lands, along with sergeant Braxton and her team, so I don't seem partial. I want you to do a thorough search! Report back to me if anything! I mean anything seems suspicious! Understand?" Edward the 2nd said. "Yes, sir!" Abdirrahim said. He put down his glass of wine and was about to leave the yacht. "Hold on, motherfucker! What I told y'all what to say when leaving my presence?" Edward the shouted. "Forgive, me, sir! Long live the house of Lassenberry! long live Edward the 2nd!!" he shouted. "Good man! Now get outta here." He said. Edward the 2nd refilled his glass halfway. He gulped the wine down in one swallow. Once he was sure Abdirrahim had left the ship, he turned to one of his agents. "Is the vial in a place where they can easily find it?" he asked the agent. "Yes, my lord." The agent said. "Good! By-the-way! What the hell he said in that funny language of his?" Edward the 2nd asked. "It was Somali, my lord. He said they will die a horrible death." The agent said. "Cool!" Edward the 2nd said.

The next day around 2am, the Pale Lands was under siege by Abdirrahim and his soldiers, along with sergeant Braxton and the royal guard. All citizens with albinism with relation to the Pale horseman were forced to evacuate their homes to search for evidence about the death of the prime minister, Jenna Jenkins. The pale horse man did not take this lying down. there was a standoff between Abdirrahim's men and the pale horseman. The standoff became more intense when 200 soldiers from the Zewde clan arrived.

"What are you doing here, Ethiopian?" Abdirrahim asked. "We were sent by Lord Lassenberry as reinforcements!" commander Menelik said.

Menelik sahle had just turned 18 when queen Kimberly promoted him to the rank of commander in the Zewde clan. He suffered from a brain tumor protruding from his skull when he migrated with his brothers and sisters from the Afder Zone. Just a shot glass of GLC cured him instantly. He revealed to the queen that he was a natural leader at such a youthful age.

Sergeant Braxton stood on the hood of one of the military vehicles. She was given a bullhorn by one of her soldiers. "Testing! Testing!" she shouted after the feedback. Everyone from all sides went silent. "By order of lord protector, Edward the 2nd, I hereby announce that soldiers of the pale horseman task force lay down your weapons, and let your homes be lawfully searched!" she said. "We take our orders from the queen!" Kiker from the pale horseman shouted. "The queen is not present at the time, and the prime minister is deceased! By the 48 laws of Lassenberia, this nation is under the authority of lord Lassenberry for the time being!" Braxton shouted.

Kiker turned to his men. "Lay down your weapons, my brothers! We will comply with their orders, for now!" he shouted before taking the initiative to lay down his weapon. The other 89 pale horseman reluctantly followed suit. "Thank you, captain." Braxton said to Kiker. Abdirrahim and his men still had their weapons drawn as they slowly moved in, while the Zewde clan lowered theirs. "What are you doing, Abdirrahim? They are unarmed!" Menelik asked. "Just a precaution! These people cannot be trusted!" Abdirrahim said. "He's right, Abdirrahim! There is no need to aim weapons at unarmed people! Especially fellow Lassenberians!" Braxton said. There was a moment of silence when a single shot came from out of nowhere, striking Braxton in the head. The bullhorn fell from her hand before she fell off the hood of the vehicle. The crowd looked on in awe as the blonde-haired sergeant fell to the ground. Suddenly, bullets began flying from Abdirrahim and his soldiers. Soldiers from the pale horseman task force began dropping like flies. Some civilians were hit in the hail of bullets. A soldier from the pale horseman named Jasper Forde did a quick tumble roll, simultaneously grabbing his machine gun from off the ground. He took down a handful of Abdirrahim's men before taking cover.

About 800 yards away, a NA agent was disassembling a high-powered rifle by first taking off the 6-24x50 rifle scope. He calmly placed the rifle parts in a hard leather case and walk off with it.

Back at the skirmish, the pale horseman were being overran. About 20 of them survived to run back into their homes to barricade themselves in. Menelik had no choice but to join in the battle on the side of Abdirrahim after one of his men was hit. Members of the royal guard tended to sergeant Braxton, dragging her body out of harm's way trying their best to revive her. Sadly, it was too late.

After 15 minutes, Abdirrahim ordered a cease fire. "This ends today! Burn these creature's homes to the ground!" he shouted to him. "Wait! This is not part of our mandate!" Menelik shouted. "You have a choice, boy! Either you join us, now or answer to lord Lassenberry later! Trust me Ethiopian! You don't have the manpower to stand against us!" Abdirrahim shouted. Menelik paused for a moment before ordering his men to slowly back away. "Cowards!! Lord Lassenberry will have your heads for this betrayal!!" Abdirrahim shouted. "When the queen returns, we'll see whose heads will be in danger!" Menelik said before having his soldier drive them away.

Miles away coming in from the opposite side of the island, Kimberly and her entourage were flying in on her private plane. About 20 miles behind them was the United States doomsday airplane carrying the Secretary of Defense and his staff. They were being escorted by 2 United States fighter jets flying out of Djibouti.

"I'm exhausted! I'll never get used to the different time zones!" Sheldon said. "I just hope you were focused enough to record every moment of our trip." Ali said. "Don't worry. I didn't miss a moment." Sheldon said. "How is the investigation on princess Teresa's whereabouts coming along?" Kimberly asked. "Last I'd check, your majesty, Abdirrahim and his men have been sweeping the countryside thoroughly." Ali said.

They were about to come in for a landing until they received word from the pilot that their landing might be delayed due to the chaos going on below. Kimberly looked of the window and saw in the distance about 15 to 20 funnels of black smoke coming from the Pale lands. "What the hell?" she said with a terrified look on her face. Ali rushed to the window. "Check your weapons!" he said to his men. Sheldon looked out the window as well. "Jenna! My kids!" he said to himself. "I think we shouldn't land, your majesty! The nearest airport is in Madagascar!" Ali suggested. "No! I'm the queen! Those are my people down there! We're landing!" Kimberly ordered. Ali ran towards the cockpit. "Radio a message to the Secretary of Defense! It might not be safe for him to land!" he said to the pilot. "I pray that everyone is safe, your majesty! One of Kimberly's handmaidens said. Ali came running back from the cockpit. "Your majesty! The Secretary of Defense refused to turn around! He said he will face whatever tragedy with us!" he said. Kimberly raised an eyebrow of suspicion to what Ali had said. "Really? That's odd for what a high leveled dignitary would do." She said. "What are you purposing, your majesty?" Ali asked. "Stay vigilant when comes to Secretary Gates." She said. "Yes, your majesty!" Ali said.

The pilot relayed a message to Lassenberian air traffic control. It took them a few minutes to respond. Finally, they were given permission to land. As the plane came in closer for a landing, the passengers noticed armed soldiers standing at the ready near the air strip. Once the plane came to a complete stop, Ali unbuckled his seatbelt. He ran to the cockpit again. He gave the pilot the order to keep the turbines running. He then ran back to the cabin area. "Your majesty. I think it would be safe if you and the staff stay on board until my men and I find out what's going on!" he said. "Ok! be safe!" Kimberly said as she held his hand. "Open the hatch!" Ali said to one of the crew members. Once the hatch opened, Ali and his men exited the plane with weapons drawn. They were approached by one of Ali's band of top men, Elmi Barre, and his crew. "Waa maxay arintan, Elmi?" Ali asked. "We are under strict orders from lord lassenberry to secure the island, sir! The only reason you were given permission to land is because lord Lassenberry would like to meet with the queen!" Elmi said. "Waxaan jeclaan lahaa in aan la hadlo sayidkayga Lassenberry!" Ali said. "I can't allow that, sir! Lord Lassenberry is lord protector! His word is law, now!" Elmi said. Elmi's men drew their weapons. "Give me a moment!" Ali said before reentering the plane. "What is it, Ali?" Kimberly asked. "This is a crazy situation, Your majesty! According to my men on the ground, lord Lassenberry has taken control of the island! He wants to meet with you, and you only!" Ali said. Kimberly turned to Sheldon! "I want you to come with me and record every moment for history's sake!" she said. "My wife and kids are out there! Of course, I'm coming!" Sheldon said. "Alright then! Tell Elmi I'll come only if Sheldon comes with me!" she said. "Very well, your majesty!" Ali sighed. Ali left the plane and explained the conditions on the queen meeting with lord lassenberry.

Miles above, the doomsday plane carrying Secretary Gates and the 2 U.S. fighter jets were still circling Lassenberian air space. "What do you think is going on down there, Mr. secretary?" his staff member asked. "I have no idea! But we have to get our hands on a sample of this miracle drug to take it back to the states and try to replicate it!" Gates said.

Kimberly and Sheldon were being driven to castle Lassenberia by Elmi and his soldier. She and Sheldon sat in the back seat as they watched the black smoke in the sky coming from the pale lands. "If you hurt my wife and kids, I'll kill every last one of you mother fuckers!" Sheldon said. "Lord Lassenberry will explain everything once we arrive at the castle, sir." Elmi said.

Once they arrived at the castle, Kimberly and Sheldon noticed a few NA agents standing guard outside the main gate. "This doesn't look good!" Kimberly said to Sheldon. Minutes passed when they were led to the throne room. Kimberly became infuriated when she saw Edward the 2nd sitting on her deceased husband's throne. "This better be some sick joke!" she said to him. Edward the 2nd looked cozy sitting on the throne as he was leaning back with his legs crossed. "Ah! The former queen of Lassenberia!" he said with a big smile on his face. There were 2 NA agents standing at parade rest on both sides of the throne. "What do you mean, former queen, and where is my family?" Sheldon asked. "Awe! I'm sorry to say that your wife is no longer with us!" Edward the 2nd said with a faux sorrowful look on his face. "You son-of-a-bitch!" Sheldon shouted before charging toward Edward the 2nd. He was stopped with the butt of Elmi's machine gun to the back of the head. Sheldon fell to the floor, being knocked unconscious. Kimberly ran to his aid. "You evil bastard! You killed my sister?" she cried. "Hold on! According to the evidence found, it was them damn albinos responsible for your sister's death!" Edward the 2nd explained. "Albinos? What are you talking about, you asshole?" Kimberly shouted. "Robot! Show the former queen the evidence!" he said to the NA agent standing by his side. The agent approached Kimberly with the empty vial that held the poison that killed her sister. "I don't believe you!" she cried. Edward the 2nd turned to Elmi for confirmation. "It's true, your majesty. I didn't believe it at first, but the vial was found in the home of council member Ukerewe." Elmi said. "Hey! You will no longer address her as your majesty! Ever!" Edward the 2nd shouted as he pointed at Elmi. Kimberly stood to her feet, wiping away her tears. "I am the queen of Lassenberia! I am the widow of king Marcus!" she said. Edward the 2nd leaned forward in his seat. "No bitch! You are no queen! As far as your husband, my cousin is concerned, he gave up his right back in the United States because he was a coward! I was chosen to save the Lassenberry organization from going under! You know it's true! Or should I show the people of Lassenberia the documents your so-called king signed?" he said. Kimberly couldn't respond. She just dropped her head in shame. Moments later, Abdirrahim and his top soldiers entered the throne room. 2 of his men had dragged in the unconscious Barron of the pale lands Ukerewe, by his feet. He was battered and bruised. "He was trying to make a run for the pier, my lord." Abdirrahim said. Kimberly ran over to Ukerewe. She kneeled to console him. "I should've stayed!" she whispered to Ukerewe as she caressed his beach blonde hair. "Enough of this bullshit! Take his ass away and lock him up!" Edward the 2nd said to Abdirrahim. "Yes, my lord! You heard him! Take this creature to the prison and chain him up!" Abdirrahim said proudly. His men dragged Ukerewe away. Kimberly looked at her hands. They were covered with his blood. She stood and turned to Edward the 2nd. "Where's my family?" she asked. "Your kids, nieces, and nephew are fine! You on the other hand, I'm not too sure about!" Edward the 2nd chuckled. "I would think twice before you lay a hand on me! Ali and his men won't stand for this insurrection!" Kimberly said. "Insurrection? What the fuck is an insurrection?" Edward the 2nd asked he scratched his bald head. The NA agent leaned in toward Edward the 2nd and whispered into his ear. "Oh! That's what it mean?" he asked. "You're pathetic!" Kimberly said. "Bitch! I'll show your ass pathetic! Elmi! Go back to the airport and take all of Ali and his soldier's weapons! If they give y'all any problems, arrest all of them for treason" Edward the 2nd ordered. "What about the plane and 2 American fighter jets above, my lord?" Elmi asked. "Fuck them! Tell air traffic control that the queen said to turn their asses back around to the United States! If they do not leave, blow their asses out of the sky!" Edward the 2nd said. "Yes, my lord!" Elmi said before leaving. "The Braxton family won't stand for this either!" Kimberly said. "Bitch, please! One of them albinos just assassinated lady Ellen's niece, Christina! I have no doubt that she'll have my back!" Edward the 2nd said. "No! No! Christina!" Kimberly cried. "Sad, ain't it?" Edward the 2nd said. "You'll never be a king!" Kimberly said. "Why be a king, when I can be a god!" he said. "I just made a deal with United States! If we do not fulfill our end of the bargain, there will be serious repercussions!" Kimberly said. "Fuck the United States! They need us! The entire world needs us! We do not need them! You fell for the okey-doke, bitch!" Edward the 2nd chuckled. "What do you want us to do with this albino lover, my lord?" Abdirrahim asked. Edward the 2nd stood from his throne. He gracefully walked over toward Kimberly. "You know I always wanted you to myself. Let us spend some alone time together, and I'll think about letting you rule by my side." He whispered in her ear. Kimberly looked disgusted after hearing his offer. So disgusted that she spit in his face. Edward the 2nd smiled as he wiped the saliva from his cheek and licked it. "I saw that in a movie!" he chuckled. "You're not even half the man my husband was!" she said. "Lock her ass up! A matter of fact! Put her in solitary confinement!" Edward the 2nd said before Abdirrahim's men took her away. Edward the 2nd returned to his throne. "It's all mine now, robot!" Edward the 2nd said to the NA agent. "My lord. To take total control of the island, you need to get the access codes for the GLC supply from her." The NA agent said. "Mother fucker! Don't you think I know that? Besides, she ain't going nowhere no time soon!" he shouted. "Of course, my lord." The agent said.

Back at the airport, Elmi approached air traffic control supervisor Jubba Gacayte. Jubba used to be a helicopter pilot in the Somali Air force until he was shot down by enemy forces during the Ogaden War. after his release from a Ethiopian prison, he was betrayed by his commanding officers for losing his helicopter to the enemy and was sent back to the civilian world where he roamed the continent until he found work in the petroleum industry as a laborer. He saved enough money and headed to South Africa in 1995 where he went to air traffic control school at the age of 52. He worked his way up the later as a night shift supervisor until he ran into Kimberly while she was looking for contractors to begin construction on the desolate island of Lassenberia once she discovered the power of the GLC. Once the Somalian refugees started pouring in, and the airport was completed, Jubba was given the nickname Sky father by Ali.

"Sky father! I have a message from the queen!" Elmi said. "Hadal, wiil! Waa maxay?" Jubba asked. "She want s you to tell the Americans above to leave our airspace, at once!" Elmi said. Jubba looked at Elmi with suspicion. "What are you waiting for, old man? It is the queen's wish!" Elmi said. Some of Jubba's staff turned in their direction. "Elmi! Do not be disrespectful to the Sky father!" the female radio operator said. "It's alright, Meesha! If it is the queen's wish, so shall it be done!" Jubba said.

Miles above Lassenberia, Secretary Gates was looking at his watch, waiting patiently for the word from his crew that they could land. One of his staff members approached him, telling Gates they were denied permission to land. Secretary Gates was outraged. "I can't go back empty handed!" he shouted. "Empty handed, sir?" the staff member asked. "Never mind! Get us out of here!" he shouted. "Yes, sir." The staff member said.

Everyone on board the doomsday plane were unaware of Gates' true intentions to get his hands on a GLC sample and get it back to Doctor Zachmont. "So, the reneging nigger wants to play hard ball! Very well!" Gates said to himself.

Later that evening, Edward the 2nd went to pay a visit to Kimberly in her cell. She was stripped of her clothing and forced to wear tattered rags. Her cell had dim lights with poor air conditioning, made so under his orders. 2 NA agents went with him. "Leave me alone with the former queen." He said to his agents. "Yes, my lord." They said simultaneously before leaving. "You didn't think when you had this place built, Yo ass would be the one behind these bars!" Edward the 2nd said. "You're going to destroy us all!" Kimberly said. "Damn! Even in rags, you look sexy as hell! I wanna come in there and fuck your brains out!" he said in a soft creepy tone as he rubbed his genitals. "You one step foot in here, and I guarantee you'll lose every part of your manhood!" she said. Edward the 2nd began chuckling. "What's crazy, is that I believe you!" he continued chuckling. "What…do…you…want asshole?" Kimberly asked. "Somethings been bugging the fuck out of me! My people in intel say it was the secretary of defense on board that plane! I ain't to knowledgeable on American politics, but ain't the secretary of state the one supposed to be visiting different countries?" he asked. "That's why I said you're going to destroy us! One day he'll return with an army!" she said. "Thanks to you, we have strong allies!" he said. "I've worked too hard to see you tear down what I've built!" Kimberly said. "Here's the deal, beautiful. It is a new day for Lassenberia. I will create a new language for future generations! I will create a new religion, where the name Lassenberry will be god!" he said. "What about the free will of the people? What about the laws?" Kimberly asked. "Bitch! I am the nephew of the great Eddie Lassenberry!! I am…the law!!" he shouted. "No!" Kimberly shouted. "My daughter will be the law, and queen one day! One of your sons will be her king, keeping the Lassenberry bloodline pure! As for your brother-in-law, nieces, and nephew, sorry but I can't have them around me." He said. "That's the only family we have left!" she cried. "That's your family, not mine!" he said in a nonchalant manner. In a fit of rage, Kimberly rushed toward the cell bars and tried to grab Edward the 2nd. "I'll kill you!" she cried. "They will die, unless!" he said. "Unless what?" she asked as she wiped the tears from her eyes. "Unless you hand over the codes so I can have total access to the GLC." He said. "Why are you doing this? The GLC is my discovery! "Kimberly cried. "I'll give you 24 hours to decide their fate, bitch!" Edward the 2nd said before walking away. Kimberly fell to the cement floor covering her face as she continued sobbing.

The next morning, Edward the 2nd was standing in front of the mirror in the throne room. He had in his hand his deceased cousin's crown. He donned the crown. The size of the crown impaired his vision. "Damn! My cousin had a big fucking head!" he said. He turned to his agent. "What do you think, robot?" he asked while wearing the crown. "It's not a good fit, my lord." He said. Edward the 2nd took off the crown and threw it across the room. Abdirrahim entered the throne room. "What's on the agenda?" Edward the 2nd asked. "The albinos are almost ready for removal, my lord!" Abdirrahim said proudly. "What does almost mean?" Edward the 2nd asked. "2 days at the most, my lord." Abdirrahim said.

Moments later, a NA agent entered the room. "What is it?" Abdirrahim asked the agent. "Hold on! My agents don't answer to you!" Edward the 2nd said. "Forgive me, my lord!" Abdirrahim said. "What is it?" Edward the 2nd asked the agent. "Lady Ellen of the Borough of Braxton is here to see you, my lord." The agent said. "Send her in!" Edward the 2nd sighed. "Yes, my lord." The agent said before leaving. "Do you want me to leave, my lord?" Abdirrahim asked. "Nah." he said.

Lady Ellen entered the throne room wearing a long flower printed summer dress with sandals. "Don't we look lovely this day!" Edward the 2nd said. Lady Ellen didn't look pleased.

She had a grieving look on her face. "The ceremony for my niece's passing will begin exactly at noon tomorrow." She said. "I'm sorry, but you'll have to postpone it due to security reasons." Edward the 2nd said. Lady Ellen looked bewildered. "Postpone? Security reasons?" she asked. "Yeah! I should've told you earlier, but we're going to ship all the albinos back to the motherland. We need all citizens on alert for the next 2 days in case they start some fucking revolution, or something!" He said. "We'll be rid of those creatures once and for all!" Abdirrahim said. "Take it easy!" Edward the 2nd chuckled as he gently punched Abdirrahim in the shoulder. From the expression on Lady Ellen's face, she didn't find it funny. She glanced around the room and saw the crown of king Marcus on the floor. "Is it necessary that the queen be imprisoned?" she asked. "Former queen! Former queen, Lady Ellen!" He said with a sinister smile. "The former queen once said Lassenberia is a place where prejudice nor racism will not be tolerated." She said. "With-all-do-respect Lady Ellen, your niece is dead because of these cursed people!" Abdirrahim said. "From what I have heard, she died from a stray bullet. No one knows what direction it came from. I want officials from the United Nations to come in and do a proper crime scene investigation!" Lady Ellen said." That is enough! We have all been through some traumatic shit in the past few days! Let us just do one thing at a time! Lady Ellen. I promise I will personally see to it that your niece has an exuberant, and extravagant send off! Ok?" Edward the 2nd said. "Extravagant send off?" She asked. Edward the 2nd turned to his agent. "Agent! Escort Lady Ellen out of the castle! I'm busy!" he said. "Yes, my lord. The agent said. The agent approached Lady Ellen, putting his hand on her elbow to escort her out of the throne room. She quickly smacked the agent's hand away. "Just make sure you take care of the funeral arrangements as you promised! I will inform my people of the delay!" she said before leaving. Once she left the throne room, Abdirrahim turned to Edward the 2nd. "Do you think she will be a problem, my lord?" he asked. "Nah, besides, we need her and her family. The United States will think twice before attacking a country with white folks living in it." He said. "What about Commander Ali and his men, my lord? Should we continue to detain them?" Abdirrahim asked. Edward the 2nd sighed as he scratched his bald head. "Yes. Just make sure they are well fed and treated fairly. Soon he and his people will come around and see things my way. Now, leave me so I can think." He said. "Yes, my lord!" Abdirrahim said. Once Abdirrahim left the room. Edward the 2nd turned to his other NA agent. "I want you and a couple more agents to rock Ali and his men to sleep! Forever!" he said. "Rock them to sleep, my lord?" the agent asked with a confused look on his face. "Kill them! But do it quietly! I can't risk them mother fuckers turning on me!" Edward the 2nd said. "Yes, my lord." The agent said. "Remember! Do it quietly! Ninja style!" Edward the 2nd said with a silly grin on his face. "Yes, my lord." The agent said. After the agent had left the throne room, Edward the 2nd went to sit back on the throne. He slumped back, closing his eyes. "I'm gonna make you proud of me, Uncle Eddie. You just watch." He said to himself in a soft exhausted voice.

Later that evening, Edward the 2nd went to visit Kimberly in her cell with a pen and pad in his hand. "So, beautiful! You know why I'm here! What are the codes?" he asked. "I have your word that my nieces and nephew won't be harmed?" she asked as she slowly approached the cell bars. "I promise I won't lay a hand on their heads!" he sighed. There was a moment of silence. "7890-20 Alpha!" she said with a defeated look on her face. "Now let me see my family!" she demanded. "7890-20 Alpha. Got it." He said as he jotted down the information. "I said let me see my family!" she shouted. "After I gain access, then you can see them." He said before leaving.

Once Edward the 2nd returned to the castle, he used the code that Kimberly gave him to enter a room called the vault. It was designed to electronically have the flow of GLC shoot up from the GLC well. He quickly ran back to the throne room, having a smile from ear-to-ear when he saw the that the flow of GLC had stopped. "I am God!!" he shouted as he spread his arms spinning around. At that moment, he was approached by one of his NA agents. "Hey, robot!! How is the albino removal?" he asked the agent. "Everything is going according to your orders, my lord. "Fucking great!" he shouted. Edward the 2nd put his arm around the agent. "You see that! That is my divine right!" he said as he pointed at the GLC fountain. "I need you to gather up the former queen's family, except for her sons and bring them to the prison." Edward the 2nd said. "Yes, my lord." The agent said.

It was around 2 in the morning Lassenberian time when Jenna's children, Oliver, Corina, and Jamila were dragged out of bed. "Lord Lassenberry requests your presence." The agent said. Oliver put up a struggle as the agents physically took him away. Elsewhere, the girls were scared and confused as other agents told them to come with them. "Where's my daddy?" Corina asked the agents. Neither agent gave her an answer. She and her sister were just shoved along.

They were taken to the prison where their aunt was being held. The girls were in their pajamas, and Oliver was barefoot in pajama pants. "You hurt my sisters, and I'll kick all of your asses!" Oliver shouted as the girls were being handled. Neither agent responded to his threats. Moments later Edward the 2nd arrived with more agents. "Hey, kids! Wanna see your auntie? She wants to see you!" he said with smile on his face. "Where's my father?" Oliver asked. "Oh! He's on his way!" Edward the 2nd said.

Just as Edward the 2nd said, Oliver's father Sheldon was being carried in by 2 more NA agents. There was a total of 10 agents there. "Great! The whole family is here!" Edward the 2nd shouted in a joyful manner. Sheldon was unconscious as his daughters were crying out to him. Sheldon had a bandage wrapped around his head with blotches of blood stains on it. "Well! Let's get this over with!" Edward the 2nd sighed. The family was taken down the corridor of the prison to Kimberly's cell. Edward the 2nd followed close behind.

Moments later they arrived at Kimberly's cell. Kimberly was sleeping on the cot. "Wake the fuck up, your majesty!" Edward the 2nd shouted. Kimberly slowly came out of her slumber. She jumped up when the first person she saw was her niece Jamila. She rushed to the bars of the cell. Jamila and Corina ran to the cell clutching the bars. Kimberly grabbed their fingers. "Auntie!" Corina shouted. "How are my girls? Did they hurt you?" she asked them. Edward the 2nd rolled his eyes as he sighed. "We're fine!" Jamila said. "How are you doing, young man?" Kimberly asked Oliver. Oliver glanced around at the agents. "I'm good, auntie!" he said. "Ok, beautiful! The gangs all here! Are you happy now?" Edward the 2nd asked Kimberly. "Let my aunt go! We'll leave your stupid island!" Oliver said. "Can't do that, young man! By the way! This stupid island will lead the way into a new world!" Edward the 2nd said. "I gave you what you've wanted! At least let the kids go!" Kimberly said. "The only place they're going, is into a cell with their soon to be dead father! They will not be fed or given water!" Edward the 2nd said. Oliver began to fight the agents but had no effect against their combat skills. The girls began to scream as the agents stripped them away from Kimberly's touch. Kimberly fell to her needs, helplessly crying her eyes out. The girls could be heard screaming down the corridor as they were being dragged away until their screams faded out of existence. "I hate you!!" Kimberly cried. Edward the 2nd looked down at her. "Why? You should be thanking me! One day your of your sons will be my daughter's husband!" he said before walking away. Kimberly fell to the floor on her back crying as she covered her face.

on the other side of the prison, the girls were shoved inside one of the cells. Their father was shot in the head by one of the agents before his body was tossed in the cell as well. Jamila and Corina rushed to their father's lifeless body. "Daddy! Daddy! Don't leave us!" Jamila cried. Corina grabbed her sister, holding her firmly. "He's gone Jamila! He's gone to heaven!" Corina cried. Oliver was unconscious after being punched in the face. He was dragged into the cell by his feet. One of the agents locked the cell and left the family to their fate.

A day later, the last of the albino citizens were forced to board the same ships the refugees from India arrived in. "Tell commander Abdirrahim that all citizens of the pale lands have boarded the ship and are ready to be moved out." One somalin soldier said to his subordinate.

The albino citizens were packed like sardines on the huge cargo ships. Children and babies were crying. The young men who tried to fight back were beaten by the Somalian soldiers. When the 10 cargo ships sailed out to sea in the dark of night, they were purposely driven off course towards the uninhabited islands of Antipodes. The former citizens of Lassenberia where forced by the armed Somalian soldiers to disembark the cargo ships and set foot on the volcanic islands. Unbeknownst to the rest of the world, the islands of Antipodes were used as military training bases for Russian special forces weeks later. Unfortunately for the people with albinism, they were used as live targets for the Spetsnaz's military training exercises. Young men, women and children were slaughtered like animals until they were wiped out of existence. Until this day, the Russian government has denied to the World Court that such an atrocity has taken place.

It was the end of June 2004 when the former Queen of Lassenberia was crawling around on her hands and knees in her cell, weak from being denied bread and only allowed fresh water within the past 2 weeks. Her beauty was fading as her skeletal features became more prominent. Prior to this, Edward the 2nd approached her, giving her a ultimatum to be intimate with him. Like so many times before, she refused. This was the final straw for him. He maliciously allowed her to slip away into nothing.

It was July 1st, 2004 when Edward the 2nd was at the castle playing with his daughter when he was approached by one of his NA agents. "My lord. There's a mob outside the castle grounds chanting absurdities about you." the agent said. "Shit! They're probably Kimberly and Ali followers!" Edward the 2nd sighed. "What are your orders pertaining to the hostile environment, my lord?" the agent asked. "Fuck! fuck! fuck! I can't have anyone killed for the time being when I'm just getting started! I want the people to love me as much as they loved her! Where is Abdirrahim and his men?" he asked the agent. "They're on the other side of the island doing what they call military exercises, my lord." The agent said. "Good!" Edward the 2nd said with a sigh of relief. "Have a hand full of your men go through the crowd and offer the women, especially the younger ones the opportunity to be one of my wives and live the life of a queen, if they would just go back to their homes! My uncle used to tell us when we were kids that women love the material world!... Now go!" Edward the 2nd said. "Yes, my lord." The agent said.

There were a few thousand Lassenberian citizens shouting, pumping their fists, demanding answers on queen Kimberly and her royal guard's whereabouts. Just as ordered, only 10 agents roamed the crowd whispering Edward the 2nd's message into the ears of mostly teenage girls. As Edward the 2nd predicted, the young ladies were flabbergasted from what they were being told. A few minutes passed as the crowd shrunk. The agents were whispering in the native languages of these young ladies. Even the ones who had boyfriends and potential husbands began to retreat to their homes with big smiles on their faces. Their male companions followed them. More time passed, reducing the crowd to just over a hundred. The citizens left standing were the elderly and the preadolescent. "I'll tell lord lassenberry, mission accomplished." The head NA agent said to the other agents.

— CHAPTER .48 THE GREAT SPEECH —

Back in the United States, Secretary Gates was summoned by Dr. Zachmont to the NA facility out near Lerado Texas. Gates was dressed in a ceremonial robe provided by one of the NA servants before entering Zachmont's chambers. The servant opened the door announcing Gates's presence to the doctor. "Ah, Carter, my boy! Come in!" Zachmont said joyfully. Gates looked nervous when he glanced over at a pile of human skulls in the corner of the room. Some of the skulls still had bits of muscle tissue and flesh attached to them. "Leave us" Zachmont said to the female servant. Yes, doctor." She said before leaving the room. Gates approached Zachmont before dropping to his knees. "Sir! I can explain!" Gates pleaded. Zachmont consoled the secretary of defense by patting him on the head like a pet. "What is there to explain? You've done your best! That's all I can expect of you!" Zachmont said with a convincing smile. "You're not disappointed in me?" Gates asked. "No! in fact! I want you to come with me and meet the master! Having a man on the inside, giving us intel on this wretched government is a plus, despite what did, or shall I say, what didn't take place in Lassenberia!" Zachmont explained. "Oh, thank you sir!! Thank you so much!!" Gates shouted as he folded his hands together. "Now, get off your knees!" Zachmont said. Gates looked surprised when the doctor helped him to his feet. "Let me get dressed, and we'll be on our way!" Zachmont said.

A few hours later, the doctor and Gates were on a private jet cruising toward the north eastern part of the country. The jet was miles above the dense forests of Maine. There were 8 NA agents sitting Across the aisle from the Zachmont and Gates while they were being served lunch by the doctor's servant.

"Once again sir, I can't thank you enough for this, sir!" Gates said. "Carter, my boy! You think being Secretary of defense is an honor and a privilege? Wait until you have a one-on-one meeting with the master!" Zachmont said as he patted Gates on the knee.

Finally, the private jet had landed on the outskirts of the NA palace property. Waiting at the landing zone for the doctor and his entourage were 3 black limousines. The drivers, who were 3 NA agents, stood outside of the vehicles at attention. Zachmont, his servant and Carter entered the limo parked in the middle. The Na agents that arrived with them piled into the other limos. All 3 vehicles slowly drove off into the wilderness.

When they arrived at the palace, the NA agents scattered about throughout the palace grounds except for one. Zachmont, his servant and Gates stood outside gazing at the magnificent design of the palace. "As many times as I've been here, I'm always in awe of this wonderous structure!" Zachmont said. "And how!" Gates said. Zachmont reached into his pants pocket and pulled out a small vial filled with a blue liquid. He handed it to Gates. "What's this?" Gates asked. "It's just a little something you should ingest to make you see things differently before meeting the master." Zachmont said. Gates reluctantly swallowed the blue liquid. "Now, if you would my follow my agent. He will lead you inside!" Zachmont said with an elated expression on his face. "Aren't you coming with me, sir?" Gates asked. "Of course not, my boy! I told you earlier it was a one-on-one meeting. This is your moment to shine. Not mine!" Zachmont said as he gently stroked Gates's arm. Carter followed the agent to the main entrance pass the sentry detail. He turned his head, staring at the Zachmont with a worried look on his face. Zachmont reassured him that everything was fine with a smile and a hand gesture to keep moving forward.

Moments later, the NA agent and Carter Gates arrived outside the master's chamber. Standing outside the giant steel doors of the chamber at attention, were 6 Na agents wearing high-tech body armor, with military machine guns strapped to their shoulders. "This is where my journey ends, and yours begin, sir." The agent said. Carter nodded his head at the agent before turning towards the chamber door. He nervously straightened his necktie. It took 3 Na agents on either side to open the heavy steel doors after one of the agents punched in an access code on a keypad located on the wall nearby. Once the sound of the locks on the doors were disabled, this gave the agents the signal to pull open the doors. Once the doors were opened, Carter stepped inside the chamber. There was total darkness in front of him. The only light was the light coming in from behind him until the agents closed the steel doors. Carter could not see his hand before his face. The only sound in the chamber was his heavy breathing,

Suddenly, Carter looked up and saw the flickering of light and the sound of electrical energy surging through the odd shaped fixtures. These lights were way different from the norm, which covered every inch of the high ceiling. There were swirling shades of light within the main source of light. After gazing at the ceiling in awe, Carter looked down noticing that the floor was clear, made of a thick glass like substance. He kneeled to touch the floor. As soon as he touched the floor with his fingertips, the floor appeared to ripple like water in a lake after a stone was tossed in it. Carter looked at his hand and noticed that his fingertips were as dry as the time he stepped inside the chamber. "This can't be real!" Carter said to himself.

"That is correct, Secretary Gates! It is an illusion!" a thunderous voice said from out of nowhere. Carter slowly turned, looking in all directions. "What you see, is what you perceive to be real, young one!" the voice said. "Master?" Carter said as he continued to turn to pinpoint where the voice was coming from. Suddenly, the lights were turned out. The chamber became pitch black again. Carter Gates began to panic until a beam of light in a pyramid shape came from above. Standing in the center of that light was a tall thin figure. The male figure stood with his hands by his side wearing a white 3-piece suit with a white necktie.

The strange looking man's smile showed off his stained teeth, which looked more like fangs across the top row. His hair, which was white as fresh fallen snow, was pulled back into a ponytail. His shoes were white padded leather with diamond studs on the tip of each shoe. His fingernails looked more like discolored claws.

"Master!" Carter Gates said before falling to his knees. The master approached Carter and began stroking Carter's hair like a pet. "Forgive me if I've failed you, master!" Carter cried. "My son. Your image is too dear to me to be considered a failure. Now rise." The master said. Carter stood before the master with a look of relief on his face. "Give me another chance at retrieving what we need from Lassenberia, master!" Carter said. "Would you be so kind, Secretary Gates to turn around." The master said. Carter looked terrified as he slowly turned around. What he saw caused him to clutch his chest. Once again, he fell to his knees. Standing before him was the mirror image of himself. "Amazing, isn't he? It took years to perfect, but we've finally brought to fruition what conspiracy theorists have been rambling about for years!" the master said. "Oh, my god! How could this be?!!" Carter said as his breathing went out of control.

The mirror image of Carter Gates standing before the master and the original Gates, not only looked like Gates but wore the exact same attire the original Gates was wearing. Gates fell to his knees having the look of agonizing pain on his face. The master began to chuckle as Gates laid on the floor as his life force left his eyes.

"He was worthless. But you, my beautiful creation, will not fail me! You will continue to work on infiltrating Lassenberia and get me that miracle drug! Now, go and meet with Doctor Zachmont outside! He will fill you in on the details!" the master said. "Yes, my master. The duplicate Gates said. Before leaving the chamber.

Outside the palace, doctor Zachmont was leaning up against the limousine with his arms folded when the new Carter Gates emerged from inside the palace entrance. "I am ready for my orders, doctor." The new Gates said. Zachmont stood before the new Carter Gates. He placed his hands on the new Carter's shoulders. "I can't believe my eyes! He said it could be done, and he did it! You are magnificent!' Zachmont said with a huge smile on his face. The duplicate Gates didn't show any emotion. He just nodded his head and entered the limousine. Zachmont rubbed his hands together as he laughed hysterically before entering the limousine.

It was July 20th when Butch called a meeting with Sammy Perez at one of his safehouses in Newark, New Jersey. Fearing that his life was in danger from what the FBI had brought to his attention, Sammy showed up at the meeting with a dozen hired guns who were standing outside the meeting place. He himself was strapped with 3 pistols on his person, which one was in a holster on his belt strap.

He came into the room where Butch was standing alone. There were no bodyguards nor his cousin Dubbs anywhere to be found. "General Perez!!" Butch shouted as he smiled before embracing Sammy with a hug. "Butch! It's good to see you, my dude!" Sammy said. Before releasing him from the firm hug, Butch felt him up. He could feel the bulge on Sammy's waist. "What's with the artillery, brother?" Butch asked. "I'm a multi-millionaire, my dude! The world don't wanna see a Spanish man like me make that kind of paper! You of all people know how that is!" Sammy explained. "Yeah! It comes with the territory. Take a seat! Can I get you anything to drink?" Butch asked. "Nah, I'm good, my dude." Sammy said. "First of all, I liked to say you been doing a great job out on the streets! No violence. No coming up short with your refill payments! Damn! You got really got it together, man!" Butch said. "So, why did you call this meeting, my dude?" Sammy asked with a suspicious look. "It's Mookie, man. I hate to say It, but the brother ain't got that flare like he used to!" Butch said. "What you mean, my dude?" Sammy asked. "His people are complaining that they ain't eating! That Mookie is giving his top guys crumbs!" Butch said. "That's a new one on me, my dude! From what I know, Mookie got the upmost respect on the streets!" he said. Butch sighed as he looked up towards the ceiling. He then stared Sammy in his eyes. "Bottom line! Mookie gotta go! He's still bitter about what happened to his father a long time ago! I think me and my cousin's lives are in danger. Since the Lassenberry people been out of the picture, there's been talk about him saying that me and Dubbs are the final move for his revenge on what happened." Butch said. Sammy rubbed his hands together as the palm of his hands began to sweat. He having a worried look on his face. "Here's the deal! You make our problem disappear, and you get more property under your belt! Understand?" Butch said. "I'm gonna have to take some time to think on that one, my dude! Mookie and his pop were, and still are a big inspiration to me!" Sammy said. Butch didn't show any signs of disappointment or anger. He made a quick drumroll with his hands on the table. "Cool!

Later that evening, Sammy was in bed staring at the ceiling. He briefly turned his head towards his wife. He turned towards the ceiling once more. "¡Yo puedo hacer esto! ¡Puedo hacer esto!" he whispered to himself.

3 days later around 11pm, a huge block party was being given for one of Mookie's top soldiers nicknamed Bravo, who just came home after doing 7 years in prison for getting caught with 10 pounds of weed in a duffle bag. Because of his loyalty to Mookie's crew and not snitching, Mookie decided to throw him a coming home party.

It was a cool breezy evening in North Hudson Park. The Stonehenge building in the background, which Mookie became part owner of, was decorated with giant green neon lights spelling out the name Bravo. Giant speakers were hooked up in the surrounding area blasting all different styles of Latino music. Occasionally, gunshots were fired into the air from certain intoxicated members of Mookie's crew as they were screaming and yelling in a festive manner.

Mookie was being moved through the crowd in his wheelchair by his trusted bodyguard. There were a few other bodyguards surrounding him as he made his way through the crowd. Mookie's trusted bodyguard leaned over to say something in his boss's ear. "Seguro que viene, jefe.?" the bodyguard whispered. "Tan pronto como veas a este hijo de puta rata, ¡quiero que los chicos lo lleven por la calle y se fumen el culo!" Mookie said. "I can't believe he's trying to move against you after all you've been through!" whispered the bodyguard. Don't worry! it'll all be straightened out." Mookie said as he patted his bodyguard on the shoulder.

Suddenly, the man of the hour and his girlfriend approached Mookie and his bodyguards. The burly man who went by the name Bravo could barely walk a straight line. He had enjoyed himself a little too much indulging in alcohol. Mookie gave his bodyguards the ok to let him come forward. Bravo released his girlfriend's hand and purposely fell to his knees in front of Mookie. "¡Jefe! ¡No puedo agradecerte lo suficiente por todo esto! ¡Te seguiré hasta mi último aliento!" Bravo cried. "¡Basta! ¡Parada! De rodillas, hermano. No vamos a hacer nada de esa mierda de Lassenberry por aquí." Mookie chuckled. Bravo tried his best to stand to his feet. Mookie leaned to the side, looking behind Bravo to see what a small crowd in the party was cheering about. He noticed that it was Butch who was causing the uproar. Butch made his way through the crowd with his arms spread and a big smile on his face. "What's up, my amigo?" Butch shouted. Mookie gave off a suspicious grin. He then turned to his bodyguards, giving them the signal to proceed with his plans. One of the bodyguards grabbed Butch by the shoulder, leading him away from the party, followed by the other bodyguards. Butch had a confused expression on his face as he was being lead away. The crowd thought his abuction was part of a gag of sorts. Mookie pulled out his cell phone to make a call. After a couple of rings, someone on the other end picked up. *"Hey, my dude!"* the voice said. "Yeah! The old mans' on his way out." Mookie said. *"Good! We Puerto Ricans gotta stick together, my dude!"* the voice said. "Now, i have to go talk to these wierd motherfuckers about turning over the operation to me." Mookie said. *"My dude! You mean us, right?"* the voice said. "Sammy, listen! You're getting a big chunk of territory! Be happy!" Mookie said before clicking his phone off.

"Motherfucker!" Sammy said in anger as he looked at his phone. He was sitting in his brand new Boeman Sedan, which was parked in his driveway. Moments later, there was a tapping on the passenger side window. At first, this startled Sammy until he realized it was Butch's cousin Dubbs. Sammy reached for his pistol which was hidden between the car door and his seat. He didn't expose it, but had his finger on the trigger. Sammy rolled down his window quarter of the way. "What the fuck, my dude? I told you i would call you!" Sammy shouted. "Let me in, man!" Dubbs shouted. Sammy unlocked the door to let him inside. Dubbs jumped into the passenger seat. "So, what happened? Did it happen?" Dubbs asked. "It's done, my dude!" Sammy said. Dubbs fell back into his seat with a terrified look on his face. He covered his mouth with his hands, shaking his head. "Damn! Do you realize how much shit we gonna be in with them secret society motherfuckers?" Dubbs cried. Sammy looked at Dubbs with fury in his eyes. "My dude! Now you're scared? You're the one who help set this shit up!" Sammy shouted. "You're right! You're right, man! I gotta stay focused! I gotta stay focused!" Dubbs shouted as he was fidgeting around in his seat. Suddenly, Dubbs became still. He just gazed into Sammy's eyes. "He's really gone, huh?" Dubbs asked. "Now, we wait for Mookie to talk to these people, and then we split the pie 3 ways, my dude!" Sammy said as he gave Dubbs dap. Dubbs looked worried before expressing a nervous smile.

It was the 3rd of August when Lord Lassenberry gave the order to his agents to gather the citizens of Lassenberia in front of the castle. The agents were equiped with bullhorns, driving slowly down the streets of Lassenberia yelling out orders for the citizens to attend the great meeting, as Lord Lassenberry called it.

Back at the castle, an elaborate podium was set up outside the castle grounds. There were several microphones hooked up to the podium, along with a huge banner of the Lassenberry family crest draped in front of it.

Inside the castle were a couple of members from the royal council talking amongst themselves. "This meeting, is a waste of time, if you ask me." One council member said to the other. "Javed! Quiet down! These men in black suits are all around us! At least speak in our native tongue!" the other council member whispered. "You know it doesn't matter brother! These men, if you want to call them that, speak in many tongues!" Javed said. Javed took a deep breath to calm himself. "Listen Jaish! Your my brother, and i love you! The only reason i joined the council as your personal aid was to look after you! Lord Lassenberry is a really dark spirited man! He chose you to be apart of the council because of your lightheartedness! You don't pose a threat to him! That's why i demanded to be by your side!" Javed explained. "So, brother. It is not me who should be worried about Lord Lassenberry. It's you." Jaish said. Javed smiled. "Let's head outside, brother!" Javed said.

Outside the castle grounds thousands of citizens gathered in front of the podium. Javed and Jaish stood off to the side of the podium with the other 10 new members of the council. There were 10 NA agents spread out through the crowd monitoring the citizens of Lassenberia. On the outskirts of the crowd were hundreds of Abdirrahim's soldiers dressed in new uniforms emulating Lord Lassenberry's.

The crowd became quiet as a dozen young men, dressed in the same uniforms emerged from the castle holding midieval trumpets with Lassenberry family crest banners attached to them. The young men raised their trumpets and began to play the introduction for the head of Lassenberia. Many of the citiizens began chuckling as the trumpeters sound was off-kilter. After the trumpeters stopped playing their instruments, Abdirrahim approached the podium.

"Good day citizens of Lassenberia! I hope you are all doing well! It is my honor to introduce to you his majesty, king of Lassenberry, Edward the Great!!!" Abdirrahim said. Javed and Jaish looked turned to each other with a bewildered look on their faces, as did other members of the council. "Great? I heard it was queen Kimberly who developed all of this!" one citizen in the crowd whispered to another. Abdirrahim backed away from the podium, where he ended up standing next to Lord Lassenberry's main NA agent. Lord Lassenberry took to the podium.

He took to the podium, standing tall and proud with his chest out. He had a smirk on his face as he gazed uponed the crowd. He wore the traditional Lassenberry uniform with the green belt and red sash. He wore medals given to him by over a dozen nations hoping to gain his favor. There was no teleprompter in front of him. He didn't pull out a written speech.

"Citizens! Council members! Warriors of our grand military! Today is a new day for Lassenberia! Today my people, you will be the first generation of Lassenberians to witness the kingdom of Lassenberia lead the world into the future of medicine! But first, i want to discuss the 48 laws of Lassenberia! From this day on, the 48 laws of Lassenberia will be eradicated! The only law, or laws will come directly from me! This land is a paradise! I will not allow this land to be tainted by the outside world! So, my dear subjects! Leaving this land to travel to other parts of the world, is not a option! The boarders will be permanently closed! Only dignitaries, foreign or domestic, will be allowed to come and go, only at my discretion!

I would also like to say, my subjects! From this day on, the diversity of language and faiths will be no longer tolerated! A new universal language will be enforced! What you all call a higher power or God, from now on resides, in me!" Edward the Great shouted.

The crowd looked bewildered. Those amongst the crowd that couldn't interpret the english language that well looked towards those standing next to them for a better understanding of what Edward the Great was saying.

"**Best believe, my loyal subjects! In years to come, the rest of the world will follow suit! The rest of the world will follow suit because we have something they not only want, but need! The of the world will be ours once their leaders kneel in front of this great symbol my uncle the late great Sir Edward Lassenberry created.**" Edward the Great shouted as he pointed to the lassenberry family crest,

"**My loyal subects! For a long time, there has been a dark force infultrating the united States of America, and in other pockets of the civilized world!**" he shouted. The NA agent standing behind lord Lassenberry turned his head in his master's direction with a suspicious look on his face. Standing next to the NA agent was Abdirrahim. Abdirrahim slowly drew his pistol from his holster.

"**Now, my loyal subjects! You will bare witness today on how i will shut that fucking dark force down before it infests our precious land!**" Edward the Great shouted before giving the signal to Abdirrahim. Once the signal was given, which was putting his hands to the microphones and clapping his hands together 3 times. Abdirrahim pointed his pistol to the NA agent's temple. Then squeezed the trigger. Before anyone in the crowd could blink twice, weapons were drawn and fired upon the other 18 NA agents in the crowd. All of the NA agents were caught off guard. They were put down almost simultaneously. There were screams and citizens scrambling to take cover.

"**People! People! My loyal subjects! Stay calm! Come back! Don't run!**" Edward the Great shouted. The crowd settled down, slowly making their way back in front of the podium. Abdirrahim gave his soldiers the order to pick up the dead NA agent's bodies and carry them away.

"**Take heed, my loyal subjects! These men, or whatever you wanna call them, were loyal to me! They've would've given their lives for me within less than a second! They had to fucking die because they served their purpose! Now! You all serve a purpose!... to me! Never forget this day! Never forget what just took place!**" Edward the Great shouted. "Long live the house of Lassenberry! Long live Edward the Great!!" Abdirrahim shouted as he grabbed his king's hand and raised it in the air. He reapeated the chant until the crowd fell into place. "Long live the house of Lassenberry! Long live Edward the Great!" most of the crowd chanted. There was still a combination of fear and bewilderment thoughout the crowd.

"**Now, go to your homes or daily routine! Be assured! You are all safe now, and can enjoy paradise for generations to come!**" Edward the Great said before the crowd dispursed. One of Abdirrahim's soldiers turned off the microphones on the podium. "Great speech, my Lord." Abdirrahim said. "You Goddamn right it was a great speech!" Edward the Great said boldly. "So, my Lord. Do i still have your word that i have total control over the armed forces?" Abdirrahim asked. "Nigga! Didn't i tell you we have a deal? You keep Lassenberia safe, and i won't blow this whole island to kingdom come!" Edward the Great said as he showed Abdirrahim a small device attached to the palm of his hand.

Atfer queen Kimberly was removed from the throne, Edward the Great had a meeting with one of the top nuclear engineers Kimberly hired to build 2 nuclear warheads to defend

Lassenberia from otside threats. The device was remotely connected to his heart like a pacemaker. Edward the Great's philosophy was that if he was taken out by outside forces, that the entire island nation of Lassenberia should meet its demise with him.

Moments later, Edward the Great was being followed back to the castle by members of his council. Jaish was one of the council members who was fuming about Edward the Great's actions. He walked along side his king expressing his feelings about the situation that had taken place. His body was frail in comparison to Edward the Great's frame, but that didn't stop him from saying what was on his mind.

"My lord! This act of violence, in front of all these people! How could you?" Jaish asked. For his brother's sake, Javish grabbed Jaish by the arm, trying to pull him away. Jaish yanked away from his brother. "i demand an answer, my lord!" Jaish shouted. Edward the Great stopped, turning towards Jaish with fury in his eyes. "Listen, african boy! All of you listen! All you motherfuckers are in your positions because all of the old council members are no longer with us! So, be thankful you get to see another day in paradise! Now, get the fuck out of my face!" Edward the Great shouted before walking away.

Inside the castle, Edward the Great was walking down the corridor along with his personal aid and Abdirrahim. His aid was an elderly woman from Lucknow. She looked shakened by what had taken place outside the castle. Edward the Great was comforting by putting his arm around her. "It's ok, little mamma! Those bad men are gone for good!" Edward the Great assured her. "Excuse me, my lord. i have to go feed princess Niyale now." She said as she wiped the tears from eyes.

The elderly woman was Zilda Modi, an indian refugee who was cast out at the age of 12 by her wealthy family to Lucknow due to her servere case of leprosy. She was the first Indian refugee Kimberly cured by using the GLC. Edward the Great noiticed her loyalty to Kimberly and used it to his advantage by making her his persoanal aid. Edward the Great said she was like a mother figure to him. Some of the council members were saying behind closed doors that their relationship was more like slavemaster and slave.

As Zilda was walking away, another council member approached Edward the Great. "Lord Lassenberry!" the council member said. "Yeah, what's up?" Edward the great said. "The sky father demands to see you at once!" the council member said nervously. Edward the Great looked infuriated. The council member responded to his facial expression by taking a step back. "He demands?!" Edward the Great shouted. "Yes, my Lord!" the council member whimpered. Edward the Great smiled. "Well, tell the sky father to meet me in throne room in a half hour!" he said. "Yes, my Lord!" the counci member said before walking away. Edward the Great rubbed his hands together, smiling aty the same time. "He demands, huh?' he said to himself before heading towards the throne room.

Later on in the throne room, Edward the Great was sitting on his throne waiting for the sky father to arrive. He had one of his servants, who was a young dark skinned lady brush off whatever remants of lint off of his uniform. He couldn't help notice her beautiful drown eyes, her long legs and her soft curly afro. "Damn, girl! You don't look like the typical african chick! What's your name, and how you get this job, baby?" he asked. She smiled. Her smile was so seductive, Edward the Great began salivating, licking his lips. "I'm Mahasin Wingo!" she said with a perky attitude. "Wow! Mahasin? What does that mean?" he asked. "It's Islamic, meaning beauty!" she said. "Your english is normal as fuck!" he said as he leaned back in his throne. "It's because i was raised by my mother back in the United States until the age of 10!" she said. "So, how did you end up here, by my side?" he asked. "Jubba Gacayte is my uncle. He rasied me after my mother died." She said. Edward the Great leaned forward. "Who the fuck is Jubba?" he shouted. "He is known as the sky father!" she said. Edward the Great's head snapped back. "Oh, shit! I just known him as the sky father" he said. "Yes, that's him! But don't mention that we're related to him! He wants to keep the nepotism quiet!" she said. "Damn! i need to step up my game and socialize more!" he said to himself.

— CHAPTER .49 STANDING ALONE —

It was officially the first day of the Fall season. Trees were beginning to bloom with red, brown and orange leaves throughout Newark. In the downtown area some abandoned buildings were sprayed with graffiti saying fuck the house of Lassenberry in spanish. The words larga vida a Vasquez were written underneath. By this time, north jersey was called. El terreno que construyó Vásquez.

Dipsite of the vandalism in the hood, the New Jersey drug empire Edward the Great left behind was now shared between Mookie Vasquez, Dubbs Watson and Sammy perez. The problem for them had arrived when the powers that be within the National Agreement didn't take lightly the unsanctioned hit on Butch Watson. The NA representative for new jersey, Doug reed was ordered to deal with the situation.

Sammy perez was at his home, mingling with family members drinking and partying over his success after taking over a third of new jersey's drug game. "¡Escucha! ¡Escucha!" Sammy shouted as he raised his glass of liqour. Everyone in the room went silent. "I told y'all! Didn't i tell y'all i was gonna make my mark?" he shouted. "¡Lo hiciste, hermano mío!"one of his soldiers shouted. "You damn right, my dude!" Sammy shouted. "We got this shit in the bag, bro!" another soldier shouted. "Eat, drink and be merry, my people! I gotta go take a leak!" Sammy shouted. As sammy put down his glass, the salsa music began to blast. He made his way through the crowd, heading to one of his many bathrooms.

While in the bathroom alone standing in front of the urinal, Sammy was tapped on the shoulder by a Latino man in a black suit and tie. "What the fuck, my dude? Can't you see i'm taking a leak?" Sammy shouted. "Mr. Reed would like to speak with you outside." The man said. "Who?" Sammy shouted. "If you do not comply mr. Perez, everyone at your gathering will die. Including your wife." The man said in a calm voice. Sammy became nervous to the point that his flow of urine missed the urinal, hitting the marble floor. He quickly zipped up his pants and turned towards the man. "What is this about, my dude? Who the fuck are you?" he asked. "Una vez más, el señor Pérez. Si no me sigues afuera, todos aquí en tu casa morirán." The man said. "How do i know this ain't no shake down, my dude?" Sammy asked. The man showed no emotion. He just pointed to the window in the bathroom. Sammy reluctantly walked to the window. He opened the window and saw a black helicopter hovering in the distance. The man gave sammy a pair of binoculars. Sammy nervously took the binoculars from the man and put it to his eyes. He was shocked to see a man in the helicopter pointing a rocket launcher at his home. "Ok! I'll go with you. My dude!" sammy shouted. "Don't cause a scene. Just follow me outside into a black SUV." The man said. Sammy followed the man as ordered. He took the backway to his home to avoid the crowd gathered in his living room until he was approached by his uncle ralph, who was staggering drunk. "¿Adónde vas, sobrino? ¡La fiesta está saltando!" ralph slurred. "I got some business to attend to right now, uncle ralph!" sammy said. "Who is this?" ralph asked pointing to the man in the black suit. "Uncle ralph, please! Just go back and party with everyone else!" Sammy pleaded. Ralph put his arm around sammy. "I'm proud of you, nephew! It's about time we ran this shit!" ralph shouted in his ear. Sammy noticed that the man in the black suit unveil a pistol from inside his suit jacket. "Uncle ralph! Just go back and enjoy the party! Please!" sammy cried. Ralph was wobbling as he took a few steps back. "Ok, nephew! I see you got some serious business to talk about!" ralph said as he staggered away. Sammy let out a sigh of relief. "Let's go, Mr. Perez." The man said.

Sammy and the strange man stepped outside when a black SUV pulled up in front of them. The man opened the rear passenger door. "If you would, mr. Perez." The man said as he gestured sammy to enter the vehicle. Before sammy entered the SUV, one of his soldiers, who was patroling the area. "¡Oye, jefe! ¿Adónde vas?" the soldier shoted. "I'll be back! Make sure my wife has whatever she needs!" sammy shouted before entering the vehicle. Inside the vehicle sammy noticed there were 2 NA agents of African American descent in the driver and passenger seat. "Oh shit. I'm a dead man!" he whispered to himself before being injected in the neck with a syring from the NA agent that escorted him outside. Sammy passed out within seconds.

When sammy woke up, he found himself in a small room tied to a office chair. He noticed across from him Dubbs was also tied to a chair but unconscious. "Dubbs! Dubbs!" he shouted. Sammy tried to get free from his bindings, but found it futile. Dubbs finally woke up, looking confused. "What the fuck happened?" Dubbs asked. "My dude! I think we're fucked!" Sammy said. "Why? I ain't do nothing!" dubbs shouted. "My dude! Are you serious?" sammy said. Sammy looked over and saw the entrance door knob turn. "When they come in! Don't say shit, my dude!" sammy whispered. Suddenly, a burly NA agent entered the room followed by Doug Reed. He was dressed in a blue suit and tie. The NA agent pulled up a chair for doug, positioning him between sammy and dubbs. Doug with a smile on his face slapped dubbs on his lap. "Well, boys! Which one of you did it?" he asked them. Neither one of them gave him an answer. Dubbs looked confused. "I don't know what you talkin about, man!" dubbs said. Doug began laughing. "You're a good actor, i'll give you that!" he chuckled. "My dude! What's this about?" sammy asked. Doug turned his head towards sammy. Sammy saw the fury in his eyes. "What's this about? What's this about?!!" doug shouted as he stood from his seat. He leaned over with his face inches apart from sammy's. "Ok. let me fill you in on what happened. Butch. Remember him? The guy you used to work for? The guy who used to work for me? Well, his body was found by one of my agnets who always kept a close eye on him." He said.

Doug began slowly pacing the floor, rubbing his hands together. "Now, i know you're asking yourselves, where's Mookie? Well, mookie is no longer with us in physical form, may he rest in peace. The murder of Butch happened on his turf. But, something tells me that you 2 were in on it." Doug explained. "My dude!" sammy shouted. "It's doug. Doug reed. Mr. Reed to you." He said to sammy. "Mr. Reed! That's fucked up what happened to Butch, but sware i ain't had nothing to do with his death!" sammy cried. "Butch was my cousin! My blood! If you let me go, i'll continue to look for his killer!" dubbs cried. Doug walked over towards dubbs. He leaned over, putting his hand on dubb's shoulder. "Well, you filthy nigger, you should start by looking in the mirror." Doug said in a calm voice. Sweat began popping off of dubb's face. Doug sat back in chair. "I don't give 2 fucks about your cousin. It's just that my bosses are upset that you 3 took control without our blessing. There are procedures to this, rituals to be preformed! So, by not coming to me to starighten this whole mess out, your'e guilty as charged! I know you 2 have hundreds of people depending on you. So, to be fair, i'll let you and sammy decide your fate." Doug said. "You mean, you ain't gonna killk us?" sammy asked. "The Lassenberry name is no longer relevant in New Jersey. From what i've heard, there's a land called Lassenberia. A land on the rise of being the most powetful nation in the world. I'm an expert on how the human mind works. I know you 2 will eventually turn on each other for absolute power. That means one of you will have the choice to either be exlied to Lassenberia, or stay here and stand alone to run the narcotics business in New Jersey. Choose wisely! The one who decides to stay, will not be able to make any moves without the say so of the National Agreement. You and your family will belong to us, forever." Doug explained. "You telling us that one of us can stay as long as we obey you?" sammy asked with a wide eyed look on his face. "Yeah! The other will live the rest of his time on Lassenberia without any contact from his loved ones." Doug said. "Fuck! I already know what i wanna do!" dubbsa said in a cheerful voice. "I'll give you guys a few minutes alone to come to a conclusion." Doug said before he and the agent lkeft the room.

"So, what you thinking, my dude?" sammy asked. "I'm tired of this shit! It's hard to look my family in the face after what i did!" dubbs confessed. "I served a lot of time in the joint! You didn't! i earned this shit, and everything that comes with it, my dude!" sammy said. "All i ask, is that you take care of my whole family! Do i have your word?' dubbs asked. "My dude! Standing alone? Not having to split any loot with anybody?!! I see no problem sliding your people 2 million a month!" sammy said. "Make it 10 million! I gotta big family!" dubbs said. Sammy sighed as he thought for a few seconds about the deal. "Ok, my dude, 10 million!" sammy said. "I have your word?" dubbs asked. "My dude! After we get outta here, i'm gonna pocket at least 50 mill a month! You got my word!" sammy said. "If i'm gonna be sent away, i rather be sent to the most powerful nation. I was always loyal to the Lassenberry family. I'm sure i'll be fine. I would also like to say, Long live the house of Perez, my brother!" Dubbs shouted. "Whatever, my dude." Sammy said as he shrugged his shoulders. Moments later. "Here he comes!" dubbs said. Doug and the NA agent returned. "So, gentlemen! What's the verdict?" he asked. "I'm staying, my dude! I mean Mr. Reed!" sammy said. "He told me he would take care of my family financially." Dubbs said. "Very well!" doug said. Doug whispered into the agent's ear. "Tomorrow at noon mr. Perez, you'll report to me at castle

Lassenberry in Cherry Hill." He said. "What about me, mr. Reed?" dubbs asked. "Oh, yes! Tonight you will be escorted by my agents to a place to be vaccinated. After that you will board a oil tanker heading towards Yamoussoukro." He said. "Where the fuck is that?" dubbs asked. "It's the capital city off the Ivory coast, West Africa. There, a guide will lead you on a trek to South Africa." Doug said. "Why can't y'all just take me strsight to Lassenberia?" dubbs asked. "Like i said, it is, or soon will be the most powerful nation on the face of the planet. I doubt very much anyone in The National Agreement is welcomed in Lassenberia!" doug chuckled. Why i have to get vaccinated?" dubbs asked. There was a silence in the room, which lasted for only a few seconds. Doug just stared at dubbs with a creepy smile on his face. "I Just like leaving wierd messages." He said before leaving the room. "What the hell does that mean?" dubbs shouted. The agent pulled out a switchblade from his jacket and tossed it on the floor between sammy and dubbs. "Free yourselves." The agent said before leaving the room. Sammy tipped over in his chair, causing him to fall to the floor. "I got this, my dude!" he said as he scooched toward the blade. "My gut tells me that this is gonna turn out bad!" dubbs said, having a sorrowful look on his face.

Later that evening, dubbs was being escorted to a private airport in jersey by 6 NA agents. Before reaching the airport, dubbs was in the back of the SUV sitting between two agents sobbing like a baby because he wasn't aloud to say goodbye to his family. When the vehicle reached the airport, dubbs litery had to be dragged to the private jet to fly him out of the country. When he was forced to be seated on the jet, he began to laugh histerically. "He warned me! Butch warned me!" he said to himself.

after the SUV parked on the tarmac, dubbs was manhandled by the agents towards the private jet. A black sack cloth was placed over his head before he was bound and seated to one of the aircraft seats. Dubbs started panicing, breathing heavily through the sack cloth.

A while later, the private jet landed in a undiscosled place. Just like brandon hart before him, dubbs was led to the creepy laboratory. Just like brandon, dubbs was confronted by a man in a lab coat. Just like brandon, dubbs was injected with the same deadly microscopic weapon.

The next morning sammy arrived at his home. He was comfronted by one of his soldiers he told to guard his home before being taken away. "¿Estás bien, jefe? ¿Dónde diablos has estado? ¡Tu esposa estaba preocupada!" the soldier said. "Where's my wife at right now?" sammy asked. "she's inside, taking a nap. By-the-way, boss. An old creepy looking white guy showed up in a limo about a hour before you got here! He gave her a gold envelope!" The soldier said. "Alright then. Keep patroling the area." Sammy said before entering his home.

Once inside, sammy looked around the livingroom. He shook his head as he saw the aftermath of food scraps, liquor and wine glasses everywhere from last night. He stormed up the stairs yelling out his wife's name. He burst into the master bedroom. "Baby! Why the hell you ain't call the help to come over and clean up that shit downstairs?" he shouted. Elizabeth was lying on her side in the bed. She slowly turned over. "Where the hell have you been? You had me and everybody worried sick. You realize how long it took me to convince your family and your boys to go home?" she shouted. Sammy took a deep breath. "I'm sorry, baby. I had to leave on some big business type shit!" he said. "You couldn't tell me, of all people?" she shouted. Sammy smiles as he started salsa dancing. "Guess what, baby! New Jersey! It's all mine! All mine!" he said as he continued dancing. Elizabeth looked furious. "Go fuck yourself!" she said as she flung the gold envelope at him. Sammy stopped dancing and looked at the envelope. He picked it up. "Thanks baby! I was just about to ask you about this!" he said before leaving the bedroom. As he was walking down the corridor, he found it hard to open the envelope with his bare hands. He went downstairs to the kitchen and opened it with a steak knife. He began to smile as he read the letter. He started dancing again. As the letter instructed, he pulled out a cigarette lighter from his back pocket and went over to the sink, setting the envelope and letter on fire. He watched as both burned in the sink before turning on the faucet.

Back on the island nation of Lassenberia, the newly Lassenberian coast guard cutter the LSS JABBO was setting sail from the eastern harbor. It's captain, Johannes Usman and his one hundred man crew were preparing for search and rescue excercises when the boatswain's mate spotted a South African Naval ship 5 miles off their port side. The signalman from the south african ship was sending a message to the JABBO. "Captain. We have communication from the SAS Drakensberg." The helmsman from the LSS JABBO reported. "Very well. Translate message." Captain Usman ordered. The orders were relayed back to the signalman. "The Drakensberg reports that she has a very important foreign dignitary with a message for Lord Lassenberry. His wish is to come aboard, sir." The helmsman reported. Captain Usman leaned back in his chair for a moment to ponder what to do next. "Get me Abdirrahim on the radio!" Usman ordered.

When captain Usman made contact with Abdirrahim, it took about an hour of back-n-forth communication to allow this foreign dignitary to board the LSS JABBO. When Abdirrahim recieved the approval directly from Lord Lassenberry, it was only on the grounds that this outsider never step foot on Lassenberian soil. Lord Lassenberry prepared for this visit by taking the time to have his servants donn him with a flexible bodyarmour from head-to-toe. "You look worried, my Lord!" Mahasin said as she slid his arm through his elbow pads. Lord lassenberry gave her a look that she realized was the wrong thing to say. "Get out!" Lord Lassenberry said to the other 2 servants. The 2 young ladies back out of his chamber with their heads bowed down. "Leave us alone!" he said to the soldier stsanding guard by the door. The soldier gave the traditional salute by bowing his head while putting his right fist over his heart. Once they were alone, Lord Lassenberry grabbed her by the arm. "If you wanna have my baby, you best not make me look weak in front of anybody! Understand?" he said. Mahasin went from looking terrified to looking confident. "So, my king! Do you want to make me your queen?" she asked. He released her arm. "I gotta go! Just remember what i said!" he shouted before leaving the room.

Shortly after, captain Usman recieved a radio message that Lord Lassenberry was on his way by motorboat with a tight security team. The boatswain's mate looking through his binoculars, spotted a small motorboat come towards the JABBO with the Lassenberia flag flying, waving in the breeze.

Lord Lassenberry and his 5 man security team were about a 100 yards away from their destination when one of his bodyguards recieved a urgent radio message from the JABBO. "Lord Lassenberry! There seems to have been an incident on board the JABBO! It wouldn't be wise to board her until we get further information!" the bodyguard shouted. "Fuck that!

I have on full body armor! Tell them i'm coming on board! Just watch my back!" Lord Lassenberry ordered. "Yes, mylord!" the security team shouted all at once.

4 crew members from the JABBO tied the motor boat to the ship and lowered a rope ladder so Lord Lasssenberry could come aboard. *"Coming on board, His Majesty, Lord Lassenberry!"* was announced over the ship's PA system. Once on aboard, Lord Lassenberry was escorted by his security team and armed crew members of the JABBO to the bridge to meet captain Usman. As he was making his way towards the ship's bridge, crew members of the JABBO stood at attention, giving him the Lassenberian salute. When Lord Lassenberry reached the bridge, every crew member, even the captain stood at attention. "I wish wee could've met under better circumstances, my Lord!" Usman said as he and Lord Lassenberry shook hands. Lord Lassenberry was awe struck as he looked around at the carnage on the bridge. "What the hell happened here, captain?" he asked. There was a headless body lying on the bridge's deck. There were crew members recieving medical attention from acid burns caused by the headless victim. "He said his name was William dubbs watson. He handed me this envelope. I excused myself to go to the restroom. As i was relieving myself, i heard a loud pop! Then i heard some of my crew yelling and screaming! I came running out with my pants around my ankles, and i saw this mess!" Usman said as he handed Lord Lassenberry the manila envelope. "Dubbs was his name?" Lord Lassenberry asked. "Yes, my Lord!" Usman said. Lord Lassenberry opened the envelope. He was shocked as he read the message. *We miss you Krayton. Come back home so we can talk things out.* The message said. "Is everything ok, my Lord? who is this Krayton person?" Usman asked as he leaned over to read the message as well. "No one is to leave this ship! Not even the injured!" Lord Lassenberry said. "We have no GLC on board, my Lord!" Usman said. "I'll have some sent to you! Make a written report on what took place! Have it sent to me before the day is out!" Lord Lassenberry said before ripping the message in pieces. "Of course, my Lord!" Usman said with a look of confusion.

After returning to the motor boat, Lord Lassenberry told the man incharge of his security team to have Abdirrahim report to his throne room at once. He also told him not to allow anyone from the JABBO to leave.

A few hours later, Abdirrahim reported to the throne room. "What took you so long?" Lord Lassenberry asked. "Lady Ellen and i were going over the supply list for the Braxton territory, my Lord." Abdirrahim explained. "Anyway, i have an important mission for you! I need you to destroy the Jabbo!" Lord lassenberry said as he sat comfortably on his throne. "What?!" Abdirrahim shouted. "You heard me! There was a terrorist attack on board today! The person responsible is dead but spread some type of contaminant on board! The crew of the JABBO can never step foot on Lassenberian soil!" Lord Lassenberry said. "We have enough GLC to cure the world! We can most certainly save the crew!" Abdirrahim said. Lord Lassenberry leaned forward. "I don't want to risk it! It was most likely an attack from my enemies back in the United States! I want you to get intouch with the South African media! I want the destruction of the JABBO caught on camera to show the world how fucked up and evil the United States is! Now, go make it happen!" Lord Lassenberry ordered. "My Lord! i beg you! There are good men on board the JABBO! Men with families! It's just not right!" Abdirrahim shouted. "You either destroy the JABBO, or Lassenberia will fall!" Lord

Lassenberry shouted as he pointed to the device connected to his chest. "Very well, my Lord!" Abdirrahim sighed.

A couple of hours later, Lord Lassenberry was enteraining his daughter, princess Niyale in her play room. He held her up in the air, spinning her around. "You're gonna rule the world, little girl! Daddy will make sure of that!" he shouted. Little Niyale began giggling until the continuous spinning caused her to spit up on her father's face. "That's enough of that!" he chuckled. He walked over to the dresser drawer, with his daughter in his arms. He grabbed a box of wet wipes out of the drawer. While wiping his daughter clean, Zilda came running in the room. "They killed them! They killed them, Lord Lassenberry!" she screamed. Niyale reacted to her screams by screaming herself. "Calm down, Zilda! Tell me what happened?!" Lord Lassenberry shouted. Zilda begasn clutching her chest as she tried to catch her breath. At that moment, one of Lord Lassenberry's guards came running in the room. "Are you and the princess ok, my Lord?" he asked. "Yeah, i'm good! Now go back to your post!" Lord Lassenberry said. Zilda caught her breath and explained to her king what had took place. "The ship! The ship! They say the Americans did!" she said. "What ship?" Lord Lassenberry asked. "I think it was the JEEBU or JABBO, or something!" she said. "The JABBO or something, huh?" he said with a smirk. Lord Lassenberry handed his crying daughter over to Zilda. "Now, let's go see what all the comotion is about. You get the princess a fresh set of clothes." He said before leaving. "You be careful, my Lord!" Zilda shouted as he left the room.

Thousands of Lassenbians stood at the pier in awe as what was left of the LLS JABBO went up in flames a couple of miles off the coast. There were news helicoptors circling over the horrific scene, as well as rescue ships and fishing boats trying their best in search of survivors.

While being driven to the catastrophy, Lord Lassenberry kicked up his boots as he sat in the back of his armored vehicle and lit a cigar. Sitting across from him, was a young soldier of Somalian descent. Lord Lassenberry could see the fear in his eyes. "Don't worry, kid. Those from the United States responsible for what happened, will pay. We'll soon have the rest of the world on our side." He said with confidence. He leaned over to console the young soldier by rubbing his shoulder. "You're a soldier! Look the part! That's an order!" he said. "Of course, my Lord!" the young man replied.

Once he arrived on the scene, a path was being made through the crowd by Abdirrahim's men. "Make way for his majesty, Lord Lassenberry!!" one soldier shouted as he pushed a citizen out of the way. Standing in the backround away from the crowd were the royal council members. Lady Ellen of Braxton was the last council member to show up with her entourage. After he exited the vehicle, Lord Lassenberry approached her. "Lady Ellen! It's been awhile since we were face-to-face!" he said. "It certainly has, your majesty." She said. He turned towards the sea. "Sad day for our naval forces. But, we will get revenge." He said calmly. "Who do you think is responsible?" Lady Ellen asked. "We'll discuss that at the next council meeting. But for now, i have to ease the minds of the people." Lord Lassenberry said as his servants set up the podium for him to speak on. Once one of his servants did a microphone check, Lord Lassenberry took his place upon the the podium.

"My dear citizens! I know it seems frightening to see members of our great military perish at the hands of an enemy that i thought was considered an ally! I promise you all, that this act of terrostism will be avenged! I promise you, we will get through this! Regardless of what just happened, this is still a paradise! All i ask, is that you put your trust in me! This will never happen again under my leadership! Now, go to your homes, and let our officials continue to investigate this tragedy! Long live the house of Lassenberry!" he shouted before stepping down from the podium. "Long live the house of Lassenberry!" the crowd chanted as he walked through the crowd. The women began to swoon, reaching out, just to touch him. Far off in the distance Abdirrahim was sitting in a rowboat, wearing a black wetsuit. His scuba gear and fins were placed at his feet. He watched the fire coming from the LSS JABBO. In his hand was a device the size of a tv remote. He stared at the device, which was actually a detonator, and in a fit of rage snapped it in half with his bare hands, tossing the pieces into the water. He held his head in his hands and began sobbing.

The next day Lord Lassenberry held a meeting with the council members at Castle Lassenberry. In attendance were council members Javish, his brother Jaish, Lady Ellen of Braxton, the sky father, Akshay Devgn, who was once a poliitcal prisoner from northern India now appointed prime minister of the former Pale lands, Carlos Mondlane, who owned a fishing company back in Mozambique until his health began failing. He traded his company, which was suffering financially to Lord Lassenberry for a vial of GLC, Ayub who was a teenage engineering prodigy from Zimbabwe was healed of terminal cancer after arriving on the Lassenberian shores in a life raft, mother Talon from Benin, who was the voodoo priestess of the Fon people traveled to lassenberia out of curiosity. Her spiritual healing powers were challenged by Lord Lassenberry's use of GLC. Once she witnessed the powers of the GLC, she surrendered her beliefs until Lord Lassenberry oppointed her head of the new age faith. Matamela Cyril, a former political prisoner of aparteid was summoned by Lord Lassenberry for being a famous polyglot in south africa. He was assigned to form the new language for the people of lassenberia. Sitting at the opposite end of the table in her high chair across from lord Lassenberry was princess Niyale. Lord lassenberry recently gave her the title of council member. In private, certain members of the council found it insulting a baby could hold a seat at the table. She spent her time at the meeting chewing on dry cereal, continuously throwing her sippy cup on the floor for someone to pick it up. Unkown to the rest of the council, there were 4 more council members that gathered with Lord Lassenberry only to speak on evacuating the island nation.

"i want to start out by saying, that was some fucked up shit! Those men dyiing like that, scared the shit out of me!" Lord Lassenberry chuckled. The council members looked around the table at each other in a confused state. "What happened to the words of encouragment you told the people, my Lord?" Lady Ellen asked. "Lady Ellen!! Don't mean to change the conversation, but i'mabout to change the conversation!!" he shouted with a big smile on his face. "The floor is yours, my Lord." she said. "Thank you! Now. Concerning the Burough of Braxton! I realize that you and your family members are the only caucasians on the island. The only way i can see keeping Lassenberia safe from our adversaries in the United states, is showing the world that you and your family are citizens of Lassenberia." He said as he paced back-n-forth behind his chair with his arms folded. "So, you will invite the media here, my Lord?" Ayub asked. "Damn skippy, young man!" Lord Lassenberry shouted as he pointed to Ayub. "What is this thing called damn skippy?" Ayub whispered to the sky father. "Pay attention!" the sky fathwer whispered. "I will arrange to have American and British Journalists come to the island and do a expose on the Braxton family. The public will be sympathetic to our way of living if any future attacks occur." He said as his daugther threw her sippy cup on the floor again. "The saftey of Lassenberia depends on a handfull of white people? Is this what you're telling us, my Lord?" Javed asked. "Crazy, ain't it?" Lord Lassenberry said. Javed just shook his head." Lady ellen! I should've told you this before the meeting, but for the saftey of you and your family, i have to put in effect a lock down on the burrough of Braxton until further notice." Lord Lassenberry said. Lady Ellen looked shocked. "Sorry it has come down to this, but i see no other way around it." Lord Lassenberry said. "My family, especially my nephew will not allow us to be confined to one area of what you call paradise!" Ellen shouted. Lord Lassenberry leaned over the table giving Lady Ellen direct eye contact. "May i remind you again, if it wasn't for me, you and your family would be back in the states in a ditch somewhere out in Mormon land!" He shouted. Princess Niyale reacted to her father's shouting by crying. "Don't just stand there like a dope! Don't you see my daughter crying? Pick up her sippy cup!" he said to one of his soldiers standing guard. "Yes. Of course, my Lord!" the soldier said before picking up the cup, giving it back to princess Niyale. "Can we focus on the matter at hand, my Lord?" Lady Ellen asked with a furious tone in her voice. Lord Lassenberry stood there with fury in his eyes. "My baby girl, the future ruler of this great land is all that matters!!" he shouted. Lady ellen didn't say a word. She got up from her seat and headed for the exit. Before walking out the door, she turned toward the council. "I pray for you, Lord Lassenberry! I pray for you all!" she said before leaving the room. Despite baby Niyale cooing, there was a moment of silence in the room. Lord Lassenberry began to grimace, rubbing his chest due to the discomfort of the nuclear detonator implanted in his chest. "Are you ok, my Lord?" one council member asked. He looked at the council member, shaking off the pain. "Of course i'm ok! I'm a lassenberry!" he shouted. "Very well, my Lord." the council member said. "Well, anyway! Cyril! Mother Talon! How we're coming along with the Lasserian language in the schools and the church of Lassenberry?" Lord Lassenberry asked.

It was the moment Sammy Perez was waiting for. There he was, standing alone dressed in a sparkling black tuxedo, sporting a diamond incrusted watch and a diamond pinky ring on his left hand in front of the infamous palace entrance owned by the National Agreement. The letter in the gold envelope given to him said he was to come to the National Agreement alone. Except for a few celebrities he had seen on TV, the other guests arriving to the gathering were unknown to him. "This the shit i'm talking about!" he said to himself as he smiled from ear-to-ear.

It was a couple of days before thanksgiving 2004, and the air in the deep forests of Maine was frigid. Sammy didn't seem to mind the cold air. He was just too in awe of the exterior of the palace until a chubby caucasian man dressed in a black and white checkered suit, wearing a white fedora approached him. "If you think the outside is fancy, wait until you see the inside!" the man said to Sammy. Sammy's trance was interupted by the oddly dressed man. "What? What you say, my dude?" sammy responded. "forget it! My name is Angus! You must be Sammy Perez!" Angus said. "How you know my name, my dude?" Sammy asked with a suspicious look on his face. Angus chuckled. "It's my job, at least one of my jobs to know who's going to be a potenial member!" he said as the both of them shook hands. "I hope you also know that i run the dope game in all of new jersey!" Sammy boasted. "That's just terrific! By the way! What are you, Cuban?" Angus asked. "Puerto Rican, my dude! Why?" sammy asked. "Oh! No offence! We've have quite a few of you spanish guys as members!" Angus said. "Yeah! I just saw Ricardo Ramirez over in the distance! My dude got the record for the most grand slams in baseball! He's dominican though! Nobody's perfect!" sammy chuckled as he nudged Angus on the shoulder. "Oh! I get it!" Angus chuckled. "That was a long plane ride and drive up here, my dude! I'm hungry than a motherfucker!" Sammy said. "Let's go inside, gets some fine food in your belly, some drinks and get aquainted with the other members before the festivities begin!" Angus said. "I thought they was gonna bring me here in one of thoughs luxury jets, instead they bring me here in a cramped ass prop plane!" sammy said. "After tonight, every inconvience in your life will change for the better, if you release and go with the flow!" Angus said as he lead Sammy inside.

Back in New Jersey around 2 in the morning, 2 black men around in their twenties were conversing outside in front of the Ivy Hill Park apartments in Newark about the state of the drug game, and who was running the show. "Man, shit is crazy out here, my nigga! Since the Lassenberry family left the game, shit ain't been the same! You got these spanish niggas on Roseville ave. Living it up because of what happened to old man Butch!" the man said. "What happened to Butch?" the othe guy asked. "You ain't hear?" he said. "You know i'm just getting back from doing sea trials! I don't know shit going on out here now-a-days!" the other guy said. "Oh, my nigga! They got'em!" the first man said. "What do you mean, they got him?" the other guy asked. They made that nigga disappear! I don't know for sure, but from what i heard, he's dead!" the first man shouted. "I don't believe that! Butch was one of the most feared guys on the streets before i was born!" the other guy said. "Hold up!" the first man whispered. The 2 men became quiet when a few strangers walked by to enter the building, fearing that their conversation might be heard. "Like i was saying, the old man was taken out! Right now, i don't know who's running shit right about now! I overheard from my nigga down neck that it was that cat Sammy!" the first man said. "Sammy?" the other guy asked. "Yeah! He used to run product out of bloomfield!" the first man said. "Oh! I remember him!" the other guy said. "Just recently, my man clyde was found in a dumpster out in Irvington with a bullet in his temple! Few other niggas from his crew bodies showed up in fucked up places! On top of that shit, i heard a few spanish niggas got his spot now!" the first man said. "Daaaamn!" the other guy said. "All i know as long as i get my product, and get it on time when i need it, i ain't got no problem with the ricans!" the first man said. "Damn! I'm glad i got out of the game when i did!" the other guy said. "Where you said you was stationed at again?" the first guy asked. "The submarine base up in Connecticut! Why?" the other guy asked. "i need a back up plan, my nigga! I don't know what my future is with these spanish niggas!" the first guy said. "So what you saying?" the other guy asked. The first guy cautiously looked around before speaking. "Just so happens i got my hands on a couple of bricks! I caught these niggas sleeping, so i had to make my move! Understand? What i need from you is to help me move the product up where you stationed at! We flip it, and flip it, and flip it some more so i can become independent from all this shit! You feel me?" the first guy explained. "I feel you. I feel you." The other guy said as he rubbed his chin. "I plan to get the fuck out of Jersey, go over to the caribbean to one of them islands!" the first guy said. The other guy stood there pondering what he was just told. "What's my cut?" he asked. "10 percent, my nigga!" the first man said. "Nigga! I work for the United States Navy now! I'm not gonna risk my career moving product across state lines for only 10 percent!" he said. "Alright…15 percent!" the first man said. "30!" the other guy demanded. "25!" the first man said. The other guy went silent for a moment. He extended his arm toward the first man. "Deal" he said. The 2 men shake hands to finalize the deal. "You still have my number?" the first man asked. "Yeah. I still got it." The other guy said. "Cool! Give me a call tomorrow at noon. I'll tell you when and where to meet up. The product will be chopped up and ready to go by then!" the first man said before the other guy left him standing alone.

CHAPTER .50 MAHASIN WINGO

K eeping his word, the runner rendezvoused with the dealer at midnight near Weequahic Lake. Both men pulled up, stopping their vehicles parallel to each other facing in oppisite directions. The dealer didn't say a word. He just tossed the backpack filled with hundreds of plastic packets of cut cocaine in the runner's back seat." Don't come up short, nigga!" the dealer shouted before driving off. The runner took the exit out of the park leading to Meeker Street.

20 minutes later, the runner was about to leave Weehawken, heading toward Manhattan when he saw flashing blue and red lights in his rear view mirror. "Fuck! I gotta toss this shit!" he shouted as he tried to reach for the backpack in the back seat. He found it impossible to drive and reach for the backpack. "Shit! This can't be happening!" he said to himself. Realizing it was a lost cause, he decided to pull over on the side of the road. He leaned over toward the back seat, trying to stuff the backpack under the front passenger seat. Once that was accomplished, he breathed a sigh of relief. When he looked through the rear view mirror. To his surprise the 2 figures coming out of the squad car didn't look like regular cops. They were actual NA agents dressed in their standard black suit and neck-tie. "What the fuck is this shit?" the runner said to himself. The 2 agents, one being a black man and the other being caucasian. The black man, who was wearing dark shades approached the driver's side. The runner was prepared. He had his license, registration and military ID at the ready. The caucasian agent approached the passenger's side. The runner rolled down the window. He extended his arm out the window with license and registration in hand. "There will be no need for that, mr. Daniels." The agent said. "If y'all don't want my paperwork, why you pull me the fuck over, and how the fuck you know my name before checking my shit, officer?" he said in a bold manner. "Step out of the vehicle, sir." The agent said. "Officer! I'm a non commissioned officer in the Navy! I'm stationed up in connecticut! I'm on my way there now!" he said. "Sir. Take your key out of the ignition and Step out of the vehicle." The agent said. "Damn!" the Daniels said as he took the key out of the ignition. He unbuckled his seat belt and stepped out of the vehicle. The agent took his car keys and tossed them into the tall weeds off the side of the road. "What the fuck you do that for?" Daniels shouted. The caucasion agent came around the driver's side

helping his partner restrsin Daniels, cuffing him from behind. They took Daniels back to their sqaud car. once he was tossed in the back of the sqaud car the agents entered the vehicle, locking the passenger doors. Before the sqaud car drove off, the caucasian agent turned toward Daniels. "We were ordered to tell you, mr. Daniels that the narcotics you were about to take over state lines was infused with a tracer using nano technology. Thats why we were able to find you." The agent said. "What the fuck is nano technology?" Daniels asked. "You left the collective to join the military. Just yesterday you decided to get involved again. The rules are, ever since the lassenberry family took control of New Jersey, it is prohibited for anyone to sell narcotics outside of their territory." The agent explained." How the fuck was i supposed to know, man?" Daniels shouted. "Just because Sammy Perez is head of running narcotics for New Jersey doesn't mean the rules have changed." The agent said. "Sammy? Sammy Perez? Let me get a chance to talk to him! I can explain everything!" Daniels shouted. "It's too late, mr. Daniels. We are ordered to take you to a undisclosed location, execute you and dismember your remains." The agent said. Daniels went balistic. He began sobbing, banging his head against the grated partition. "Please! Please let me go! I promise to stay away from the product! Please just let me go!" Daniels cried. His cries fell on deaf ears. The squad car made a quick u-turn, heading south toward I-95.

The next day around around 3 in the morning, a man is sitting on a bench in Watsessing Park located in Bloomfield New Jersey. Standing a few yards away from him were 4 NA agents watching him sob. "I can't believe i did that shit! God help me! God help me!" the man said to himself. The man sitting on the bench was the official head of New Jersey's drug cartel.

Sammy Perez cried as he stared at the dry blood on the palm of his hands. He still had on the same sparkling black tuxedo he wore a couple of days ago when he arrived at the NA palace. The NA agents had to stand their watching their new boss wimper without any further orders until a black SUV appeared off into the distance. The windows were a rinted dark making it impossible for anyone to see inside. The rear passenger window rolled down. The man sitting in the back seat summoned the head agent over to the vehicle. "Mr. Reed." The agent said. "What's the problem, agent?" Doug Reed asked. "Mr. Perez is still distraught. We haven't recieved any further orders from him, sir." The agent said. "Jesus! Why can't people be more like Eddie Lassenberry? That was one hardcore motherfucker!" Doug reed said to the man sitting next to him. "Hey. Try this. Tell the agents to kneel in front of him. I guarantee his lust for power will drown out those pathetic emotions." The man sitting next to Doug Reed suggested. "You know we had the same problem 10 years ago with the guy out in Houston?" Doug Reed said to the man. Doug Reed thought about for a moment. "You heard the man! Go over there and kneel in front of the cock sucker! Say something to make him feel powerful, too!" he said. "Yes, mr. Reed." The agent said before walking away. The agent went back to where Sammy was sitting. He stood about 5 feet in front of him. Before saying anything, he dropped to one knee. Without hesitation, the other agents followed suit. This caused Sammy to look up. For that moment he ignored his blood stained hands. He wiped away his tears with the sleeve of his tuxedo. "We are here to serve you…Master Perez. What are your orders, sir?" the agent said. At first, Sammy had a surprised look on his face. From the time they left Maine, to the time arriving in New Jersey, the agents hardly said a word to him, let alone anything with such praise. Sammy stood tall, brushing off his tuxedo. He had the proud look of a boss. "Did i lie?" the man next to Doug Reed said. "Good call! Lets say we grab a late night dinner! The type of df dinner that doesn't scream for their mommy!'"' Doug chuckled. The man next to him started laughing. "That sounds like a great idea, my firend!" the man said. "Driver! Get us the fuck out of here!" Doug chuckled.

"Sir. The sun will come up very soon. We need to retreat before the public comes out in droves." The agent said to Sammy. Sammy began to focus. "I gotta get cleaned up! Take me home!" Sammy ordered. The agents stood to their feet and escorted their new boss to the other SUV parked on the sidewalk.

About a hour later, Sammy and the agents arrive at his home in Vineland. One of the agents sitting up front get out of the SUV and open the door for him. 2 of the agents stand guard by the vehicle while the other 2 escort him to his front door. Sammy puts his hand on the door knob. His hands started trembling as he hesitated on putting the key in the lock. He just stood there with his eyes closed. "Are you ok, sir?" the agent said. "I'm cool! Just go back to the car!" Sammy said as he stared at the door. Once the agents went back to the vehicle, Sammy drew up enough courage to unlock the door and enter his home. As soon as he step foot in the house his eyes started to tear up again. There was a dead silence. He slammed the door closed. He looked up at the top of the staircase. He slowly treked his way from the living room, to the dining room to the kitchen. He stood in front of the sink flipping the faucet on and off. Suddenly he reguritated into the sink while the water was running. After wiping his mouth, he turned off the faucet. He then dragged his feet, slowly peeled off his blood stained clothes as he headed up stairs. He went into one of his 4 bathrooms and stepped into the shower. He turned on the water. The water from the gold plated shower head came shooting down on his head. He didn't bother to wash off the blood at first. Eventually grabbed the soap and shampoo and began to wash the blood and the smell of alcohol off of his body. Moments later he stepped out of the shower, drying himself off. He stood in front of the medicine cabinet mirror and wiped the mist off of it. He grabbed his monographed towel from off the hook, wrapping it around his waist. He was so disgusted with his image in the mirror, cracked the mirror with his fist. He then made his way toward the master bedroom. He found it hard to approach the bed. He just stood there with his hand wrapped in a gauze.

He stood there in a daze for about an hour until he heard the doorbell. He snapped out of his daze and ran into his walk-in closet where his gun safe was located. He punched in the digital code to unlock the safe. Out of all the 30 weapons in his arsenal he chose a high caliber revolver. He quickly checked to makesure it was fully loaded. He dropped the towel and went into the dresser drawer and pulled out a pair of sweat pants and t-shirt. The doorbell was still ringing.as he was getting dressed.

He crept down the stairs with weapon in hand. He suddenly stopped at the bottom of the stairs. "¿Quién está ahí?" he shouted. "Es el agente 143, señor!" the agent shouted. Sammy felt a sigh of relief. He went to open the door. Standing there was the head agent of his security team. "Shit! I thought you were the cops! I was about to go out in a blaze of glory, my dude! What you want? I was…resting!" he shouted. The agent ingored his rant. "Sir! Mr. Reed thought you would need to relieve some stress." the agent said as he made a hand gesture toward the parked

SUV. Coming out of the SUV were 2 gorgeous young ladies covered in full length fur coats. One was a caucasian girl with long blonde hair flowing in the breeze. The other young lady was asian with long jet black hair. The ladies headed toward Sammy showing sexual hunger on their faces. "My dude! Are you serious? You realize what i just been through?" Sammy said. "They are a gift from mr. Reed, sir. The agent said." "No! get them outta here!" he shouted. "Sir." The agent said. "¡Aléjalos de mí!" Sammy shouted. The agent gave the girls the signal to stop in their tracks before they came to the front entrance. "Sir. I was ordered to tell you that if you do not eccept this gift from mr. Reed, we will have to torture and dispose of these women immediately." The agent said. Sammy glanced over the agent's shoulder at the young ladies. They were smiling and winking at him, not knowing their fate if he decided to reject them. "Come on, my dude! This shit ain't right! Those girls didn't do shit to me!" Sammy said. "Sir. I have my orders. Do you want these women or not?" the agent said. "¡A la mierda! ¡Siento que estoy en una maldita pesadilla!"Sammy said to himself. "What will it be, sir?" the agent asked. "Fuckit! Bring'em here!" he said to the agent. The agent gave the women the signal to come forward. Sammy stepped to the side to let the women enter his home. Sammy looked depressed and tired as the Asian woman gave him a kiss on the cheek before entering. "Enjoy, sir." The agent said. "Fuck you!" Sammy said before slamming the door in his face.

The night Sammy entered the NA palace, was the most exciting moment in his life, he said to Angus. Just like previous years, the NA went all out to entertain it's guests with expensive fine wines, expensive and exotic cuisine, music palitable to the ear, and the company of beautiful women a handsome studs for whom ever preferred them.

The women were of super model and porn star status, wearing nothing but string bikinis and high heels. The studs walking around strutting, showing off their chiseled abs and muscular physic. Like his predescssors Sammy got the chance to rub elbows with other narcotic kingpins from around the country. The top male actors, athletes and politicians were in attendance as well.

Sammy had the gift of gab. He really let his hair down after a few drinks and seeing the man he concidered an underworld legend. Jose(chi-chi) Mendez ran the drug game in southern California. Next to Eddie Lassenberry, Sammy thought chi-chi was the man. Sammy stumbled his way through the crowd to meet chi-chi. Once he came within of few inches of chi-chi, he tapped him on the shoulder. Chi-chi turned around and Sammy gave him a hug. "What the fuck?" chi-chi said as he pushed him away. "My dude! i've been hearing about you since i was a kid!" Sammy shouted. "Who are you, again? Chi-chi asked. "My fault, my dude! I'm Sammy Perez! I run New Jersey now!" "Is that so?" chi-chi said as they shook hands. "Yeah, my dude! Your stories are legendary! I heard you saved the Lassenberry family from some gangbangers back-n-the day!" Sammy said. "The thing is, they never returned the favor!" chi-chi chuckled. "My dude! I run shit now! I'm here for you!" Sammy said. "Ya veremos. Disfruta de las festividades de esta noche, mi nuevo amigo." Chi-chi said. "¡De eso estoy hablando!" Sammy said before chi-chi walked away.

The night at the NA palace was like the production of a very expensive porn movie. Both women and studs were servicing these powerful men in very unconventional, sexualiy explicit ways. Sammy himself had 2 beautiful Asian women giving him fellatio at the same time. He looked over to his left and saw a well known politician screwing one of the studly men from behind. The sight of the spectical made Sammy cringe, to the point he had to speak on it. "My dude! You look halfway decent! Why you fucking a dude?" he asked. "Do you know who i am, son?" the man said. "Yeah, i know you governor!" Sammy said. "Since you know me! Take those 2 bitches with you and go over to the other side of the room! I can't concentrate while you're yapping!" the governor shouted. "Lucky for you i'm getting my dick sucked, my dude! Lets go bitches!" Sammy said before taking the 2 girls away with a smile on his face.

Moments later, Sammy walked away from the ladies after getting his rocks off to go over to the extravagant bar to more to drink. He noticed while standing by the bar that some of the agents doing security were carrying thick chains and padlocks. He saw them walk to all the entrances and chain the doors. "What the fuck?" he said to himself. Sammy looked really concerned to the point he nudged the guy standing next to him looking for answers. "My dude! What's with the securtiy detail locking the doors?" Sammy asked. "It's time." The man said before walking away. "Time for what?" Sammy shouted. What caused Sammy to look more freaked out was that more agents came out of a room with ancient daggers placed of xilver platters. "This shit is getting fucking weird!" he said to himself. As the agents carried the silver platters around the room, most of the guests began taking to daggers off of them. Moments later, chi-chi approached Sammy carrying 2 daggers in his hand. "Chi-chi, my dude! What's going on here?" he asked. "Take this and shut the fuck up!" chi-chi said as he handed Sammy a dagger.

Suddenly after the master of ceremonies finished his monologue, the caos began. Sammy was so terrified, that he dropped his drink. Chi-chi began to laugh histerically. "No hay vuelta atrás ahora hermano!" he said to Sammy as he continued to laugh. Sammy was overwhelmed by the screams and the blood spewing everywhere. "I gotta to get the fuck outta here!" he said to himself. Sammy looked over in the distance and saw a couple of giant stained glass windows. He dropped the dagger and maneuvered his way through the killings. Once he reached the windows, he picked up a solid oak victorian chair and threw it at the window. Unfortunately the windows were shatter proof. "Fuck!" he shouted as he looked for another exit. He was startled when one of the women ran in his direction, being chased by one of the sexual predators. She grabbed Sammy, trying to hide behind him to dodge capture. "Help me, please!!" she cried as she pulled on his tuxedo. Sammy ignored her cries when he spotted an A list actor that he recognized from the movies coming in their direction weilding a dagger. "Get the fuck away from me lady!!" Sammy shouted in fear of being stabbed. "Where you think you're going young lady?" the actor chuckled. He drove the dagger into the young lady's back repeatedly. Sammy cringed as the her blood splattered on his tuxedo. The actor grabbed the young lady by her hair, dragging her lifeless body, tossing her onto a pile of other dead bodies. Sammy was then approached by Angus, whose checkered outfit was covered in blood. His face had numerous scratch marks from his victims. "Sammy! You better get in on this before we run out of bodies!" he chuckled. "What the fuck?" Sammy shouted. "Just kidding, son. We still have a plethora of little kids in the dungeon waiting to be plucked like chest hairs!" Angus chuckled. The melee was so much for Sammy, he just fainted on the spot. "Get over! Wake this son of a bitch up!" Angus said to 2 NA agents. The 2 agents ran over and picked

Sammy from off the floor and place him upright in a chair. They administered him smelling salts to bring him to consciousness. Sammy quickly woke up. "What the fuck happened, my dude?" Sammy said in a groggystate. "You can't cop-out on us now! Gag himand Tie him up!" Angus ordered the agents. Coincidentally the agents had a set handcuffs and a roll of duct tape near by. They strapped him to the chair and sealed his mouth shut. None of the other guests came to his aid. There was so much masochistic activity carnage going on that Sammy's situation blended in. "Bring her in boys!" Angus shouted. 2 more agents went to one of the closets, and to Sammy's dismay the agents brought before him the last person he thought he would see in a enviroment like this. Sammy couldn't say a word, nor scream when the love of his life was dragged out of the closet, bound and gagged as well. "You see, son… When you want to be apart of this world, you have to pay big. I mean big!" Angus said. Sammy tried to his best to break free from the handcuffs but failed. "You have a choice, son. You either pick up the dagger you dropped on the floor and plunge it through your wife's stomach, or we'll torture her some more and kill her ourslves!" Angus said. Sammy began shaking his head, making muffled noises in desperation as his tears trickled down to the duct tape covering his mouth. "What's that? I can't hear yoooou?" Angus said in a melodic voice. All Sammy could do was stomp his feet in a frenzy. "Take the tape off!" Angus said to one of the agents. The agent snatched the duct tape off of Sammy's mouth. "Come on, my dude! That's my wife! She ain't got nothing to do with my business!" Sammy cried. "You just don't get it, do you? All of these men here are here because they sacrificed what they loved the most to live lavish in paradise. Our paradise! Thanks be to the master!" Angus shouted.

It was the last week of february, 2010.Tensions between the United States and the island nation of Lassenberia have grown over the years. There have been reports of Skirmishes between U.S. speciel forces and Lassenberian naval forces within the media. Back in the United States these reports have been kept from the American public.

Lassenberia had economically flourished into a world super power, despite not being involved in foreign trade with the United States, Isreal and the European Union. Lassenberia now owned one third of the realistate in india in exchange for 208 liters of GLC, owned property in Tanzania, Russia, South Africa and had a 3 mile artificial island near the island Palm Jumerah Lord Lassenberry named Edward Island. All of this property was not for this citizens of Lassenberia, but for the royal family consisting of Lord Lassenberry and his 52 children.

Over the yearsLord Lassenberry had chosen 17 of the most beautiful eligble women of Lassenberia as concubines. The names of his 18 sons and 34 daughters were picked by Lord Lassenberry himself. He had put into law that at the time of his death, his eldest son Prince Edward rashawn, who was 5 years old at the time would ascend to the throne.

Princess Niyale, who was 6 years old, had learned to speak the Lasserian language fluently. She was programmed by her caretakers not to address the citizens of lassenberia unless they spoke the language. Her programming taught her that any other language, especially english was inferior. The programming also taught her and her brother Edward that those who didn't share the Lassenberry bloodline were inferior, until she came under the care of Mahasin Wingo.

To Lord Lassenberry, Mahasin was so physically attractive, he didn't want to impregnate her thinking it would ruin her figure, making her flawed in his eyes. She wasn't aware that he saw her only as a sex doll. A year earlier, princess Niyale's former nanny, Zilda Modi was found dead at the bottom of one of the staircases in the castle. Her death puzzled a lot of members of the council, castle security and the help. Castle Lassenberry was a modern marvel. It was equiped with technological conveniences, which included elevators. Ever since she was hired to take care of the princess, it was known to all who worked in the castle that she had never taken the staircases.

Prior to her untimely death, Zilda was the only non combatant staff member that was around Lord Lassenberry most of the day. Mahasin only saw him when he needed to relieve stress. Mahasin yearned for more time with the king. It was rumored by Abdirrahim of her and the king's sexual escapades coming to the attention of her uncle, the Sky father. He advised Lord Lassenberry to have her transfered to the Bravo Military base, working with the civilian staff as a secretary. Lord Lassenberry became infuriated. Yet, he thought it would be unwise to have his lust for Mahasin known to the populace causing him to butt heads with the more beloved Sky Father. Mahasin resented the transfer for a while until Lord Lassenberry came up with an-idea involving Abdirrahim, one of the few people on the island that he could absolutely trust to be the messenger between him and Mahasin.

It was 2 weeks before Princess Niyale's 5th birthday when Lord Lassenberry summoned commander Abdirrahim to the throne room. When Abdirrahim entered the throne room Lord Lassenberry was sitting on throne in a slouching position with one leg dangling over the arm of his throne feeding his pet cockatoo he named Kimberly. Abdirrahim stood at attention for a moment as Lord Lassenberry continued to feed his pet. "You summoned me, sir?" Abdirrahim shouted after clearing his throat. "Yeah. Leave me and the commander alone!" Lord Lassenberry said to his 6 man security team. Lord Lassenberry placed his pet on his shoulder as he stood from his throne. He stood before Abdirrahim as he continued to feed his pet. "I love this fucking bird!" he said. "How can i be of service, my Lord?" Abdirrahim asked. Oh yeah! I need someone i can trust. That someone is you." He said. "What is it, my Lord?" the commander asked. "Right about now, i not only need you as a soldier, but as a messenger." Lord Lassenberry said. Abdirrahim looked confused.

The following day Mahasin was typing out her part of the daily planner for the citizens of the former Pale lands. She was one out 35 administrators and digital illustrators at the Bravo command center. Like others in the working class of Lassenberia, Mahasin worked for free. All citizens of the island nation recieved food, clothing and shelter at it's finest. Lassenberians that chose to work, done so out of boredom than necessity. Only high ranking military personnal recieved small territories called sub-buroughs. Mahasin on the other hand found it boring sitting at a desk dressed in conseritive garb. She'd rather be back at castle Lassenberia bringing comfort to her king provocatively dressed. That day Abdirrahim paid a visit to the facility, walking straight toward Mahasin's work area. Before approaching her, he pulled out a gold envelope from inside his uniform jacket. Once in front of her cubicle, Abdirrahim just stood there. Her back was turned to him as she working on the computer. Mahasin felt a presence behind her causing her to quickly turn around. "Commander! What are you doing here?" she asked in a bright and cheerful manner. Abdirrahim just stood there looking unsure of himself. "Well, commander?" she said in a pushy manner. "Just passing through to have a word with management!" he said. "Ok! You have a good day!" She said as she swiveled her chair back around to her desk. Abdirriham marched off. He took the gold envelope and tore it into small pieces before exiting thefacility.

Back at the castle, Lord Lassenberry waited anxiously for a response from Abdirriham. While waiting in his private chamber, he was visited by 4 of his children and their nannies, including Princess Niyale and her nanny Zilda. Lord Lassenberry's persona changed as he set eyes on his babies. "Come give daddy a great…big…hug!" he shouted in a joyful manner. He kneeled down to their size. The 4 toddlers ran into the arms of their king, their daddy. He noticed a cut above the eye of his 3 year old son Jake Zakari. Lord Lassenberry looked pissed. "What's this? Who did this to you, Baby boy? Who did this to my boy?" he shouted, giving his nanny a evil stare. "My Lord! i sware it was an accident! He was playing with the other children from the Jersey burrough!" the elderly woman said. Lord Lassenberry stood up and went nose to nose with the elderly woman. "Nami! What did i tell you and the other nannies about having the princes and princesses playing with the subjects?" he screamed in her face. "I am so sorry, my Lord!: she said. "Why do you think i had a whole platoon full of kid? Huh?!! So they can pay with each other!!! That's why!!!" he screamed. Princess Niyale tugged on her father's shirt. "What is it, baby girl?" "Lyx zot miz skz meez kiz!" Niyale said. "I'm not angry, baby girl! i just don't wanna see you and your brothers and sisters get hurt." He said in a calm voice. WhenAbdirrahim entered the room Lord Lassenberry was elated. "Please! Everybody out! Please! I have very important business to deal with!" he shouted. "Si ca sheme po taz zia iny ton kiz?" Niyale asked. "Yes baby girl. I'll play with you and your brothers and sisters when i'm done." He said before giving her a kiss on the head.

After everyone had left the room, Lord Lassenberry rubbed his hands together in a giddy manner. "So, did she get the envelope?" he asked Abdirraham. "Ah…yes my Lord!" abdirrahim said. Lord Lassenberry noticed that his answer was wavering. "Don't fuck with me! Did you give her the envelope?" he asked again. "Yes, My Lord!" he said this time in a convincing voice. "Ok…ok." was Lord Lassenberry's response. "I Just promoted a few of my men to move up in rank, my Lord. The ceremony is next week. I need you to present their insignias to them." He said. Lord Lassenberry looked agitated. "Can't you get one of the council members to do that shit?" he said. "My Lord, itwill be wise to do this." Abdirrahim said. "What the fuck for?" Lord Lassenberry asked. "Queen Kimberly would've done it." Abdirrahim said with a smirk. "Don't you ever mention that name around me again, Do you understand me, commander?" he shouted. "Yes…My Lord." Abdirrahim said. Lord Lassenberry paced back-n-forth to calm himself. "Ok. I'll do the damn ceremony!" he said. "Thank you, My Lord!" "Tell all my assistants i said write a speech for me to congradulate your men, and get my uniform ready." Lord Lassenberry ordered. "Right away, My Lord!" Abdirraham said with a big smile on his face. "Now, get the fuck outta here, man." He said. "Yes, MY Lord." Abdirraham said before leaving. Lord Lassenberry shook his head with a smirk.

Days after the ceremony Abdirrahim's soldiers was ordered to retrieve the parents of the child who injured Lord Lassenberry's son. "Por favor! O meu filho é apenas um bebé! Porque estamos a ser castigados pelas suas ações?" the woman cried. "No more of that Portugese gibberish, woman! You either speak Lasserian, or at least english!" the soldier shouted as he grabbed her by the wrist. Her husband was helpless to defend her as he was being carried by 4 other soldiers. They were both dragged out of their home, and tossed into the back of a military truck as other civilians gathered in awe. They couldn't come to their aid if they wanted to because of the 20 other soldiers doiung crown control.

One of many new laws that Lord Lassenberry put into effect after this incident was that any child showing any type of aggression or violence toward anyone of his children, the parents would be exiled to a part of Antartica which Lord Lassenberry claimed 2 percent of the landmass, making Lassenberia the 8th sovereign state to own a piece of the continent. It wasn't hard for Lord Lassenberry to claim such an exclusive peice of property due to the value of GLC. He heard of conspiracy theories growing up that there were actual tropical regions deep in the frozen continent. He wanted to fund a team of South African scientists to explore the deepest reaches of the continent until he was talked out of it by certain council members because it might cause conflict with the other claimers who owned much more land. There were a handful of orphans in Lassenberia until the citizens got the message.

After all of the beautiful women he impregnated, all the property and wealth he accumulated, Lord Lassenberry wasn't satisfied until he had control of Mahasin Wingo, mind body and soul. Still, he conducted business perfectively with his allies. India, madagascar, all the African contries lining the east coast, all the south east asian countries, russia, and a majority of the middle eastern countries.

These countries were his protection from the National Agreement until the U.S. government wanted in on the action. By this time, the president of the United States was a 40 year old named Allan Anangu Harrison. He was born to a caucasian man from Nebraska, and a woman of Aboriginal descent. He was the change the liberals were looking for. A man of color in the Whitehouse turned the tables on how the world saw America. But behind the scenes he was no different from his predecessors.

President Harrison was swayed by lobbyists to hire former Secretary of Defense, Carter Gates. Even though he was a republican, his political reputation was impeccable. Gates convinced the president to put him in position of Secretary of State. Unknown to president Harrison and his cabinet Gates wasn't the man everyone thought he was. His mind and body belonged to serving the American public. His soul, his essence belonged to the National Agreement.

It was the middle of April when Lord Lassenberry and Princess Niyale went to visit Mahasin at her place of employment. The whole workforce stood at attention once the royal family entered the facility. The princess remembered Mahasin and ran over to give her a hug. Lord Lassenberry stood off in the background, not making it obvious that is was he who wanted to see mahasin. The princess spoke only in Lasserian at the time. Mahasin wasn't as fluent in the new language. She turned to Lord Lassenberry to help with translation. Lord Lassenberry was so engaged with Mahasin's beauty, he forgot that all the employees and management were still standing at attention. Mahasin cleared her throat to remind him. "Oh shit! Y'all can go back to what y'all was doing!!" he shouted to the crowd. Lord Lassenberry had the look of embarrassement. Mahasin covered her mouth trying to hold back her laughter.

After a few minutes of talking to the princess, mahasin told the king that she was in safe hands and would bring the princess back to the castle later. "Yej fiekj ide kiz." The princess said to her father. "I love you too, baby girl." Lord Lassenberry said. Before he left, the all the workers stood as he exited the room.

In a short time afterwards Lord Lassenberry and Mahasin figured out a way to meet up with each other in secret. Lord Lassenberry was so frustrated under these conditions that he devised a plan to assassinate the sky father. His plans were thwarted when Abdirrahim talked himout of it after a night of them drinking off the southern coast of Lassenberia aboard the royal yacht. That night of indulging heavily in alcohol, Lord Lassenberry began staggering up and down the port side of the yacht with a fresh bottle of beer in his hand. Abdirrahim walked closely behind him so he wouldn't fall overboard. Lord Lassenberry began mumbling and crying like a baby as he pounded his fist on the ship's railing. "That motherfucker fucked me!!" he shouted. "Excuse me, my Lord?" Abdirrahim responded looking confused. Lord Lassenberry wobbled, turning toward the commander. He grabbed Abdirrahim by the collar. "That fagot, Terrance!! I hate that motherfucker!! I'm gonna kill that white boy!! Watch!!" he shouted slurring his words. "Terrance? Who's Terrance, my Lord?" Abdirrahim asked. Lord Lassenberry was silent as he closely examined the bottle of beer in his hand. "What the fuck is this i'm drinking, man? What's this shit on the label?" he asked his commander. "They're horses, my Lord." Abdirrahim said. "Horses? What the fuck?" Lord Lassenberry shouted. "Yes, my Lord.it comes from Madagascar." Abdirrahim said. "This is some powerful shit! But, you know what's more powerful? Me!" Lord Lassenberry shouted as he repeatedly jabbed his index finger in Abdirrahim's chest. Abdirrahim firmly grabbed his king's wrist. "Please, my Lord. don't dothat again." Abdirrahim whispered. Lord Lassenberry yanked his arm away. He took a swig of his beer. He smiled at Abdirrahim. He then guzzled down the rest of the beer and tossed the empty bottle over the side of the yacht. "I know what to do now, commander. I know what to do." Lord Lassenberry said in a soft voice. The following day, the elderly nanny of princess Niyale was found dead. Shortly after, Lord Lassenberry convinced the sky father his daughter Niyale was inconsolable, and only Mahasin's company could heal the grief-stricken little girl.

Mahasin quickly had her belongings moved into Zilda's quarters at the far end of the castle. Some of the council members found it odd there was no formal ceremony held for Zilda, concidering how close she and the princess were. Also, investigators at the scene of death found it odd as well that Zilda's body was found yards away from the bottom of the staircase. They concluded that if she fell ill her body would have landed at least on the stairs. It was ruled a homocide. The day Mahasin moved into the castle, Abirrahim advised the king it would be wise to take the suspicion of Zilda's death from himself by honoring her in a more extravagant manner. Heeding his commander's words, Lord Lassenberry ordered to have a road built from east to west in Zilda's name. During the construction of the road, Lord Lassenberry stayed in his castle hoping the rumors about Zilda's death would settle down a bit. Months later, he made a public appearance to christen the new Zilda road. The true cause of her death was never solved.

Near the end of August 2010, through months of negotiation defense secretary Gates arranged talks with the hiearchy of Lassenberia. Since outsiders were forbidden at this time to visit Lassenberia, the meeting would take place in Accra, the capital city of Ghana. Every major media outlet in the free world considered this the most important event since the Japanese surrender after second world war.

This was going to be an historical event for the president and the people of Ghana having 2 super powers visit their nation. Great steps were taken to accommdate both nations. Security forces from the United States, Lassenberia and Ghana were to be set at the highest level for September 2, 2010 coincidently. It was mandated that all citizens within a 50 mile radius of the Golden Jubilee House clear the streets and stay in their homes while the meeting would take place.

It was around 1am when Lord Lassenberry was lying in bed naked. He was staring at the ceiling, covered from the waist down in silk sheets. There were lit medieval style torches mounted on the walls even though there was modern electricity installed throughout the castle. 15 minutes later a dark figure wrapped in a cloak entered his bedroom. Lord Lassenberry looked up and began smiling. The person took off the cloak, letting it fall to the floor. It was Mahasin Wingo standing in the nude, showing off her petite figure with a sexy pose. "Bring that ass over here, girl!" he said before biting his bottom lip. Mahasin took her time, switching her hips as she approached the bed.

She slowly slithered onto the bed from his feet, toward his erect penis, which was bulging from underneath the sheets. Mahasin quickly snatched the sheet unveiling his private area. She began massaging his penis with her tongue, then her mouth. He grapped the back of her hair, thrusting her mouth toward the base of his penis. She began gagging. He allowed her head to rise just enough that her lips were touching the tip of his penis. There was a string of saliva bridging her mouth and his penis. "I didn't tell you to stop! Put that dick back in your mouth, girl!" he whispered. Mahasin smiled as she slowly stroked it before puttting it back into her mouth. "Come here and turn yo ass over!" he said as he was pulling her by the hair. She turned around arching her back as she laid on her stomach. Lord Lassenberry got up on his knees behind her and began rubbing his penis on her ass cheeks. "Stop teasing me, my Lord! put it in me!" she shouted. "Beg for it. Beg for it!" he said. "Please, my Lord! give me that black dick!" she shouted. He then grabbed the base of his penis and slid it into her anus. Her eyes grew wide as saucers. Her mouth opened up as if she was gasping for air. He started drilling her in the anus like a savage. Her screaming pearced his ears to the point where he had to put his thumb in her mouth. She began sucking on his thumb as her screams were muffled. "You want it in yo pussy?! That's what you want, bitch?!" he shouted. "Yes! Yes, my Lord!" she squealed. He yanked his penis out of her anus and shoved it in her wet vagina. He began drilling her faster and faster until the sweat from his face dripped down between her ass cheeks. "Turn over! Turn the fuck over!" he shouted as he smacked her on her ass. Mahasin quickly turned over her back. He then moved up placing his penis between her smooth, brown breasts. "You want me to cum on your titties... huh?" he shouted. "Yes, my Lord! cum on me! Cum inside me! Cum all over me!" she screamed. He squeezed her breasts together to slide his penis in between them. Back-n-forth his penis slid between her breasts as she squeezed them together. Lord Lassenberry had the look of a predator about to devour its prey as he grabbed her by the throat. "You're mine! You belong to me, right?!" he said as he began to squeeze her neck tighter. "Yes, my Lord!! yeeees!!" she shouted as she was gasping for air. As he continued choking her, he moved his penis closer to her face, tracing her lips with the tip of his penis. He then released her from his grasp. Her eyes were teary as she fought for air. He got up off of her, standing at the edge of the bed, dripping with sweat. He began masturbating. With his penis aimed at her face. "You ready? You want this cum?" he said breathing heavily. "Yes, my Lord!! give it to me, please!" she shouted. "Fuck! Fuck! Fuck!" Were his last words before unloading his cum in her mouth, and on her face. "That's it! Rub it all over your face and titties!" he ordered. He watched as she obeyed, massaging his semen on her breasts and cheeks. Lord Lassenberry stepped away from the bed as he continued to stroke himself. He smiled. "You can go Now." He said. Mahasin looked enraged as his cum dripped from her nipples. "No!! I want your cum in me!!" she screamed. Lord Lassenberry began laughing like a mad man as he put on his diamond studded silk robe. "Next time. Now, go back to your room." He chuckled. "No! No! No! She screamed as she fell off the bed and crawled toward him, grabbing his ankle. Lord Lassenberry yanked his foot away as he walked toward the his bathroom. He shut the bathroom door, leaving Mahasin outside begging for him. Moments later after cleaning himself off, he came out of the bathroom. Mahasin was sitting on the floor outside the bathroom naked with her arms folded pouting. "You still here? i thought i told you to go back to your room!" he said. She looked up at him. "I'm not leaving until you cum inside me!" she shouted. "Oh really?" he said. Lord Lassenberry went over to the wall and put his finger on the silent alarm button. "If i press this button, my guards will come in here and drag you the fuck out! Do you wanna be embarrassed?" he said. She sighed, finally heeding his words. Mahasin stood up and snatched her cloak off the floor before storming out of the bedroom. One of his armed guards, who looked like a scrawny teenager was standing outside the bedroom as Mahasin walked passed and down the corridor. "Your married, right?" Lord Lassenberry asked the guard. "Yes, my Lord." the guard said. "Remember, some women are meant for breeding, others are meant for entertainment purposes only, understand?" he said. "Yes, my Lord!" he said with a jittery response. Lord Lassenberry didn't say a word. He just place his idex finger over his lips reminding the guard to keep what just took place quiet as always. He then shut his bedroom door.

It was theSeptember 10th when the free world came to a stand still. It was the day Secretary of State Gates and Lord Lassenberry were to meet in Ghana for a the trade agreement. Gates and his staff had already arrived in Ghana a couple of days prior to the event. During this time he was given a tour of the country by the president of Ghana and his staff. Because of the shut down within a 50 mile radius of the capital, it was safe for Gates to tour. There were secret service agents scattered strategically within the city of Accra and the shores of Labadi Beach. There was also a U.S. aircraft carrier and 2 U.S. destroyers sharing the shores with Ghana's fast attack crafts 20 miles off the Cape Coast. Unbeknownst to anyone, there were 50 NA agents of African American descent dressed in civilian clothes strategically scattered within the city of Accra, in hotels and at the Kotoka International Airport. Hundreds of miles above were 2 Ghanaian fighter jets streaming from coast to coast. Hundreds of journalists and cameramen from the main stream media were set up outside the Golden Jubilee House simultaneously yelling out questions at the president of Ghana and Secretary Gates as they returned from touring the country side. Secretary Gates was so sure of himself that he turned to the media to give a brief statement. "I can be certain that after today, relations between the United States and the island nation of Lassenberia will benefit not just certain entities but all of humanity! Thank you!" he said before entering the presidential palace.

Hours had passed. Secretary Gates and the president of Ghana were still waiting for the arrival of Lord Lassenberry and his staff. Many attemps were made to contact from Lassenberia. To no avail; no response came from the island nation.

Even more time passed. The sun was beginning to set over the Atlantic ocean. The media grew weary of broadcasting repetitive news feeds. The fighter jets had to land at the naval base to refuel. There were 2 more fighter jets taking off to relieve them of duty. In fact every ghanaian soldier was relieved from their posts.

Inside one of the conference rooms of the presidential palace. Secretary Gates was becoming belligerrent. "What is this? What the hell is going here?" Secretary Gates shouted. His staff members looked nervous because know one could give him any answers. Gates began to feel woozy. "Ron, You stay! Everyone else, get out!" he shouted. The 20 staff members and security detail rushed out of the room.

"Mr Secretary, sir! Maybe the king was caught between a rock and a hard place! You can't out rule it!" ron said as she shrugged his shoulders. "A coup d'état? Bullshit! You've heard the report from our person on the inside! He called it a paradise, and the people cheered!" Gates shouted. Ron glanced at the door. "Sir! Please keep it down!" ron whispered. "I'm malfunctioning! I need my fix!" Gates said as he leaned against the chair. Ron reahed into his breifcase and pulled out a syringe filled with 12 cc's of a orange liquid. He walked over to Gates and ijected the orange substance behind his right ear. Ron pulled out his handkerchief and dabbed behind Gates's ear. Gates began trembling until the drugs took effect. He straightened his necktie and inhaled through his nose. "Are you ok, sir?" ron asked. "I'm fine! I'm fine!" Gates said as he shooed him away. Suddenly there was a knock on the door. Ron went to answer it. It was Ron's assistant. He wispered in Ron's ear. Ron looked shocked as Gates looked concerned about what was being whispered. The assistant left the room. "What is it?" Gates asked. "Sir! You're not going to beleve this!" ron said.

20 miles away, arriving from the east were 4 of the biggest helicopters in the world. Ghanaian armed forces identified them as being from Russia. Across the land people watched as the copters flew over in formation toward their destination. 5 miles, away everyone from the president, his staff, Gates and his staff watched the squadron of helicopters from the stairs of the presidential palace, what really captured the attention of the masses was the 500 foot jumbtron being carried by 4 thick,100 foot iron cables connected to the copters. "I think we should leave, sir!" Ron whispered in Gates's ear. "Not on your life! I want to stay for this!" Gates said with a evil grin as the copters hovered above them.

The lead pilot of the squadron gave the order to power up the jumbotron. The night sky within seconds was so bright it could be seen as far as Madina. Some in the crowd at the palace had to squint from the bright lights, while others came equiped with sunglasses such as secretary Gates. Not only was the video out of this world, there were hundreds of speakers lining the bottom of the jumbotron. When they were turned on the feedback could be heard a mile away. The crowd had to cover their ears.

The figure that appeared on the jumbotron was Lord Lassenberry. He was shown from the chest up. The crowd could see he was wearing the traditional Lassenberry uniform. For an added digital effect, sun beams shot from behind his head.

"People of earth!" were Lord Lassenberry's first words. His voice carried like thunder within a mile radius. The crowd had to cover their ears to muffle the sound of his voice.

"I'm just fucking with y'all!" he chuckled. **"On a serious note, i'm here to tell all of you that a time for real change has come! Lassenberia will not compromise nor trade with a nation or nations that harbor extremely evil entities! Secretary Gates! I know you're amongst the audience! I would like to say to you, and that weak president you serve, that we the people of Lassenberia and our allies are aware that the United States has been infiltrated by a force or secret society for numerous decades! You've allowed this scourge to turn a great nation into giant crack house! You've allowed the evil money grubbing pharmaceutical industry to add fuel to the fire, by not finding cures to many illnesses but pseudo treaments that cause major painful side effects or temporary relief! My messege to you America, is that Lassenberia is the cure! My message to you America, is that if you want the cure, you must rid yourselves of this scouge and the pharmaceutical companies that are in partnership with these demons! To be more specific, i want you, Secretary Gates, your weak president and your allies to bring forth men such as Terrance Haggerty, Dragan Serpiente and Doug Reed to name a few! Check your phone, mr. Secretary! A complete list of names have been sent to you! When these people are sent before the Lassenberian court of justice, then and only then the people of the United States and its allies around the world will have the cure to end their suffering! Do not take this message as a threat, but as a message toward salvation! I, Lord Lassenberry have spoken!"** were his last words before transmission was shut down.

"Incredible!" the president of Ghana said to himself. There was a silence amongst the crowd as the squadron of helicopters flew off. Moments after, Ron's phone starts ringing. He answers it. "Mr. Secretary! It's the president! He wants to speak with you!" Ron said before handing the phone over. The silence was broken when the media started replaying the coverage and giving commentary on what just took place. The crowd of dignitaries were all shouting at each other in a unorderly fashion. After speaking with the president, secretary Gates And Ron walked away from the crowd. "Get me the hell out of here!" he said to Ron.

Back in the United States Sammy Perez was sitting in his living room along side his new girl friend Giovana Flores watching the event that took place in Ghana on TV. Giovana was so intrigued that she stood up to walk closer to the TV. "Nunca vi nada como esto en mi vida! ¡El mundo tal como lo conocemos ha terminado!" she said as she touched the TV screen. "Come on, baby! Move out the way!" Sammy shouted as he threw a magazine at her. Wearing nothing but a bra and panties, she seductively walked over towards him. "No te pongas celoso, papito! ¡Sabes que soy todo tuyo!" she said as she fell on his lap. "I ain't jealous! The nigga came a long way! My dude got the world by the balls now!" Sammy said. "¿Crees que esta gente blanca va a dejar que se salga con la suya?" she asked. "Whatever cure my dude got, i think them white boys will give up their mothers for that shit!" Sammy said.

Later that evening, Sammy was in his kid's bedroom getting them ready for bed. He kneeled down along side his 5 year old twin sons to pray, when suddenly he heard gunshots coming from outside. Giovana came running out of the bedroom towards the kids room. "¿Has oído eso? ¿Quieres que consiga el arma, nena?" she asked. "No! Just stay in here with the boys, and lock the door behind me!" Sammy said before giving the boys a kiss on the head and Giovana a kiss on the lips. Sammy quickly ran to the master bedroom, to the gun safe. He punched in the code tio open it. He pulled out a shotgun, a machine gun, 2 pistols and 2 boxes of ammo. He was loading his weapons until he heard someone banging on his front door. He was so nervous as the banging continued, he kept dropping shells. When he finally got locked and loaded, he crepted down the long staircase. All he could was the beat of his heart, beating faster and faster. He was so terrified it drowned out the sound of the banging on the door. Sammy came to the door with his pistol drawn. "Who the fuck is it?" he shouted. "Sammy, its me doug! Doug Reed!" the voice cried. Sammy looked bewildered. "What the fuck?" he said to himself. With his pistol pointed at the peephole, he slowly opened the door. As soon as the door opened wide enough, Doug Reed rushed in and gave Sammy a firm hug. "You have to save me!! They're coimg to kill me!! Please help me!!" Doug cried as he held on tightly to Sammy's arm. Doug looked disheveled. His nose was bloody, his lip busted and his right eye blackened. His clothes were grimy covered with blood stains. Sammy noticed the glock in his hand and the 2 dead NA agents lying dead on his front lawn. "Calm down, my dude!" he said to Doug. "No, no! You don't understand! They're coming to kill me!" Doug cried. "It's all good, my dude!" Sammy said as he gently took the glock out of his hand. Sammy pulled him inside. He looked around the landscape before closing the door. Once inside the house, Doug fell to his knees. "Come over here and sit down, my dude!" Sammy said as he lured him to the dining room table. "Come sit down, my dude! Let me get you some water," he said as Doug was shaking like a leaf. Doug was sitting at the dining room table twiddling his thumbs. "God help me, please!" he said to himself in prayer. Sammy came back from the kitchen with a glass of water. "Here you go, my dude. Take a sip." He said. Doug grabbed the glass of water and began to guzzle it like it was his last. "Take it easy, my dude! There's plenty more where that came from!" Sammy chuckled. Sammy pulled out his cell phone. Doug started to panic. "What are you doing?" he asked. "I gotta make a phone call! There's 2 dead bodies on my property! I gotta clean that shit up, my dude!" Sammy said. "I understand! Do watch you have to do!" Doug said before taking another sip of water. Sammy hit speed dial. "Yo shaq! I need you and the boys at my spot, pronto!" Sammy said. *"Got you, boss man! I'm there!"* Shaq said before clicking off.

Garry L. Hinton was a landscaper by day, but to the underworld he was known as Shaq. To his family and co-workers Gary Hinton was a big teddy bear. Shaq on the other hand was the head of a crew called the cleaners. He started out as a shooter for Eddie Lassenberry when he was only 15. At the age of 19 he was arrested for domestic violence against his baby's mother. After serving a year in prison, he was arrested again for selling guns to an undercover cop out in Irvington, New Jersey. He came home in 2008 and pledged his loyalty to the new boss of the Lassenberry organization, Sammy Perez.

The cleaners came on the scene as soon as Shaq came home from doing a bid. Certain people in the Lassenberry organization made it loud and clear that Sammy wasn't fit to rule over the entire New Jersey drug game. Those non believers were delt with by the NA, and disposed of by Shaq and his team.

Giovana came out of the bedroom. "¿Está todo bien, nena? ¿Con quién estás hablando?" she yelled from the top of the stairs. "I"m good, baby! Go back in the room!" he shouted. "Who's that upstairs?" Doug asked. "Its my lady." Sammy said. "Oh, ok!" Doug said. "How the hell you get pass my alarm system?" Sammy asked. Doug chuckled. "I dugg under the gate!" he said as he showed his bloody fingertips. "Jesus, my dude! That's some crazy shit!" Sammy chuckled. Doug began to cry. They killed my wife and dog in front of me! After they ruffed me up, i escaped by jumping out of the window!" he continued to cry. "Damn, my dude! Sorry to hear that!" Sammy said. "She was the love of my life!" Doug cried. "I'm sure she was! But don't worry, my dude! You're safe here!" Sammy said. "Safe? Did you watch the news? That fucking lassenberry kid is out for blood! My blood!" Doug cried. "Yeah, i saw that shit. Who is Terrance Haggerty and the other guy he mentioned?" sammy asked. "Terrance? He's dead. Been dead for a long time. The other guy? Something other than human! You've must have ran into him when you went to the gathering!" Doug said. "All i remember is that bitch ass Angus guy! I hope lassenberry cut that sick fuck into a million pieces!" Sammy said. "What about me?" Doug asked. "What about you?" Sammy asked. "I'm one of them, until now!" Doug said. Sammy gazed around the house. "Like i said, my dude. You're safe here." he said. "Thank you." Doug said in a soft voice. "You can stay in the basement. It's real nice! Like having your own apartment!" Sammy said. "Thank you, again." Doug said. "i'll bring you down some fresh sheets and pillows. Another thing. Once you're in the basement, you stay in the basement. You come out for any reason! You come near my family! I'll kill you! You understand, my dude?" Sammy said. Doug stood up as he wiped away his tears with his shirt sleeve. He extended his hand in a friendly gesture. Sammy gave off a smirk before shaking his hand. "Go down in the basement and clean yourself off! Its down the hall, second door on your right, my dude! You look like shit!" he said. "You're a good kid, Sammy!" Doug said as he placed his hand on Sammy's shoulder.

A week had passed when Sammy recieved a call from someone who said she was his new National Agreement connection. The y were to rendezvous at a diner in Hope, New Jersey, which used to be owned by Butch Watson.

After getting dressed, he informed Giovana to tell the boys time again not to go down into the basement. Waiting for him outside were 2 NA agents and a limo driver. After giving Giovana a kiss he made his way down the driveway, looking down at the specks of dried blood that Shaq and his crew missed when disposing of the 2 dead NA agents.

When his limo arrived outside the diner, he sent one of the NA agents inside to check out the surroundings. Moments later the agent came out. "There are 10 patrons dining inside, sir." The agent reported. Suddenly, Sammy's cell phone began to vibrate. He looked at the incoming number and answered it. "Hello?" he said. Noone answered. "Hello? Hello? Fuck this! He said to himself before hanging up. "Are we ready to go inside, sir?" one of the agents said. "Let's go!" Sammy sighed.

   Once inside the diner Sammy sat at the booth facing the entrance. The agent accompanying him stood outside the entrance. The waitress approached Sammy. Good morning, sir! Can i start you off with a cup of coffee?" she asked with a bubbly attitude. "Yeah sweetheart, sure!" he said. She handed him a menu. As he was looking at the menu 2 caucasian men walked in. Both men strutted in wearing quality suits. One looked in his 30's, while the other guy he was following looked around 60 years old. Before they were offered a seat by the waitress, the older gentleman noticed Sammy sitting alone. "Hey Sammy!" he shouted. Sammy looked confused. "Do i know you?" Sammy asked. Both men walked over toward him. "Its me! Larry! Larry Cusumano!" he shouted. Sammy squinted his eyes to get a better visual on the man. "Oh, its you!" Sammy sighed.

   Larry Cusumano was one of the 6 capos from the Gatano crime family. He ran certain aspects of criminal activity, besides drugs in the most northern part of Jersey. Since the end of it's heyday, the Gatano family's income was shared by a crew from New York. Extortion, illegal gambling, construction, loan sharking and waste management were lucrative businesses at this time for New Jersey mob guys until New York came in with greater numbers as far as membership. This particular New York crew finagled their way into these businesses. Since Eddie Lassenberry devistated the Gatano's rule over the narcotics game years ago, it was a financial struggle for them to stay afloat. The 50 member crime family had to deal with New York in north jersey and Philadelphia in central and south jersey.

   "Crazy meeting you here!" Cusumano said. "Yeah, it is. What brings you into a diner, my dude. You was always concidered a classy guy." Sammy said. "I'm here on business!" Larry said as his henchman went over toward the counter and asked for the manager. Sammy watched as the manager came out and handed the mob guy an envelope. He gave larry the nod after he checked for the cash inside.

   "Hey! Since i'm here, maybe we can talk business for a moment!" Larry said. Sammy looked outside at the NA agent. For some strange reason the NA agent went back toward the limo. He entered the limo. The limo drives off. Sammy is looking nervous now. His muscle just abandoned him. "Mind if we sit down?" Larry asked. Larry's henchman sat down next to Sammy, having him boxed in while Larry sat across from him. "Lets cut to the chase! Some crazy bitch came to me saying you might be harboring some whack job mentioned on TV. Is it true?" Larry said in a lighthearted manner. "If that's true, why didn't this bitch come to me herself?" Sammy asked. "Well, i was offered a substantial amount of cash to burn your house down unless this fucker resurfaces. Fuck her! I'm here to make my own deal. You bring me and my people back into the fold as partners. For any reason this guy is brought to us, your house stays intact. You get protection from us." Larry said. "You threatening me, my dude?" Sammy asked with hostility in his voice. "I'm just telling you what it is, chico." Larry said. "I don't know what you talkin about, my dude!" Sammy said. The waitress brings Sammy's coffee. Before he could grab the cup larry's henchman grabbed the cup of coffee and poured it on the floor. "What the fuck, my dude?" Sammy shouted. "Here's a number where you can reach me. You have 3 days to do the right thing." Larry said before he and his henchman left the diner. The patrons were glancing over at Sammy as he held his head looking stressed out. The waitress came over to him. "Is everything ok, sir?" she asked. "Yeah, i'm good! Could you call me a cab?" he asked.

Later that evening, Sammy was sitting in his backyard with Giovana. There were no NA agents around. He noticed the same black Boeman SUV driving passing by the estate numerous times. Next to him was a case of beer, which half of the bottles were empty. "Al final del día, es un hombre malvado! ¡No te sientas culpable entrenándolo para proteger a tu familia!" Giovana said. "Baby! There's never a second thought when it comes to protecting my family!" he said

Inside Sammy's mansion, his boys were running around playing with water guns. One of his sons tried to escape from his brother by running down in the basement to hide. Once the little boy came to the bottom of the steps, he saw Doug standing in the center of the room smacking himself in the face. The boy was in awe. "Who are you? What are you doing?" the boy asked. Doug began crying as he continued smacking himself. "What are you doing down here?" Doug asked as he continued sobbing. "This is my house! I can go wherever i want!" the boy said. "Where's your mommy and daddy?" he asked. "They're outside." The boy said. Doug's self abuse became more intense. He began hearing voices in his head. "I'm hungry! But i know it is forbidden to do harm to this child! Master! Help me!" he said to himself. "You're crazy!" the boy said.

Moments later, the little boy came running out of the basement wiping his face. He dropped his water gun at the bottom of the basement stairs. He ran into his brother who sprayed him in the face with his water gun, removing evidence of Doug's interaction with him.

Outside Giovana was tired of Sammy incoherently rambling on about the past. She kissed him on the cheek and went inside. Sammy was sitting alone looking at the night sky. He stood up from dthe patio chair. He stared into the darkness of the quiet upscale neighborhood. "Yo soy Sammy Pérez! ¡Jefe de Nueva Jersey! ¿Me oyes, mundo?" he shouted before throwing the empty bottle of beer into the air. It was so quiet in this gated community that the smashing sound of the beer bottle echoed. He was so intoxicated, it was a struggle for him to make his way back to the mansion. His mind was willing but his body gave out.

Hours later, the sun was rising from the east. The sunlight was beaming down on his Sammy's face as he lay unconscious. Suddenly he was awakened by a splash of cold water to the face. He sprung into consciousness looking bewildered of his surroundings. "What the fuck?" he shouted as Giovana stood over him with empty bucket in her hand. "Levántate! ¡Tenemos que hablar!" she said with sadness in her eyes. "What's wrong, baby?" he said while wiping the water from his face. "Levántate y ven a la casa!" she said. "Ok! I'm coming!" he said as he struggled to get off the ground. Giovana walked away, heading back towards the house. Feeling groggy, Sammy dragged his feet as he followed Giovana. Inside the house, Giovana lead him to the basement door. She pointed at the floor. Sammy looked confused. "What am i looking at?" he asked. "Hay un charco de agua en la base de la puerta, que conduce al otro lado de la puerta!" she whispered. Sammy shook his head, looking disappointed. "Go upstairs. I'll handle this." He said. Giovana slowly made her way upstairs. Sammy placed his hand on the door knob. He stood there in a daze until he took his ahnd off the knob and headed upstairs he went into the safe and grabbed one of his guns. He put a full clip in, placing one in the chamber. He then hid the gun behind his back in his belt, covering it with the tale of his shirt. He headed down stairs. He stood in front of the basement door, took a deep breath and opened the door. It was dark as he stared down into the basement. He covered his nose and mouth from the stench which hit him like a fist. He clicked on the light switch before he made his way down stairs. "Yo, my dude! You ok down there?" Sammy shouted as his eyes were squinting from the smell of bad body oder. There was no answer from Doug. To be on the safe side, Sammy pulled out his gun. "Yo! Answer me, my dude! I ain't fucking around." He shouted. When sammy reached the bottom of the stairs. He was shocked at what was in front of him. He found Doug face down naked on the floor in a pool of blood with broken piece of his son's water gun lodged in his neck. "Fuck!!" he shouted as he stood over the body. He rushed back upstairs and went outside to find his cell phone. When he fopund his phone, he looked pissed to see that his phone had a low battery. He went back into the house and charged it. He made a phone call to the man who wanted Doug.

A couple of hours later, Sammy met up with Larry and members of his crew on a back road in Washington Valley Park in Bridgewatwer Township, New Jersey. Larry and his crew of 4 guys stepped out their vehicle before Sammy stepped out of his. He approached the crew with a nervous look ln his face. "I just wanna tell you guys that i ain't come alone!" he said with a trembling voice. "Alright tough guy, where is he?" Larry asked as his men slowly surrounded Sammy. "He's in the trunk!" Sammy said. "The trunk? What the fuck is he doing in the trunk?" Larry asked. Sammy put his head down as he sighed. "Hey! Look at me! What the fuck is he doing in the trunk? If this is some kind of set up i guarantee you won't leave here alive!" Larry said. "Something went wrong, my dude!" Sammy said. "Open the trunk!" Larry shouted. Sammy went over to his car and popped open the trunk with Larry's men standing behind him. When Sammy opened the trunk, there they saw Doug's body wrapped in sheets with his face unvailed. "What is this shit? He's fucking dead! I can't bring back a dead body!" Larry shouted. "My dude! You didn't say bring him to you alive!" Sammy said. "So you killed the fucker just to spite me?" Larry asked. "My dude! He did himself! I think he felt guilty about whatever, and said fuckit!" Sammy said. "How do we know this is the guy?" one of Larry's guys asked. Larry turned to his henchman. "Go get that thing out of the glove compartment!" Larry said. Moments later the henchman came back with a device that looked like a computer notepad and handed it to Larry. "What's that?" a crew member asked. "These people equiped me with this thing to identify this guy." Larry explained. He pulled out Doug's hand from underneath the sheet and placed the palm of his hand on the notepad. Seconds later, Doug's face and his information was displayed on the notepad. "It's him! We're taking the car!" Larry said. "You can't take my car!" Sammy said. "You think we're putting him in ours?" Larry said as he snatched the car keyes from him. He tossed the keys to one of his men. He went nose-to-nose with Sammy. "You and i know this shit won't go smoothly with these people! I expect 10 million from you every month, or New jersey will be looking for a new drug lord! i think i have a very good feeling your protection will be null and void since this fucker is being handed over D.O.A!" he whispered. Sammy stood there as Larry and his crew drove off with both cars. Sammy began walking down the road as he pulled out his cellphone. He hit speed dial. "Yo manny! ¡Ven a buscarme! ¡Estoy en el parque de Washington en Bridgewater!" he said before hanging up the phone.

Back in Lassenberia, Lord Lassenberry just recieved word from his intelligence officer that the body of Doug Reed was being flown from the United States to South Africa. He was infuriated when he heard this. He left the council room, heading back to his chamber. The 2 guards standing outside his chamber stood at attention, soluting him. He went in and was surprised to see Mahasin in his bed naked covered in his silk sheets. "What the hell you doing in here?" he asked. "The guards let me in. Do you mind?" she said giving him a seductive look. Lord Lassenberry couldn't resist her sexiness. He immediatly took off his clothes and hopped into to bed with her.

As they were kissing, Mahasin pushed him away. "What's wrong?" he asked. "So, what happened with those people you asked to be turned over to you?" she asked. "What?" he said with a bewildered look. "The people you wanted to bring to justice!" she said. "Don't concern yourself with that. Your'e in paradise. Enjoy it!" he said before he began kissing on her neck. She stopped him once again. "What now?" he asked sounding frustrated. "You don't trust me enough to talk about it?" she asked. Lord Lassenberry sighed as he stared at the ceiling. "Ok!" he sighed as he got out of bed and went over to his vault. He punched in the digital code which allowed him to access what was inside. Inside the vault was a safe with a combonation lock. He opened it. Inside was a beaker of GLC, the B.O.I and a pistol. He took out the B.o.I and headed back to bed. "What that's?" she asked. "This, young lady is the history of all Lassenberry business events dating back 60 years." He said. She began turning the pages, having an impressive look on her face. "It's called the BOOK OF IMFORMATION." He mentioned. "The book of imformation?" she asked. "Yeah! The B.O.I." he said. "Boy, as in young man?" she asked. He began laughing. "B.O.I, not b.o.y!" he explained. Mahasin began reading more as Lord Lassenberry began kissing on her arm. "Tell me about Benny Lassenberry!" she said. "Oh! He was my grandfather! A great man. But my uncle Eddie! That nigga started all this!" he proudly stated. "How's that? She asked. "He wanted a place for our family to escape. But he came up short, financially, until i stepped up to the plate!" He said. "What did you do?" she asked. "I simply turned a negative into a positive! These fucking pharmaceutical companies dumped their waste on our land! But the universe flipped it on them! The waste has become a godsend! Guess who's God now, young lady?" he said. Mahasin said nothing. She just pointed her finger at Lord lassenberry. "You damn right!" he shouted. "Can i read more of this?" she asked. "i think you've seen enough young lady! Let's get back to the reason we're in here." he said as he took the B.O.I out of her hands and tossed it on the floor. Soon as Mahasin spread her legs, they went at it like animals in the wild.

The next day around noon, a military amphibious helicopter carrying the body of Doug Reed landed 5 miles off the coast of Lassenberia by order of Lord Lassenberry himself. Not only was the body of Doug Reed on board the aircraft, but also the notorious Dragan Serpiente. He was bound, gagged and shackled in heavy chains from head-to-toe on Lord Lassenberry's orders as well. When the Lassenberian naval ship LSS Cherry Hill received communication from the aircraft, the captain of the ship deployed a motor whaleboat from it's portside. The small boat carried a crew of 8 heavily armed Lassenberian sailors. For an extra precaution 2 Lassenberian helicopters were deployed to hover over the aircraft. The waters of the Mozambique Channel were choppy that day. It took the motor whaleboat crew tremendous effort to attach cables to the aircraft utility floats for a stable transition. Once the cables were connected, the motor whaleboat boarded the aircraft locked and loaded. "I am lieutenant Usman of the Lassenberian navy! I'm here to take Dragan Serpiente and the body of Doug Reed into custody under his majesty Lord Lassenberry's orders!" he said with a deep african accent. The soldiers handing over prisoner and the body were dressed in all black military gear. He noticed Usman's patch on his uniform sleeve. "Your from Kenya?" one of the soldiers asked. "I am Lassenberian!" Usman said proudly." Amazing! Well, here they are!" the soldier said. Doug Reed's body was wrapped in tarp. Usman checked to see if the body was legitimate before unloading it from the aircraft. Serpiente was unable to walk, so he was carried off the aircraft. The Lassenberian sailors frowned from the pungent coming from Serpiente's body. It didn't bother the soldiers on the aircraft because they were wearing gas masks. "Yeye harufu mbaya zaidi kuliko mwili wafu!" Usman said. The other sailors began laughing. "We will contact your superiors once the prisoners are brought before Lord Lassenberry!" Usman said. "Fine!" the soldier said. Once the transaction was made the motor whaleboat crew unhooked the cables from the aircraft and drifted back toward the LSS Cherry Hill.

Waiting by the shore for the prisoners to arrive were the lassenberian council and their staff members. Lady Ellen's long blonde hair was flowing in the strong breeze as the motor whaleboat was coming full speed toward the peir. Standing next to her was council member Ayub. He was dressed in his uniform resembling that of Lord Lassenberry's but the color of the uniform was dark brown with white sashes and dark drown jack boots.

"Do you think the king will actually trade the cure for these prisoners with the United States?" Ayub asked. Lady Ellen turned to him. "If Queen Kimberly were here, i promise you there would be a trade. With this king, i make no promises." She said. Ayub was speechless.

Elsewhere on the island, Abdirrahim was in a hangar which stored all the extravagant planes and jets from world leaders as gifts to Lord Lassenberry. Abdirrahim was inside one of these airchaft, but not alone. Mahasin was fogging up the window of a prop plane she and Abdirrahim were having wild sex in. He took her from behind thrusting his penis into her very violently as he was pulling her hair. "Give it to me! Harder! Harder! Don't stop!" she shouted passionately. "You're mine! Say it!" he said as sweat poured down his feace. Mahasin didn't answer. She looked back at him with a sexy devilish smile. "Are you cumming yet? I want to see it!" she said. "You one look at her beautiful face caused him to explode inside her. He quickly pulled out and shot his remaining load on her ass. Both of them were breathing heavy as he smeared his seman all over her ass. When they were done she pulled up her panties. And turned on her back. "So, are you going to get me that book?" she asked. "I thought you said you read it!" he said trying to control his breathing. "I only read a few pages in front of him! Remember, the more i get to know about him, the more i can get into his head and heart, the better my chances i will become his queen! I get rid of him for good, then you can be my king slave!" she chuckled. "Oh shit!" he shouted. "What's wrong?" she asked. "The prisoners! They should be arriving at any moment! I must go!" he said as he pulled up his uniform trousers. Rermember! You get me that book, you can get more of this!" she said as she pointed to her vagina. He looked at her for a moment and spat in her face. "You, are one beautiful slut, my future queen!" he said before exiting the plane. She smiled as she wiped the spit off of her face and licked it off her hand. Abdirrahim could hear her laughter as he was leaving the hangar.

Moments later the motor whaleboat docked at the shore. Lord Lassenberry arrived with a convoy of military vehicles and troops. He hopped out of the vehicle before his assistant could open the door for him. "Hey! Where the fuck is Abdirrahim?" he shouted. The council members and their staff just stood there in silence. "Your prisoners have arrived, my lord." Lady Ellen said. "Great!" he said. She had a blank stare on her face as he approached her. "Smile! Today is a beautiful goddamn day!" he shouted wth his arms spread. "language!" she said. "Well excuse me, my lady!" he said as he bowed his head. Others around them began chuckling.

Lieutenant Usman approached Lord Lassenberry. "My Lord! I salute you!" He said as he bowed his head, putting his right fist over his heart. Lord Lassenberry placed his hand on his shoulder. "Good job, young man! Your father would be proud! He was a great captain. I miss him dearly." He said with a sad expression on his face. Suddenly his facial expression changed within a millisecond showing off his pearly whites. "Now! Bring me these creeps, lieutenant!" he said as he rubbed his hands together. Usman gave his men the signal to bring the prisoners over. Lord Lassenberry's facial expression changed once again when he saw the unexpected. A burly body rapped in a body bag was laid before him. Dragan Serpiente was forced to kneel before him. "What the fuck is this?" Lord Lassenberry shouted. "Language, Lord Lassenberry!" Lady Ellen shouted. "Fuck that!! Why is there a dead body in front of me? Where the fuck is Terrance Haggerty?" He shouted. "My Lord! I thought you received the message!" Usman said. Jaish kneeled over the body and unveiled Doug Reed's face. "Is this him, my Lord?" he asked. Lord Lassenberry tried his best to hold in his rage. "Fuck no!! That's fucking Doug Reed, and he's dead! I want Terrance Haggerty!" he shouted as he stomped his feet in a childish tantrum. Suddenly Abdirrahim appeared on the scene. "Where the fuck you been?" Lord Lassenberry shouted. "Please calm yourself, my Lord! What's wrong?" Abdirrahim asked. "Don't tell me to calm the fuck down! Look at that! It's Doug Reed! He's fucking dead!" he shouted. "My apologies, my Lord! I should have warned you of the outcome!" Abdirrahim said. "Where is Haggerty? I want Terrance Haggerty!!" Lord Lassenberry shouted. "Our associates from United States presume he is dead, my Lord!" Abdirrahim said. "So, where's the body?" Lord Lassenberry asked. "Ever since your grand announcement in Ghana it was rumored he had left the United States or was murdered." Abdirrahim said. Lord Lassenberry looked around the crowd. He kneeled in front of Serpiente. He told one of his soldiers to remove Serpiente's gag from his mouth. "God! You are one hideous motherfucker!" Lord Lassenberry whispered as he stared into his eyes. Lord Lassenberry had to pinch his own nose shut because of Serpiente's breath. "Listen, creature! I know what you fucking did to all those children in the past! I got the report from my cousin, may he rest in peace!" Lord Lassenberry said. Serpiente smiled, showing off his rotted teeth and sharp fangs. "Yeeessss! Sir Marcusssss! I rember him! He was great! A great...coward! i look into your eyessss, and see the same greatnesssss!" Serpiente chuckled. Lord Lassenberry glanced at his subjects! Feeling embarrassed, he stood up and punched Serpiente in the jaw. Serpiente fell over on his side. "Pick him up!" Lord lassenberry ordered his soldiers as he rubbed his knuckles to relieve the pain of striking Serpiente. 2 of his soldiers bring Serpiente back to his knees. "Something tells me that this monster is too fucking dumb to run a shawdow government!" Lord Lassenberry said. "I agree, my Lord." Abdirrahim said. "It don't matter. Soon he'll end up like Mr. Reed." Lord Lassenberry said as he continued to rub his knuckles. "My, lord! Look at your hand!" Ayub shouted. Everyone around Lord Lassenberry was in awe of what they saw. His hand began to swell with giant reddish blisters. "You must have scraped his teeth, my Lord!" Abdirrahim said. "No problem." Lord Lassenberry said. He reached in his pants pocket and pulled out a small vial of GLC. He unscrewed the cap with his teeth and emptied the vial on to his wound. Within seconds the blisters shrunk out of sight, and the swelling of his hand healed. Serpiente salivated as he gazed upon the miracle. "What a splendid gift from the Godsssss!" he said. "Gods?!! Lord Lassenberry chuckled.

It was a couple of hours before the execution when Lord Lassenberry personally paid a visit to his communications officer. Lord Lassenberry wanted the death of Serpiente to be televised around the world.

Pamela Bethea, former secretary General for Global Communications at the united Nations had retired 3 years earlier. She and a few loyal members of her staff were responsible for secretly bringing all heads of state in Africa together in becoming a subsidiary to the Lassenberian movement. Her accomplishment was rewarded with a Lassenberian school named in her honor . The carribean born U.N. secretary was about to enjoy retirement with her husband, 3 children and 8 grandchildren until tragedy struck. Her entire family was wiped out when a russian military helicopter crashed into her home in Antigua and Barbuda, killing all of her family members. She miraculously survived with third degree burns over 80% of her body. Lord Lassenberry quickly had her transported back to Lassenberia when he heard that she survived the tragedy. What was unknown the the public and the media that the remaines of the pilot were never found. Some Lassenberian council members had their suspicions that this was no freak accident. Lord Lassenberry officially made her a citizen of Lassenberia after the investigation.

Lord Lassenberry returned to the castle with Abdirrahim. "Listen! After this shit is done, it'll be crucial for you to stay close to me! According to my cousin's notes, we're about to knock off a big wig! The repercussions might be catastrophic, understand?!!" Lord Lassenberry said as he was about to open the safe containing the B.O.I. "I understand, my Lord." Abdirrahim said. He stood back as Lord Lassenberry opened the safe. Lord Lassenberry went to his desk and began to log in what was about to take place. "My Lord." Abdirrahim said. "What?" Lord Lassenberry asked as he was writing. "I don't mean to intrude, but i think it would wise to give me access to the safe just in case something were to happen to you." Abdirrahim suggested. Lord Lassenberry stopped writing. He stepped away from his desk and approached Abdirrahim. He was silent as he looked his top soldier up and down, from head-to-toe. "Say if something was to happen to me. What would you do with it?" he asked. "My Lord! I will pass it on to your eldest child, obviously!" Abdirrahim said as he stood at attention. "Obviously, huh?" was Lord Lassenberry's response. The silence continued as he stared into Abdirrahim's eyes. Suddenly Lord Lassenberry cracked a smile. "If i can't trust you with my family's legacy, who can i trust?" he said as he slapped Abdirrahim on the arm. "Thank you, my Lord! I will not disappoint you!" he said. "I'm sure you won't. Now kneel!" Lord Lassenberry said. "My, Lord?" Abdirrahim with a shocked look on his face. "You heard me, soldier! Kneel before me!" his king ordered. Abdirrahim slowly kneeled. Lord Lassenberry went to his desk and grabbed a knife from one of the drawers. He went back and stood before Abdirrahm. He took the knife and slit the palm of his hand. "What you are about to have access to is more divine then the Bible, the Quran and the Torah combined! May the spirit of my uncle expose your innards if you ever betray the Book Of Information!" he said as he smeared his blood on Abdirrahim's forehead. "You may stand." Lord Lassenberry said. Abdirrahim looked shakened from the ritual as he stood up. Lord Lassenberry took out a handkerchief and wiped the blood from his hand. He showed Abdirrahim how to gain access to the safe before placing the B.O.I back. "Now, let's show the world we don't fuck around!" Lord Lassenberry said with a smile.

An hour later troops from different branches of the military had gathered on the east end of the island. The execution was about to take place in one of the 5 parks named Marcus Park. The troops were hand picked on Abdirrahim's orders. The crowd, along with3 camera men surrounded a giant cauldron filled to the rim with water. Underneath the cauldron was a neatly stacked pile of teak wood shipped from India on Lord Lassenberry's orders. About 4 feet away from stood a 50 foot flagpole. Instead of rope used to hoist up the Lassenberry flag,a long thick linked chain was used in its place with a meat hook attached to the end of it.

Moments later, all 12 council members arrive on the scene with their entourages. They were escorted to accordion-like bleachers which were covered with rows of cushion for the elites to sit comforablyt. As being the most senior member of the council, Lady Ellen and her entourage sat at the top of the bleachers.

Another council member, Akshay Devgn sat on the bleachers with a proud look on his face. Earlier he convinced Lord Lassenberry to quickly expose of Serpient's body after the execution, according to hindu tradition. "I don't know how you convinced Lord Lassenberry to bend to your will!" one of his staff members said. "Preneet! Do not say such things in front of others! Speak Punjabi, or hold your tongue, please!" Devgn whispered. "Sir! I thought we were only aloud to speak English and Lasserian! I haven't taken one course in Lasserian since i've arrived, sir!" the young lady whispered.

The park was closed off to the rest of the public by having the 20 foot fence surrounding the park covered with red, green. And black velvet drapes. There were soldiers posted outside the fences to make sure citizens passing by didn't try to peek through the drapes.

Some of the council members made comments about how odd it was that refreshments and hor d'oeuves were being served for all in attendance, even military personnal. "I guess we're reenacting acient Rome?" one council member said sarcastically. Just as soon as the council member made that comment a team of bass drum players came marching into the park. They were mostly teenagers dressed in traditional Lassenberian uniforms. They replicated old nazi youth film footage from World War 2. The council member turned to one of his staff members. "This is definitely Romanesque! I'm just waiting for the lions!" he shouted over the drum play.

As the drummers were banging their instruments, Lord Lassenberry was being carried into the park on a 12 porter litter (vehicle). Each porter, with carrying poles resting on their shoulders wore a black hooded robe. He sat in the seat of the litter clutching the armrests with a serious look on his face. He wore a silk black robe with red and green sashes resembling his uniform. Lady Ellen was speechless even though her jaw had dropped. Some of the other council members, like Devgn just rolled their eyes. All military personnal stood at attention and saluted their king as he passed by. The council members stood out of respect as well. When the porters stopped and lowered the litter in front of the bleachers, Lord Lassenberry jumped off the vehicle like a kid on a swing in midair.

"That was cool! Don't y'all think?" Lord Lassenberry proudly said. The council members stood in silence until Jaish started applauding. The other council members reluctantly followed suit. "Y'all better clap!" he shouted. Suddenly he cracked a smile. "I'm just fucking with y'all!" he chuckled. "My Lord! Can we proceed with the execution? Most of us have busy schedules!" Matamela said. "Damn Mat! You got big balls! But you're right! We need to bring this freak out here and get it over with!" Lord Lassenberry said. The litter that carried Lord Lassenberry into the park was quickly converted into a throne which was place to the left of the bleachers. Lord Lassenberry sat on the throne with 2 armed soldiers standing behind him on both sides. He gave Abdirrahim the signal to bring forth the prisoner. Abdirrahim gave one of his lieutenants the signal to bring the prisoner into the park.

Moments later, 2 soldiers bring in Serpiente who was chained by the neck and his hands cuffed in thick custom made shackles. The violent sounds of the drums played loud as Serpiente was dragged before Lord Lassenberry. The drums stopped, which was well rehearsed as soon as he gave them the signal by raising his right hand.

Once again serpiente was forced to his knees. Lord Lassenberry cleard his throat after pulling out a prepared speech written on asheet of notebook paper. "I Lord Lassenberry, King of the great island nation of Lassenberia condemn you, you disgusting, foul subhuman motherfucker to death for crimes against humanity! These cameras are here to make sure your death will be humiliating to those in your organization, and to let the world know there is no greater power on this planet than me!" he shouted. Serpiente began laughing histerically. The council members looked at each other, looking shocked drom Serpiente's response. They then turned to their king to see how he would respond. "Oh! You think this shit is funny? Hook his ass up to the pole!" Lord Lassenberry shouted. The soldiers took serpiente over to the flagpole and hooked him from behind. The signal was given for the drum roll as he was being hoisted into the air. Abdirrahim had lit the fire prior to this. The water in the cauldron began to boil. Serpiente continued laughing as he was slowly being lowered to his death. Lady ellen closed her eyes, putting her hands together and began praying in silence. Once his feet touched the boiling water Serpiente's laughter turned into a horrific scream. He began to squirm to free himself from his bindings as his flesh separated from his bones. The site of the execusion was so grotesque some of the spectators had to turn away while others reguritated where they stood. As for Lord Lassenberry, he just sat there motionless staring into Serpiente's face as he was being submerged into the boiling water. As soon as the water reached his chest Lord Lassenberry gave the order to his soldiers to stop lowering him. Lord Lassenberry stood from his throne and walked toward the cauldron. He came so close, he could feel the heat from the fire on his face. Serpiente was gasping for air. It took everything in him to keep from passing out even though he and everyone there knew his death was inevitable.

"I know you're in a lot of pain but i know you can still hear me! Where is Terrance Haggerty?" Lord Lassenberry asked. Serpiente looked Lord Lassenberry in his eyes. He tried to speak but the pain was overwhelming. His hands rose from the water showing the skin on his fingers falling from his bones. "I'll ask you again, motherfucker! Where is Terrance Haggerty?!!" Lord Lassenberry shouted. Lady Ellen stood from the bleachers. "Lord Lassenberry!! End this now!!" she cried. Lord Lassenberry looked at Lady Ellen with fury in his eyes. He turned to his soldier, giving him the signal to fully submerge Serpiente to his death. There was a dead silence in the park. The only thing that can be heard was the sound of boiling water. Lord Lassenberry was so upset that he didn't go with his instinct to allow Serpiente to answer, he just stormed out of the park on foot. "Where are you going, my Lord?" Abdirrahim shouted. "Back to the castle!" Lord Lassenberry shouted as he pushed a drummer out of his way. "Why are you just standing there? Go escort your king!!" Abdirrahim shouted to one of the soldiers. "Why me, sir?" the soldier asked looking confused. Abdirrahim approached the young soldier. "Don't ever question my orders! Just obey them!" he whispered standing inches away from the soldier's face. "We are done here! Dispose of the remains!" Abdirrahim shouted to his men. "I guess thats our que to leave." Lady Ellen said to the other council members. "Follow me!" Abdirrahim said to the soldier that questioned him.

Back at castle Lassenberry, Masahin was walking toward Lord Lassenberry's chamber. The 2 soldiers standing guard at the chamber entrance saw her coming in their direction. Both guards were wielding machine guns across their chests. As soon as she approached them they crossed thiers weapons to block her from entering. "What is this? How dare you block me from entering!" she said. "Sorry maam. We have our orders not to let anyone enter his majesty's chamber if he is not present." One of the guards said. Mahasin smirked. "How do you think it would sound if the king heard you didn't allow the future queen Lassenberia access to her king's chamber?" she said with pride in her voice. The 2 guards looked at each other, not knowing how to respond at first. They reluctantly lowered their weapons to let her pass. "Don't just stand there you fool! Open the door for me!" she said to the guard. "Yes, maam!" the guard to her left said nervously. When he opened the door there was squeaky sound coming from one of the hinges. "Have someone take care of that squeaking! It annoys me everytime!" she shouted before entering. "Yes, maam!" the guard said.

Once inside the chamber, Mahasin locked the door. She quickly went over to where the vault was stationed. She lifted up her dress and pulled out a piece of paper from her panties. written the paper was the code to the vault and the combination to the safe that Abdirrahim had given her. After opening the safe she pulled out a tiny device from her panties as well. It was a mini camera. She glanced at the pistol and beaker of GLC. But it was the B.O.I she was after. She took it out of the safe and went over the bed. She opened to the first page. She only had to use her thumb and index fingure to snap pictures as she turned page after page.

Coming down the corridor was Lord Lassenberry, cursing to himself with regret for listening to Lady Ellen. "I'm the king! I'm the king! I need to listen to my gut instead of that white bitch yapping all the fucking time!" he said to himself. As he was walking, castle staff members who were walking in the opposite direction going about their business moved out of his way, fearing his disturbed looks and mumbling. When he made a right turn down the corridor he saw his first born Princess Niyale leaning up against the wall holding a laptop. His whole demeanor changed. His frown instantly turned up side down. "Hey, young lady! What are doing standing here alone?" he asked as he gently pulled on her pigtail. "Ysi zuyi klsz Mahasin." She said. "Why did she tell you to stay here? Where is she?" he asked. The princess pointed towards his chamber. Lord Lassenberry didn't say a word to the princess. He stormed down the corridor.

Lord Lassenberry noticed that one the guards posted at the door looked nervous. "What the fuck is your problem, soldier?" he asked. The soldier presented the Lassenberian salute to his king before answering. "Your future queen is in your chamber, my Lord!" he said. "My future queen? What the fuck?" he said bedore storming into his chamber. When he entered the room he was shocked to see Mahasin standing by the vault trying put the B.O.I back. "What the fuck are you doing?!!" he shouted. Mahasin was so terrified she dropped the B.O.I on the floor. He rushed over to her. As soon as she picked up the B.O.I he snatched it from her. "Bitch! How the fuck you get into my vault? You better not kie!" he shouted. Mahasin was speechless. Her eyes began to tear up. The more silent she was, the more it infuriated the king to the point him greabbing her by the neck. Suddenly her fear turned to anger."Take your hand off of me!!" she shouted before slapping him across the face. He dropped the B.O.I on the floor and slapped her back. She took the beaker of GLC from the vault and cracked it over his head. Lord Lassenberry fell back as shards of glass pierced his face and eyes. Before the GLC could heal his vision and skin he heard a gunshot that echoed down the corridor."What the fuck is going on?!!" he shouted as his vision was clearing. When his vision returned, he saw standing at the door Abdirrahim with a pistol in his hand. The 2 guards and the soldier standing behind Abdirrahim were shocked to see Mahasin on the floor, eyes wide open with blood oozing from the side of her head. "What did you do?!! What the fuck did you Do?!!" Lord Lassenberry cried. "She attacked you,My Lord!" Abdirrahim said. Lord Lassenberry snatched the pistol from out of Abdirrahim's hand and pointed it at his head. Abdirrahim backed away, putting his hands in the air. "Taking it easy, my Lord! I was just doing my duty to protect you!" he shouted. With the pistol still pointed at Abdirrahim's face, lord Lassenberry glanced at the soldiers standing in the doorway. "Get the fuck out! Now!!" he said to them. "My Lord! Please don't do this!" one of the guards shouted. "I said get the fuck out!! That's an order!!" Lord Lassenberry shouted. The 2 guards and the soldier slowly backed out of the chamber. "Now! Tell me how the fuck this bitch have access to my vault?" he asked Abdirrahim. "My Lord, please!" Abdirrahim said. "Tell me the truth, nigga!!" Lord Lassenberry shouted. Abdirrahim dropped to his knees. Tears trickled down his cheek as his arms were spread. He didn't utter a word to his king. Lord Lassenberry slowly lowered the pistol. "Guards!!" he shouted. The guards came back into the chamber. Lord Lassenberry kneeled down to look Abdirrahim in his eyes. "You know what. You don't have to say nothing. I think i get it. Her shit was amazing, huh? Anyway, you'll have to stand before the council, for appeaerances only. Like i told you earlier, i'm going to need you by my side. Our enemy oversees will be pissed when they find out they ain't getting shit from us because i ain't get Terrance Haggerty." Lord Lassenberry whispered to him. He and Abdirrahim stood up. "Take him to the holding cell. Take him through the tunnels. Make sure he ain't seen by the public on his way there." He said. "Yes, my Lord." One of the guards said as he and the other guard apprehended Abdirrahim.

Standing alone in his chamber, Lord Lassenberry stood over the body of Mahasin Wingo. He began sobbing for a moment until his emotions quickly switched. "What a waste of good pussy!" he chuckled as he wiped the tears from his eyes. He pressed the com-link on his wrist watch, putting the watch close to his mouth. "Lord Lassenberry to sky father. Lord Lassenberry to sky father. Come in." He said. *"Yes, Lord Lassenberry. Sky father here."* The voice said. Lord Lassenberry took a deep breath. "I have some bad news! There's been a accident! Your niece was shot!" he said. *"My niece?"* the sky father responded. "Yeah, Mahasin!" Lord lassenberry said. *"My lord! I don't have a niece! I don't have any family members here!"* the sky father said. Lord Lassenberry just stood silent as if he was staring into the abyss. *"Lord Lassenberry! Lord Lassenberry! My lord! Are you there?"* the sky father shouted. Lord Lassenberry shut off communication. "Fuck!! What did i do?" he said to himself. As he turned to leave his chamber, stasnding in the dooorway next to the soldier was his first pride and joy. Kdizs Mahasin!!!" Princess Niyale shouted as she saw Mahasin lying on the floor and the a gun in her father's hand. "Take it easy, young lady! You don't understand!" he shouted. Lord Lassenberry struggled to grab her as she ran passed him to get to Mahasin. Before Niyale could kneel by her side, her father dropped the gun and grabbed her. "Let go of me! Hse hwkzzzils kieed!" she shouted. "Watch your mouth, young lady!" he said. "Mahasin! Mahasin! Eissd djt zee Mahasin!!" she screamed. "I did not kill her, young lady! I found her like this!" he said as he grabbed her by the shoulders. Niyale pulled away from her father and picked the gun off the floor. She pointed the gun in his face, holding it with 2 hands. "Come on, young lady! You can't be serious!" he chuckled. Before he could utter another word to her the gun went off. She fired a shot passed his ear."What the fuck?" he shouted before smacking her down to the floor. He grabbed the gun. "Take her outta here! Lock her in her room and stand guard outside her door until i clean up this shit!" he said to the soldier standing in the doorway. "Yes, my Lord." The soldier said.

About an hour later.Abdirrahim was sitting in a holding cell until one of his lieutenants approached the guards and ordered his release on behalf of Lord Lassenberry. "General! Lord Lassnenberry would like to see you." The lieutenant said.

Abdirrahim entered Lord Lassenberry's office. He stood at attention in front of his king's desk. "Relax, general. Take a seat." Lord Lassenberry said. Abdirrahim pulled up a chair and sat across from his king.

"I just recieved word from Pamela Bethea. She recieved a message from the president of the United States. He wants his shipment within 24 hours. I say fuck him." Lord Lassenberry said. Before Abdirrahim responded he leaned back in his chair, folding his arms. "What about Mahasin, my Lord?" Abdirrahim asked. "Did you just hear what i said? You fucked her! I fucked her,and now she's dead! One thing i learned from my uncle is that pussy will come and go! We're running a nation! But, there is one thing i need you to do!" Lord Lassenberry said. "What is that, my Lord?" Abdirrahim asked as he leaned forward in his chair. Lord Lassenberry opened the drawer to his desk and pulled out a automatic pistol with a suppressor attached to it. He slid it across the desk toward Abdirrahim. "What do you want me to do with this, my Lord?" he asked. "The guards that witnessed what went down with the Mahasin situation. It will be a problem if and when they start to gossip. I can't let this get back to the council. We can't let this get back to the council! Understand?" Lord Lassenberry explained. Abdirrahim looked sad as he took a deep breath. "I know these men are loyal to you, but i can't risk it." Lord Lassenberry said. Abdirrahim took the weapon and checked the magazine. He then nodded his head. "Of course i understand, my Lord." He said. "Good! Just make sure it's done quietly! You know what to do!" Lord Lassenberry said. Abdirrahim stood from his chair. Lord Lassenberry stopped him before he was about to leave the office. "Remember young man. The world is ours. Now, what do you say about that?" Lord Lassenberry asked. Abdirrahim stood at attention after tucking the weapon inside his uniform jacket. "Long live the House of Lassenberry!!" he shouted. "Now, you're dismissed. ":Lord lassenberry said.

Once abdirrahim left the office Lord Lassenberry made contact on his com-link to his communications officer, Pamela Bethea. "Hey, sweety! Did you edit the execution video yet?" he asked her."We're working on it now, my Lord." She said. "I can't let the world see me look weak under some white woman, even though she's a council member. Understand?" he said. "Yes, my Lord." Bethea said before cutting off communication.

— CHAPTER .51 WHEN GODS MEET —

Sitting in the oval office surrounded by members of his cabinet, president Harrison looked very unhappy after receiving the message from Lassenberia that Lord Lassenberry was unsatified with the deal the 2 governing bodies had made earlier. "Dammit! He did it to us again, Mr. President!!" Secretary Gates shouted as he pounded his fist on the president's desk. President Harrison looked up at Gates, shaking his head. "No, Mr. Secretary. The first time, he did it to you." The president said in a calm voice. Gates took a couple of steps back from the desk with a infuriated look on his face. Gated turned to face the other cabinet members. "So, do the rest of you feel the same?" he asked. "It was embarrassing that you came face to face with a jumbotron insted of lassenberry himself." Secretary of Health and Human Services, Leroy jackson said.

There was no response from the 4 other cabinet members. "Lassenberia has Russia, India, as well as other unsavory diplomats in their back pocket. I will not sign an executive order for millitary action." Harrison said. Gates smacked himself on the forehead looking at the president in disbelief. "Mr. President! Correct me if i'm wrong, but i thought this country was a superpower!" Gates shouted. "Iv'e given it some thought. Yes we can go into Lassenberia, and take it's resource by force! But, sooner or later we'll be painted as bullies to the American people which the rest of the world already sees us. I can't have that, not in my administration! Besides, certain friends of ours in the Senate and Congress say that big pharma pays well." The president said. "I have a prediction, sir. In time, Lassenberia will surrender its resource. I also predict just like you said, it will not be in your administration, sir. Will you all excuse me. I need to go gather my thoughts." Gates said before leaving the oval office. "Do you see him as a problem in the near future, sir?" Secretary Jackson asked. "He's just an old man with a big ego. Nothing to be concerned about." The president said with confidence. Secretary Jackson witnessed the president's concerned expression as saying otherwise.

Back in Lassenberia 3 days had passed when Princess Niyale was confined to her room. She was summoned by her father to his office on the 4th day. She was escorted to his office by 2 soldiers. "have a seat, young lady." Lord Lassenberry said once she entered the room. "You can leave us." He said to the soldiers. "Yes, my Lord." One of the soldeirs said as they bowed their heads. Niyale sat in the chair as her feet dangled barely touching the floor. "Yis xeep kenm ditp?" he asked her. She nodded her head. "I know i told you to speak the new langauge, but i wanna go old school for right now. This bilingual shit is giving me a headache." He said. "Do you know what this is, young lady?" he asked as he pointed to the B.O.I on his desk. "Noooo!" she said with a sassy tone in her voice. "This book or binder, or whatever you wanna call it will show you everthing about your family history. We have enemies overseas, young lady. Very powerful enemies. One day you will be queen. No time like the present for you to prepare for your future." He said. "What if i don't want to be queen?" she asked. "Don't be silly, young lady! It's your divine right!" he said. "My what?" she asked with a cofused look on her face. "Nevermind. Starting today the both of us will read this binder together covering decades of our family history. You may have a lot of younger brothers and sisters but you are special. Pure Lassenberry blood runs through your veins, young lady. You may not understand what that means now but one day you will continue our family bloodline. The catch is that you won't bond with some citizen of Lassenberia or anyone regular guy. There is another Lassneberry out there and when the time comes you will summon him and he will be your consort." He said . "Daddy!! What are you talking about?" she shouted. "Just remember what i said. Now, do you have to use the bathroom?" he asked. "Noooo!!" she said. "Are you hungry?" he asked. "Ysa hegf ot seemd!" she said. "Ok. I'll have the help make you sandwich. Right now i need you to roll that chair over here and sit next to daddy so we can begin reading this." He said. "Why did you kill Mahasin? She was like a mother to me!" she said before pushing the chair next to her father. Lord Lassenberry sighed. "Listen. Today you will know the truth about her. She wasn't who you think she was." He said as his eyes teared up.

It was a week after halloween when Secretary of Defense Gateswas sitting in his office at the Pentagon shaking uncontrollably. A few minutes earlier he had summoned his personal assistant Ron to his office. Ron saw his condition and new exactly what to do. He went into his briefcase and pulled out the syringe that secretary Gates so desperately craved, and needed. "Hurry, ron! It's getting worse!" the Gates shouted. With the right amount of dosage, ron rushed over and injected the syringe behind his boss's ear. After the injection Gates leaned back in his chair breathing a sigh of relief. "You're a good boy ron! Thank you!" he panted. "Anything for you sir. Anything!" ron said. "I will report your deeds to the master! You will be remembered a thousand lifetimes!" Gates said. "Thank you, sir!" ron said. "Now! I need to go over project Trudeau with you. How far along are we?" Gates asked. "The boys are beyong peak physical condition. Weapons training will start within the next 2 weeks, sir" Ron said. Excellent!" Gates said as he rubbed his clammy hands together. "I always wondered, sir! Why the name Trudeau?" ron asked. Gates began to chuckle. "It was June 14, 1940. The master was visiting Paris for the 10th time. He came across a woman walking with her son, who seemed to be no more than 5 or 6 years old a the time. His impulses got the best of him. He grabs the mother by the neck! The pressure from his hand immediately crushed her throat! He snatched the boy, putting him under his arm to take him,god knows where! Suddely, he's stopped in his tracks as German troops come marching in his direction! This startled the master! The master was so impressed, he tossed the boy over the side of the Pont de Bercy bridge and gave off a loud Sieg Heil salute as the troops marched by!" Gates said. "Still, sir. Where did the name

Trudeau come about?" ron asked. "Oh! He asked the little boy his name before he tossing him over the side of the bridge!" Gates chuckled. Ron didn't know how to take the story. He just gave off a nervous grin.

The Trudeau project was overseen by Dr. Hugo R. Schouten. 20 boys from the ages of 10 to 13 years of age were selected to head a private army under the guise of U.S. Army rangers. The rumors spread throughout the American media about skirmishes with Lassenberia in the past was about to come to a deadly realization. Due to the lack of technology, the master could only develope a clone for one subject which happened to be Secretary Gates. The soldiers in training had to be developed like the other NA agents, which meant it would take a long period of time for them to spring into action.

About a month later Secretary Gates, his assistant ron and other members of his staff met with a big time film director and his leading man to discuss the details of an upcoming spy movie. The meeting was held in the V.I.P section of a fancy restaurant in SoHo. There were a dozen federal agents posted outside the restaurant and a half dozen federal agents posted outside the VIP section. The party of 10 were having a good time conversing about the entertainment business. When it came to the dining part, the movie director noticed Gates hadn't touched anything on his plate. The film director was a brash old school jewish guy from the golden age of hollywood. "Excuse me Mr.secretary, but i didn't invite you to dinner so you could waste a 3 hundred dollar plate of food!" he said. "My apologies. I should've told you i've already had a quick bite to eat a couple of hours ago. I did tell you we could've talked about consulting on the golf course!" Gates chuckled. Ron, who was sitting next to his boss noticed his hand start to tremble. Ron purposely tipped his wine glass over, spilling his drink on his boss's lap. Gates calmly looked down at his lap smilimg as one of the female staff members gasped in awe. Ron jumped up from his seat with a faux look of fear on his face. "I'm so sorry sir! Lets get you to the restroom to get the stain out!" ron said. At this time both of secretary's hands began to tremble. He just sat there still smiling, looking at his lap. Ron grabbed the Secretary by the forearm, pulling him out of his seat. He gave everyone at the table the impression that he was fearful of spilling the drink, but the scowl on his face and his gritting teeth showed his frustration. "Excuse us, please!" ron said before leading Gates to the restroom.

Once in the restroom, ron noticed Gates's trembling became more intense. Gates still had a smile on his face, as well as a dazed look. "Shit! It's getting worse!" ron said to himself. He had to lean Gates up against the sink before checking his pockets. "Fuck! " he shouted before running out of the restroom. Ron approached one of the federal agents. "Do not let anyone into that restroom!" ron shouted. He ran outside to the Boeman SUV. He climbed into the back seat and reached for his breifcase. He pulled out the syringe and raced back into the restaurant. He pushed the federal agent, who was guarding the door to the restroom out of the way. Inside the restroom ron found Gates face down on the floor, flopping like a fish out of water. He quickly injected the syringe behind his boss's ear. Instantly Gates stood up from the floor wiping off his suit as if nothing had occured prior. Ron noticed that there were bruises on his forehead from the fall. "What's the problem?" Gates asked as ron was staring at him. "Sir! I have to tell the our guests that you're not feeling well and that we have to go!" ron said. "What the hell are you talking about? I'm about to be a consultant on a big budget movie!" Gates shouted. "Look in the mirror, sir." Ron said. Gates shook his head at his image as he straightened his necktie. "Well, what are you standing there for? Tell them the meeting is one!" Gates shouted. "Right away, sir!" ron said before rushing out of the restroom.

Once inside the SUV Gates and ron sat next to each other. Their vehicle was followed by the other federal agents in the other vehicles. Ron turned to Gates. "You know it's over, sir." He said. Gates reached behind his ear. He looked at his fingertips before rubbing them together. Ron took out his cell phone. He dialed only 3 digits. Unlike normal cell phones making a ringing sound on the other end, his cell phone made a continuous buzzing sound. "*What is it?*" the voice on the on the other end asked. "Replica has failed to the point of no return. Must be discarded." Ron said. "*Standby for further instructions.*" The voice said. Ron stayed on the line. At this time Gates began to tremble again. "I need another fix." He said in a calm voice. Ron dropped his head as he sighed. "It's over, sir. Time to close up shop." Ron said. "Regardless whats to come of my fate, it still feels great to be the first of my kind," Gates said as he stared out the window while trembling. Ron still had the cell phone to his ear when he received his instructions. "*Return replica to the source for disposal* " the voice said before hanging up. "Driver! Take us to Teterboro airport!" ron shouted.

The following day, somewhere in Middle America a middle-aged couple sat in the livingroom of their colonial home to watch the evening news. "*Breaking news. Secretary of Defense, Carter Gates was found dead in his Washington home this morning. At this time, cause of death is unknown. It has been reported that Secretary Gates was taking medication for heart complications for years.we will continue this breaking story once we've receive more infromation on his cause of death. Again. Secretary of Defense Carter Gates has passed away at the age of 62. This is Chanda Webb reporting live outside the Pentagon.*" The reporter said. "Jesus! I was looking forward to him running for President in the next election!" the man said to his wife.

The next day ron and the Rest of his staff were at the pentegon cleaning out his former boss's office. making room for the next Secretary of Defense. "Did anyone notice Secretary Gates acting strange in the past few months, or it's just me?" one staff member asked. "Its just you, Beverly. It's you.now, let's finish up here!" Ron said.

Later that day, ron was called to the oval office. After contacting Dr. Zachmont his plan was to pack his belongings and head up to Maine to put his bid in for master of ceremony at the NA palace. Zachmont told him that he'd have a great chance of getting the position due to being a successful handler to Gates.

At the Whitehouse ron stood outside the oval office waiting to meet with the president. There were 2 secret service agents standing outside the office as well. Ron was looking nervous as time went on and because the 2 agents kept their eyes locked on him. Finally, the door to the oval office opened. First to step out of the office was Assistant Secretary of Defense For Legislative Affairs, Jovita Pence. She and president Harrison shook hands as he congradulated her on her promotion. As soon as Harrison locked eyes on ron he gave him the same stare as the secret service agents. "Good evening, Madam Secretary!" ron said to Pence. "How are you this evening, Mr. Oliver?" she said. "I presume that you're next in line to defend this great nation!" he chuckled. "I was wondering, would you like to continue your career as part of my staff?" she asked. "Thank you Madam Secretary, but i think it's time i put in my paperwork and ride off into the sunset!" he sighed. President Harrison stood there watching the 2 converse like a tennis match until he interrupted. "Excuse me Jovita but i must speakwith ron in my office at once." He said. "Sure thing, Mr. President! Contact my secretary if you change your mind!" she said to ron before heading down the corridor. "Would you?" Harrison said as he made a hand gesture for ron to enter his office. "Do not let anyone disturb us." Harrison said to the secret service agents. "Yes, Mr. President." One of the agents said.

"Take a seat!" Harrison said before sitting at his desk. Harrison sat backcomfortably in his chair, interlocking his fingers. Ron sat back in his chair as well, crossing his legs. "What i'm about to say to you is just between the 2 of us. I've received the autopsy on Gates. Now, tell me what the hell is going on!" Harrison shouted. "What do you mean, Mr. President?" ron asked. Harrison leaned forward, placing his elbows on the desk with his arms folded. "I went to view the body myself. That's not the same Secretary Gates that was in my office days ago!" Harrison said. "With all due respect, sir! That doesn't make any sense!" ron said. The autopsy said he died from heart failure. The pathologist found an orange crusty substance clogging his external jugular vein! He said himself that he had never seen anything like it!" Harrison said. "Wow! I don't know what to tell, sir!" ron said. "So, you didn't witness any kind of substance abuse?" Harrison asked. "Nothing but the occasional glass of wine!" ron said as he shrugged his shoulders. Harrison leaned back and began tapping his fingers on the desk as sweat began trickling from ron's forehead. Harrison displayed the biggest smile. "So, where are you planning to ride off into the sunset?" He asked. "Oh! Well. Sir! There's a nice little town outside of Abbot Maine!" he said. "Abbot is a small town! What town could be smaller?" Harrison chuckled. " i forget, sir! It's some Native American name i can't pronounce!" ron chuckled. "Oh really?" Harrison said. "The great thing about it, there are no roads leading to it! You have to be flown in!" ron said. Harrison paused for a moment before standing from his chair. "Well! Don't let me stop you from heading towards the sun." Harrison said as he extended hand in friendship. Ron stood from his chair to shake hands with the president. "It's been a pleasure, sir." Ron said. "Good luck and god speed!" Harrison said before escorting ron out of the oval office.

2 days later a group of men in a motor boat spotted a black helicopter flying over Wyman Lake located in the great state of Maine while they were night fishing. It was flying low, heading due north. "Looks like a news chopper?" one of the men said. "Nah! That's definitely military!" another guy said.

The group of fishermen got off the subject about the helicopter and continued drinking a waiting for a bite on their fishing lines. What they didn't notice 20 minutes later the 4 black hang gliders passing over a couple of miles above.

The hang gliding team used high tech night vision goggles to keep track of the black helicopter. Prior to this a cargo plane had took off from US Air Force Base Exchange. The glider team jumped out of the cargo plane at a very high altitude once the helicopter was picked up on radar.

"Leader one to glider team. Prepare to drop in 5 minutes." The hang glider said on his wrist comlink. The 4 man glider team landed in a field on the outskirts Abbot. Dressed in all black the glider team's mission was to do recon on the passenger of the helicopter, which happened to be ron oliver. Soon after the team secured their gear they ran through the field before they

made their way to a wooded area. As they crepted through the woods the team leader gave the order for them to split up within a mile radius of each other. *"Remember. Stay clear of civilians."* The team leader said on his comlink.

When the glider team came upon the small town, one of the team members noticed something odd. *"Glider 4, to team leader."* The team said. *"Team leader to glider 4. Report."* He said. *"This is strange. I'm looking into the home of one of the residence. They look like mannequins!"* he said. *"Glider 2 to team leader. I'm seeing same thing simular from my position!"* he said. *"Glider 3 to team leader! What's more weird, there's no sign of the aircraft!"* he said. *"Glider 2, Glider 4. Move in. Stay in stealth mode."* The team leader said.

As the team members crepted through the town they reported the same occurence in each home they passed by. Glider team member 2 crepted across the lawn of one of the house when unknowingly hit a trip wire. This trip wire set off the sprinkler system of every lawn in the town. The pressure from the sprinklers was more powerful than usual causing the fluid to shoot a100 feet into the air. *"Glider 2 to team leader! This is weird!"* he said. *"Team leader to glider 3. Let's move in!"* he ordered.

As the fluid came down the entire team gathered in the middle of the street."Mannequins in every home, and powerful sprinker systems. What the hell is this place?" the team leader said as the fluid rained down on them. Suddenly, one of the members noticed smoke coming from his uniform. The other team members had the same experience. "What the hell is this?" glider member 2 said. The fluid began to burn through their uniforms. "My skin is burning!!" glider member 3 shouted. "Let's get out of here!" the team leader shouted. As the glider team tried to make a run for it to leave town, they began to feel the fluid eat through their flesh. The pain was so excruciating it stopped them in their tracks. The team leader fell to his knees as his flesh began to bubble and fall from his bones until he was no more. This fluid short ciruited his comlink. The same occured to his teamates as their screams went unheard. The sprinkler system throughout the town ceased once the 4 bodies ended up as clumps of flesh.

The weather was a frigid 20 degrees as the streets were flooded with this fluid which for some strange reason didn't freeze. It then subsided into the drainage system. At the other end of the small town there was a huge metal plate in the middle of the street. About a mile beneath this plate was the black helicopter, along with other aircraft stationed on top of a elevator platform. The area surrounding the helicopter was dimly-lit with blue neon cables lining the base of the area. There was one giant thick wooden door resembling something built from medieval times. On the other side of this door was as trail made out of concrete. This trail which was the width of a vehicle, stretched for over 50 miles. The trail branched off in several directions. One path lead to the NA palace.

Beneath the palace was a small stadium resembling an updated version of the roman colosseum was able to seat 2 thousand people. In the center of the colosseum stood a giant tri-sided jumbotron mounted on top of a 50 foot stone pillar. Ron arrived at this stadium, like many others to listen to a message from the their master. Sammy Perez was another one amongst the crowd of criminal sorts. There were hundreds of NA agents roaming the outskirts of the crowd.

Once the crowd was settled in their seats, the jumbotron was turned on. A silence grew amongst the crowd when a scrambled signal appeared on all 3 screens. Suddenly, a figure appeared.

"Good evening, my children! I am so pleased to see you! I apologize to you all for not being there in the physical! But, i have so much human love for you all! Tonight i must admit the set back named Carter Gates! It was an experiment that has not been attempted in the past 2 thousand years! I promise you, this time my children the plans i have for us will not fail! Soon America will bend to our will, and the rest of the world will be ours!" the master said before pausing to a thunderous applause. "This plan i have devised will take some time! Some of you will not make it due to your limited existence! But i promise you my children, those who believe in me and have faith in me will be remembered throughout the ages! So wait and be patient, my children!" the master said. He closed his eyes. "i see victory! I see victory! I see victory!" he continued to chant until the jumbotron transmission turned off. "He sure didn't say much!" one man standing next to Sammy Perez said. "Too me, he said enough, my dude!" Sammy replied.

The year 2019 had come to a close. Lassenberia was the econimic leader in the world. It was just a rumor to the majority around the world. America's government, it's allies, Russia's government, other world super powers as well as big corporations kept this fact from the masses through false media. There were a few conspiracy theorists around the world who had made plans to make the pilgrimage to the land of second chances as it was dubbed until the pandemic struck.

Some say it came from hi-tech planes flying above earth's troposphere but was dismissed as a conspiracy theory. The effects of this scourge caused major respiratory problems, especially amongst the eldery. Just like China, government officials in America sought to shut down traveling and quarantine it's citizens. Crop dusters flying above Lassenberian skies showered the island nation with GLC to protect it's people.

Jubba Gacayte, known as the sky father had a team of cryptologists decipher coded messages from the Untied States that they were preparing to invade and rape Lassenberia of its most precious resource. Lord Lassenberry knew this day was coming. Even though Lassenberia was protected by the Russian government and the governments and tribes of East Africa, the idea of invasion was so overwhelming to Lord Lassenberry to point he began to fall into a depression. His old habit of binge drinking resurfaced. He had lost focus on who he was and what was his responsibilty to his people. Just like in the old castle lassenberry back in the United States, Lord Lassenberry roamed the corridors of the new castle in a drunken stupor with a bottle of vodka in one hand and a pistol in the other. "They're coming for us!! I'll kill all them bitch ass mother fuckers!!! Fuck you Terrance!!!" he shouted in the halls as he randomly shot off his pistol. The castle's staff took cover until Abdirrahim and his men tackled him.The pistol accidentally went off before Lord Lassenberry fell to the floor.

One the other side of the island in the borough of Braxton Princess Niyale and Lady Ellen were having tea, discussing the King's downward spiral. "Yheer xes pleax t gie!" Niyale said as her right leg was trembling. "Please, your highness! I know you have a lot on your mind, but must i keep reminding you that i'm from the older generation! Can i send in one of my grandchildren to translate?" Lady Ellen chuckled. "I'm sorry! But my father is driving me crazy!" the princess said. Lady Ellen placed her cup of tea on the coaster. She placed her hand on Niyale's shoulder. "You are not a child anymore. Soon it will be time for you to take charge and be the woman you were destined to be. Now, lets pray to our lord and savior together." Lady Ellen said. Suddenly Princess Niyale had a dour look on her face. "I am the future queen of lassenberia! I am the savior!" she said before one of Lady Ellen's aides entered the room breathing heavily. "What is it, Aknil?" Lady ellen asked. "My lady! It's the king! Something terrible just happened!" he cried.

"Bullshit!" Queen Niyale shouted. "Your majesty! What do you mean, bullshit?" Captain Trudeau said. "Your whole story about your daughter! You do not represent the United States Army! Do you think i'm some kind of simpleton? I am Queen Niyale!!! Absolute ruler of this great land, you pathetic creature!!!" she shouted. The captain's facial expression changed from the deer in the headlights, to a more sinister look. "The master was right about you." He said. Captain Trudeau removed a laptop from his backpack. He turned it on, punched in a code on the keyboard and turned the screen to face the queen. Suddenly the image of the being responsible for all the comotion and death that occured appeared on the screen.

"Queen Niyale, i presume!" the master said with a joyful look on his face. "Who are you, creature?" she asked. "Jid feot svic aiesh." The master said. With her thumb on the detonator Niyale approached Captain Trudeau, standing 5 feet from the laptop he was holding. "My father mentioned your name to me when i was a child! He said he heard it in a dream." She said. The master smiled. "i came to your father in his sleep long before you were born, long before Lassenberia became the great nation that it is! I whispered my existence into his ear, using an ancient mystic belief taught to me as a child! I can teach you, if you'd like!" he said. "Why would a foul creature such as yourself teach me this gift?" Niyale asked. "Simply, because i need you! This world needs you, your highness!" he explained. "Why do you care about the world? You're the cause of all of this chaos!" she said. "It boils down to the ends justifying the means!" he said. "Explain yourself, creature!" she said. "With your permission, your highness, may we speak to one another face-to-face? This form of communication is beneath me!" he said. Niyale didn't respond. "I promise you, as a superior being that no harm will come to you!" he said. "A superior being doesn't make promises! He or she gives orders and makes demands!" Niyale said with a smirk. The master began clapping. "Braaavo, your highness! You are certainly divine material!" he chuckled. "Now show yourself, creature!" she said.

Moments later, the transmission clicked off from the laptop. Captain Trudeau placed it back into his backpack. Niyale looked up towards the ceiling when she heard a rumbling noise coming from above. The rumbling noise ceased after a few minutes. Coming out of the rubble of the destroyed castle wall was the being that was responsible for destroying 1/3 of Lassenberia. Trudeau's men stepped to the side for their master. He patted Trudeau on the head like a pet as he walked by him.

He stood a couple of feet from the queen, towering over her. Niyale firmly gripped the detonator as she had her hands folded behind her back."I'll get straight to the point! Ages ago my squadron was sent to this...this rock you call a planet on a surveillance mission. Your fresh water supply was desperately, or maybe still needed for trade with one of our allies in the galactic council. While on our mission here, our enemies from another quadrant of this galaxy were preparing to attack us. As we went above and engaged in battle, they deprived us our findings by manifesting a dome over the earth, incasing your sun and moon as well, which are quite smaller than humans were told. This dome is mentioned in the Christian bible as the firmament. Before the dome was completed, my ship was bombarded and badly damaged. I crashed to earth like a bolt of lightning, separated from my squadron. I've been here ever since." He explained with sadness in his eyes. Niyale had a suspicious look on her face. "So, you are looking for sympathy after all the trouble you've caused? Is that what you're telling me?" she asked. The master became irate. "I'm...looking...for...a...way...out of this prison!!!" he shouted as black saliva spewed from his mouth. Niyale calmly wiped the residue of his fluids from her cheek. "I admit, i interfered with humans out of bordem! But at the same time i was looking for a way to penetrate the dome, which happened to be 2 thousand miles of solid ice at its peak!" he said. "What do you need from me, and what can you offer?" Niyale asked. "In my prime i possessed the strength of a thousand men! Now, i am old and withered! That precious resource you have in your possession may give me the strength to penetrate the dome with my bare hands!" he explained. "So you can fly,now? Great!!" Niyale said sarcastically. "Who do you think gave humans the idea to make jetpacks, young lady?" he said. Niyale pondered his case for a minute. "What can you do for me in return, creature?" she asked. "What do you desire?" he sasked. The master smiled. Niyale couldn't answer him quick enough. "You can have full control of my troops! But most importantly, once i'm gone you can be responsible for healing the world of this pandemic! If i do not receive the resource, i will give the order to commence a second wave of the pandemic!" he explained. The master extended his hand in a friendly gesture to seal the deal. "No need for that! We are are gods in our own right. Our words are enough." She said. "Very well, your highness!" the master said as he put his hand down by his side. "How much of the resource do you think you will need to rejuvenate yourself?" Niyale asked. "I have know idea!" he chuckled. "In that case, I will decide the amount. We shall meet here alone in 24 hours." The queen said. "Jasx esaoi blivix, your highness." The master said as he bowed his head to her. "Jasx esaoi blivix, to you as well." Niyale said as she bowed her head. The master turned and walked away with his troops following behind. Niyale remained in her power during their conversation. Once she was alone, the young queen fell to her knees and began hyperventilating.

Later that day, Niyale along with a small group of her surviving soldiers walked the main roads of the north side of the island tending to the wounded and easing the fears of the distraught. Shortly after easing the fears of a little girl of indian descent Niyale was approached by Pamela Bethea and the sky father. "Any communication from the russian government?" she asked pamela. "No, your highness! All of our allies are in fear of the pandemic! I've received messages from world leaders that they have taken refuge underground!" she explained. As pamela and the queen were speaking, more and more citizens of Lassenberia came out of hiding. At the end of the conversation there were thousands of citizens and military personnel surrounding the queen. "Would you assist me?" she asked the sky father. He helped her stand on the hood of one of the military vehicles. She was handed a bullhorn from lieutenant Anwar.

"My dear subjects! Shix yih whoseer naqe! I know our situation seems grim now! But i assure you all that we will pull through this setback! After tomorrow we will

bring light to the world! It is a great time to be alive! It is a time to heal the world! Not only from the pandemic that has streched across the world, but the mindset that has plagued the world for centuries! Those souls we have lost today will not be avenged! Those souls will be canonized as saints because we live in paradise! We will spread our attributes to the rest of the world! After tomorrow the world will be renamed Lassenberia! There are others beyond our relm! There are trillions of souls out there that will be touched by us, cured by us and praised by us! So, lets rebuild from the ashes and take the universe head on!" she said before handing over the bullhorn to Pamela Bethea. **"Long live the house of Lassenberry! Long live the house of lassenberry! Long live the house of Lassenberry!"** pamela shouted as Queen Niyale stepped down from the vehicle with the aide of the sky father.everyone chanted Pamela's cries as the queen walked through the crowd. Niyale approached Lady Ellen who was standing on the outskirts of the crowd. They held each other firmly. "Soon i will need you to go to Russia and deliver a very important message for me, ok?" She whispered in Lady Ellen's ear. The leader of the Borough of Braxton looked confused but nodded her head to reassure her queen that the task, whatever it may be will be carried out.

The next day around the same time where queen Niyale and the master had met for the first time, Niyale watched as the royal private jet flew overhead heading north. Flying in from the opposite direction was a more advanced aircraft. It looked unlike anything the queen had even seen due to the astonished expression on her face. It came to a complete stop as it hovered over a mile above the castle.

The queen didn't get any sleep. She did have time to change her attire. She went from formal to rugged, wearing a flannel shirt with the sleeves rolled up, hiking pants and boots. Her sidearm was a glock in a holster attached to her belt.her hair was pinned up into a bun. In her hand was the nuclear detonator. The only thing giving her leverage against the master. By her feet was a gallon of GLC in a clear jar.

She watched as a shiney pod slowly descended from the aircraft. It appeared to have 4 propuulsion thrusters spewing blue flames guiding it's descention. The pod landed about 50 yards away from the queen. The entrance of the pod opened. The master stepped out. He approached the queen wearing the same uniform he wore when he first arrived on earth. It loosely fit his decrepit body.

"It seems like yesterday since we've met, your highness!" the master chuckled. Niyale didn't find humor in his words. "i thought you were coming alone! Who's in the wierd looking ship above?" she asked. The master looked up at the aircraft. "It's on automatic pilot! It took me over a century to perfect it. Another innovation of mine to the world!" he said. He looked down at her feet. "Is that it? Is that the cure to give me the strength to head home?" he asked. "It's yours, if you want it." She said. The master went to pick up the jar. The jar of green goop had a swirl of blue liquid floating in the middle, which the master didn't pay any attention to. "Remember, creature! If you make any foul moves, i will end us all!" she said. He held the jar in his hands. "Here's to going home!" he said before taking a sip of the GLC. Both the young queen and the master stood in silence, waiting for the green goop to take effect. A minute had passed. The master felt no difference in his body. He became frustrated.

"Why isn't anything happening?" he shouted. "Maybe it's because you're not human. Drink more." Niyale suggested. The master began to guzzle the GLC, spilling some on his chin and uniform. He had consumed 90 percent of what was in the jar until it fell from his hands, shattering on the ground. "Yeeees!! I can feel my strength returning!!" he shouted as his muscles grew, causing his uniform to fit more snug. He clenched his fists as he stared into the queen's eyes. Niyale revealed the detonator to reassure him that she wasn't afraid to press the plunger. The master smiled as he took a step back. "Oh! I should inform you there are others who have been living amongst you humans far longer than i have, young queen! I suggest you hold on to that!" he said. Niyale looked puzzled. I have something for you! Catch!" he said before tossing a small object to her. "What's this?" Niyale asked. The master looked up at his floating aircraft. "The keys to the car!!" he said. The object looked like a 4 inch glass wand with a glowing violet fluid inside it. "Well, farewell Terra! Its been... an adventure!!" he shouted towards the sky with his arms spread. With his strength rejuvenated, the master turned and made a dash to his pod. "I wish you well, young queen!!" he shouted before closing the hatch to the pod..

Once inside the pod, the master strapped himself in. He activated the pod, then punched in the coordinates he needed to get home. The last thing he did before taking off was to activate a device that caused the outer shell of the oblong shaped pod to generate enough heat that it turned glowing white. Even though the young queen was standing yards away from the pod, the heat was so intense she had to run another hundred yards away to keep from disintegrating. The heat turned the sand below its thrusters into a giant sheet of glass. The pod went from 0 to 1000 mph within 3 seconds. The pod's takeoff was so fast, Lassenberia's radar lacked the ability to track it.

The distance between ground level and the dome was about 14,000 miles which took the master very little time to reach. The difficult part was to pierce through thousands of miles of solid ice. The master's pod made it through 100 miles of ice before systems started to fail. The heat of the pod was overpowered by the more intense cold of the dome which read -200 degrees on his monitor. Realizing his pod had failed him, he donned his jetpack. He waited until the pod's outer shell cooled to the touch. Once it cooled the top hatch opened. With the force of the jetpack pushing him forward and his super strength, he began punching his way through the ice. "Nothing can stop me from reaching my destiny!!" he shouted to himself as he continued punching his way to freedom.

The following day, the master's super punches allowed him to move forward half a mile until he felt a change in his body. He looked at his hands and noticed them drying up, becoming wrinkly. His ability to breathe became harder as he continued punching. He paused for a moment as he looked back at the flat earth surrounded by the wall of artic ice. "Curse you humans!! Curse the house of Lassenberry!!" he shouted before passing out. The being who caused so much caos on earth for the past 6 thousand years became a fixture in the ice dome he so wanted to be free from.

Back on the surface of flat earth, queen Niyale was in her chamber sitting on her throne as she was in talks with the leaders of the free world via satellite. "The world owes you much more than you can imagine, your majesty!" the new President of the United States said. "We here in the United Kingdom share the same debt of gratitude!" the prime minister said. Other world leaders in the conference gave similar praise. "I thank you all for the pleasantries, but our work is far from over. From my father's notes this creature from beyond left behind a network of treachery, i call a cabal. It must be annihilated!" the queen explained. "The disappearance of our special forces in Maine gave our people in the intelligence community the lead we need to snuff out this threat! Trust the United States and its allies are on the job!" the president said. "I have a question. How long did your government have knowledge of the dome, Mr. President?" the queen asked. Except for the president, every other world leader's communication was cut off. "What just happened?" the queen asked. "What dome, your majesty?" the president asked."The creature mentioned a dome covering the earth!" she explained. The president leaned into the camera, making his face look bigger on the monitor. "What...dome?" he asked again before communication was lost.

As the leaders of the world were thanking the young queen, thousands of water bombers and crop dusters were spreading GLC over every inhabitied area of what mankind thought was a globe.

THE END

Near the Indigirka river the small town of Oymyakon, known as the coldest place on earth located in Russia, a group of russian soldiers were sitting around a camp fire devouring huge rations of Pelmeni. Among this group of young soldiers was one who stood out like a sore thumb. This man in his early 20's wasn't eastern european. His brown-skinned face poked through the layers of fur he wore to protect him from the extreme cold. He was continuing his survival skills from the russian soldiers. "Так, мой черный друг. Когда вы закончили с вашей подготовки, куда вы идете дальше?" one soldier asked him. "I don't know, my pale conrad! Wherever the wind takes me!" the black man chuckled. The other soldiers chuckled.

Suddenly, out of nowhere a white woman wearing a fur coat approached the group. She was followed by 10 soldiers in fur attire from Lassenberia. "I finally found you!" she said. The senior russian soldier stood from the campfire. "Who are you? What can we do for you?" he asked. "I am Lady Ellen of the Borough of Braxton, from the nation of Lassenberia! I am here for Prince Marcus!" she said. Following his gut instinct, the young black man slowly stood from the campfire. He pulled back his fur hood. "Wow! You look like your mother!" she said. "Are you talking about me?" he asked. "Yes! You are Prince Marcus, future consort to your cousin, queen Niyale of Lassenberia!" she said with pride. Moments later, everyone looked up as a green mist fell from the sky.

Now, The End

Thank you
The Most High/ The Creator
My Family
Gary L. Hinton Jr. aka Shaq
Spinner(I didn't touch the money!!)
Marjani Jones
Adrienne V. Carr
Dirk Miller and Connie Daly
Clark Stoeckley
Jimmy cupo
Ralph Fernandez and Carmen B. Parrilla
Bernadette Keith
Ray Rosa
Faby
Cory Cenci
Mike Rico
Little Joe
Anthony Travis
The People of Bloomfield N.J.
The People of New Jersey
People around the world
The man i see in the mirror

Printed in the United States
By Bookmasters